PRAISE FOR *THE PAIN TOURIST*

'Riveting from start to finish, I thoroughly enjoyed the roller-coaster ride. Smart and twisty, this book will get under your skin' Liz Nugent

'I LOVED *The Pain Tourist* – such a brilliantly unique concept, with wonderful, emotional writing ... I was hooked on the story from the word go. BRILLIANT' Lisa Hall

'The most original and intense thriller ever!' Michael Wood

'An absolute BELTER of a book ... I'd forgotten how good Paul Cleave is!' Sarah Pinborough

'Tense, thrilling, touching. Paul Cleave is very good indeed' John Connolly

'Paul Cleave is an automatic must-read for me' Lee Child

'You can't be a true fan of crime fiction if you're not reading Cleave's books' Tom Wood

'Uses words as lethal weapons' *New York Times*

WHAT READERS ARE SAYING...

★ ★ ★ ★ ★

'Paul Cleave has ripped up the genre's rhythms and given us something entirely new ... *The Pain Tourist* is a masterpiece' Café Thinking

'A heart-pounding, jaw-dropping thrill ride that will blow your mind' Emma's Bibliotreasures

'A brilliantly executed, thrilling, twisty, nerve-shredding serial-killer chiller with one hell of a plot. Perfect for fans of Dean Koontz' Live & Deadly

'Tense, suspenseful, emotional and jam-packed with unforgettable characters ... A red-hot, sleep-stealing, pulse-pounding read' Jen Med's Book Reviews

'An addictive trip from the very first page' The First Eleven Minutes

'I have never read a thriller that has felt so real, yet so surreal at the same time ... addictive' PRDG Reads

'Number-one TOP read of the year ... amazing storytelling' Ian Dixon

'Cleave has made my heart pound, pulse race and jaw drop with this book' Little Miss Book Lover

PRAISE FOR PAUL CLEAVE

WINNER of the Thriller & Suspense Gold Foreword Indie Award
SHORTLISTED for the Ngaio Marsh Award
THRILLER OF THE YEAR: Crime Fiction Lover Awards

'A true page-turner, with an intriguing premise, a rollercoaster plot and a cast of believably flawed characters' *Guardian*

'The psychological depth of the leads bolsters the complex plot. This merits comparison with the work of Patricia Highsmith' *Publishers Weekly* STARRED review

'What is really compelling about *The Quiet People* is neither its neat twists nor the topical examination of mob rule, but Cleave's portrait of Cameron as he goes rogue' *The Times*

'A true page-turner filled with dread, rage, doubt and more twists than the Remutaka Pass' Linwood Barclay

'It grabbed me by the throat, shook me around, and left me breathing hard. Fantastic, and highly recommended' Lee Child

The Pain Tourist

ABOUT THE AUTHOR

Paul is an award-winning author who often divides his time between his home city of Christchurch, New Zealand, where most of his novels are set, and Europe. He's won the New Zealand Ngaio Marsh Award three times, the Saint-Maur book festival's crime novel of the year award in France, and has been shortlisted for the Edgar and the Barry in the US and the Ned Kelly in Australia. His books have been translated into more than twenty languages. He's thrown his Frisbee in more than forty countries, plays tennis badly, golf even worse, and has two cats – which is often two too many. The critically acclaimed *The Quiet People* was published in 2021. Follow Paul on Twitter @PaulCleave, Facebook: facebook.com/PaulCleave, Instagram @paul.cleave and his website: paulcleave.com/

Also by Paul Cleave and available from Orenda Books
The Quiet People

The Pain Tourist

PAUL CLEAVE

**ORENDA
BOOKS**

Orenda Books
16 Carson Road
West Dulwich
London SE21 8HU
www.orendabooks.co.uk

First published in the United Kingdom by Orenda Books 2022
Copyright © Paul Cleave 2022

A catalogue record for this book is available from the British Library.

ISBN 978-1-914585-48-7
eISBN 978-1-914585-49-4

Typeset in Garamond by Elaine Sharples

Printed and bound by CPI Group (UK) Ltd, Croydon CR0 4YY

*For sales and distribution, please contact info@orendabooks.co.uk or visit
www.orendabooks.co.uk.*

PART ONE

Chapter One

James's thoughts as he lies in bed tend to gravitate toward what he's just watched or read – which isn't great if what he's just watched or read is a story about killer clowns hiding in the closet. Fully aware that night-time noises only make it harder for him to fall asleep, his parents keep their voices to a whisper and movements to a shuffle, but what he's hearing now are daytime noises: knocking on the door, followed by voices, followed by arguing, all at – he glances at his bedside clock – 11.00pm. He can't make out what the argument is about, but he doesn't like how it sounds, nor does he like the thumps and bumps that follow.

What is going on down there?

The question gets him to his feet. His room is in darkness. His nightlight has been living in his wardrobe for the last two years, after Hazel teased him for still using it. He picks his way slowly through the minefield of toys to the door, toys he was meant to put away but didn't. He can't see them, but doesn't need to. He has one of those memories where he can walk out of a room and months later tell you the location of everything that was in it. His memory is so good he's frightened his brain will pop one day from hanging on to everything. He opens the door slowly and steps into the hallway. He passes Hazel's room; unsurprisingly, she has slept through all the noise.

From downstairs, his mother says, 'Please don't do this.'

The fear in her voice makes his blood run cold, but the *smack* that follows turns it to ice, so much so that when he goes to take another step toward the stairs, his legs give out, and he has to clutch at the wall to slow his descent to the ground.

'Don't,' his dad says, the same fear in his voice as his mum's. 'Please, don't.'

James's chest tightens around his banging heart. The world blurs as he fights to get a decent breath. Ahead of him there's an angle from which one can see downstairs into the lounge – something he's done when his parents are watching horror movies. Since his legs are useless anyway, he rolls onto his belly and slowly slinks along the carpet.

Smack. He jumps at the sound.

'Where is it?'

'I don't know what you're talking about,' his dad says. 'Please, you have the wrong house, you have the—'

Another smack, and James covers his mouth to stifle the building scream. More banging and bumping from downstairs. He needs to call the police, but can't – his parents say he's too young for a cellphone, and the same goes for Hazel, even though all their friends have them. And to make things worse, his parents got rid of the landline years ago. Best he could do would be to send a message to one of his friends online from his computer, but they'd all be asleep. Can you send an email to the police?

He keeps shimmying forward. The lounge comes into view. It's lit up. He can see somebody's lower half, dressed in black pants and black shoes. A stranger. Another shimmy forward, and now he can see somebody the size and shape of his dad, in his dad's clothing, kneeling on the floor with a pillowcase over his head. There's a spot of blood on the pillowcase. That somebody is next to another somebody, this one also on their knees, also with a pillowcase over their head, this one dressed in his mother's clothes.

The stranger says, 'Just tell us where it is.'

'There is no—'

His dad rocks back when he is smacked across the face, but

before he can fall, the man who hit him grabs his shirt to keep him upright. James can't tell who he's talking to when he says, 'Go and get the kids,' but then a second man comes into view, this one also in dark clothing, and a ski mask too. In movies, monsters are always zombies, or vampires, or some weird kind of mutant, but in this moment his eleven-year-old brain tells him he's been wrong all this time. What he's looking at now are monsters. *Real monsters.*

The second man – the second monster – comes toward the stairs.

'Don't!' his dad yells, and the first monster turns back and hits him again.

If you don't get up, they're going to hurt you. They're going to kill you.

He wiggles away from the stairs. His legs are jelly, the floor quicksand, the walls are the sides of a sinking boat. But to stay on the floor means capture. He grabs at the wall and gets to his feet, then stumbles to Hazel's room. He gets the door open and closes it gently behind him. There's no way to lock it, and he's not strong enough to block it with heavy furniture. He crosses the room. Hazel doesn't stir until he's pulling back the curtains and opening the window. Is there time to climb out onto the roof? He can hear the second monster on the stairs.

'Wha ... wha soo doing? James?'

He shakes her, and, voice low, he hisses, 'We have to go.'

'Wha...?'

He puts his finger to his lips and grabs her hand.

'There are monsters in the house. We have to climb out the window.'

Hazel is fourteen, but acts like she's sixteen. She snatches her hand back, and, more alert now, she says, 'It's too late to be playing one of your immature games, James.'

During the last year she's discovered she likes saying 'games' and 'James' in the same sentence.

'We have to go!' he says, giving up on the whispering in the hope what he can't convey in words he can convey in volume. He grabs at her again.

'I'm not going anywhere. Now get out of my room!'

She pushes him away. A strip of light appears beneath the bedroom door as the hallway light clicks on.

Crying now, he says, 'Please, Hazel, please.'

His tears give her pause. She can't see them, but can hear them. But it's too late. The door opens. The second monster is backlit by the hallway light. He's huge. Twice as big as anybody he's ever seen. Like something Doctor Frankenstein put together from dead bodybuilders.

Hazel freezes. James does the same.

'Come with me now,' the monster says, his voice deep, like those bodybuilders were chugging back the steroids.

'No,' James says, so scared he's not sure he's spoken loud enough to be heard.

But he must have been, because the monster points at them and says, 'Say no to me again and I'm going to kill you.'

Hazel takes James's hand.

'You got three seconds. After that I'm breaking bones.'

James casts his memory over the books he's read – there have been so many, but he can't recall a scene like this. In them, all the kids, who are often around his age, are so brave. Some of them even solve mysteries.

'We're coming,' he says, but he has no intention of that. The open window gives them access to the roof, and then to the fence, then the street, the neighbours, the police.

Can you both make it through?

No. Not both.

He pulls on Hazel's arm and she gets out of bed. She's shaking.

'One,' the monster says.

If a kid was brave, wouldn't he do anything he could to protect his sister?

'Two.'

Even a sister who wished their parents would drive their little brother to an abandoned farm and leave him behind?

'Three.'

He twists Hazel toward the window. 'Go!'

She doesn't go. Instead she turns back to James.

'Go!' This time he shoves her, then he charges the monster, because that's what brave boys do, it's David and Goliath, but David won, and so can—

The monster scoops James off the floor and hurls him into the bookcase. He bounces and lands heavily on the floor; books, photo frames, a lamp, some dolls, all raining down around him. A yell from his dad downstairs is cut short. The monster reaches the window and grabs Hazel as she's climbing through it. Despite James's fall, the floor no longer feels like quicksand nor his legs like jelly; it's as if being tossed across the room has centred his balance. He picks up the lamp and gets to his feet and smashes it against the monster's back. The reaction is instant, with the monster spinning and backhanding James so hard across the face he ends up back on the floor, but the motion does make him lose his grip on Hazel. She disappears through the window, off balance, the roof tiles rattling as she tumbles out of sight. Was she able to stop her fall? Or is she lying in a puddle of broken bones?

The monster puts his head out the window to check, then comes back to James. He grabs his leg and drags him into the hallway and down the stairs, his head banging off each one. He's hauled into the lounge and forced up onto his knees.

Dad is opposite, pillowcase over his face, his arms behind him. Mum is on her side, a pillowcase over her face too, but her hands have been restrained in front of her with a cable tie. He can't tell if she's dead or unconscious. The first monster he saw is standing over them with a gun in his hand. He's seen a thousand guns on TV, but never one for real. This one has a silencer on it. Furniture has been pulled in from the walls and tipped over. His mum's paintings have been tossed onto the floor.

'The girl got out the window,' Monster Two says. 'She's going for help.'

'Find her.'

There aren't just two monsters, but three, which he discovers when Monster Two steps away and a third takes his place. That monster wrenches James's hands behind him and locks them together with another cable tie. The whole time he keeps staring at the blood on the pillowcase hiding his dad's face.

'Please,' his dad says. He sounds out of breath. Panicked. Scared. 'Don't hurt my family. I have money. It's not a lot, twenty thousand maybe, maybe a little more. I can go to the bank in the morning. You can have it all. You can look at my accounts online. You can see what I have. You can. Just don't hurt them. We can transfer it if that's what you want.'

'Tell us where it is.'

'There isn't any safe,' his dad says. If there were a safe James would know about it. The year he found out Santa wasn't real, he searched the house all December long, looking everywhere a present could be hidden. He didn't see any safe.

'There an office upstairs?'

'There is, but there's no safe.'

'I wanted to do this without having to kill your kids, but you're leaving me no choice,' Monster One says.

James's bladder lets go. His chest hurts so bad. He's going to die, and he's always going to be known as the kid who wet himself first.

Please, Hazel, run. You have to run and get help.

'For the love of God, there's no safe!' his dad says, his voice higher, panicked, desperate. 'Take anything else you want, anything.'

Monster Two returns. 'The little bitch got away.'

Relief washes over James. The police will come, and these men know it. This is as far as things go.

'Shit,' Monster One says.

'We gotta go,' Monster Three says. 'She's probably banging on somebody's door right now.'

'It'll take a few minutes for the police to arrive,' Monster One says.

'We don't know that,' Monster Three says. 'And for all we know that neighbour is coming over here right now.'

'Which would be a mistake for the neighbour,' Monster Two says.

'Either way, we gotta go,' Monster Three says.

'Not until we get what we came for.'

'What if he's not lying? What if this is the wrong house?'

'We haven't seen your faces,' his dad says. 'We can't identify you. Please, just go.'

Monster One pulls the pillowcase from his dad's head. It barely looks like his dad. His right eye is swollen shut, his hair is ruffled, his lips are swollen, there's blood over his chin.

'Last chance.'

'There is no safe!'

Monster One points the gun at James's mum. There's a *pfft*, and his mum's body does the smallest of jerks, and then a red patch the size of a coin appears in the middle of the pillowcase.

His dad is halfway to his feet when there's another *pfft*. His nose disappears into a mist of blood and his face slackens and his eyes lose focus. He falls into a lump. James screams. He barely hears Monster One when he says, 'Do the kid.'

James closes his eyes tight and he waits for the *pfft*.

He doesn't have to wait long.

Chapter Two

The street is lit up – patrol cars, ambulances, media – all mixed in with the lights from the neighbouring houses, where folks watch from porches and front lawns. Barriers are set up in the street, people pressed up against them, some on tiptoes, while others stretch their necks for a better view. A few have brought binoculars. Some have coffee. All have cellphones, and most of those phones are pointing toward the crime scene.

The barriers are pulled aside so Detectives Theodore Tate and Carl Schroder can drive through. The media yell questions. The two detectives ignore them. Tate is driving. He parks up opposite the house. The night is warm, the air heavy, it's been one of those rare summer days that pops up in the middle of winter.

'You ready for this?' Schroder asks.

Tate shakes his head. 'You?'

'No.'

They get out of the car. The buzz of voices from folks watching on carries in the warm air. Lights erected in the garden and along the boundary of the house are so bright a plane could safely land. The house is two-storey, as are most on the block. Similar designs too – like the architect gave a community discount. The neighbourhood is ten years old, no front fences, but lots of manicured gardens and lawns drained of colour thanks to winter. The front door is wide open. There are half a dozen officers scattered around the house, guarding it, but none inside. The house has been cleared and left as undisturbed as possible. Both men pause at the door to pull on latex gloves and nylon booties before going in. To the left an open-plan kitchen and dining room, modern furniture, modern appliances. Straight ahead a staircase, a white wooden rail, narrow, black steel balusters. To the right a lounge, and in the lounge the bodies of the Garrets. Tate shudders.

'Jesus,' Schroder whispers.

Knowing what they're about to see doesn't soften the blow, and yet they both know if Hazel Garrett hadn't got away, the scene would have been worse. The neighbour whose house she ran to – Brian Mann – raced over here after watching three men fleeing out the front door. James was still alive – though barely. A retired ER doctor, Mann used all his skills to keep him alive until the ambulances arrived.

There was nothing that could be done for Frank and Avah Garrett.

Frank and Avah are slumped on the floor. Mann told the first officers on the scene that Avah had a pillowcase over her head, which he removed so he could check on her condition. The pillowcase is next to her body. She's on her side, face against the carpet, eyes open, a bullet hole in her cheek, the hair between her face and the carpet matted with blood, her hands bound ahead of her. Tate wants to tell her he's going to find the people who did this, but he says nothing. Nobody is saying anything. The only noise is coming from the folks outside. Avah Garrett looks familiar.

He pivots to Frank. There's a pillowcase next to his body too, but Mann said that one had already been removed. He's on his back, his legs buckled beneath him. There's a bullet hole where his nose ought to be. Hard to tell if he also looks familiar.

Another pivot to a patch of floor where there is gauze and bandaging and bloody towels from where James was kept alive. Among them is a cricket bat Mann brought over as a weapon. There's a plastic cable tie among the mess that match the ones on the parents, these ones removed from James by the paramedics. Tate has never seen so much blood come from somebody who wasn't already dead. He can smell urine. Hard to know if Hazel escaping is why the rest of the family were shot, or if they were all going to be shot anyway. People capable of doing this, it's probably the latter.

'You recognise them?' Tate asks.

Schroder shakes his head. 'Why? Do you?'

'Avah maybe, but not sure from where.'

Tate does a three-sixty. More modern furniture flipped over, a smashed TV on the ground, artwork pulled down, holes in the canvases, a bookcase tipped over.

'They were looking for something,' Schroder says. 'Maybe some kind of wall safe.'

'So why not tell them? Three men come into your house with guns – you're going to give them whatever it is they're looking for.'

'Maybe they did, and got killed anyway, in which case the safe is in a different room.'

They split up. Schroder takes downstairs, and Tate heads up. First room upstairs is an office with a view out over the backyard. The paintings are on the walls and the furniture is in place. The paintings are done by the same artist and match the ones downstairs. A closer look and he can see a signature. He thinks it's Avah Garrett. The landscapes are beautiful. He wants to bury whoever is responsible for this in one of those landscapes.

A search of the office doesn't reveal a safe, but it does tell him why he recognises Avah. Avah and Frank Garrett are the real-estate agents who sold him and Bridget their house. He remembers them being warm and friendly with big smiles. It's a horrible reminder that one moment you can be selling a house, the next you're lying executed on the floor of one.

Hazel's bedroom is next. He pictures how it all played out. Mum and dad held at gun point, not revealing what the men wanted to hear. The killers decide to use the kids as leverage, but the daughter escapes. The three men go from having all night to having to get the hell out of there. They could have just left, but instead chose to execute the family. It's cold. Colder than anything he's ever seen.

He finds Schroder in the master bedroom. 'Anything?'

'I found some business cards,' Schroder says. 'The Garretts are real-estate agents.'

'I saw. We bought our house from them.'

'Small world. You remember much about them?'

'Only that we liked them a lot. I'm going to go chat to the daughter.'

'You want me to go with you?'

'I'll manage,' he says, and heads back downstairs.

Chapter Three

James Garrett is on his knees in the lounge. Monster Two can't find Hazel, which means she didn't fall from the roof, she didn't break any bones, she's got help. He's scared, his pyjamas are wet, and he can feel the barrel of the gun against his head ... He's waiting ... waiting...

The headache that explodes into being is like nothing he has ever experienced – it's like people are screaming into a canyon, the echoes bottled up and released en masse into the centre of his brain. His skull is tearing open. His brain is expanding and pressing at the jagged edges of the tear. The lounge lights are flickering, they blink off, and—

The surgeons lose James Garrett at 11:39pm. The blood loss and the severity of the injury is making this one of the hardest surgeries Doctor Wolfgang McCoy has ever had to perform. The bullet has entered through the back of James's skull, creating a fingertip hole that has expanded in a spiderweb of fractures. James's head has been shaved and that web cut away, opening a window to the brain and the wound below. The bullet has entered on a downward trajectory, furrowing through the occipital lobe and into the cerebellum, and is either lodged in there or against the jaw bone. There hasn't been time to x-ray the boy to see if the bullet is in one piece or a dozen.

The surgeons attempt resuscitation and are successful.

James is in the dark for only a few moments before the lights in the lounge blink back to life. The loud ringing in his ears – the bottled screams – have dulled. He's lying on his side, mirroring his mum's position. His dad is still on his knees with Monster One now pointing his gun at him. What do these men, these monsters, want?

A slight movement from his right. His mum? Yes, there it is again, a twitch. She's still alive! Monster One also sees the twitch, and turns toward her. He takes aim—

His dad screams, the muscles in his neck tighten, and he snaps the restraints behind his back. Monster One is too slow to react as his dad leaps up and grabs his gun hand and gets it pointing at the ceiling.

Bang!

A hole appears next to the light and plaster dust rains down on them.

Bang!

The light explodes. Monster Two opens fire, bullet holes lining the wall. His dad twists Monster One around and uses him as a shield. The monster jerks back and forth as his chest is torn open by gunfire. The lights in the lounge flicker ... they stay on ... they flicker some more, then die.

The second time the surgeons lose James Garrett is at 11:44pm.

The occipital lobe's primary function is vision. Even if the boy were to survive the surgery, there is every chance he would be partially or fully blind, with blindness only one of a multitude of life-changing – or life-ending – scenarios. With all the possibilities, the only thing Doctor Wolfgang McCoy is confident about is James will never be the boy he was this morning. Most people who get shot in the head don't live to tell the tale, and those that do don't get to tell it well. There is a whine as the defibrillator is fired up, somebody yells clear, and James's body jerks as hundreds of volts race through it. His heart starts beating, and...

The lights come back on. James can hear sirens. They're getting loud fast. His mum sits up and pulls the pillowcase off her head. There's a bloody graze running the side of her face from the bullet.

'Shit,' Monster Two says, and he turns and runs for the door.

James rolls over to see Monster Three staring at his dad. There's a term he's come across in the books he read – fight or flight. Monster Three lands on fight. He grabs at the gun buried in the waistband of his black jeans. At the same time his mum picks up Monster One's gun. It's like one of the old westerns his dad likes to watch on TV, where two men face off in the street, reading each other's expressions as to when to draw.

'Don't,' his mum says.

Only Monster Three does. He takes aim.

Mum fires, and Monster Three drops like a rock.

Dad rushes over and kicks the gun away from Monster Three's hand, but there's no need – there's a bullet hole in the centre of his forehead. James has never seen a dead body before, never thought he would, and doesn't know how he feels about seeing one now. Pleased, he thinks – especially when compared to the alternatives.

His mum helps James sit up. 'Are you okay?'

'I think so,' he says. Except for the headache.

His mum disappears into the kitchen while his dad stands guard at the door with the gun. The sirens are getting louder. His mum returns with a pair of scissors. She cuts his wrists free, then he does the same for her. He rubs his wrists. He feels cold.

'Hazel must have got help,' his dad says.

'Everything is going to be okay,' his mum says.

The lights from the police cars reflect into the room. His dad puts the gun on the ground so the officers don't open fire on him. They come inside, and James hopes the conclusions they're coming to are the right ones. He recognises them. They spoke at his school last week about the dangers of drugs. Officer Bligh and Officer May. Bligh is overweight, his uniform stretching at the seams. May has a tightly knotted ponytail that sways as she looks quickly around the room.

They take it all in, and they do the math, and they do the math right, because Bligh says, 'You've done a great job.'

'You guys were lucky to survive this,' May adds.

'You can thank our kids,' his dad says. 'They're the ones who figured out we were in danger, and it was Hazel who got help.'

'We know,' Bligh says.

'Your kids are heroes,' May says.

The lights in the lounge flicker.

The third time they lose James Garrett is 11:48pm.

The cerebellum's primary job is to control motion. If they can stop the bleeding, if they patch the torn parts of brain back together, even if there is a day when the kid leaves the hospital breathing, he's unlikely to be doing it on his own two feet. When it comes to the brain, it's like the Wild West – anything can happen – and that includes miracles. Doctor McCoy isn't a religious man, but that hasn't stopped him from praying in the past when he's been wrist deep inside a patient, holding the pieces together, and he prays now, he prays this kid can pull through.

They ride out the darkness in silence until the lights come back on. For a moment there, James didn't think they were going to.

'There was another man,' his mum says.

'We know,' Bligh says. 'We already arrested him.'

'He will go to jail for a very long time,' May says. 'Possibly forever.'

James likes the officers. A lot. Sometimes he thinks he wants to grow up to be a cop. Other times he thinks he'd like to be a fireman, or an actor, or a musician, but mostly what he wants is to be a writer. He wants to write books, or maybe movies. He'd be good at it. The teachers at school are always telling him he has an incredible imagination. It's probably why at night his mind is restless when he's trying to get to sleep.

Hazel shows up, followed by Doctor Mann. Doctor Mann takes in the scene and comes to the same conclusions the officers came to. Two dead bodies, two police officers, and the Garrett family safe and sound.

'I think we should look at getting you patched up,' Doctor Mann says to James's mum. 'How about we get you to my house and disinfect that wound, then make us all some hot chocolates? How does that sound?'

James thinks it sounds as good as anything he's ever heard. The others agree. He will have two hot chocolates if his parents will let him, and hopefully some cake too. Doctor Mann makes the best hot chocolates, but Mrs Mann makes the best cakes. He hopes they're—
The lights flicker. The world pauses. He still feels cold.

James's blood pressure drops, the machine flatlines, and Doctor McCoy keeps on fighting.

Chapter Four

A six-foot-tall Dr Brian Mann's hand swallows Tate's when they shake, making him think that any wound Mann touches would be made all the larger for it.

'It's truly horrible, truly a horrible thing,' Mann says. 'I hope you catch these men.'

Tate is invited inside. The house is warm, cosy, every horizontal plane graced by a framed family photograph. They pause outside the lounge, where he can see Hazel Garrett sitting with Pauline Mann, Pauline trying to get her to drink tea. Pauline is shorter, and thin, with small hands, as though over the years her husband has absorbed parts of her.

'Hazel has been withdrawing into herself at the same pace the crowds have been growing outside,' Mann says, keeping his voice low. 'I feel like going out there with the garden hose and spraying it over all of them.'

'Does Hazel know?'

'We haven't told her, but she's a smart kid and knows there's a reason her parents haven't come to get her. She's asked over and over what I found, but all I've said is her parents have been hurt, her brother too, and I did everything I could to help them.'

He runs a hand through his hair before resting it on the back of his neck, his elbow pointing at Tate. 'I couldn't bring myself to tell her the truth. After I retired I thought my days of giving bad news were over, but I can tell her now, if you like. It will be better coming from me than from you.'

It's a lot to ask, but Doctor Mann is right. 'Okay. But first, does she have other family?'

'Grandparents. I ... I was going to call them, but wasn't sure if you'd have wanted me to.'

'We'll take care of that. The three people fleeing the house, did you get a good look at them?'

'All I can tell you is one was bigger than the other two, and when I say bigger, I mean big. Guy had to be six and a half feet, easy, and solid too, not the kind of guy you'd want to tangle with.'

'You could judge his height from your window?'

'I judged it when he folded himself in half to get into the back of the car.'

'What were they wearing?'

'Black, all of them, black tops, black pants, black ski masks.'

'And the vehicle?'

'A blue SUV. I'm not good with cars, so I couldn't tell you what kind, but it looked modern. It was parked outside Grant and Nancy's house.'

'Grant and Nancy?'

'Frank and Avah's next-door neighbours.'

Tate jots the names in his pad.

'Talk me through it from the moment Hazel showed up.'

Mann tells Tate they were watching TV when there was tapping at the French doors that open onto the back deck. Urgent, but not loud. Hazel was there, her face red from running. She was crying. They let her in and she quickly closed the curtain behind her and told them they needed to call the police, that there were people in her house, that some of them were probably looking for her.

'It's why she didn't bang and scream on the front door, because she knew they'd find her, and she said not to turn the lights off because it'd draw attention. We didn't doubt her for a second. She's a smart kid, and that's why I'm here telling you the story and not a coroner.'

It's a grim assessment, and not one Tate can argue with.

'I went to our bedroom to peak through the curtains. There was a man in a ski mask running up and down the street, looking for Hazel. I watched him give up and head back into the house. By then Pauline was on the phone to the police.'

'How long until they came out of the house after that?'

'Couldn't have been much more than a minute.'

'You said the big one was male – what about the other two? Could you tell?'

'They moved like men, but maybe that's just my preconception. I mean, what kind of woman would have done what these three did? What kind of woman would shoot a boy in the back of the head?'

Probably the same kind of woman who would drown her children, Tate thinks, or gas them in her car, or let them be abused by some deadbeat guy she's dating. When it comes to hurting children, it's equality all the way.

'Could you make out the licence plate?'

'Thirty years ago I could have from that distance, but not now.'

'You didn't hear any of the shots?'

'Nothing. We were still up watching TV – we're both night owls. I guess we just didn't hear them over the TV.'

'How's your hearing?'

'A lot better than my eyesight, that's for sure. So is Pauline's.'

The killers must have used silencers, otherwise half the neighbourhood would have heard.

Mann looks down at his hands. They're red from where he's scrubbed them clean, and there's still blood under his fingernails. 'As soon as they were gone, I grabbed the cricket bat and went over. I wasn't expecting to find what I found. There was nothing I could do for Avah and Frank. I didn't think there'd be anything I could do for James either, but he had a pulse, and then it was just a matter of fighting to keep it until the paramedics arrived.' He looks back to Tate. 'They're such a nice family, all of them. I can't believe this happened to them.'

Nobody ever can.

'Let's talk to Hazel.'

Chapter Five

Hazel Garrett is on the couch with her arms around her legs and her knees under her chin. A blanket hangs over her shoulders like a cape. She's thin, pale, a pixie haircut blending into a lightly freckled face. She's staring at a coffee table, where there are untouched hot drinks. Pauline Mann has her arm around her. The air is so thick with grief Tate wouldn't be surprised to see the walls bowing outward from it. He makes room on the coffee table and sits on the edge.

Hazel doesn't look up, and her voice sounds hollow when she asks, 'Mum and Dad are dead, aren't they? And James too?'

Mann crouches next to her. He goes to talk, but his voice catches. He coughs into his hand and clears his throat, and tries again. 'I'm sorry, Hazel, but yes, both your parents have passed away, but James is in hospital, fighting for his life.'

Hazel wipes a palm beneath one eye, then the other, and with a voice still hollow while she stares at the coffee table, she asks, 'Is he going to be okay?'

'The doctors are doing everything they can, just as we will do everything we can to help you get through this. You need to know you're not alone.'

She wipes at her eyes again and looks at Tate. 'You're a detective?'

'I am.'

'You catch monsters?'

'I do.'

'James said there were monsters in the house. I didn't believe him.' Pauline tightens her grip on Hazel, but Hazel carries on. 'He was trying to save me while I was being mean to him.'

She keeps wiping at her eyes, but it's no good, the tears are coming thick and fast. Soon she will be inconsolable, making Tate question if he should back away and leave her be or push forward. He's torn.

Before he can make a decision, Hazel takes a deep breath, and carries on. 'If I had acted right away he would be okay, and Mum and Dad would still be alive. It's my fault what happened.'

'I can promise you, Hazel, that none of this is your fault.'

'Then why does it feel like it is? Can I go to the hospital to be with James?'

'Of course. But first, if you're able to, I need you to tell me everything you can remember so we can find the people who did this?'

'Perhaps this isn't the best time,' Pauline says.

'Will it help find who did this?' Hazel asks.

'It will.'

She wipes at her eyes, and she takes more deep breaths, and wipes at her eyes some more. Then she tells him in fast sentences that James came into her room, that she didn't believe him when he said they were in danger, and that he pushed her out the window when the bad man tried to get them. The bad man had a ski mask on, and was dressed in black, and was big enough to fill the doorway, and James tried to attack him. He wasn't holding a gun, but he may have had one on him.

To Tate, the ski masks suggest the men, at least originally, were planning on leaving the family alive. There's no point in wearing masks if you're going to kill the only people who can identify you. Did things change when Frank and Avah wouldn't tell them what they needed to know?

'Is there a wall safe anywhere in your house?'

'What?'

'A wall safe. Or a safe. Somewhere that your parents would hide valuables.'

She shakes her head. 'Nothing like that. I saw the licence plate of the car they got into,' she adds.

'You did?'

'We watched them as they ran to the car. I knew you'd want to know it, and I was able to make it out, but ... but I can't remember it,' she says, and her tears are coming harder now. 'I could have helped James and didn't. I could have told you the licence plate number, but now I can't.'

She becomes inconsolable at that point, and it breaks his heart to watch her.

He wonders what will happen to her now and who will take her in. This morning she woke up with a family, and tonight she will go to sleep an orphan. It makes him think of his own daughter. He has the urge to drive home and hug her, maybe wrap her in cotton wool, maybe board up the house to protect her from the outside world.

Mann walks him out. 'Given everything she's gone through, it's a miracle she hasn't completely shut down. But it's coming. That I can promise you.'

Tate hands him his card. 'If you can think of anything else, give me a call.'

Mann looks at the card before pocketing it. 'You really think they were looking for a wall safe?'

'It's a working theory.'

Tate is turning away when Mann puts a hand on his arm. 'I don't know for sure if the Garretts have a safe or not, but I'm pretty sure I know another of our neighbours has one. What if these men came for something that wasn't even there? What if all of this is the result of them going to the wrong house?'

Chapter Six

Tate meets Schroder on the street. The group beyond the barriers has grown as more folks have ventured into the warm night to watch the show. The coroner's van is parked out front of the house. He wonders if the autopsy will find that this is one of those cases that comes down to millimetres – where a millimetre to the left or right would mean there wouldn't be an autopsy.

'If there's a safe in the house I can't find it,' Schroder says. 'How's the girl doing?'

'About as well as can be expected. Walk with me.'

Schroder falls in alongside. Wednesday has ticked over into Thursday, but the night hasn't cooled any.

'Anybody see anything of note?'

'It's possible they got into a dark blue SUV that was parked one house along. I figure it was probably stolen.'

'It also figures we'll find it on fire somewhere,' Schroder says. 'Where are we going?'

Tate comes a stop. 'We're already there.'

There in this case is three houses down – another two-storey place, this one with a concrete tile roof and pale, porous Oamaru stone. The garden is full of small hibernating shrubs and the grass looks like a bowling green. All the lights inside are on. Everybody in the block is awake, having answered the door to officers who have been looking for witnesses.

'The guy who lives here is Blair Crawford,' Tate says. 'Doctor Mann says he's a diamond wholesaler.'

Schroder takes a moment with that, then, 'You think this is a case of mistaken identity? These guys go to the Garrett house expecting diamonds, then lose their shit over getting nothing?'

'It's possible. Mann says the Crawfords moved in a month or two back, that he knows Crawford is in the diamond business because they have a friend in common. He says it's not something Crawford talks about. Which means the Garretts probably didn't know. They couldn't tell their killers they had the wrong house, that what they were looking for was three doors down.'

'Wouldn't the Garretts just say they weren't in the diamond business? It wouldn't have been hard to prove they were real-estate agents.'

'That I don't have an answer for, but lots of people must know Crawford. Dealers he sells to. Somebody mentions it to a friend, it gets passed down the chain, and like kids playing "telephone", the details get mixed up, and suddenly you got three guys looking for diamonds where there aren't any.'

It only takes a few seconds for Blair Crawford to answer the door. He's a burley guy dressed in a flannel shirt and jeans, with a big beard and hair that touches his shoulders. He looks like he doesn't just supply diamonds, but makes them by crushing coal in his fists. If the killers had come here, maybe it would be three bad people on their way to the morgue instead of two good ones. Crawford leads them into the lounge, where Alice Crawford is also dressed in a flannel shirt and jeans, her sleeves rolled up, revealing sleeves of tattoos that start at the wrists and disappear beneath the flannel. The kids are upstairs in bed, probably in flannel pyjamas, Tate thinks. Husband and wife sit side by side on the couch, and Schroder and Tate sit in armchairs opposite.

'I'm not really sure what more help we can be,' Crawford says. 'Like I told the other officers, we didn't see anything. We were in bed at the time. We still don't even know what's happened, only that people are dead.'

'Do you have a safe in the house?' Schroder asks.

'Excuse me?'

'A safe. Do you have one where you keep valuables? Perhaps diamonds?'

Crawford frowns. He leans forward. 'What has that got to do with anything?'

'There was a home invasion,' Tate says. 'A husband and wife were executed, and their young son is fighting for his life in hospital. We think three men came to their house looking for a safe, only we think it's possible they had the wrong address.'

Both the Crawfords go pale. Alice raises her hands to her mouth, like she's about to pray and is worried about being lipread.

Blair Crawford interlocks his fingers behind his neck and looks up at the ceiling. 'It's a floor safe,' he says.

'And you store diamonds in it?' Schroder asks.

'Cash too,' Crawford says. 'At any given time I can have fifty thousand dollars' worth of diamonds. Sometimes more.'

'You're comfortable with that kind of value being here?' Schroder asks.

'It's why we have the safe, and it's not like we advertise it.'

'But people who know what you do for a living might have figured it out. Who are your customers?'

'Mostly retailers. I'm a middleman. I don't sell direct to the public. And the retailers, they don't know where I live. I always use a PO box too. My address isn't listed anywhere, not even in the phonebook. They probably assume I have an office somewhere. Trust me, having diamonds at home isn't something I want people to know.'

'But surely your friends know what you do for a living,' Tate says, 'and some might talk. Your address may not be in the phonebook, but it'll be listed on your council rates, your driver's licences, your house insurance, your voting registration papers, taxes, bank...'

'I get the point,' Crawford says. 'And it's why I have a gun.'

'You have a licence for it?' Schroder asks.

'Of course. And I keep that in the safe too. I wish they had come here.'

'Don't say that,' Alice says.

'It's true. I could have handled them. I know I could have. I'd have unlocked the safe for them, and I would have gotten the gun, and—'

'And you and your family could be dead because of it,' Schroder says.

Crawford shakes his head. 'I practise at the range every two weeks. I could have taken them down before they even knew what was happening.'

It's not Tate's job to pop Crawford's bubble by pointing out targets at a range don't shoot back, or that guns would have been held against his children's heads while he was opening the safe, or he may have been forced to give the code to somebody else who'd unlock it.

They go through the questions. The Crawfords moved here six weeks ago. They haven't noticed anything out of place in the neighbourhood. Nobody has said or done anything to make them any more cautious than usual.

'This floor safe,' Tate asks, 'you brought from your previous house, or buy a new one?'

'I got a new one. I wanted something more secure.'

'You pick it up yourself? Install it yourself?'

Crawford shakes his head. 'I bought it through a store that specialises in house security. They gave me the name of a guy they use for installations. Because it was being put into the floor, I needed the floorboards to be removable, but not obviously so. When it comes to DIY, that was—'

Alice puts her hand on his arm, and says, 'The installer.'

'What about him?'

'Don't you remember?'

He looks confused for a moment, then nods eagerly. 'Yes. He had the wrong place. He was knocking on the door, and when I didn't answer, he called me. Turns out he was at...' He stops as the reality of what he's saying hits him. He looks at his wife, then at both of Schroder and Tate. 'Umm ... everything that happened tonight, was it at number forty-one?'

'Yes,' Tate says, his pulse quickening.

'We're forty-seven. The guy, he had written down a seven when we spoke to him on the phone, but it got typed up as a one on the invoice. He'd filled it out before he arrived, everything but the price. I remember him making a joke that his handwriting is so bad it's why he married a pharmacist.'

Everybody lets that sink in, then Alice asks the question they're all thinking. 'Is that why those people are dead? Because of a typo?'

Chapter Seven

Along with two patrol cars for backup, Schroder and Tate drive to Sebastian Patrick's house. They don't think Patrick – the safe installer – was one of the men at the house tonight, not unless his memory was as bad as his handwriting, but that doesn't mean he didn't pass the information on to somebody. Whether that was voluntarily or not is another question.

Nobody answers the door. Schroder shines a flashlight through the garage window and lights up a car inside. The house is single-storey with four bedrooms, modern, with the kind of plaster cladding you can kick a football through – which isn't quite what has happened around the back of the house, but close enough, because officers discover a hole has been cut through the exterior wall to give access to the backdoor lock. The six of them enter, and split up into two teams of three, Schroder with one pair of officers, Tate with the other. There's nobody home. They turn on the lights. For a guy who deals with security firms, Sebastian Patrick doesn't have a lot of security. A key left in the deadbolt inside the back door, no alarm, no lockable latches on the windows, car keys in the ignition.

The computer in the office is lit up. It's the only thing in the house showing any life. There are a series of installation receipts on display, and Tate clicks through them, stopping on the one for Blair Crawford. Sure enough, his address is listed as forty-one. It means there's nothing the Garrets could have said to convince the three men they didn't own a safe. Also on the screen is a display warning from the printer, saying it's out of ink, suggesting whoever broke in tried to print the receipts but failed. Six receipts have been opened on the display covering the last year, all for safes that have been installed.

'This wasn't about diamonds. It's more of a lucky dip,'

Schroder says. 'People don't install safes unless they have something to hide, and these guys wanted whatever that something was.'

'We need to get people out to these other addresses,' Tate says.

'On it,' one of the officers replies, and radios it in.

'If we're lucky they started with the Garretts,' Schroder says. 'It's a one in six chance. Hopefully they panicked after that and called it quits.'

'Maybe they wrote down the addresses,' Tate says, and he picks up the notepad next to the keyboard. Rather than using the pencil next to it, which they will print, he finds another one in the top desk drawer. He is scuffing it over the notepad when Schroder's phone goes off. Schroder puts it on speaker. A burned-out SUV has been found. Licence plates match a report of a stolen vehicle from earlier in the night. It's a coin toss as to whether the guns used are in the ocean or buried in the forest.

The six addresses from the invoices on the computer monitor come up from the imprints on the pad, but not the names. The Garretts' is the top one. A further search of the computer shows Sebastian and Nathalie Patrick left for France this morning for a three-week vacation. Right now they're somewhere over the Pacific Ocean.

'Let's get forensics through here,' Schroder says.

'You want to talk with some of the neighbours?'

'We can get others to do that. Let's figure out the stolen car.'

Chapter Eight

Gary Lee is the owner of what started the day as a dark-blue, six-year-old Toyota SUV, but ended it as a blackened shell parked in the sand dunes of New Brighton beach. On the drive to Lee's house the news comes in that the other five addresses the safe installer did work at haven't been hit. Officers are posted at each.

Lee doesn't appreciate being woken at two in the morning, and appreciates it even less when Tate and Schroder tell him the reason why. He's late twenties, thin, and fidgets when he talks. Sitting in the lounge, he tells them he had parked the SUV in a parking building in town before meeting his girlfriend for dinner. He hadn't taken the ticket with him.

'I know it's stupid leaving the ticket in the car,' he says, 'but once I lost it, and the parking guys pinged me an extra fifty dollars because of it. Parking places are like that, right? A law unto themselves.'

Truer words have never been spoken, Tate thinks. 'Was the ticket on display?'

'It would have been in the centre console. So, yeah, it's on display if you're looking for it. Which I guess somebody was.'

Tate writes down the name of the car parking building, and the floor Lee thinks he parked on, then thanks him for his time. Hopefully security cameras will reveal something.

They head back to the car. While Tate drives, Schroder gets the after-hours number for the parking building. He's bounced around until he lands on a manager who agrees to meet them right away, along with their IT guy. Schroder has gotten photographs of the burned-out car on his phone, and shows them to Tate at the next red light. There's not much to see – a black shell, plastic melted beyond recognition, vinyl and foam burned away, revealing springs and twisted metal.

'Forensics said the lock pins on the ignition were drilled out and a screwdriver jammed in,' Schroder says.

The car-parking building is a colourless five floors of concrete and steel. There's an office on the ground floor, the windows and walls stained with exhaust. A guy in his sixties steps out of it. He keeps running his hand over the top of his head as if confirming what he woke up with is still there, which isn't much. His name is Calvin Misk. Misk sounds proud when he tells them their security cameras were upgraded a few months ago, covering every angle of the parking building. Which turns out to be true, because a minute later they're in the office, with the IT guy showing them the setup. The IT guy is early twenties, pale, with fingers covered in ketchup from the burger he bought on the way here.

'What are we looking for?' the IT guy asks.

Schroder describes the SUV and reads out the licence plate. 'It came in around seven o'clock, and parked up on the second floor.'

'Shouldn't be hard to find,' the IT guy says, and thirty seconds later he has Gary Lee's Toyota loaded up on the screen.

They follow its progression as it passes across multiple cameras before finding a space on the second floor, just like Lee said. Lee exits the car, checks his phone, then makes his way to the stairwell rather than taking the elevator. A camera catches him on the stairs, another at the bottom, and another as he disappears onto the sidewalk and out of frame.

'We need to check three things,' Tate says. 'Was he followed in? When was the ticket stolen from his car? And how was the ticket paid for?'

The IT guy runs the footage. Ten minutes after it's parked, a guy makes his way toward it, looking through the side-windows of every car along the way. He's dressed in black with his hoodie pulled up and a baseball cap pulled low. He's also wearing thin leather gloves. He keeps his head down as he walks. When he looks through Lee's car window he must spot the ticket, because then he reaches into his jacket and pulls out a slim-jim. Opening the door takes him ten seconds. He grabs the ticket and heads for the pay machine. He is halfway there when suddenly he drops between two cars. Twenty seconds later a car drives past, coming from a level above. When it's gone, he stands up and carries on.

'Show that again,' Tate says.

The IT guy rolls the same footage. The guy on screen doesn't get any kind of call. Either he hears the car coming, or he has an ear piece. Tate's phone rings. He doesn't recognise the number. He steps out of the office and takes the call. It's Doctor Mann.

'You said to call if I could think of anything odd,' Mann says.

'I did. What have you remembered?'

'It's probably nothing, but it did seem a little weird. When the three men came out of the house, one of them ran across the front yard and two of them ran down the driveway.'

Tate closes his eyes and pictures the house, the driveway, and where the car was parked out on the street. 'Okay,' he says, wondering where Mann is going with this.

'Quickest distance between two points is a straight line,' Mann says. 'Which is what the big guy took. But the other two went down the driveway. It would have taken them a few more seconds, which isn't much, but in the scheme of things I'd have thought every second counted.'

Tate isn't sure if it means anything, but he files it away and thanks Mann for the call. When he goes back into the office, Schroder has been working with the IT guy and has figured out that there were two spotters working with the car thief, one on the ground floor and one on the top. Tate watches footage of the thief approach the pay machine. He pulls a small zip-lock bag from his pocket and extracts a five-dollar note. He puts the ticket into the machine, and then the money, and a moment later the ticket comes back out. He doesn't collect his change. He returns to the car, and sixty seconds later he's driving away.

The IT guy fiddles with the controls and shows Tate the

spotters. One has to be the big guy Doctor Mann and Hazel saw. The timing shows all three entering the building two minutes apart from each other. All are dressed in hoodies and baseball caps. One stays on the ground floor, one goes to the roof, and the third patrols the levels, looking for a car where the ticket has been left behind.

'We're going to need copies of this footage,' Schroder says.

'Won't be a problem,' Misk says.

'How far back does the footage go?'

'A month. After that it's deleted to make space,' the IT guy says.

'Then give us everything you have from the last month. These guys might have been in here checking the place out in that time.'

Out of the office they discuss what they have. The car thief was experienced. The three men worked well as a unit. They knew to wear gloves and keep their faces down. They have access to firearms and silencers. The money they used to pay for the ticket came from a sealed bag. They were careful. They could have stolen the safe-installer's car, but probably felt it was too big a risk in case a neighbour called it in. A car-parking building gave them anonymity in an environment they could control, rather than having a neighbour look out their window and see the car of somebody who was on holiday rolling down the driveway. The ticket for the car will have been swallowed up by the exit machine on the way out of the parking building but will only have Lee's fingerprints on it.

'Guys this good, they have to be in the system somewhere,' Schroder says.

'Unless they're so good they've never been caught.'

'Can't be a lot of people willing to execute children, and there sure can't be that many as big as that guy we just saw. Let's head to the station and run some records. If we're lucky, we'll get a hit on one of them.'

'Sure,' Tate says, 'but first let's go to the hospital and check in on James.'

Chapter Nine

Though stabilised, Doctor McCoy knows James Garrett is by no means out of the woods, though there has been some good news. X-rays have shown they've been lucky with the bullet and that it hasn't fragmented. Right now it's resting above the back of the jaw. With the bleeding stopped, it's now their job to patch up as much as they can, then back out of the wound carefully before any attempts are made to retrieve the bullet.

The adrenaline flooding his system as he fought to save James's life has disappeared. It's four in the morning. He is both mentally and physically fatigued. He hands things over to another surgeon and steps out, needing a coffee or some fresh air or possibly both.

He peels his gloves off and tosses them into a bin. His mask and hat and scrubs go into a separate one. He steps into the waiting room and isn't surprised to see people waiting on him. The two in suits are no doubt detectives, and the two older folks sitting with their arms around a young girl will be family. The men in suits introduce themselves. Detective Inspector Carl Schroder and Detective Inspector Theodore Tate. Nobody shakes hands.

'Doctor McCoy, like in *Star Trek*?' Tate asks.

'People around here call me Bones, but I wish they wouldn't. I've never seen the show.' The surprise on Tate's face is a look he's seen a thousand times before. It's like they think he was raised on another planet.

He tells them what James has gone through, describes the injuries, cutting away the skull, how the bullet tunnelled through the back of the brain to the jaw. 'We lost him four times on the table, but he kept coming back. I've never seen such a strong will to survive.'

'And will he?' Schroder asks.

'We've done everything we can. The rest is up to him.'

'If he pulls through, what's his prognosis?' Tate asks.

Doctor McCoy sighs heavily. The fatigue has a weight to it, and right now it's trying to pull him into the floor. He looks over at the family. The younger sister, probably, and her grandparents. They look nervous. Anxious. He isn't surprised they haven't rushed up to him yet for an update. Sometimes people are desperate to know. Other times they're too frightened to find out.

'It's not good, and we won't know for some time how bad things may be. He could be blind, or mute, or paralysed. He might have the intellect of a toddler, or not even that. The poor kid might never wake up. But there's hope. The human brain has the ability to rewire itself. It can do some miraculous things, and that's what it will take here – a miracle. There's a lot of damage, a lot of inflammation, and he lost a lot of blood. If you're thinking he's going to be able to give you answers as to what happened, then you need to think again. Even if we do get that miracle, there's every chance the bullet has wiped out the day's memories, or even a lifetime's worth.'

The two detectives look solemn as they take that on board. The three of them say nothing for several seconds, then Tate asks about the condition of the bullet.

'It's in one piece. Right now another surgeon is formulating a plan on how to retrieve it, and as soon as he does, you'll have it. Is that the sister?' he asks, glancing over at the girl.

'Hazel,' Tate says.

'A hell of a thing for anybody to go though, let alone a young teenager. You figured out who did this?'

'We're working on it,' Schroder says.

'Somebody capable of shooting a child in the back of the head is capable of anything.'

'That's why—'

'Yeah, yeah, I get it,' McCoy says. 'That's why you need the bullet. Look, I better go update the family. You'll have your bullet soon, I promise, but as far as talking to James, you're going to have to wait. Whether it's days, or weeks, or months, I don't know. It could be years, or it may never happen at all.'

PART TWO

Chapter Ten

Home will be a hotel suite for the days that follow the attack while the house is processed. It's a nice room, and all the expenses are paid for, including the mini bar, which contains Toblerones that James fights Hazel for – a fight she happily loses on account of him pushing her to the window last night. Things all turned out okay, but they might not have if she had been dragged downstairs too, and that alone entitles him to eat all the chocolate he wants – hers too.

The hotel has a heated pool on the roof, and a view of the city in one direction and the Port Hills in the other. While the police interview his parents, he and Hazel have the entire pool to themselves. They order hamburgers for lunch and hit repeat for dinner. After the interviews his mum goes into hospital to have the dressing on her wound changed, and Dad comes up to the pool to remind them not to talk to strangers – of which there are many, they are told – downstairs with cameras and microphones, wanting the story. It's a good day – but one marred by the bad headache that hasn't left since the blow he took last night. The pills help, but only a little. The headlines that evening are all about what happened to his family. Everyone at school will be talking about it. He wonders if the kids who are sometimes mean to him will now be nice.

Day two and the mini bar is restocked and the room is tidied. Winter has kicked back in, so no more swimming. He reads a lot, and Hazel watches TV. The police have told them they're heroes – Hazel for getting help, James for helping Hazel, his dad for fighting off the attackers, his mum for opening fire. They eat hamburgers for lunch, and again for dinner. He could get used to this. The headache persists. He takes more pills.

Day three and they return home, the police sneaking them out the back of the hotel and past the media. The carpet throughout their ground floor has been replaced, and the bullet holes in the walls patched and painted. The only evidence a crime happened here is the growing crowd of reporters in the street who have gotten wind the family has returned.

He goes back to school ten days after the shooting, and by now something new and shiny has distracted the reporters, making him old news. But he's still a hit at school, and his classmates ask for his story, which he would be happy to tell a million times, but soon finds himself quickly tiring of the telling. He thinks he should write it up. He can talk to the police officers involved and learn more about the three men who attacked his family to give his words some backstory. His mum sees a plastic surgeon about the wound on her face, and is told it can be made almost invisible.

Over the following month the headaches fade, but the dreams start. The first dream, he's lying on a bed in a bright room. A spaceship? No. He only thinks it is because the book he's currently reading is a science-fiction novel about a boy abducted by aliens. In the book the boy escapes and finds other abductees on board taken from across different periods of time.

He has the same dream a few days later, only this time there's a figure in the room next to him. He can't turn to see who, because the aliens have injected him with a paralytic. He can't move, can't talk, can barely open his eyes.

The dream changes from a spaceship, and to a government laboratory, no doubt, he imagines, because of the new book he's reading – he's finished the alien one and moved onto one about a teenager with a mutant gene that gives him the ability to walk through walls. The imagery is similar: a bright room, he can't move, a figure next to him, only instead of an alien-injected paralytic, it's a government one.

The dreams evolve over the weeks before settling in the end not on the spaceship, or the laboratory, but in a hospital room, and the figure in the room is no longer an alien, or a government agent, but his sister. Hazel is reading books to him, which makes no sense, because Hazel has never read him a book in her life, and never would, not unless the book was about a boy named James whose parents kept him locked in a cage.

Six months after the shooting, he tells Hazel about the dreams. She asks why he is blaming her? He isn't, but that doesn't stop her from calling him an idiot. For his birthday she buys him a collection of short stories, so perhaps she doesn't hate him at all. For Christmas she gets him a second volume, and for his birthday the following year she gets him nothing.

His parents invest in a piece of property with an old warehouse on it, the goal being to tear it down and develop an apartment complex. The warehouse has long wooden floorboards and wooden walls, lined with windows up high. It was used for importing office furniture. It reminds him of the one used at the end of Raiders of the Lost Ark, only instead of there being thousands of wooden crates, there are hundreds of abandoned filing cabinets.

High school starts. He navigates through his first year. He has friends. He has bullies. This is what high school is. As his first year turns into a second, he is reminded over and over that he needs to choose a direction, and that means thinking about university. When he tells his English teacher he wants to be a novelist, she tells him people can't make money from writing, and to choose something else. The following year a different teacher, while on holiday, falls from a hotel balcony and lands in a coma. All the students sign get-well cards to send Mrs Perry good thoughts.

As school progresses, he can't think of what he wants to do with his future. He can't figure out how anybody could. Hazel graduates from high school and goes to university, and isn't around as much. She dates a guy named Jeff, or Geoff, she never tells James how it's *spelled. Hazel had broken her ankle playing netball, and Mum drove her to the hospital, and that's where they met – her in the waiting room with a broken ankle, Geoff Jeff with a broken leg. It surprises him that he misses seeing her.*

His parents don't develop the warehouse. There are issues with the permits, and development may not go ahead, which means the eyesore remains an eyesore. James doesn't understand all the terminology, but does understand what his dad means when he says they may end up taking a bath on the deal.

Seven years after the night when men tried to kill them, he graduates high school, then starts a gap year. He considers travel, but can't decide where to go. He thinks about getting a job, but doesn't know what. He gets to work on the novel he's always wanted to write. Hazel moves out, and his dad turns her bedroom into a library. It becomes James's favourite room in the house.

His parents leave the real-estate firm they are working for and branch out on their own. At the same time, his mum shows her paintings after her friend introduces her to an art-gallery owner. Eight years after the shooting, she sells her first piece. James finishes his novel, sends it to some publishers, but doesn't hear back. He starts a second. That same year, GJ proposes to Hazel. She says yes.

The gap year ends. James enrols in university, focusing on English and psychology. He still has the dreams, but way less frequently, as if not only is Hazel too busy for him when he's awake, but also now when he's asleep.

Nine years after the attack, the headaches come back. All these years it's the first he's been sick. The same goes for his parents, and Hazel. Well, there was that time Hazel broke her ankle, and that time his dad stood on a nail that went through his foot, but nothing else. No colds. No sniffles. No hay fever.

The headaches intensify the dreams.

He is back in the government lab.

He is back in the spacecraft.
He can hear voices
Voices...
Voices that follow him into the dreams and back out. He can
Can—

Can...

...turn his head to the side, but only just. His neck hurts. His head hurts. He can move his fingers and toes, but nothing else, the paralytic the aliens have used is coursing through his body. This dream – it's different from the others. And he's thirsty, so thirsty. When he goes to speak, he can't. Something is down his throat. *You're being choked!* He panics. Why can't he wake up? Footsteps. An elevator dinging. Tapping. He can't breathe. He focuses on his arms. Nothing. He focuses on his legs. Nothing there either. Have they been amputated? He can't even look down his body to check, so maybe ... no, if he can feel his fingers and toes then that means he has his arms and legs, unless ... unless it's both? Can aliens amputate and still have you feel what's missing?

Why can't he wake up?

His body isn't his body. The spacemen, have they transplanted his brain? He's read books where that has happened, and seen it in TV shows. It must be what's giving him the imagery for this dream...

This dream that doesn't feel like a dream.

He tries to lift his head. Can't do it. But he can turn it a little more than a moment ago. There is a doorway to his left, and beyond it a brightly lit corridor. Somebody walks past – a nurse! He bites his lip and feels the pain. So not a dream. What's the last thing he can remember? He was driving to university ... then what? He strains his eyes to look down his body. He's flat on a bed. His arms are on top of a white blanket. He has them, which comes as a huge relief. But they are thinner than they should be, and the same shade of white as the sheet. *How can that be? How can they look so thin but feel so heavy? What accident has landed you here?*

He rolls his head to the right. Five other beds, five other patients, all of them asleep, all of them pale.

'Oh my God, James?'

He turns his head back to the door. A nurse is coming toward him, a woman his mum's age maybe, but with greyer hair. He doesn't recognise her, but her voice sounds familiar.

'You're awake,' she says.

Yes, he's awake, and when he goes to say that, he finds he can't. All he can do is groan.

She takes his hand. 'Don't panic. You have a feeding tube down your throat. You're in a hospital. You're safe. You need to relax. I know you're confused, and scared, but you need to stay calm.'

He can't stay calm. Something isn't right here. Not right at all. He knows what a feeding tube is, but doesn't understand why he would need one.

'I'm going to remove the tube, okay?'

His neck feels tired. The tube down his throat tickles. He had thought it had gone through his mouth, but it's down his throat through his nose. It's uncomfortable and tickles more as she pulls on it. He can still feel it after it's gone.

'Do you know who you are?'

He nods. He knows. He's James Garrett, university student, a man who once almost lost his family, a man who used to have headaches and recurring dreams, who one day will be a writer.

'You've been in a coma.'

A coma? Like Mrs Perry from school? How can that be?

'I'll get your doctor, and I'll call Hazel, and I'll be right back. They'll be excited you're awake,' she says, smiling so hard he wouldn't be surprised if her face broke in half. 'They can explain everything.'

He tries to ask her to tell him now, but nothing comes out. She squeezes his hand one more time, then heads for the door.

Chapter Eleven

He's bored and he's broke – two bad things made worse when combined, even more so when they result in him focusing on why his wife left him. Though, technically, she didn't leave him – she forced him to leave her, kicking him out of the house along with the suitcases she had packed for him. He isn't sure what he loved more – his wife, or his house – and three years on he's not sure which of those two he now hates the most. Easy to think it should be the wife – but, damn, if there aren't days he'd like to see the townhouse on fire, and days where he'd like to see Jessica screaming from the window while it was.

It's late. He's still in his police uniform, lying on his couch, where he's been since getting home from work hours ago. He's been listening to the rain outside, knowing there's no point in going to bed because he wouldn't sleep anyway – not when his thoughts are a tornado of anger that won't blow itself out, brought on by today being the day the divorce became final, meaning they're no longer thoughts of his wife, but of his ex-wife. He's also been listening to a drip in the hallway that he ought to do something about, only he did something about it weeks ago when he patched the broken roof tile above it with silicon, but it seems the silicon hasn't taken hold. He had Googled it before attempting the repair, and fifty percent of people said this was the best idea ever and those who disagreed were assholes, and fifty percent said it was the worst idea ever, and those who disagreed could go fuck themselves. He's hungry, but doesn't feel like going to the effort of making anything. He could order something, but doesn't know what he feels like having. Plus – there's the broke thing.

The drip, drip, drip from the hallway. He climbs off the couch. The carpet is so thin it hurts his feet. He puts on a pair of slippers and goes to the laundry. He has to shove the door to get it to open because it's swollen in the damp. He grabs a bucket and sets it beneath the leak in the hallway. The insulation in the ceiling is paper thin, worn down by sixty years of neglect and the spiders and birds that sneak in under the eaves. The ceiling has bowed and discoloured from where water has pooled above it, the drips seeping from the bottom of that bow and landing – thud, thud, thud – in the bucket.

He grabs a beer, the fridge light not coming on because it burned out over a year ago. He pops open the beer, hoping it will quench his appetite for food, and goddamn it, it sprays foam over his uniform. Even though Jess isn't here, he can still hear her asking, *Why the hell didn't you get changed when you got home? Did you want to make a mess?*

To which he would have said yes, that's exactly what he wanted to do, which wouldn't have helped. In hindsight, they're the kind of conversations that had her cheating on him with Stephen, and then with Craig, before leaving him for Wayne and telling him about all three when she took the house, as if she needed to hurl one more fuck-you at him in a long string of fuck-yous. She even blamed him for the affairs. She said he was distant, emotionally stunted, that he lacked empathy, that he focused too much on his job, which sent her looking for affection elsewhere. She got angry at him when he laughed at her for crying at the end of rom-coms, and concerned when he'd root for the bad guy in horror movies. But don't you want teenagers to get sliced and diced in ways you haven't seen before? He thought so. Jess didn't. Then there was the fight they had when he didn't understand why she was so upset when her grandmother died. She was acting like she was the only person in the world who had lost somebody, and it wasn't as if she had visited the old trout since she'd gone into the care home anyway. In that moment he wondered if he had a type. Years earlier he'd dated a woman who liked going to funerals of people she barely knew just for the contact sympathy.

In the end Jess blamed herself for the marriage falling apart, telling him she should have known better, that she had ignored all the signs going in. He had asked her to reconsider. She had told him about Wayne. He forgave her. Then she told him about Craig. And Stephen.

He strips out of his uniform and bunches it into the machine. He puts it on a hot wash because Jessica always hated it when he did hot washes, after all, the detergent was designed for cold water, and didn't he want to save the planet? She made it sound as though every time he turned on a hot tap, somewhere a dolphin would pop.

He finishes his beer and grabs another. It's not as cold as he'd like it – nothing in the fridge ever is because of the seal peeling away. He hates the fridge. Hates the ceiling. Hates this house that he can barely afford the mortgage for. He's always fancied himself a bit of a handyman, but hasn't been able to put it into practice. This house, so it seems, was scarified by the gods so others could increase in value.

He flicks on the TV because it's one thing in the house that works as it should. There's a piece on the news about Joe Middleton – dubbed the Christchurch Carver – who terrorised the city for years, picking off women while working as a janitor at the police department. Three years ago Middleton was arrested, and two years ago he escaped, and as of today nobody has any idea where he is – or even if he's still in Christchurch ... or New

Zealand. Documentaries and books and articles and online forums have given Middleton cult-like celebrity status. There isn't a week that goes by he won't see somebody wearing an *I survived the Christchurch Carver* T-shirt, and every time there is another murder in the city, Middleton trends on social media as people theorise if he could have just added to the eleven victims they know of. And now the news is talking about a movie that will soon go into production about him. It will cover his childhood, follow him through his killings, and on to his eventual escape from the police. He turns off the TV – he can't watch this shit. He heard about the movie a month ago; it pissed him off back then and it's going to piss him off even more moving forward.

What would it be like to be the Carver? Not to care about anything but yourself? He thinks it must be pretty damn good, and he'd be lying if he said he wasn't jealous of the guy's fame – and the greater fame to come if the movie goes ahead. Sometimes, when he's a few beers in and hating Jess more than when he's sober, he lets his imagination take hold and wonders if he really could light that fire, and watch the townhouse and Jessica burn. He imagines what it would be like to have his hands around her throat, having her writhe beneath him, her eyes bulging as she glances to Wayne for help – only Wayne can't help because Wayne has been nailed to the wall.

Three years ago his fantasy was less about strangling Jess and more about being the one to catch the Carver. He even had a box full of notes he'd made after his visits to the crime scenes, notes detailing what the detectives were telling him, dozens of photos he snapped and articles printed from the Internet. He used to picture himself on the news, folks fawning over him, folks calling him a hero. He used to imagine busting the case open, becoming famous, and it'd be him Hollywood would be focusing on, not the Carver. But he never made any headway, and then Middleton was caught. He hasn't looked through the box in over two years, but he still has it, buried in his wardrobe somewhere.

There is a creaking sound from the hallway, followed by a grinding. He gets there as the ceiling stretches, like a balloon being inflated. He can't do anything but watch as it tears open, the drywall falls away, and old insulation and dirty rainwater splash into the hall.

Chapter Twelve

The marlin Doctor Wolfgang McCoy has hooked is leaping into the sky and blotting out the sun. Caroline is offering encouragement, as is his accountant, and a patient he removed a brain tumour from over a month ago. The marlin hits the water and leaps again, all while his phone is ringing ... ringing ... and Caroline grabs him by the shoulder and shakes him...

'Wolfie,' she says, 'your phone.'

'My phone what?' he grumbles, the marlin landing, but there's no splash, no boat, no ocean, then no marlin. It's all been replaced by his pillow, his bed, his nightstand, his phone.

'Your phone,' she says.

He groans into his pillow. He wants to go back to the marlin, but at this time of night it's going to be the hospital, and that means somebody is fighting to survive. He rolls over and takes the call. 'McCoy here.'

'Doctor, it's Bianca Sadler.' He pictures Nurse Sadler at the nurses' station on the third floor, gripping the phone. 'It's James Garrett,' she says, and he goes from picturing Nurse Sadler to picturing James Garrett, first as the boy he operated on, then as the young man he has grown into – albeit in a bed in the coma ward.

'He woke up a few minutes ago.'

It takes a moment for her words to make sense, so sure was he that she was about to say James had passed away. 'Are you sure?' he asks, which is a stupid question, because of course she's sure, but it's been so long.

So long.

'Very. He's weak, but he's lucid.'

'What does he know?'

'Only that he's been in a coma, but not for how long. I haven't told him anything about his family.'

'Have you called Hazel?'

'I thought you'd want to.'

He's on his feet, moving around the bedroom. He doesn't remember standing. 'And cognitively? How is he?'

'He's aware. Confused and scared, but aware.'

'Find Hazel's number and text it to me. I'll call her when I'm on my way.'

Caroline has fallen asleep during the phone call. He grabs his clothes and sneaks downstairs to get dressed. His phone beeps with Hazel Garrett's number. The same way he has seen James grow up, he has seen Hazel grow up too. She was taken in by her grandparents, who would drive her to the hospital every day to sit with James and read to him. Once she had read him all his favourite books, she used her pocket money to buy more. Back then Wolfgang hunted through his home and found boxes of books from his own childhood for her, books he had kept for his own children back when he thought he could have children. Other doctors and nurses did the same. Hazel was more dedicated than anybody he has ever met in his time as a surgeon, but a daily ritual becomes impossible to maintain, and after two years her daily visits became every second day, then weekly, and ultimately monthly. His heart broke for her, this young woman whose parents were brutally killed and whose brother was alive only in the technical sense of the word. He last saw her two weeks ago. She didn't ask how James was doing – she hasn't asked that question in years, because the answer was always the same: there was no change.

And now, in the middle of a Monday night the same as any other, there is.

Chapter Thirteen

The nurse introduces herself as Bianca. She tells him he can call her B, which he can, because over the last twenty minutes James's voice has gained enough strength to make single syllable sounds. When he says 'B', it doesn't sound like 'be', but 'ba'. All the letters sound different to how they feel when he says them.

Surely you should be able to speak better than this after a week in a coma?

But his arms – his stick-like arms make him think the coma might have been longer.

A month?

Maybe.

Longer?

You're about to find out.

The headache has faded. Nurse Ba tells him feeling will return to his body, but doesn't say when. She tells him his doctor, Wolfgang McCoy, is on his way, and he's never met a Wolfgang before.

Is this even real?

A great question. Where are his parents? Where's Hazel? As he waits, other nurses come and go, peering in the doorway and smiling at him like he's a carnival attraction. He doesn't know what he feels more – hunger, exhaustion, fear or confusion – only that he feels all of them. He's frustrated Nurse Ba won't tell him what happened, instead telling him Doctor Wolfgang and Hazel will be here soon. He is extremely aware she hasn't mentioned his parents.

He plays over the last thing he remembers – the drive to university. No. Strike that, he had been to university, and he was home, he had gone to bed. He remembers that, but not what came next. What could have happened to have landed him here? The harder he tries to force the memory, the more frustrated he becomes. Perhaps he drove to university the next day, where an accident wiped his memories along with his sense of time. Or perhaps he had a brain embolism during the night.

It takes a few moments to realise the woman in the pyjamas who comes into his room isn't another patient, but Hazel. Her hair is significantly longer since last week at dinner. She must be wearing a wig. She's taller too, even though she's only wearing slippers. Weird she would rush out in her slippers and flannel pyjamas, wrapped up in a thick jacket, yet have taken time to cover her freckles with makeup. She leans in and hugs him fierce, her arms slipping beneath him. The makeup, the wig, Hazel being taller – that's all weird enough on its own, but hugging him? If he wasn't sure this was his sister a moment ago, now he's convinced she isn't. He doesn't have the strength to pull away.

'Be careful with him,' Nurse Ba says, as though Hazel might break him in half. She releases her grip. When she pulls back she's crying.

'I always knew you were going to wake up,' she says.

She makes it sound like you've been asleep a year!

'Ha,' he says.

'Are you laughing?' she asks, smiling, but still with the tears.

'Ha,' he says again.

'He's trying to say your name,' Nurse Ba says. 'I'm Ba, for Bianca, and you're Ha, for Hazel.'

'He can't talk?'

'He's had a feeding tube down his throat for...' she says, but pulls up short of saying for how long. She lowers her voice, but even so, James hears her say, 'He doesn't know yet.'

Hazel, her voice to match, asks, 'Any of it?'

Nurse Ba shakes her head.

The panic building inside him builds some more. If he could, he would yell, *What is going on here?* Nurse Ba moves aside, and a man who isn't dressed like a doctor but probably is comes in. Doctor Wolfgang maybe? James stares at him while Hazel drags a chair over so she can sit and hold his hand in both of hers. She keeps smiling, the same trying-to-break-her-face-in-half smile Nurse Ba gave him earlier.

'I'm so glad you're back,' Hazel says.

Back from where?

She smiles. She cries. She tightens her grip on his hand. She looks up at the doctor, and he has one of those stupid smiles too.

'Hello, James, my name is Doctor Wolfgang McCoy,' he says. 'I know you have questions, and I know you're scared, and I want to assure you that even though you can barely move right now, and can't talk, these things are hopefully only temporary.'

Hopefully?

'Together we're going to work at getting you back on your feet.'

Doctor Wolfgang looks at Hazel, and Hazel nods, and tightens her grip on James's hand so much he groans with pain. She quickly relaxes. 'Sorry.'

'Wh ha?' he asks, and it sounds enough like *what happened* for Hazel to get it – but what else would he be asking?

'You've been in a coma for ... for nine years, and...'

Nine years?

NINE YEARS?

He's been here since he was twenty? Impossible. That makes

him ... twenty-nine, and Hazel thirty-two, but she doesn't look thirty-two.

'James?'

It doesn't make sense. None of this does. He looks at her. He blinks back tears.

'Can you hear me?'

He nods. He can't imagine how this can possibly get any worse. And then it does.

Chapter Fourteen

Wolfgang watches as James struggles to process the information, his face riddled with the pain of what he's being told. Ironically, this is a good thing because it tells McCoy the damage he feared all those years ago may have been avoided. But for James, it's as though his parents only died two minutes ago. Over the years Hazel has always said she would be the one to break the news when James woke up. It was always 'when', and never 'if'. Wolfgang has admired her optimism, even if he couldn't share it, and has on occasion reminded her that if James were to wake, he will not have progressed mentally beyond the age of eleven – and that was a best-case scenario. Tomorrow he will try to determine where James is at; and despite never wanting to have given false hope, he's now hopeful.

James cries as he listens, and moves his head from side to side in small movements. His fingers twitch. Over the years a physiotherapist has routinely exercised James in an attempt to avoid atrophy, but nevertheless, most of his muscles have worn away. Even if the head trauma hasn't removed James's ability to walk, it will be months before he can even try.

Hazel doesn't go into detail, but she does tell James the men who did this were never caught. Wolfgang remembers how confident both Tate and Schroder were in the beginning, and how that confidence turned into frustration and ultimately defeat when every avenue dried up. The likelihood of them solving the case seemed as slim as James waking up, and perhaps the two were linked somehow, in which case now that one thing has happened, perhaps the other will too. They will be eager to talk to him in the hope that can happen. Or at least Tate will.

Wolfgang has had a career of breaking bad news to people, but watching Hazel give the news to James hurts deeper than those other times. He can't be here. He briefly interrupts them:

'I'm going to come back in the morning, James, to check on you. I really can't tell you how pleased I am that you're here,' he says. He wishes he could add something more to help, but there's nothing. He can't remember the last time he felt so useless.

Hazel hugs him. She hugged him the night he told her James was going to survive, and it caught on, with her hugging him hello and goodbye every time she sees him, but this time she's squeezing the air out of him. 'Thank you for everything,' she says.

It's not often he's lost for words, but he's lost now. She goes back to her brother, and he slips out of the room, telling Nurse Sadler to walk the line between giving them privacy while keeping an eye on them, and in fifteen minutes to remind Hazel her brother will need rest.

His footfalls echo down the corridor as he walks to his office. He turns the desk lamp on and sits down heavily. He retrieves a metal tin from his desk drawer, full of business cards he's collected over the years. He goes through them now, first finding the card for Detective Inspector Carl Schroder and then the one for Detective Inspector Theodore Tate. He drops the one for Schroder in the bin. He considers calling Tate, but it's one in the morning – Tate has waited nine years, he can wait another nine hours. The last thing James needs right now is the police showing up full of questions.

Chapter Fifteen

After Nurse Ba tells I lazel it's time to leave, and Hazel has hugged him and told him she will be back in the morning, James stares at the ceiling, wondering how can any of what Hazel has told him be real. The last nine years are so solid, so set in stone, that it will take more than words to shake those foundations. Knowing this isn't real, knowing his parents are alive, that this is some kind of trick, calms him somewhat, but still leaves him concerned as to what is going on here. His parents are fine. The real Hazel is engaged to a man named GJ. His mum is selling paintings and his dad turned Hazel's room into a library. James is a twenty-year-old university student who is either experiencing a strange kind of dream, or perhaps a psychosis. It's possible he's experiencing the very coma they told him he has woken up from.

His head hurts thinking about it.

Perhaps the only way out of this dream – or coma – is to fall asleep, which will wake him up in the real world. Only that thought isn't comforting either. What if Hazel and the doctor aren't lying? What if one truth, one timeline, became split the night he was shot? Falling asleep now could send him back into the coma from which he just emerged. Would he ever wake from it again? Not such a bad thing if the world he returned to is the same one he just left, but what if it's different now? What if it's changed by what he's just learned? When you wake from an awesome dream, you can never return no matter how hard you try. In a world that may never have really existed, what if the Christchurch he returns to is a wasteland of crumbled buildings and bloody skies?

In the end it's a moot point. Whether he wants to fall asleep or not, the choice isn't his. The fatigue is pulling at him, which suggests this is real. The thoughts, the fears, this world, Fake Hazel or Real, soon it's all gone as his eyes close and...

Hazel is back. Real Hazel, with the pixie-cut and the freckles. They're holding hands in the warehouse his parents bought and took a bath on. It's her first time here.

'Why all the cabinets?' she asks.

'I'm not sure, but there are more than there used to be.'

'What's written on the front of them?'

'Dates.'

'Dates from what?'

'I don't know. But they go back a long way.'

She tries to open one of the drawers, only to find it won't budge.

'They're all locked,' he says.

'You can't stay here.'

'Can't I?'

'Story time is over, James. You know that, right? You know none of it was real.'

He knows, he just doesn't want to admit it. He runs his fingers across the top of the newest filing cabinet. It has today's date on it. There's no dust on it, but it will gather there, the same way it's gathered on the cabinets deeper in.

Hazel turns toward him and takes his other hand too. 'You had a good nine years, James, but you have to let us go. You have to say goodbye to us. To this life.'

'I don't want to.'

'Our parents are gone. It's hard, I know it is, but you will get through this.'

'How can I grieve for parents who, for me, never died?'

'I will be there for you every step of the way, I promise,' she says. 'It will be okay.'

'Will it?'

She doesn't answer. She fades, the warehouse fades, everything fades.

Chapter Sixteen

A younger Wolfgang had a pull-out sofa put into his office for the nights he was too tired to drive home. Now the older Wolfgang climbs off it for the first time in over ten years. In those ten years he has gone from a man in his early fifties to one in his early sixties who feels like one in his late seventies. It's seven in the morning. He didn't get to sleep until three, and the sleep he got wasn't great. He massages his knees and neck, then stretches out the aches in his back before freshening up in the staff facilities. He phones Caroline and apologises for not making it back home, and she laughs and says it's the best sleep she's had in years.

After a quick hospital-café breakfast, he's told James Garrett has woken up. James barely acknowledges his presence when he goes to check in on him. Hazel is sitting next to the bed, holding his hand. Wolfgang signals her to follow him back into the corridor.

'The more we can understand, the better we can plan a way to get him back on his feet. I know he won't feel like it, but it's important we move forward and catch any problems before they get worse. I'd like to check his sight and hearing this morning.'

'I'll tell him.'

'We have to remember that despite appearances, we're still dealing with an eleven-year-old boy. Children don't understand that the work they need to put in – or won't put in – will affect them for the rest of their lives.'

'I know.'

'It's going to take time, Hazel.'

'I know that too.'

He doesn't doubt it. 'Tell him I'll be back soon to examine him. I'm going to have him transferred into a private room, and I'll get him some clothes too.'

'Thank you.'

'I'm going to have to let the police know he's woken up.'

'He's not ready to talk to them.'

'Agreed. Let me explain the situation to them. Don't worry, I'll make sure they give him some time, but they need to know.'

He returns to his office. He stares at Tate's business card, knowing the detective will be eager to talk – and hopeful James can remember something. A long time ago Hazel told Wolfgang that James had an eidetic memory. Wolfgang has never met somebody with one before, but has always wished he had the ability to recall something he'd seen in the past in such vivid detail. It's rare among children, and almost unheard of in adults. The hope is James saw something that night that is lodged in his memory that can help. He hopes so. The police will hope so too.

He dials Tate's number while watching the rain fall against the window. He hates this time of year. Hates the cold days, the damp air, hates the colour and life stripped from the city. The number he's calling turns out to be disconnected.

He's about to call the police station when he decides to take the disconnected number as a sign from above. He still hasn't gotten around to believing in God, but with James waking up, maybe it's time to start. The police can wait.

Chapter Seventeen

Jessica hasn't come begging for him to return. He's still broke. His house hasn't got any less shitty and his career hasn't changed trajectory. He has taken advantage of the sunny day, despite the cold, to reseal the broken tile. He's put duct tape over it too, despite fifty percent of the Internet calling him a snowflake for doing so. The ceiling in the hallway is open, the damaged drywall cut away, and the beams in the ceiling exposed. Cold air flows between the tiles and swirls through the house. Something is living up there too – he thinks perhaps a possum. To top it all off, his uniform shrunk in the wash the other night – thanks, Jess. If he hadn't been so annoyed at her, he would have just done a cold wash, but...

'But nothing. But everything.'

He wrestles a large piece of drywall into his hallway. He scores and snaps it into manageable sizes for the ceiling since he is working alone. He's lucky the leak didn't spread across multiple rooms. There still won't be any insulation, but that's tomorrow's problem. Or next week's. Or, if he's being honest with himself, next summer's problem. He gets to work, a mosaic of rectangles going up over the following two hours, a job that would have taken fifteen minutes if Jess hadn't kept the cordless drill. His forearms are numb by the end of it, and the ceiling is a mess, but it sure as hell looks better than before. He is putting the ladder away when a high-pitched squeal above the ceiling makes him jump. At the same time the stereo playing music from the lounge goes dead. He flicks a light switch – nothing. Whatever is living in the ceiling isn't living anymore.

He breathes out hard and fights the temptation to stab the screwdriver through the wall, and gives into the temptation of a beer instead. He nurses it while thinking about how everything wrong in his life can be linked back to Jess. He wishes she were dead. He's heard people quip how police officers and detectives earn a living off people's heartache and pain, the same way doctors need folks to get cancer and break legs. Which means if he were to kill Jess, he could earn money by helping to solve her murder. That would make it doubly good. Not that he'd get the chance to solve anything. Two minutes after Jess's body was found he'd be dragged out of his house in handcuffs. There's no way he could get away with it.

He finishes his beer, then hunts around the junk drawer in the kitchen for a flashlight. He finds it, but the batteries are flat. Thanks, Jess. He carries the ladder to a manhole in the bedroom closet. He switches off the power at the fuse board, climbs into the ceiling, and uses the light on his cellphone to look around. It wasn't a possum, but a rat – a large one at that, its teeth still embedded in the cable going to the lights. He removes the rat, then tugs on the cable, hoping to find some slack, and what do you know, he does. He cuts the damaged section away and rewires the two ends, patching it with insulation tape. Illegal, sure, but he can't afford legal these days – and it's not like this is the first law he's broken over the last few years so he could keep paying the bills.

He climbs down and turns the power back on. The lights stay off.

Goddamn it.

Jessica. It's all goddamn Jessica's fault, and there's not a thing he can do to her.

He grabs another beer and lights some candles and puts them around the dining room. He sits at the table with the files that didn't help him catch Joe Middleton, the files that didn't make him famous, having gotten them out of the closet earlier to throw away. What a waste of time that was back then. Solve the case, get a movie deal, and play himself. Was it too much to ask?

He guesses it was.

Hell, he'd have been better off killing people and…

Shit.

Maybe it's the beer, maybe it's the whole ceiling fiasco, maybe it's the dead rat – but he returns to an idea that on bad days likes to come out and play. He couldn't be famous solving the Carver case, but ever since Jess left him he's known about another way that Middleton can make him a star. And truth be told, it's not like he hasn't imagined his hands around Jessica's neck a thousand times.

Of course, it's just an idea, and entertaining an idea doesn't make him a monster, nor is it against the law. And it couldn't hurt to play it out a little – and after all, the box with all the Middleton files is out on the table anyway.

He knocks back his beer and slams the bottle down onto the table heavier than he wanted. He still needs to figure out why the power isn't on, but for now he empties the box out onto the table and starts to read.

Chapter Eighteen

James has a private room with a view to Hagley Park, where, over the following days, he watches people jogging along one short edge of the tree-lined one-and-a-half-square-kilometre grounds, and on weekends he watches people hunting for parking spaces for the several games of rugby played there. There's a golf course in the park too; years ago he followed his dad around it while he played, and it was his job to keep score. He isn't sure if that ever happened. He can remember it, but was it before or during the coma?

In his room there's a TV bolted to the wall that in the mornings plays cartoons, and in the afternoons plays renovating shows where a steady stream of folks are shocked to find subfloors and electrical wiring in far worse condition than they had anticipated. There is a couch that Hazel spends a lot of time on, and a nightstand with some books Hazel has been reading to him. The room also has a private bathroom that he's in no condition to use. He has a catheter, which means he can pee into a bag, and he's learned during the coma he had absorbent pads beneath his body for when he pooped. The thought of that embarrasses him, but being helped into the bathroom these days to do his business is even worse.

There have been days and days of tests. He's given blood. There have been x-rays, and MRIs and reflex tests, there have been cognitive questions where his memory and awareness have been observed. He's worn headphones and listened for beeps, and he's read letters from a chart across the room, grunting out the sounds. He has passed the hearing tests, but one of his eyes, his right, is blurry, like he is looking through a window soaked with condensation. He can, however, feel every needle prodded against him.

As the days go by, he slowly comes to terms with the reality of his situation. He has spent eight years and ten months in what he now thinks of as Coma World. Everything outside of Coma World is The Real World, and in The Real World he has been lying motionless in a bed with a feeding tube down his throat while his body has wasted away. His parents were brutally murdered and are never coming back. Almost half of his life has been a fiction. He's an eleven-year-old kid who looks like a man with no idea what's going to happen to him. He no longer grunts when he tries to speak, but instead he sounds like his granddad did after the stroke. The words are slurred, difficult to pronounce and even more difficult for anybody to understand. He's scared his voice may not return, scared he won't be able to walk, scared he won't be able to move his arms, scared that The Real World is a world of fear. At least his throat doesn't hurt anymore, and the headaches seem to be a thing of the past.

Each day he spends hours in an exercise room seemingly designed to build his frustration more than his muscles – despite the posters of cats and dogs offering slogans of encouragement. He works at lifting his own body weight, first his arms, then his legs, each one weighing a ton, each one impossible until it isn't – the 'isn't' coming eight days after leaving Coma World. And when it does come, it comes quickly – one day he can barely lift his arms off the table, the next he's got them in the air above his body. Soon he can keep them raised for twenty seconds, for thirty, for a minute, which gives him more privacy in the bathroom as he can clean himself up. It takes a few more days for the same to be true for his legs, but eventually he realises that the cats and dogs of the therapy-room posters are right: he can hang in there, he can be purrsitive, he can be pawsome. Even so, no number of cats and dogs can stop him from thinking about his parents. What's the point of building his muscles back when his heart has been ripped out? At night he cries himself to sleep. Other than Hazel, the only people who come to visit are his grandparents – his dad's parents. His other grandparents aren't around – one having died, and the other in a home with dementia. Grandpa Rodney walks with a cane and has nose hairs that blend into his moustache. Grandma Elizabeth keeps baking for him, as if the weight he needs to put on isn't muscle, but cookie fat, and she can't go five minutes without hugging him. They look older than they should, and smaller than when he last saw them.

There is one positive. He has discovered he can visit Coma World whenever he likes – or, more accurately, the warehouse his parents bought. Today sunshine pours through the warehouse windows, the same way it's pouring into the hospital. In the warehouse the dust shimmers in the light when he walks through it, leaving footprints in his wake. Cobwebs hang from the rafters. The whole building looks one discarded cigarette away from destruction, which is probably why the walls are lined with fire alarms and safety axes and emergency exits. The filing cabinets that were once locked he can now open – all but one. And on the ones near the back, the labels have faded – all that's left are grooves made by a ballpoint pen. In Coma World he still has the use of his arms and legs. He can still talk.

There are almost eleven hundred cabinets, each with three drawers, and in each drawer is one day of the life he lived here. He has no memory of filing these memories, but when he reads them, he can remember those moments with such clarity it's as though he's transported into them. The single locked cabinet is in the furthest corner, not only locked, but also with *Do No Open* tape criss-crossed around it. The tape covers the labels, and therefore the dates, but the dates on the cabinet beside it tell him the locked cabinet is from the night his parents were murdered.

'Maybe it's best that you don't,' Hazel said the day after he woke up, when she'd asked if he remembered anything from what he knows the police call 'The Night Of' and he had shaken his head in reply. The part of his mind that built all of this agrees. The warehouse makes him happy, but sometimes sad too. In there he knows who he is. Outside it he barely recognises himself in the mirror.

After two weeks he has enough strength to write. Or at least he thinks he does. He keeps this to himself, because if people figure out he can communicate, they'll want to spend more time with him, and more time with them means less time taking vacations into his past. Hazel – who he reminds himself went through a grieving process perhaps worse than his own – is here more often than not, and Doctor Wolfgang can't go an hour without checking in. His work with the speech therapist hasn't produced the kind of rewards he was hoping for. There's a disconnect between his brain and his mouth. He can form the words, he knows how to say them, only he can't. As Doctor Wolfgang often reminds him, his body has to relearn the fundamentals. He practises when he's by himself, and with the therapist, but not around others.

Three weeks after waking up, and to the joy of Doctor Wolfgang, he mimics he wants a pen. Doctor Wolfgang brings him one, and a pad.

He writes, *Hello,* and it's a relief to see the letters appear. The pen is heavy, but comfortable, and his arm moves well. It's the

Hello of a three-year-old, but it's a start. He writes his name out in full with big wobbly letters, misjudging the edge of the page so only leaving room for half the T. But it's a good opening effort. His arm is tired, but there is still some gas in the tank, so he carries on, focusing on writing smaller, happy to use up one line for one or two words. *Thank you for saving me.*

For a moment Doctor Wolfgang looks sad, which James doesn't understand, but then he smiles, and he says, 'You're welcome.'

He asks one of the questions he's been wanting to ask since joining The Real World. He knows the basics about what happened to his parents, but not the details. *Can I read the news about what happened to my family?*

'I'm not so sure that's a good idea, James. Soon, but not yet, okay?'

The answer doesn't surprise him. *How soon?*

'Let's give it a few more days at least, okay?'

Which James figures means a week, at least. *Can I go home?*

'Not for a while. A month perhaps.'

Which probably means two. He wants to leave here and claw his way back into what is left of his life. He wants to go to the cemetery to say goodbye to his parents. He wants to see his friends from school, to see where they are now, what they're doing. They don't even know he's woken up – nobody does, outside of the doctors and nurses treating him. There will be questions from the police, then from the media, and Doctor Wolfgang and Hazel want to protect him from that for as long as possible.

The two things he has asked for, Doctor Wolfgang has shot down. So he tries a third. *Can I have ice cream?*

Doctor Wolfgang laughs. 'What flavour?'

Chocolate.

'Let me see what I can do.'

Four weeks to the day after waking up, as he's having dinner –

he can use a knife and fork easily now – Doctor Wolfgang comes to see him.

'I think it's time,' he says. 'The men who did this are out there, and it's possible the detective may ask something that can trigger a memory that can help find them.'

James closes his eyes and looks at the locked cabinet wrapped in 'Do Not Open' tape. He was always going to be forced to open it.

Tomorrow.

'Are you sure?'

He nods. He's sure.

'I'll call them in the morning.'

Chapter Nineteen

Thermal curtains block the Tuesday morning light, as well as the view of the rain, the patrol cars, the growing crowd in the street below. The vomit by the bedroom door masks the smell of death and wet clothes. The bedroom is on the top floor of a two-storey house, set back deep on the section, a paddock behind it with large oak trees and hay, and where, perhaps, a killer escaped.

Detective Inspector Rebecca Kent watches as Acting Superintendent Eric Wilson tucks his phone back into his pocket. Tall, gaunt and pale, she's always thought Wilson looked more suited to selling coffins to the bereaved than figuring out what made them bereaved in the first place. She's overheard the call, but her focus has been on the naked body of Denise Laughton, found earlier by her paramedic husband when he came home from a night shift. Denise's legs are bound to her bed, her hands now cut free from the headboard, her eyes open, staring at her killer, for help, at the ceiling, all three. There are bruises on her face, her arms, her legs, her throat. Her pyjamas have been cut away and dumped on the floor by the bed. Whatever blade did that cutting isn't here. On top of the pyjamas is a cracked hardboiled egg.

'You'll never guess who that was,' Wilson says.

Unless it was the killer, or somebody who saw him, she doesn't really care. She also doesn't care for the fact Wilson is even here. He's a good detective, but not a great detective, with the difference between the two often being the difference between finding a killer and not finding one. Worse – these days he outranks her. He has been made acting superintendent while the actual superintendent, Dominic Stevens, takes time off to recover from double-bypass surgery. She's often thought Wilson could move from good to great if he spent more time working the cases and less taking credit for others' successes. She thinks the only reason he was given the job is because he's so concerned with budgets, spending most of his time trying to achieve the most by spending the least.

She realises he's still waiting for her to answer his question. 'Who?'

'Name Doctor Wolfgang McCoy mean anything to you?'

'Isn't he the guy who operated on Schroder?' she asks, reaching up to the scar that runs down the side of her face. She got it two years ago after a car she and Schroder had just stepped out of exploded. She was lucky to survive. Later that afternoon Schroder would take a bullet that, thanks to McCoy's surgical skills, he would survive – albeit temporally. The bullet couldn't be removed from his brain, and last year it finished the job. She still misses him. They all do. Especially today, being here at this crime scene staged to look identical to one Schroder once attended.

'Yes, but that's not why he called. You remember the Garrett case from nine years ago?'

Nine years ago she was a patrol officer in Auckland. She shakes her head.

'It was a home invasion here, parents were—'

'Shot in the head. I remember it now,' she says. 'The boy was shot, and the sister, didn't she get away?'

'She did,' Wilson says, 'and the boy just woke up from his coma.'

'After nine years? Wow. How is he?'

'Okay, it seems. He actually woke up a month ago, only the good doctor wanted him to build up some strength before telling us.'

'It was your case?'

'Schroder and Tate's.'

'Shit.'

'Exactly. McCoy got put through to me after he couldn't get hold of Tate. He says the boy can't talk, but he can write. He stressed that for James, it's like he just lost his parents. I want you to get up to speed on the case.'

'Excuse me?'

'I'm sure you're capable of giving your best to both the victim here,' he nods toward Denise Laughton, 'as well as seeing if James Garrett can offer something to close that case out. It would be a win for—'

'But—'

'I want you to interview him today.'

'Today?'

'We've already lost a month.'

She says nothing for a few seconds, then, 'I'll talk to him this afternoon.'

'Thank you, Detective.'

She turns her attention back to Denise Laughton. The husband, Derek Laughton, cut the binds and removed the egg from her mouth, and attempted to revive her even though it was clear to him she had been dead most if not all of the night. Distraught and incoherent, he is downstairs with Detectives Audrey Vega and Brian Travers.

'You think this was him?' Wilson asks, nodding to the victim. 'Middleton?'

The Carver Joe Middleton – New Zealand's most notorious serial killer, and one who many in the police force saw every day as he waltzed up and down the hallways of the department, mopping floors and cleaning windows, flying under the radar with his Slow Joe act. He came to this house three years ago and killed the woman who lived here back then. Angela Durry was found dead in this bedroom, in the same fashion, hands tied to the bed with a phone cable torn from the bedroom landline and feet secured to the bed with underwear. The knots used were those a child would make stronger through repetition – in this case triple knotted. She also had an egg in her mouth. The Carver was Schroder's case, one the department couldn't close until a lot of innocent people had suffered. Middleton is still out there, and nobody knows where. Could this have been him? The crime-scene photos from that night must be almost identical to what she's looking at right now. Back then Matthew Durry put the house on the market and moved overseas with the kids. Months later Derek and Denise Laughton bought it.

She looks at the photographs in the room. Most are of Denise and her husband, but others are of friends and family members. 'I can imagine Middleton would get a kick out of coming back to one of his former scenes to start all over. Maybe this was always his plan. Maybe he took a key when he left last time so he could come back. I'll check with the husband and see if the locks were changed.'

She heads downstairs and pauses outside the lounge where Vega and Travers are talking to Derek Laughton. She remembers another detective once saying Vega looked more like a wrestler than a cop, a thought Kent has never been able to shake, mainly because the guy was right – Vega's gym hours have crafted her into somebody who could tear your arm off and slap you silly with it. Next to her but saying nothing is Detective Brian Travers. Travers is good-looking, clean shaven, hair short on the sides and long on top, big at the front. He's dressed like he's on his way to or from a fashion shoot. He's one of the few men in the department who never hit on her back before flying shrapnel and glass put an end to that kind of thing. Sitting opposite is Derek Laughton in his paramedic's uniform, his face in his hands, his receding blond hair on display. His words are mumbled as he talks around his fingers. Kent struggles to make them out, but can tell he's saying they bought the house eighteen months ago, its dark history making it affordable. The vomit upstairs belongs to him, having thrown up after he couldn't save Denise.

'We don't believe in ghosts or bad juju,' he says, his words clearer now as he looks up. His face is pale and wet, and pained, every word sounds like agony. 'What we believed in was getting a house we could never afford under other circumstances. But it was stupid, right? If we had never bought it...' He trails off. 'I mean, Jesus, I ... I...'

He bursts into tears, and Kent carries on into the kitchen.

Chapter Twenty

He puts two fingers to the artery in his neck – Jesus, is he going to survive this? His pulse is racing so hard he's frightened the artery is going to burst. But at the same time ... wow, he has never felt so alive. So powerful! If he had to, he could go out onto the street and flip a car. He could hurl his neighbour – the one who always has his stereo up loud on Saturday nights – a hundred metres into the air. He could smash a cinderblock with his forehead. He wasn't expecting to feel this way – like ... like a god!

He is still in shock. In shock he did it. In shock it went how he thought it would – hell, *easier* than he had thought. *See, Jess? I'm not a failure at all.* Though perhaps he is, because it wasn't Jess he killed, but a stranger he started following weeks ago – Fake Jess. His picking Fake Jess had nothing to do with who she was, but where she lived. She was unlucky – but the world was full of unlucky people. He could attest to that, Amen. Somebody unlucky enough to get murdered by him would sure as hell have been unlucky enough to have gotten themselves killed in some other way soon enough, whether from a brain tumour ticking in the background, or from a piano falling from the sky. He had followed her. Had learned her routine. Had learned her husband's routine. The house had the same layout as the day Detective Schroder walked him through it.

No, not Jess, but rewarding nonetheless, and a step in the right direction. This is what he's like sometimes, only seeing the negative – the one thing he has in common with Jess, he supposes, since that's all she ever saw in him too.

His body is buzzing. His skin is tingling. His lips are numb. His chest is tight, like there is no longer enough room for his heart. He can't stop smiling. He grabbed a beer when he got home, but hasn't opened it in case it dulls this feeling. His hands are shaking. When he put them around her throat, he saw Jess – the image so powerful, for a moment he almost convinced himself he had actually driven to her house by mistake. He's pacing his lounge, thinning the already worn-to-shit carpet. He should have filmed all that he did. He could have watched it back and relived every moment. What was he thinking, letting an opportunity like that slip by?

Stop focusing on the negative.

Take pride in the positive.

And learn from the experience.

He's taken a big step to being famous. The second step is waiting for the detectives. It won't be Schroder this time. He wonders who it will be.

Chapter Twenty-One

The entire room needs painting, and of course there are a thousand holes that need to be patched from James's old posters Hazel pulled down yesterday, dark rectangles left in their wake where the wallpaper hasn't been exposed to light. She has a heater running in the room, otherwise in this temperature the filler for the holes will take three months to dry. She hasn't put down any drop cloths because the carpet still needs to be replaced – it needs to be all through the house.

Over the last five years, since moving in, she's been pouring any spare money she has into the renovations, battling with the wear and tear of time in what neighbourhood kids call *The Murder House*. Those kids often cross the road rather than walk past it, and she's seen them stand in groups daring each other to run up to the door and ring the bell. After the shooting, insurance covered the expense of replacing the carpet in the lounge, but the remainder wasn't updated, meaning there's a mismatch. Hazel's parents had life-insurance policies that paid off the mortgage, but little beyond it. Back then her grandparents wanted to sell the place, only to find the shooting had devalued it so much that it wasn't worth selling. She was fine with keeping it – the house was a connection to her parents – and her grandparents were fine with keeping it too: people had short term memories, so, over time, the house would recover the value it had lost. That was the hope. They had tried to rent it out, but they struck the same problem – nobody wanted to live in a house where people had been executed, especially when those doing the executing had never been found. In the end the house stayed empty and fell into disrepair, though mostly the damage was cosmetic. When she turned eighteen, she moved out of her grandparents' house and came back. She loved her grandparents, and they loved her, but that didn't mean she wasn't clawing at the walls to escape.

She finishes patching the holes, and if she's lucky she'll be able to sand them back later today. She heads downstairs for coffee. She needs the boost. Between law school, working part-time at the bar at night, and the renovations, it isn't just her credit card that is maxed out, but her energy levels too. She could sleep for a week.

That's why when she checks the letterbox while the jug boils, she could scream. There's a letter from the insurance company saying that due to policy changes over the years, the medical insurances that came into play the night James went into a coma have expired now that he's woken up. The bills over the last four weeks are to be forwarded on to her. She doesn't know what they will be, but it won't be cheap.

She can't afford to keep James in the hospital.

She closes her eyes, and for the first time in a very long time, she feels completely broken.

Chapter Twenty-Two

The kitchen window overlooks the garden in the backyard, where persistent rain has drowned anything not above ankle height. Kent imagines Denise Laughton in this same spot, maybe a coffee in her hand, thinking about the day that's just been, or the one ahead. Hard to imagine something so routine can have a last time, but one day there's going to be your last ever piece of toast, your last ever kiss goodbye, your final smile. The thought gives her the chills.

She opens the fridge. On the bottom shelf is a six-pack of beer with two bottles missing. One of those bottles – empty – is on the dining table. The other – also empty – is on the nightstand upstairs. Three years ago Joe Middleton drank two beers from the fridge that was here, and left the bottles in the same places. Which is just one more detail about all of this that is nagging her. Perhaps Middleton would get a thrill from killing here, but would he really focus on the small details and stage them as he once did? It's a lot of effort to go to in order to prove you were here, when DNA would do the same. But maybe it amuses him somehow.

Or maybe there's something else going on here.

She goes into the lounge. Everybody turns toward her. She looks at Laughton. 'Did you have a beer or two when you got home? Before you went upstairs?'

'I would never drink in the morning.'

'Did Denise drink beer?'

The husband looks confused.

'There's an empty beer bottle on the kitchen table and one on the nightstand,' she says.

He shakes his head. 'Denise doesn't drink beer. Wine, sometimes. But we don't have any beer in the house at the moment. Which must mean the person who killed her brought it with him, right?'

'It's possible.'

'Then his DNA will be all over them. Fingerprints too. It means you can run them. Or look at security footage from supermarkets and bottle stores. It means you can find this guy today, and then you can give me five minutes alone with him.'

The first part of that is true, and the second unlikely, and the third isn't going to happen in a million years. Thousands of those six-packs have probably been bought this week alone from a thousand different places, and even though she understands Laughton's urge for revenge, he's going to have to rely on the system.

'Would Denise open the door to a stranger at night?'

The change in direction confuses him for a moment, and then: 'Never. She was paranoid about that. You think she answered the door to somebody?'

'Did you change the locks when you bought the house?'

'Of course. The real-estate agent advised us, but we would have done it anyway after what happened here.'

'How many keys are there?'

He thinks on it. 'Two. I have one and Denise has one.'

'No spare?'

'No. Wait,' he says, then thinks on it for a moment more, then: 'There's a spare in the junk drawer in the kitchen.'

'There's one on the inside of the lock for the front door. Is that one of the three?'

'No. That one lives there so we can come and go.'

'So four keys.'

'I guess so. The person who did this, you think he had a key?'

'None with friends or neighbours?'

'No. Only the four.'

'Was the door locked when you came home?'

'I came in through the garage, so I don't know.'

'What about when you let the paramedics in?'

'Oh yeah, of course. I let them in through the front. I ... I think it was locked, but I can't be sure. I wasn't really thinking about it. I abused them, you know. The paramedics. They're friends of mine, but I called them every name under the sun for not being able to help Denise even though I already knew she was well beyond help.'

She waits a moment after that, then: 'Did you change all the locks? Or just the front and back doors?'

'Front and back, because it was the same key.'

She looks at the patio, where French doors open onto a patio and the backyard. Earlier an officer found footprints leading up to them. 'What about them?'

He looks at the doors and shakes his head. 'We didn't change those ones.'

'Do they work on the same key as the original locks for the other doors?'

'No, and there are no spares. The one in the door is the only one. You think it's The Carver, don't you?'

'We're looking into it,' she says.

'He used to pick locks, right?'

'He did,' she says, and if one here was picked, forensics will figure it out. 'Excuse me a moment,' she says, and she nods at Vega and steps into the hallway. A moment later Vega joins her.

'You think she might have known her killer and let him in?' Kent asks.

'You don't think it's Middleton?'

'I'm not convinced.'

'Husband says as far as he knows she wasn't expecting any friends. An affair is possible. She's having one, it ends badly, her killer stages everything to look like Middleton was here. Wouldn't be hard – between news articles and documentaries, there's an abundance of information out there. Could be he comes to the patio door so the neighbours don't see him, and she lets him in. He parks on the other side of the paddock behind the house, walks through it, knocks on the door. Why don't you think it's Middleton?'

'I'm not saying it's not him. But the thing with the beer bottles seems forced.'

'Agreed,' Vega says.

'Listen, I gotta take off for a bit. You remember the Garrett case from years ago?'

'Sounds familiar.'

Kent reminds her, then tells her about the phone call to Wilson and how she's been asked to follow it up.

'I thought people only woke up after years in a coma in movies,' Vega says. 'Does Tate know?'

'I have no idea.'

Vega slowly nods, taking it all in. 'You going to tell him?'

'I want to, but you know what he's like.'

'As in, he'll want to get involved?'

'Exactly.' Kent likes Tate a lot – perhaps more than she should – but he can be a real pain in the arse.

'You should tell him. Hearing what he has to say will be quicker than going through all the case files. And as you know, there'll be stuff that didn't make it in there.'

Vega is right. There will be theories Tate and Schroder will have had that weren't recorded. She would like to hear them.

'I'll talk to him,' she says.

'I'm glad Garrett has woken up,' Vega says, 'but he sure picked a bad time for it.'

'Ain't that the truth,' Kent says. Leaving here is a betrayal to Denise Laughton, but on the other hand, the justice for James Garrett and his family is long overdue.

Chapter Twenty-Three

Tate is making notes on a script when Rebecca Kent shows up at the door. After Schroder died last year, Tate left the department, stepping into a role that saw him providing technical answers about police procedures for TV shows and movies. It's a challenging job – writers and directors often don't like the truth getting in the way of the story they want to tell. The latest project is an episode of *The Cleaner*, a show filmed in Christchurch that follows the lives of two crime-scene cleaners finding themselves solving the crimes they're there to clean up. In the same way TV audiences are willing to overlook small English villages having a different serial killer every week, they have so far been willing to overlook *The Cleaner*'s main characters finding and solving things the police can't. The work may not be as rewarding as when he was a cop, but the pay is sure better, and he doesn't miss having people trying to kill him. Even so, like every other time he's seen Kent since he quit the force, he feels a stab of regret for having left that life behind.

They hug briefly once she's out of the rain, then he leads her through to the lounge. She looks wired, and he wonders if she's working the murder that's had the media excited all morning. She says no to a coffee.

'It's good to see you,' he says, and he means it.

'How's Bridget?'

'She's doing okay,' he says, but she isn't. Four years ago his wife was in a horrific accident that she barely survived – an accident their seven year old daughter, Emily, didn't. Bridget's head injuries were so bad that for the few years that followed, she was in a catatonic state the doctors gave her almost zero chance of coming out of. But last year she did come out of it, and she was able to leave the care home, and they had six months when life was good, when life was normal, when they thought Bridget had fully recovered. They spoke about having another family. The decision was painful – they had lost one daughter, and the world was cruel enough it could take another. But they both wanted to try, and the trying was successful. Bridget's memory lapses started not long after she became pregnant: small things at first, then larger things, like forgetting their daughter had died in the same accident that had hurt Bridget so badly. He would have to remind her. It was heart-breaking. For the last two months she's been back at the care home that looked after her after the accident, and now they're a month out from the baby arriving. There are good days and bad days, with the latter rapidly outnumbering the former.

'I take it this isn't a social call?'

'James Garrett woke up a month ago. Before you say anything,' she says, putting up her hand, 'we only found out about it today. Doctor McCoy didn't want us anywhere near him.'

The night of the shooting rushes back to him. He can see the lounge, the bodies, the blood. He can see Hazel in shock with a blanket wrapped around her on the couch in the neighbour's house. Over the following hours they had ridden the momentum to the Crawfords, to the safe-installer's house, to the parking garage, to the hospital, and they had been hopeful they would close out the case. But in the end all they found were brick walls, no matter what direction they turned.

He understands why McCoy made his decision, but he's also excited at the prospect of closing out one of the few cases they were never able to solve. 'How is he? Is he talking? Does he remember anything that can help?'

'I'm on my way to see him now. With Schroder gone, and you gone, the case—'

'Let me go with you.'

'That's not going to happen.'

'Come on, Rebecca, I know more about this than anybody.'

'Which is why I'm here.'

The stab of regret he felt moments ago about leaving the force intensifies. He knows why Rebecca is here, and he feels ashamed at the idea that comes next – refusing to tell her a damn thing unless she lets him help. Only he doesn't say it – he can't. He let the Garretts down by not finding them justice, and it would take a special kind of arsehole to stand in the way of that justice now.

'I literally had the case handed to me an hour ago. I came here in the hope you'd be willing to talk me through it. Will you?'

Of course he will. And he does. He tells her that over the days that followed the murders, they found nothing to contradict their belief that the killers had made a mistake with the addresses. They were never able to narrow down how the three men knew of the safe-installer. Ballistics showed Frank and Avah Garrett were shot by the same 9mm pistol, and James Garrett by another. The casings hadn't been found at the scene – just one more thing that told them they were dealing with professionals. The pillowcases tied over the victims' heads were brought to the scene, and the only DNA found on them was the victims'. When Gary Lee's car was stolen, a five-dollar note removed from a sealed plastic bag was used to pay for the parking. The theory was the same for the pillowcases – that they had been brought to the house in plastic bags – in part because of the lack of any other DNA, but also because they still had the factory creases in place. The pillowcases couldn't be traced to where they came from. They could have been bought for the occasion, or they could have been in a closet for years. The parking building gave them little. Surveillance captured thousands of drivers over the previous weeks, and they couldn't tell if the three men had cased the place out in advance, or if that was their first night there. The other houses on the list from the safe-installer's computer were never struck, due in part, Tate has always imagined, to the owners being put on notice. The day had been summer in winter, which meant no muddy footprints had been left behind, but they did find one, perfect size-fourteen print in the garden, left there when the three men had fled the house. They never figured out how the men made their way inside, whether they talked their way in or found an unlocked door or window. There were no signs of forced entry. They left no fingerprints, and DNA found at the house didn't match anybody in the system.

In the end they had spoken to more than two hundred people with criminal records that matched the attack in some way, and when they came up with nothing, they spoke to two hundred more. The leads dried up, and the case stalled. Then, like all cases over time, it got put on the back burner as new cases came in. Resources weren't infinite. He knows Kent has seen it happen many times, and will see it many more, just as he knows those occasions will haunt her the same way his have haunted him.

Kent takes it all in, asking questions along the way and making notes, and when he's done she chews on the end of her pen for a moment, then says, 'I'm interested in what isn't in the case file.'

He smiles. He had suspected as such. 'You want to know if we had somebody we couldn't prove was there.'

'Did you?'

'We did. The problem was he had an alibi.'

'A good one?'

'You could say that. He was getting arrested on the other side of the city at the same time.'

Chapter Twenty-Four

The detective is wearing tight jeans and a blue blouse and a black suit jacket. She's lean, and tough-looking, with bright-blue eyes that quickly take in the room, and dark hair tied into a ponytail. She reminds James of the PE teacher at school he and all his friends had a crush on. Only Miss Kendall didn't have a scar running down one side of her face that flexed when she spoke. She introduces herself as Detective Inspector Rebecca Kent, and she starts off by telling him she's glad that he's awake and that she is sorry for his loss, and that the detectives who originally handled the case are no longer around.

'I'll be working on it now,' she adds.

Both Hazel and Doctor Wolfgang look ready to pounce on Detective Kent if the questioning turns to badgering. James is sitting up, pillows between his back and the head of the bed. He has his notepad on his lap. His body is still tingling from the therapy earlier, and he might be imagining it, but he thinks he's put on some weight. The pen no longer feels heavy in his hand, and his writing is tighter and more controlled. His speech isn't as slurred, but he knows it's easier for everybody if he keeps writing.

He writes, *What happened to the other detectives?*

'One of them died, and the other one left the police force.'

He feels bad for the one who died, even though he never knew him. He would have known this if Hazel or Doctor Wolfgang would update him rather than trying to protect him. He has a long list of questions for Google when he gets home.

'I'm hoping you might be able to tell me about that night, if you're okay with it?'

He finds his eyes going back to her scar. He wonders if surgeons could make it almost disappear the way they did with his mum's scar in Coma World. He wonders how she got it, and figures Google can tell him that too.

'James?'

He nods. He closes his eyes. He goes into the warehouse and walks to where the dust is the thickest, where the spiders are bigger, where the filing cabinet in the furthest corner is locked and wrapped in tape. If there are any answers for Detective Kent, this is where they will be. He puts his hand on it. There is a small vibration to it, like it's being powered by a small electrical charge.

He knew the police were coming here today to talk to him, and he wanted to open these drawers earlier, only to find that he couldn't. Not because they're locked – which they are – but because he couldn't bring himself to try. He thought he was ready, but he was wrong.

'Can you write down what you remember?'

His memory of the evening starts in the cabinet next door, with him on his knees. His dad breaks the cable ties and his mum gets hold of the gun. None of it is real, yet he thinks there must be a foundation of truth to it – especially the being at gunpoint on their knees bit. He writes, *There were three men in dark clothing and ski masks.*

'You're sure they were men?'

I could hear them talking. One of them was really big.

'Did they use any names?'

He shakes his head.

'Can you remember what each man did?'

The big guy went out, looking for Hazel. She had escaped.

'Could you see their hands? Their wrists?'

He shakes his head.

'Nothing you could identify them with?'

Another head-shake.

'Do you think you could describe their voices?'

No.

'Do you remember somebody knocking on the door?'

He closes his eyes and shakes his head. These things aren't in the cabinet that's open. He flicks his nail at the edge of the tape around the cabinet that's closed. It's old, and the plastic comes away from the sticky residue beneath. He tears it away and wraps it into a ball. He opens his eyes and writes *I need a moment,* then goes back into the warehouse.

He pulls at the drawers but the locks hold. There's no key, but there are plenty of safety axes. He swings one at the lock, over and over, missing the lock more often than hitting it. The locking mechanism twists, turns, then tears away. The top drawer is empty. So is the middle. But the third is full of files from the day of the attack, starting with breakfast that morning – oats and some toast; then school – there was a math test; and dinner – roast chicken with coleslaw; and all the things between, things he couldn't remember, and things even now he can't be sure are real. How can he be sure of anything when he's inside a world that doesn't exist? He reads the file at the back. It starts with him being woken in bed by knocking on the front door, and ends with him watching his dad being shot.

In The Real World, he's breathing heavily, and his hands are shaking, and he's broken into a sweat. He opens his eyes and looks at Hazel, at Detective Kent, at Doctor Wolfgang. They all look concerned.

Somebody knocked on the door it was eleven o'clock I heard it answered then arguing then some heavy thumping sounds I went to look Mum and Dad were on their knees with pillowcases over their heads there were two men I named them Monsters One and Two and Two came upstairs for us Hazel got out the window and I didn't. Two was big and his voice was deep and he dragged me downstairs while Hazel went for help and Dad was on his knees and Mum was on her side and there was a third monster too but I didn't see him only heard him and Monster Two went looking for Hazel and One kept pointing the gun at Mum and Dad.

He wipes his tears off the pad, rips off the page and hands it to the detective. He wants to bury his face in the pillow and be left alone, but he carries on – carries on in the hope he can tell the detective something that can help find the men who did this.

One and Three had normal voices and no accent they were looking for a safe Dad told them they had the wrong house but they didn't believe him. Dad said he could get them twenty thousand dollars from the bank and One said they weren't there for twenty thousand they wanted to know where the safe was only we didn't have a safe. They didn't believe Dad then One shot Mum the gun had a silencer and Two came back in and said Hazel had escaped and put a gun against the back of my head then One shot Dad then I woke up in hospital.

He removes the second page and hands it to Detective Kent, who has handed the first page to Hazel. Hazel is crying too. Kent reads the second page, her jaw tight, then asks, 'Was there any mention of diamonds?'

Diamonds? No. He shakes his head.

She looks ready to ask more questions when Doctor Wolfgang gently puts his hand on her arm and smiles at her. Whatever follow-up question she has falls away, and she nods, and she says, 'Thank you, James. I know that was hard for you, but thank you. When you're ready I'd like to come back and see how you're doing, if that's okay?'

He gives her the thumbs-up. Hazel gives her the pages. Kent thanks him again, then Doctor Wolfgang walks her out.

I miss Mum and Dad.

'I know,' Hazel says. 'I miss them too.'

I keep expecting them to walk through the door.

Hazel sits next to the bed and she holds his hand, then she wraps her arms around him and he wraps his around hers. Her tears roll down his neck and his down hers. He has cried plenty of times over the last few weeks, but not like this, not in large, heaving convulsions that make him feel dizzy and sick. He sobs into Hazel, and he wonders what she was like the night their parents died, what she went through, how long it took her to go talk to friends, go back to school, to function.

'I always wonder what they would be doing now if they were

alive,' Hazel says, as they hold on to each other. 'Would we still be in the same house? Would they be real-estate agents? You remember Mum used to hang her paintings everywhere? She dreamed of having a showing one day and selling her art. I think she could have done it. Don't you?'

They switch from hugging to holding hands. He nods. The pain of missing them is unbearable, and the pain of remembering how it happened even more so. He goes into the warehouse and stuffs the files back into the drawer, then flips the cabinet so it's lying on its front, but it's all for nothing. He remembers a courtroom movie where a lawyer objected to something a witness said, saying you can't un-ring a bell. That's what's happened here. A bell has been rung, and he can't unhear it.

He casts his gaze out over the warehouse and reminds himself this is one cabinet of many. He has a room full of good days with his family. He walks between the cabinets, touching them, coming to a stop at one that's open. It's the one where their mum sold her first piece of art. Is it open because Hazel just mentioned it? In Coma World their mum achieved her dream. Hazel would like that.

'I would give anything to have one more day with them,' she says.

He doesn't doubt it, and in his warehouse he doesn't just have one day, but over three thousand of them. He can't open the warehouse door and let Hazel in, but he can do the next best thing.

He wipes at his eyes, and smiles at her, then he writes, *I need some notebooks.*

'How many?'

Nine.

Chapter Twenty-Five

Kent works away at a chicken salad while reading up on the man Tate told her about – Callum Hayes. Hayes has a list of assault charges to his name, having left broken bones and concussions and cracked eye sockets in his wake. There are drug possession charges, drunk-and-disorderly charges, burglary charges. Thirteen years ago he was a suspect in a house fire that killed two female university students, one of whom he had been accused of harassing, but there wasn't evidence to prosecute him, and six years ago a known associate of his went missing.

Were the Garrets part of the wake Hayes left behind?

His alibi was solid. He was being arrested at a hardware store four kilometres from the Garrett house, the trunk of his car full of boxed-up power tools from the stockroom. He was inside wrenching the cash register open when a patrol car rocked up and made the arrest. Tate and Schroder were drawn to him because of his size and his record. Though the arrest wasn't at the exact same time as the shootings, it was close enough – and they had worked on the timing. The arrest happened six minutes after Doctor Mann made the call to the police. If Hayes had sped from the scene directly to the hardware store, he could have covered the four kilometres – but only just – and only if the traffic gods smiled down on him. But it didn't allow for Hayes breaking into the premises and loading up the car – a task they had a handful of trainees from police college attempt; the fastest any one of them did it in was ten minutes. The officers who made the arrest saw nothing to suggest Hayes had an accomplice, but that didn't mean somebody else hadn't slipped away.

Only Hayes didn't have six minutes, but four, because four minutes after Doctor Mann made his call, there was another call – this one alerting police to the hardware store being broken into.

Covering the drive between the Garrett house and the hardware store in four minutes wasn't possible. And even if it were, even if the timing worked, and Hayes could not only cover that distance but also break in and load his car with goodies, the psychology didn't add up. Who leaves a botched home invasion where people were murdered to go and steal power drills and sanders? Yet neither Tate nor Schroder could shake the idea Hayes was involved. When they interviewed him, he had kept smiling and laughing off their suggestions and, according to Tate, had thrown them a wink on the way out the door when the interview was over. She knows the wink. It's where people think they're getting one over the police.

Hayes served six months for the burglary, and when he came out they put a tail on him for the following six months, and in that time he kept his nose clean.

Tate had a theory. The hardware-store robbery was a sham, and the robbery had taken place earlier in the night with the evidence left in place. It was Hayes' backup for if things went wrong. He was identifiable because of his size. Therefore he had every intention of being arrested for the hardware-store robbery if things went pear-shaped – better to go to jail for six months for theft than twenty years for murder. The anonymous call had been made from one of the only pay phones left in the city, this one opposite the store, and Tate didn't think that was a coincidence. An associate had made the call, probably after Hayes had called to say he was almost there. By the time the police arrived – which took three minutes – Hayes was in place. The math worked.

They grilled him, but got nowhere. He gave a handwriting sample that didn't match the sample they had found from the pen imprints on the pad at the safe-installer's house. They attacked the theory from every angle and interviewed everybody Hayes knew and had worked with, but couldn't find any evidence to place him at the scene. Doctor Mann had seen the three men flee the house, two of them taking the driveway, and the third – the big guy – running across the yard. It was in the garden between lawn and footpath that they found the footprint, but the footprint didn't match the shoes Hayes was wearing when he was arrested. Tate had a theory on that too. He thinks it's why Hayes ran across the front yard rather than taking the driveway – he wanted to leave behind a print. The other two did not. Then on the way to the hardware store he switched shoes.

Of course sometimes a wink is only a wink.

Even so, she finds Callum Hayes' last known address and writes it down.

Chapter Twenty-Six

Hazel uses the break in the rain to walk to a stationery store ten minutes from the hospital. James has asked for A5 notebooks, spiral bound, with at least two hundred pages each, and she finds some she thinks he will like. Is there a connection between asking for nine notebooks and the nine years he spent in his coma?

When she returns, James hands her his pad and takes the notebooks from her, along with some pens she also bought. She has been encouraged by the strength he's gained in his arms over the weeks, and shares James's hope he will be able to walk by Christmas. While he gets to work writing, she reads the message he's written and underlined for her: _I want to go home_. She doesn't blame him, and if she's being honest, it would be good to reduce the medical bills. After all, when she bought the notebooks, her credit card was rejected. Embarrassed, she had handed over the only cash she had – some wadded-up notes she earned in tips last night at the bar. How is she going to pay for James's medical bills when she can barely afford pen and paper?

Every day for the last nine years she's known two things – the first is James saved her life, and the second is if she had believed him the moment he came into her room that night, they both could have gotten away. Whether that would have led to their parents surviving she can never know, but what she does know is her inaction got James shot. If she has to work herself to the bone for the rest of her life covering medical costs and mortgages, then she will do it.

Still, if James is ready to go home sooner rather than later, it will help.

She heads to Wolfgang's office. The door is open, and he's sitting at his computer. She knocks and steps in. Over the years she has gone from calling him Doctor McCoy to Doctor Wolfgang, and finally, upon his insistence, just Wolfgang.

'James wants to go home,' she says, taking a seat.

'I bet he does.'

'He hates it here. He's been here nine years already, and he can't stand it any longer.'

Wolfgang nods. 'He's been handing me notes every time I see him saying the same thing.' He leans back and he swivels a pen between his fingertips. 'But he still has a lot of rehab to—'

'I know, but I can bring him in every day. Twice a day if that's what it takes.'

'That's good, but I don't think you're aware of how much work it will be. Your house has stairs, he'll have to—'

'I'll set up a bedroom in the lounge.'

'We still don't know what impact the bullet had on his brain. It's possible he may regress back into his coma.'

'You said that when he woke up, and that every passing day makes that less likely.'

'He will get frustrated quickly at his inability to do things,' he says.

'I can do this, Wolfgang. Really, I can.'

'There are the psychological implications. I wanted him to work with grief counsellors before going home. Then there's the fact he's returning to the house where your parents were killed, which is sure to have an effect that may stall any progress he's making. What he wants isn't the issue. The issue is what he *needs*.'

He's right. Of course he's right. She sighs, and she feels ashamed for putting her financial situation ahead of what is best for James. Earlier she was thinking she would do anything for him, and now she's attempting the opposite.

Wolfgang sighs, and puts down the pen. 'You're really sure you can do this.'

'I can.'

'And your studies? Your job?'

'Our grandparents can help look after him.'

'You've thought this through.'

'I have.'

'There will be conditions, of course, but perhaps we can help with the burden. Instead of you bringing James here twice a day you can bring him once, and I'll send a therapist out to you. I'll also want a psychologist to assess him twice a week, and to assess you too, to make sure you're coping okay. Equipment will need to be installed, the least of which are handrails and a wheelchair ramp.'

She feels buoyed at Wolfgang's change in direction, even though it does sound expensive. 'So he can come home today?'

'I'll make some calls and get some people in to make the house ready, and we'll look at getting James home tomorrow. But if things change, he comes back here.'

'Thank you.'

She stands up, and Wolfgang stands up too. 'Listen, Hazel, I hope you're not basing this decision on these bills. I learned earlier the insurance company isn't covering them, but I want you to know you don't have to worry about that. I'm going to sort it out, even if I have to cover the bills myself.'

She doesn't know what to say. 'I can't—'

'Of course you can.'

No. She can't. She's never been one to take a handout.

'Don't you worry about it,' he says. 'People do what they can for family, and that's how I see you, Hazel. As family.'

She's lost for words.

He smiles, and he says, 'He's lucky to have you.'

She holds back the tears and says, 'I'm the one who's lucky to have him.'

When she goes back to check on James, he's several pages into his notebook and still writing.

'You can come home tomorrow,' she says. She is expecting him to try and hug her, or to smile and fist-pump the air – or maybe the news will be what gets him to his feet for the first time in nine years, but there's nothing. 'I have to go home and start getting things ready for you, but I'll come back later, okay?'

Still nothing. He keeps writing. He's so focused she's not even sure he's heard.

Chapter Twenty-Seven

Kent calls Wilson on the way back to the Laughton house, only to find he's left and is now at the station, meaning they likely passed each other en route. She updates him, then listens as he shares her sense of disappointment that James Garrett hasn't offered anything to move the investigation forward – other than the fact the killers knocked on the door, then likely forced their way in. She doesn't tell him about her visit to Tate, or about Callum Hayes.

The cordon around this morning's crime scene has been enlarged, and the crowd has grown. So many questions are thrown at her she can't distinguish one from the other. Vega updates her as soon as she's inside. Evidence has been bagged and tagged and taken away, including Denise's cellphone. Her husband didn't know the passcode, but they were able to unlock the device with her fingerprint. Vega went through it earlier, finding hundreds of photos of Denise by herself, of her and her husband, of the cat. An IT expert will look for hidden folders. The same goes for the husband's phone and tablets and computers, all of which he's offered up without hesitation. They will look for secret email accounts, secret bank accounts, suspicious withdrawals, encrypted messages. Friends and family have said the idea of either of the happy couple having an affair was laughable. So far forensics have found no signs of forced entry, so it's possible Denise knew her killer, or possible she opened her door for somebody whose car had broken down, or who had fallen over or was having a heart attack, the same way the Garretts opened their door to their killers. The spare key Laughton said was in the drawer was found exactly where he said it would be. But given the locks for the French doors were never changed, it's possible there were more keys here before the house was sold and bought.

She hunts through ring binders and file boxes she finds in the office, searching for and finding the real-estate agreement for the house. The realtor's business card is stapled to the front of it. She dials the number.

'Marinda Harmon,' the realtor says, picking up.

Kent introduces herself, and before she can say anything else, Harmon says, 'This is about the Laughtons, isn't it? I saw it in the news. They weren't named, but I recognised the house. Are they okay? I know they're not, they can't be, but ... are they?'

'I can't go into detail at this stage, but yes, there has been a serious incident,' Kent says, and before Harmon can ask what that incident is, she carries on. 'Right now it would be extremely helpful if you were able to answer some questions.'

'Anything,' Harmon says.

Throughout the conversation that follows, Kent learns the house was listed three months after Angela Durry was murdered, and that the process was difficult because Matthew Durry was an emotional mess. The house hit the market at ten percent below its value, dropped an extra ten two months later, and sold for two-thirds of the market value four months after being listed, in what Harmon calls an exceptionally good deal. By that time Durry, now a borderline alcoholic, had taken the kids to England. While the house was on the market, a lockbox with the front door key was secured on the yard for agents to access. Harmon says she can come up with a list of other agents and buyers who went through the house. During this time the keys for the internal doors remained in the house so they could be opened – as did the key to the patio door – but she has no memory of any of the keys going missing. That doesn't mean somebody didn't find a spare somewhere, or an agent didn't make a copy.

'Matthew didn't care about the money,' Harmon says. 'He just wanted it gone. That's why it sold so low. The Laughtons could have...' She trails off.

'Could have what?'

'Nothing.'

'Tell me.'

'Well, I was going to say they could have gotten it even cheaper, but I guess they paid the ultimate price, didn't they – by living there?'

Kent doesn't answer that.

'The media are already guessing it was Joe Middleton,' Harmon says. 'If that's true, then it's not that he chose Denise, it's more that he chose the house. It means whoever I sold the house to ... well ... they were going to die.'

She thanks Harmon, and has barely hung up before a call comes in. It's Mason Clark, one of the forensic technicians working the scene.

'There's no DNA on the beer bottles,' he says.

'None?'

'If your guy drank from them, he wiped them down. No fingerprints either.'

'Why would Middleton do all of this, then be worried about leaving his DNA?' she asks, but she already knows the answer, and Mason goes ahead and says it too.

'He wouldn't. Look, do me a favour. Barry is still there,' he says, Barry Crowley being another member of the forensic team. 'Get him to take the trap out from under the kitchen sink. Dollars to donuts your guy tipped the beers out just so he could sit the empty bottles where Middleton had sat them.'

She finds Barry in the bedroom upstairs, fingerprinting the headboard. Two minutes later she's watching him bending under the sink in the kitchen, unscrewing the trap with a bucket beneath it. Her phone pings with an email from Harmon. It's a list of people who went through the house, from agents to clients, to people signing in at open homes. The list has more than three hundred names.

Barry frees the trap and tips it into the bucket. Like Mason predicted, it's full of beer. There's no reason for Joe Middleton to hide his DNA, or to go as far as pouring beers down a sink to make it look like he had been here. She thinks of what Harmon said about the house being chosen and not Denise Laughton. Is that what happened here? Did somebody come here to re-enact this scene just for the thrill of it? The scene wouldn't be hard to stage – there were several documentaries made about what happened here, meaning people saw how the crime scene looked, and they know how Angela Durry died.

'Faux Joe,' Vega says, when Kent runs her theory past her. 'That's what the media will call him. You just wait.'

Chapter Twenty-Eight

Hazel spends the rest of the afternoon working on James's room while tradesmen install rails in the bathroom and begin work on the wheelchair ramp for the front door. Now that there won't be time – or money – to replace the carpet, she puts down drop cloths before painting. By the time she gets back to the hospital, it's dark. Other than James's hand racing across the page, he doesn't look as though he's moved since she was here earlier.

Having skipped lunch, her stomach gurgles at the sight of his untouched dinner. She polishes off the roast carrots James hasn't touched while giving him an update on the renovations. He doesn't respond to her. He must have taken a break, though, because he's only a few pages into the notebook – but then she realises he's working on his second. The first is sitting next to the pile of fresh ones.

'Do you mind if I take a look at what you're working on?'

Now James must know she's here, because he pauses. Without looking up, he reaches for the filled notebook and hands it to her, then gets right back to work.

'Thank you.'

She takes it to the couch. He has written *Coma World* in the middle of the first page and underlined it. His handwriting is as good as it ever used to be. She flicks through the pages and sees the entire book is full of text.

'What is this?'

He doesn't answer. She reads … and breaks out in goosebumps when she sees it's the story of the night everything changed. This is what they went through moments before they were shot … only … only they're not shot. Dad breaks the binds, and Mum gets hold of the gun. What the hell? Her parents get the upper hand, and the only people to die are bad people. Help arrives.

She stares at James with the urge to ask him a question, but unsure exactly what to ask. Her heartbeat has quickened. The goosebumps make her shiver. She goes back to the notebook. Over the hours that follow her family's escape, the lights fade on and off, though there's no explanation as to why. The following day they go to a hotel. They live off room service. She hangs out with James by the rooftop pool.

The entries are dated like a diary.

She gets it now, what he's doing. 'Is this because of what I said earlier? About giving anything to have another day with them?'

He nods without looking at her.

'So you're making this up?'

He shakes his head.

'I don't understand.'

He doesn't answer.

'James?'

Nothing.

The pages have what a scriptwriting friend of hers would call the beats – the big things. It's not detailing what he has for break-fast, and it's not detailing every minute where he did homework or played video games, but it does list events beyond the tedium. She reads over the month that followed their parents' deaths – which in the notebook is the month after they survived. There are the big beats – she and James become popular at school, the house is fixed up, she turns fifteen and there's a large party at her house; but then there are the finer details too – one of the two men putting new carpet into their house has a Golden Retriever named Jim-Jim, and James is allowed to take Jim-Jim to the park to play fetch, and after the carpet is in and Jim-Jim is gone, James asks their parents if they can get a dog – to which Mum and Dad say no.

Who are these people? Where did the carpet layer come from? And the dog?

There are dreams where James is on board an alien spacecraft that then becomes a government lab before settling on being a hospital. Most pages have only a few paragraphs. If there's a big event it can take up to a page. The day of Hazel's birthday party takes up two. Because it's raining hard, the party stays inside. The windows fog up because her friends all get wet running inside after being dropped off. When she bends over to blow out the cake, her pants split. James uses his pocket money to buy her a gift – a copy of *Lord of the Flies*.

Lord of the Flies!

She looks at James. None of what he wrote happened, but *Lord of the Flies* ... she read that book to James not long after the shooting. It's one hell of a coincidence, but that's all it is ... But what about the weather? As she recalls it, the day she started reading that to James was her birthday, but it was raining so hard that she was soaked when she got here. One of the nurses gave her dry clothes to change into. The book, the rain, they were happening at the same time they were happening in Coma World.

Still just a coincidence?

'All of this, is this what happened in Coma World?'

He nods.

'You lived this life?'

He nods again.

'All of this was real to you?'

A third nod.

She taps the notebook. 'I read *Lord of the Flies* to you back then. Did you know that?'

He pauses, and she thinks he's about to try and say something, but then he carries on with the notebook. She carries on with her one. There are dates missing between the entries. A day here and there. More. Sometimes a week. She asks him about it. No response to that either. The missing days, she assumes, are the small beats.

For Christmas she gives him a copy of *The Day of the Triffids*.

She puts the notebook down.

In this world she read that book to him. Was it the same Christmas? She can't be sure, but she thinks so. It's another example of the two worlds intersecting.

This isn't a coincidence at all.

It's something else.

Chapter Twenty-Nine

Callum Hayes' last known address has a moat of dying lawn between front door and sidewalk. The house is run down, tired-looking, with chunks of guttering hanging from the roof and window frames full of rot. It's next door to a church that burned down a couple of years back and was never rebuilt. She can't imagine Hayes being the kind of guy to set down roots in the community and stick around, but even so, she has a patrol car follow her in case he's here. She only wants to talk to the guy, but when you're dealing with somebody with Hayes' record, you might just strike him on a bad day – and a bad day for him can be an even worse day for you. But today isn't that day, because the woman who answers the door hasn't seen Callum Hayes in two years. The woman, Sienna Adams, clutches a robe against her body with one hand and holds a cigarette with the other.

'That piece of shit ran out owing rent,' Sienna says, 'and he stole the washing machine while he was at it.'

'Do you know where he lives now?'

'What is this, twenty questions?'

'If that's what it takes.'

Sienna sighs. 'I have no idea where he is. Dead, for all I know. But if he isn't, and you find him, you make sure you get from him what he owes me.'

'We can try.'

'Yeah, I'm sure you will,' Sienna says. 'I know what you're thinking. Hook up with a guy like that, of course it's going to lead to problems. But it ain't so easy when you're somebody like me, which is something you wouldn't get.' But then she focuses on Kent's scar. 'Or maybe you do. I bet your options dried right up when you got that.'

Kent has heard it from others who have tried to rattle her. Sienna is right, though – men don't look at her the way they used to, but she is wrong if she thinks Kent misses being called an ice queen or a rug-muncher by some rebuffed arsehole.

'Why are you looking for him anyway?'

'We're hoping he might be willing to help us out with something.'

'What, like out of civic duty?'

'Something like that.'

'Bullshit.'

Kent hands her her card. 'If you hear from him, call me.'

'I'll be sure to do just that,' Sienna says, already screwing up the card as she closes the door.

Chapter Thirty

Wolfgang isn't sure what to say while looking at the notebook. Coma patients can hear, but the idea of living out an alternative life is ... what? Crazy? And the idea of being able to recall it in the detail James has is ... what? Ludicrous? Over the last nine years, James has regularly been tested with an EEG machine that showed brain activity, but this kind of activity? Crazy. Ludicrous. Impossible. Take your pick.

'I think he lived it,' Hazel says. 'I think he's writing it all out. Nine years, nine notebooks, one notebook per year.'

Wolfgang returns to the first page and to something that gave him pause earlier. What's crazier: the idea this could be true, or the fact he's willing to consider it? He puts the notebook on his desk and spins it around so Hazel can see the passage he's about to refer to.

'The flickering lights he writes about here,' he says, tapping the page. 'This could – and I say that word loosely – but this could line up with ... what do we call this? The Real World?'

'Why not? James probably does.'

'Agreed. You know we lost James four times on the operating table, and this could be that, the lights flickering each time we pulled him back. The accuracy here, the idea events have lined up in both worlds, it defies anything I would have thought possible. Which makes me wonder—'

'If James is making it all up now.'

'Yes.'

'I thought so too, but then there's the weather.'

'The weather?'

'See how sometimes he mentions what the day is like? I found a website with past weather reports. I checked the first twenty references in the notebook I read. Each one lined up with the weather on that day. I checked twenty more and got the same result. There's no way he could know that, and there's no way he could have looked it up. He doesn't have access to a tablet or phone, and even if he did, he's not using it when he writes.'

'Your theory is he wants to give you extra time with your parents, which means maybe he is making this up, and maybe he does have access to weather reports, and...'

'And the books I read to him in the past? How could he know that? Let alone when I read them to him?'

He doesn't have an answer.

'I know he thinks he's doing this to help me, but it hurts. I'm seeing the life Mum and Dad had, which is a reminder of what we all lost. It's confusing, because it's comforting too, but mostly I wish James hadn't started writing, but now that he has, I don't want him to stop. What happens when he gets to the end? I'll always want more.'

He spins the diary back around and flicks through the pages at random. His mind is racing. If this is real, what implications does it have for their understanding of comas? Have other patients experienced the same thing? Is it linked to James's eidetic memory?

Hazel carries on. 'His teachers always used to give James A-pluses for his stories, and Mum and Dad always used to go on about how good he was at it. James wanted to be an author when he grew up, and of course he has that crazy good memory, so maybe this ... whatever this is ... is the perfect storm. Maybe he really did live out this life.'

Wolfgang doesn't have an answer for any of that either.

'Does this change anything with him coming home tomorrow?' Hazel asks.

Wolfgang shakes his head. 'I can't see why it would.'

Chapter Thirty-One

Callum Hayes fixes a bourbon and coke. It's been a long day, and when he's done with the drink, he's going to sleep for twelve hours. He checks his phone. He has been without it since he left the house this morning. It's not that he's paranoid – it just makes sense that when you're dropping a guy wrapped in chains into the ocean it's best there's no record of where you've been. The phone lights up with a message from a woman he hasn't seen in a couple years. He groans, and knocks back the drink. There's a reason he walked out on Sienna – she's A-grade crazy. He knew it when he first met her too. It was in the eyes. Crazy bitches can't hide those crazy eyes, and yet she still managed to rope him in. That was the thing with women like Sienna – they pulled you into their messed-up worlds and you went along for the ride. You went because it started out sweet, and sweet had some damn good times, but when it soured, it soured with plates and vases hitting the wall.

He wonders what she wants. Probably something to do with the goddamn washing machine she thinks he stole from her, even though he paid for half of it. He considers deleting the message, but maybe it's important:

The police came here for you. Call me.

Could they know what he was doing today? He doesn't see how, but if they do, he's going to have to go on the run. He groans again, and pours a second drink. He doesn't want to call her, but best he does. Forewarned is forearmed. She answers after the first ring, like she's been waiting by the phone for him since the day he walked out.

'Hey, babe,' she says, which right away pisses him off.

'Hey, Sienna. What did the police want?'

'I'm good thanks, Callum. I appreciate you asking.'

He knocks back the drink. He shouldn't have called. Sometimes forewarned just isn't worth it. 'How are you, Sienna?'

'Was that so hard?'

He closes his eyes and thinks of the guy earlier slipping beneath the surface. He replaces him with Sienna and feels better for it, especially when he watches her screaming out air bubbles. 'I hope you're well. Are you?'

'I'm doing okay, you know how it is.'

He doesn't. Other crazy people might, but not him. 'Did the police say what they wanted?'

'Not they, but she. Detective Inspector Rebecca Kent.'

He knows who she is from TV: the ten who got turned into a two when she got cut up by that car explosion a while back.

'You've seen the news?'

He heard it on the drive home. 'This Carver thing?' he asks. He's always had a fondness for Joe Middleton. Seems like the kind of guy he could have a beer with. 'She's working on that?'

'She didn't say it, but I saw her on TV at the crime scene. You want to tell me you had nothing to do with that?'

'Do I need to?'

'It wouldn't hurt.'

'I had nothing to do with it, and I have no idea what she wants with me. She say anything?'

'Maybe.'

'What's that mean?'

'It means I want the money you owe me.'

'Jesus, Sienna, not this again.'

'Yes, Callum, this again. You owe me two grand and a washing machine. You give me that, then I tell you what she wanted.'

'I had nothing to do with this shit that's happening in the news.'

'I never said you did. I just wanted to hear you say it.'

He can feel a headache coming on. 'I'll pay you. I promise. What did she want?'

'Money first.'

'Goddamn it, Sienna.'

'Money first.'

'You still at the same house?'

'I'm here.'

'I'll see you soon.'

He hangs up. Whatever Kent wants, it can't have anything to do with this Carver bullshit. Which means there's another reason. Something to do with today?

Or something to do with years ago?

He goes to the bedroom and levers out a section of skirting board from behind the bed. He reaches into the gap for the burner cellphone. It's flat. He reaches for the charger too, then plugs it in. When it comes to life, he unlocks it and opens a messaging app, and taps in a phone number from memory. He sends a message:

Fishing?

He sets the phone down. Thirty seconds later it buzzes:

Let me check the weather.

His thoughts go to the night he shot James Garrett. He was assured the kid would never leave the boundaries of Vegetable Town, which has always suited Callum just fine. Finer would be if the kid had died the way he was meant to, but brain dead was a pretty good second place. Were they as careful as he remembers them being? Is there anything the kid could say to incriminate them? Back then he would have said no, but nine years later he can't be so sure. It's unlikely, but Callum has done time on things that were unlikely.

He pours a third drink while he waits. Then a fourth. Then his phone rings.

'How bad?' he asks as he picks up.

'He's been awake a month. His doctor only let the police know today. Kent spoke to him, then went looking for you.'

'He said something that can identify us?'

'This would be a very different conversation if he had. My guess is Kent got your name from Theodore Tate, and she's fishing.'

Fishing. Like their code word.

'We can't just wait this out,' he says.

'We may not have to. Remember the sister?'

Of course he does. They had a discussion about sinking her out in the ocean too, but decided there was little point in doing so as any information she could offer would have been offered right away. Her getting away that night is what messed everything up. If he'd managed to pull her back inside, they would have had more time. They could have kept cutting off fingers until the dad told them what they needed to know – or, in this case, after a big enough pile of fingers they would have come around to believing the guy when he said they had the wrong house. Which, it turned out, they did. The truth is it hadn't been their intention to kill anybody, but things just spiralled. It happens.

'What about her?'

'Turns out she's still at the original house, and right now there are tradesmen installing a wheelchair ramp outside. The fact they're busting their balls in the evening makes me think the boy is coming home soon. You're going to get the chance to do what you should have done the first time around.'

Chapter Thirty-Two

Matthew Durry pours more scotch into the glass and sips it empty. The last day and a half has seen him ruin months of hard work to get sober for the kids, but the good thing about drinking is it takes the sting away from failure. He wishes he could be a better man, and is angry he can't be. He wishes things had worked out when he took the kids overseas, and is angry they didn't. He wishes Angela hadn't died, and is angry at himself for not having been able to prevent it from happening. He wishes he could get his hands on the man responsible, and is angry at the world for not letting that happen. Three years' worth of wishes and not a single goddamn one answered. Three years' worth of anger building and festering. He's prayed too. Prayed for all the same things he wished for, in case it made a difference. He even took that praying to a church, wondering what God would think about a man desperate enough to pray for the death of another. Probably nothing – God didn't strike him as a wondering kind of guy. He was more a guy who knew everything and didn't care. If the Bible could be condensed down into one line, it would be, *Bad shit happens to good people.* Is it any wonder people turn to drink?

The drinking that, despite being bad for him, has been good for him. Without the drink he'd have jumped off a cliff long ago, the cliff that isn't always a cliff, but a noose, or a hose to a tailpipe, or a bottle of pills. There are days when he lays in bed fantasising about it. On the darkest days, the cliff becomes any one of a number of power tools.

He drinks to stay alive.

He works away at his drink while flicking through photographs of his family, stopping on one where they're ripping open Christmas presents while in their pyjamas the summer before Angela died. He looks at another: him and Angela on the doorstep of their house the day they took possession. It should be burned to the ground and the land salted so nothing can ever grow there again. Send a priest to burn some incense and hammer up a *Keep Out* fence. It's either that, or Derek Laughton will sell the house, only to have somebody show up down the line with a duffel bag full of duct tape and knives.

He finishes the drink and gets dressed. He's struggling to walk straight. Last time he looked at the clock it was after 2.00am, but he has no idea what it is now. It's still dark. People aren't driving to work yet. He heads into the garage. There are containers with fuel for the lawnmower. He grabs them, one is empty, the other close to it. He cuts away some garden hose and syphons fuel out of his mum's car, throwing up when he gets a mouthful of fumes. He gets the job done, and soon he has filled two ten-litre containers that, unless he's so messed-up he can't count, is thirty litres. Wait, Jesus, it's twenty. He really is out of it. He carries them out to the car. He takes a piss in the garden, then gets behind the wheel. He knows he shouldn't be driving, but then again, he probably shouldn't be burning his old house down either. He backs down the driveway, knocks the letterbox over, pops over the edge of the kerb and pulls away.

Chapter Thirty-Three

First thing Wednesday morning, James returns to the cabinet he was going through before falling asleep last night. He loads up on the memories from the files, then unloads them into the pages of his notebook in his hospital room, taking a break an hour in when a nurse brings him breakfast. He eats as he writes. He is halfway through his third notebook when Hazel shows up. She says hi, and asks how he's doing, but he doesn't answer. He wants to keep going. While Hazel reads the second notebook, he figures out what will make the cut for the third. At the moment he's writing about the trip to Australia that got cancelled when their grandmother died.

His mum cried during the funeral, and his dad had forgotten to turn his cellphone off, something they all discovered halfway through the eulogy when a potential client called. He knows his grandmother – his mum's mum – died in real life, and thinking about that gets him writing a message on his pad for Hazel, who is on the couch reading. He taps it to get her attention, then holds it up. *When did Grandma Agatha die?*

Hazel's face tightens as she thinks about it. 'Six or seven years ago. I'd have to check.'

Can you check the exact day?

'Grandma Elizabeth will remember.'

She steps out of the room to make the call as Doctor Wolfgang steps in. 'How you feeling today?' he asks.

James writes, *When do I get to go home?*

'Change of plans, I'm afraid. I think it's best we wait another day.'

Why? he writes, and underlines it heavily enough to tear through the page.

'The way you're going at it with these notebooks, I'm worried you're going to burn yourself out. I think it's safer to keep you here one more night just to be sure.'

Before he can object, Hazel returns. 'Six years ago,' she says. 'March the third.'

'Six years ago what?' Doctor Wolfgang asks, looking from Hazel to the notebook. 'You've found something?'

James nods, then turns his notebook so he can show them the entry he's working on – March sixth, the day of the funeral – then flicks back three days to the third. It's the same day his Grandma Agatha died. Hazel quickly explains to Doctor Wolfgang the call she just made, and neither of them looks surprised. Has he already written something they've read that has linked the two worlds?

'I have some questions,' Doctor Wolfgang says.

James is sure that he does, because he has questions too. And as much as he also wants them answered, they're all going to have to wait. If he can't go home till tomorrow, then Doctor Wolfgang can wait for his answers till tomorrow too. He knows he's acting like a kid by thinking such a thing, but then again, that's exactly what he is.

He leaves them to it, and goes back to the warehouse.

Chapter Thirty-Four

The interrogation room smells like booze and petrol, despite the fact Matthew Durry has been given some fresh overalls to change into. If people were allowed to smoke inside the building, it would have gone up in flames the moment Durry was brought in. Kent leaves the door open behind her and puts the coffees on the table. She slides one over to Durry and takes a seat. Over the last two years Durry has grown a dark beard that hides his lips and is covered in dandruff, and no two of his eyebrow hairs are pointing in the same direction. He looks more like the kind of guy who'd blow a house up rather than burn one down. His nose is red, his eyes even redder. He looks tired and broken, like the world just keeps on eating him up and spitting him out, and who could argue with that?

'I don't drink coffee,' he says, barely looking at the cup. His voice is rough.

Kent's heart goes out to him. Before Middleton came along, Durry was a decent guy living a decent life with a loving family, and now he can't escape the wake Angela's murder has created, seemingly fated to drown in it instead. Last night he got himself all liquored up, then went to his old house to burn it down. But given the house was still an active crime scene, he didn't get far. He drove through the police barriers and pulled up onto the front lawn and fell out of the car. It's a miracle he even got that far in one piece. He had twenty litres of fuel in containers, and another litre soaked into his clothes from filling them. He was lucky he didn't combust.

'Is there anything else I can get you?'

'You can get me out of here.'

'So you can try to burn down your old house again?'

'Yes.'

She wasn't expecting him to be so honest. 'It's not your house to burn, Matthew.'

'It has to go.'

She already knows why, but wants to hear it from him anyway. 'Because?'

'Because he was there. The arsehole who killed Angela.'

'It's a different arsehole,' she says.

'Doesn't matter. You get rid of the house, then neither of those arseholes, or any other arsehole, can hurt anybody in there again. If I had burned it down instead of selling it, Denise Laughton would still be alive. Get rid of the house, and Joe Middleton or whatever wannabe Joe Middleton can't go back there.' He thumbs back the hairs from his beard that get caught between his lips as he talks. 'That's what they do – they go back to old crime scenes because they get a kick out of it. I read that. They go back, or they visit the graves of people they've killed, and they jerk off, because it's all just a goddamn turn-on.'

Despite not drinking coffee, he reaches for his cup and takes a sip. Then another. She can tell he doesn't know much about coffee, because he'd recognise how bad this one was. 'That's what's happening here,' he says. 'Joe, or this new Idiot Joe, goes to the house to jerk off thinking it's empty, and it isn't, and Denise Laughton pays the price. The only way to break the chain is to make sure the house is gone, right? Then nobody can die there next year, or the following year, or any year.'

'So what's your plan, Matthew? Burn down every house Middleton went to?'

'Why not? You would think the entire world would be disgusted by what he did, but instead they make TV shows about him, and they write books, and have podcasts, and they make T-shirts with his image on them and talk about him like he's a goddamn folk hero. This guy killed my wife, and people treat him like a goddamn superstar. These pain tourists are fascinated by him. They're drawn to him. If Middleton set up a blog, he'd have a million followers by the end of the first week.'

'Pain tourists?'

He nods, and he finishes his coffee. 'Pain tourists – people who revel in the misery of others. And when the TV shows and podcasts and books aren't enough for them, they break into houses to collect souvenirs, like they did with my house after Angela died.' He slides the empty cup back across the table. 'You have anything stronger?'

Kent's heart quickens. 'Nothing. What do—?'

'Yeah, that's what I figured. I need a bathroom.'

'What do you mean that pain tourists are the ones who break into houses? That they broke into yours?'

'I tell you, you'll let me go?'

'You tell me, and I'll make sure you get some help.'

'That doesn't sound like you're letting me go at all, and the only help I need is from a bartender.'

'Please, Matthew, I'm trying to figure out who killed an innocent woman. If you have something to say that can help me, then please, say it.'

He stares at her for a few moments, then he reaches across the table and grabs Kent's coffee cup. He takes a sip. 'Okay. Bathroom first, then I'll explain.'

Chapter Thirty-Five

The Christchurch Carver was the catalyst for *New Zealand Crime Busters* coming back on the air. It had been around years earlier, made alongside the attempt to curb a growing crime pandemic, but ratings suggested curbing a crime pandemic wasn't something viewers were much interested in doing. Since then reality TV and crime podcasts have become a huge part of the landscape, millions of people entertained by the dark and the wicked of true life. On top of entertaining, rewards are routinely offered for information that leads to an arrest, almost turning *Crime Busters* into a sixty-minute game show. It's a weird balance, but one that helps get bad people off the street.

It is also a show that has produced a steady income for Tate as a liaison between the TV studio and the police department. The stab of regret he felt when Kent came to his house yesterday is somewhat dulled by his ability to use the show to make a difference, and today is an example of that.

Two weeks ago a service station was robbed at gunpoint. The young man working the counter was knocked out cold with the butt of shotgun, then had his skull cracked while kicked on the ground. The attack was brutal, the entire event caught on camera. Cameras caught the two men responsible fleeing the scene in a stolen car, having emptied the cash register and loaded up two bags with cigarettes and energy drinks. Eight minutes later they showed up at a second service station, only this time a customer and the attendant were shot and killed. In addition to taking the cash from the register, they took the victims' wallets.

Last week Tate was approached to see if there was a slot on *Crime Busters* for the story. There was, and this week they have been putting together a package that includes re-enactments, all ready to air tomorrow night – only he's just gotten off the phone having learned both those men are now in custody. It's a great result, but it does leave them with a gap.

He calls Kent. 'I got something I want to run by you.'

'If this is about James—'

'It's not. It's about Copy Joe,' he says, using the moniker he heard on the radio earlier. The police have said they believe they are looking for a copycat killer.

'Vega thought the media were going to go with Faux Joe,' she says. 'I should have made a bet. What do you want to know?'

'The service-station robberies were slated for this week's episode, but I just got a call saying an arrest has been made.'

'I hadn't heard,' she says, 'but that's good. Those men were animals.'

'It leaves us with time to fill. I can work with something from our backlog, but I wanted to offer it to you first for Copy Joe.'

She doesn't answer.

'Rebecca?'

'I'm thinking.'

'We'd have to film tonight and edit tomorrow. It'll be tight, but we can do it.'

'I'll run it past Wilson. It's his decision, but I'm betting he'll say it will look desperate, that if we're coming to you one day after a homicide it will send a message saying we don't know what we're doing.'

'It's not about that. This guy, if he's going to start replicating Middleton's crime scenes—'

'Yeah, I know. Look, I gotta go, I'm dealing with something else. But I'll try to convince him, I promise.'

'It can help,' he says. 'If this guy is planning on—'
'I get it,' she says. 'Let me call you back.'

Chapter Thirty-Six

'Pain tourists go where the Joes of this world have been,' Matthew
Durry says, once they're back in the interrogation room.

He feels better, having taken what was maybe the longest leak
of his life ... so long, in fact, that he feels more sober for it. He sips
at a fresh coffee Kent has got for him. Angela was always the coffee
drinker in the family. She used to say that thing coffee drinkers
say about not being able to function without it.

'You sure you don't have anything stronger?'

'I'm sure,' Detective Kent says.

'Don't cops always have drinking problems?'

'Only in the movies,' she says, but he doubts that's true. 'Tell
me about the pain tourists.'

The air inside the interrogation room is thick despite the door
being left wide open, and he wishes they could do the same with
a window, only there aren't any windows in here. He wonders if
that's to stop people jumping, or from being pushed. He's not an
idiot – he knows bad things happen in places like this, that suspects get ganged up on, that people plead guilty even when they
are not. After being asked the same questions over and over for
hours or even days on end, the police telling them they can go
home if they just tell them the truth, people will say anything.

'Matthew?'

'They want to get a taste of it,' he says. 'To get a sense of what it
must have been like. It's an extension of where society is at. Every
second podcast is about somebody being murdered. Every second
TV show is a true-life documentary of the same. I don't know

what Angela's last-ever thought was as she was dying, but I sure as hell know it wasn't hoping folks would package the pieces of her life into entertainment.' He can't hide the anger. People made money from Angela's death, and they were able to do so because there was an audience for it. 'There are always shows on about folks who disappeared, or were found buried in their backyard, all sorts of true-crime horror that's easy to digest when you don't have any skin in the game. Do you know how many podcasts there have been about Joe Middleton?'

'Tell me.'

'I can't, because after the first fifty I stopped checking. It compounds the pain. Compounds the grief. It picks at the scab my life has become. Do you think I like the idea of people being fascinated by him? Or idolising him? Do you think I want to be drunk all the time?' He's aware of how loud he's gotten, and dials it back. 'I miss Angela. I still have my kids, but I miss them too. I can't help it. I can't change it. I want to be better, and I try, you have no idea how hard I've tried, but the scab is always there, always being picked at.'

He drums his fingers against the table. Christ he needs a drink. 'Pain tourists are who we get when the podcasts and the true-crime novels and the documentaries aren't enough,' he says, repeating what he said earlier. 'They wonder what it's like being either killer or victim. They slake that curiosity by visiting places where the terrible happened, and the next thing you know they're going from "how did this happen?" to "how can I make this happen?" If we get rid of the locations where Joe went, then we get rid of the tourism that goes with it. We get rid of the Copy Joes.'

'You've given this a lot of thought.'

He has, in between moments where he has dreamed of killing himself and burning down the city, hunting Joe Middleton. 'I have.'

'What did you mean when you said they'd been to your house?'

'Am I going to jail?'

'No, but you don't get to walk out of here a free man either. I'm going to have you talk to somebody who might be able to help.'

'What, like a shrink?'

'I can't have you out there burning down houses, Matthew, and nor do I think you deserve to be in jail. So yes, you talk to a shrink and we get you some help. Now, tell me what you meant by a pain tourist going to your house after Angela died.'

His hangover is getting worse. He rubs at his head. 'It was before I took my kids over to England. I don't know how many came to my house, or how many times. I wasn't staying there then, but I did go back on occasion to pick up some things, like clothes for the kids, schoolbooks, things like that.' He closes his eyes and watches himself walking through the house, gathering up what his kids needed to move forward in a life that was no longer the life they wanted. He wishes he could be as brave as his children have been. Wishes he had their fortitude. Wishes he could forget the looks on their faces when he had to explain why they would never see their mother again.

He carries on. 'I went back to get their things and to arrange putting the place on the market. I had to tidy it up and make it look like nobody had ever been murdered there. The first real-estate agent I spoke to said I was lucky no blood had been spilled. I hated him, and listed with a different one.'

'Marinda Harmon?'

'That's her.'

'You remember the name of the first one?'

'It'll be on my computer somewhere.'

'You said before that the pain tourists take mementos.'

'Small things. They took my laptop and my watch.' He closes his eyes and rubs at his head as he tries to remember. 'They took some jewellery. Some CDs. Some bottles of wine.'

'I don't remember seeing any burglary reports from that address.'

'I didn't report it.'

'Why not?'

He shrugs. He's not sure she's going to get it, but he gives it a go. 'I didn't care. I mean, who gives a shit about stuff going missing when their wife has just been killed? Way I saw it, it just meant there was less for me to get rid of. Plus the real-estate agent was already super doom and gloom when it came to what we'd get for the house, given what had happened, and if potential buyers knew folks were showing up on a whim to steal stuff, it wasn't going to help. I didn't know back then about the psychology behind it, otherwise I'd have burned it down rather than sell it.' These days his most regularly recurring fantasy is him setting the place on fire, and sitting in his lounge nursing an expensive glass of whiskey while everything turns to ash around him. He still might do it, after he's spoken to the shrink that won't be able to help him.

'You're certain they broke in before you put it on the market?'

'It went on the market when I left the country with the kids, so yeah, I'm sure. I had movers go in there prior to that to put everything into storage, and all the paperwork had to happen online since I wasn't here.'

Kent leans forward. He can see her wheels turning. 'Do you know how the pain tourist got in?'

'There was a door open. I must have left it unlocked.'

'Which door?'

'The patio door.'

He can see her wheels turning faster.

'Was the key in the door after you were burgled?'

Now would be a good time to ask for those beers. 'It was.'

'You have more than the one copy?'

'There was a spare in the drawer.'

Kent nods slowly, and then she says, 'I need you to be absolutely sure about this.'

'I am. We had spare keys for everything. Angela made sure of it.'

'Did you check if the spare was missing after the pain tourist came?'

He shakes his head. 'I don't remember. Is that how you think Copy Joe got in there? You think he was the pain tourist who robbed me? That he took the key?'

She doesn't answer him.

A thought comes to him. 'What if I didn't leave the door unlocked back then? What if he already had the key and used it to get in then too?'

Still she doesn't answer him. He thinks she's thinking the same thing.

'Detective?'

'Thanks for your time,' she says, and a moment later she's gone.

Chapter Thirty-Seven

Kent smells of petrol – she tells Tate her clothes absorbed the odour during her interview with Matthew Durry after he tried torching his old house last night. It drowns out the smell of death he knows would be here otherwise. Even when no blood has been spilled, death has a way of getting caught in the weave of the carpet and the fibres of the curtains. The bed linen has been scooped up and taken away. Other than that, the room looks mostly tidy.

'We don't know if he talked his way in, found an open window or door, or if she knew him,' Kent says. 'It's also possible he had a key,' she adds, then gives him a rundown of the conversation she had earlier with Matthew Durry.

'You think somebody broke in and took a key years ago so they could come back?' Tate asks.

'It's possible. It's also possible one of the agents or potential buyers swiped a spare, or had a copy made. I got a list of everybody who went through the house when it was on the market, and it's a long list.'

'No chance this is Middleton pranking you, that he took the key and killed Denise Laughton?'

'Not according to Middleton.'

'Excuse me?'

She unlocks her phone and shows him a photograph she took earlier. It's a piece of A4 paper. At the top it says: *From the office of Joe Middleton*. Beneath that it has today's date, and halfway down the page a single line saying, *It wasn't me*, and beneath that a signature.

'He included hair, and a tissue with blood. They match the samples of him we have.'

Tate goes cold reading it. 'Where was it – the letter?'

'Under the windshield wiper of my car this morning.'

'At work?'

'At my house. The car was in my garage. He picked the lock.'

'Jesus, Rebecca...'

'I'd be lying if I said my first thought wasn't to leave the country,' she says. 'He came into my house while I was there. Probably while I was asleep. Who knows what else he did in there, or where he went?'

'You can't go back home.'

'I don't intend to.'

'You're welcome to stay with me. I have the room.'

'It's okay. The department are putting me up in a hotel.'

'Seriously, Rebecca, it's no problem.'

'I'll keep your offer in mind, okay?'

'Good. You're welcome anytime.'

'As to this being a joke, I don't think it is. The psychologists who interviewed Middleton in jail said he's incredibly narcissistic. I don't think he likes being copied, and that's why he reached out. Joe being Joe, he did it in a way that gave him a laugh.'

'And you believe him?' he asks.

'He has no reason to lie.'

'Which means somebody is copying him.'

'Yes.'

'And the crime scene is identical to last time?'

'Not identical, but close enough. The problem is your show did a recreation back then from this very room, and people learned a lot from that, but there have been other documentaries made about what happened here, and somehow crime-scene photos along with what happened here have entered the public domain.'

'Did the photos include the victim?'

'Thankfully no, but it was made public knowledge that Middleton used phone cable and underwear to bind her, along with the type of knots he used. The egg thing was made public, despite best efforts to keep that from the media. If you ever wanted to replicate a crime scene, one of Middleton's would be what you'd go with.'

Kent goes through the rest of the case with him, walking him through the house, and together they decide what to reveal to the cameras that will be here tonight. She tells him Derek Laughton is staying with family and already has plans to sell the house. He's seen it go either way in the past – people desperate to hang on, others unable to spend another night there. They make it back to the front door.

'How was James?'

'Damn it, Tate—'

'I'm just asking how he is, Rebecca, not about the case.'

'He's good. He's still learning to talk again, but he can write. He seems sharp. His muscles have atrophied over the years, and it will be months before he can walk – and even McCoy says there may be issues with motor control they don't know about yet, but they're hopeful.' They step outside and get their umbrellas. 'Look, I guess it doesn't hurt to tell you he was able to confirm what you and Schroder came up with. There were three men, one of them big, and they were asking his dad about a safe. There was no mention of any diamonds. They killed Avah when they didn't get what they wanted, then Frank. Only real addition is he heard knocking on the door before it all kicked off.'

'He remembered all that?'

'I was surprised too, but sadly none of it helps.'

'Have you spoken to Hayes?'

'Not yet, but I will.'

They reach the cars. 'Listen,' Kent says, 'I want to circle back to something. I know it was before you worked for the show, but they shot a re-enactment of the Angela Durry scene. Can you send me any of the footage you have, even the stuff that didn't go to air?'

'Anything in particular you're looking for?'

'There is, and I'll tell you if I find it.'

'I can get it uploaded for you to look at right away, but now I want something from you. What is it you're holding back from the media that you're not telling me?'

Kent nods. He's sure she would have known he was going to ask this, and will have already made the decision on what she would or wouldn't tell him. 'You know how Middleton used to turn all the photographs down inside the rooms where he committed his crimes?'

He does. It wasn't uncommon for a serial killer or serial rapist to do this. It was as if they didn't like being watched. 'Copy Joe did the same?'

'The total opposite. He gathered every photograph he could find inside the house and put them around the bedroom so they faced the bed. You didn't see them because they've been taken away to be printed.'

'That's...'

'Creepy, I know, and it gets even creepier. You saw the TV in the bedroom?'

'I did.'

'It was playing the re-enactment that was filmed here after Angela Durry was killed. It was on repeat, with the volume muted, playing off a USB drive. If Matthew Durry is right about this pain-tourist angle, then it's possible our guy went from collecting items from crime scenes to creating them, and he wanted an audience while doing it.'

Chapter Thirty-Eight

It's been a long two days since he changed his life by ending somebody else's, and most of that time has seen him nervously glued to the news. Today the media are calling him Copy Joe. They were always going to come up with something, and part of his nerves has been about them coming up with something he wouldn't like, but it turns out he likes Copy Joe very much. The more the country becomes invested in the idea this is who he is, the better this is going to go for everybody.

He has spent yesterday and today at home – time he scheduled off weeks ago, back when he wasn't even sure if he would go through with it. Police always tell folks to keep an eye out for anyone acting strange in the days that follow a homicide, becoming somebody different overnight, whether it's drinking more, or smoking more, or becoming short-tempered. So it was a good thing he booked some time away, because he's been living with frayed nerves and shaking hands, where closing car doors make him jump. This is the price of admission to the good life.

As the second day rolls on, the jumps aren't as high, and his appetite is back. By the time the phone goes late in the afternoon, his hands are no longer shaking.

The caller apologises for the late notice, but can he work tonight? It's an all-hands-on-deck situation – a re-enactment is urgently being filmed so it can go to air tomorrow night – *a re-enactment of his very crime!* He always knew this was on the cards – wanted it – but he wasn't expecting it to be so soon. He holds his hand up, and it's shaking again, but he doesn't know if it's from nerves or excitement. Yes, he says, he will do it. Of course. The filming is at the crime scene at nine o'clock. The street will be full of media, full of onlookers, perhaps full of trouble-makers, meaning extra police will be required to control the scene. He imagines standing next to Detective Kent, or Wilson, or Vega, or Travers, as they look out over the crowd wondering if Copy Joe will be a part of it – after all, some killers get off on returning to the scene. Police will have the area locked down, watching from behind car windows, from behind cameras, some will blend with the crowd, keeping their eyes and ears open.

Can he work?

Of course. He'd be happy to.

Chapter Thirty-Nine

There's an email with a link to the *Crime Busters* footage shot at Angela Durry's house waiting for Kent when she gets back to her desk. She loads it up and starts watching it. At the same time she goes online and starts downloading podcasts dedicated to Joe

Middleton to her phone. Her conversation with Matthew Durry about pain tourists has gotten her thinking more and more about how Copy Joe accessed the house. After Denise Laughton was killed, all of the owners of the houses where Middleton had struck were told that since Copy Joe broke into one, he might break into another. Each location was staked out by officers. Of the eight houses on this list, seven were sold after the crimes, all below market rate. Kent understands the compulsion to sell – after all, she's tempted to move on from her place too. Only she can't now, at least not until both Copy Joe and Middleton are either dead or behind bars – she couldn't live with the idea she'd be selling her house to somebody who might become the next victim.

With the footage muted and playing on one computer, she enters the list of addresses into another, searching the system for any reported burglaries in the years since Middleton's killings. There are two: jewellery, cash, CDs, small electrical gadgets, the reports made by the original owners, one four weeks after the homicide that took place there, the other six. In each case the houses were in the process of being put on the market while nobody was living in them. Each sale used a different real-estate agent. It's possible that there were more burglaries, and, like Matthew Durry, the owners didn't bother to report them. Are the burglaries coincidences? Or part of a pattern? Was the same pain tourist responsible? Is that pain tourist Copy Joe?

She goes about calling the new owners of the houses. Did any of them change the locks when they purchased the house? Some changed none. Others a few. Some changed all of them, including the garage-door opener. Two of the houses had alarms, the pin number being kept the same for each after the new owners took possession, and two didn't have alarms but have had them installed since. Have there been any burglaries in the time since the installations? No. When she calls the person who didn't sell, he tells her he changed the locks and put in an alarm and bought a gun. He makes a point of telling her about the gun, as though wanting her to challenge him on it. She doesn't.

She taps her pencil against the table, thinking, thinking.

She moves to the list of original owners. She's already spoken to the one who bought the gun, and she hopes the cellphone numbers listed for the remaining seven are current.

Chapter Forty

Wolfgang hates cancelling his patients' appointments, but given how distracted he is with James and these notebooks, it's for the best. He hunkers down in his office for the afternoon, scouring medical and news articles for anything similar to James's story, and finding nothing, which, while increasing his scepticism, also increases his excitement – if this goes the way he's hoping it will, then James could be a first. He makes calls and sends out emails to other doctors as the light fades outside and the lights inside the hospital take over. The closest story he finds is one that aired on TV six years ago, about a man who created an entirely fictional rugby division in his mind. This man, in his mid-thirties, created an entire world of teams, of players, of statistics. He could tell you everything from who scored what, to the weather, to where the game was played, to who was traded in the off-season – across the entire league for year after year, starting from the year he was involved in a car accident he wasn't supposed to survive. There were no medical answers. Some doctors said it was an incredible trick, while others offered the equivalent of the 'God works in mysterious ways' standby, which in Wolfgang's field was another way of saying, 'there is so much we don't know about the human brain'. It's a line he's used many times himself.

After hours at his desk, he needs to stretch his legs and heads to the cafeteria for what is either an early dinner, or a very late lunch. He swings by James's room on the way. James is sitting up in bed, the tray across his body, his eyes focused on the notebook he's writing in. After learning her brother wouldn't be going home today, Hazel took an extra shift at the bar and won't be back till tomorrow.

'How's it going?' Wolfgang asks.

He isn't expecting a response, and doesn't get one. The pile of completed notebooks is now four high, and James is a few pages into his fifth. He knows Hazel will have read the third notebook, but not the fourth.

'Can I read the third notebook?'

James nods.

'Are you sure?'

Another nod.

He decides to push his luck. 'Can I take the fourth one too?'

More nodding.

He takes the two notebooks downstairs to the cafeteria. He orders a coffee and stares at the few remaining sandwiches in the cabinet, hoping they're fresh, but knowing they won't be. But hospitals are full of hope, and miracles can happen, so he chooses the last remaining lettuce and tomato one. He sits at a table and starts on James's third year. His coffee arrives, but is too hot to sip. He keeps reading, slowly picking at the sandwich, whose texture tells him today isn't the day for miracles.

He is halfway into year three when he stops picking at the sandwich. He flicks through the pages, scanning them for key words, and finding them again in the fourth notebook. He flicks back and forth between the entries. His hands start to shake.

He abandons his coffee and the remainder of his sandwich and rushes to his office.

He finds Detective Kent's card and makes the call, then immediately has to put her mind at ease by saying James is okay.

'So he's remembered something?' she asks.

'No. I mean, yes and no,' he says. 'I can explain when I see you. Are you able to come here?'

'This isn't a good time for me, Doctor McCoy, I'm sorry.'

'I wouldn't be asking if I didn't think it was important. It will only take a few minutes. I can come and see you if that will make it easier.'

'It's that important?'

'It is.'

'I'll see you in twenty.'

Chapter Forty-One

Wolfgang is pacing his office when Kent shows up. She takes a seat, and he does the same, and then he says he's going to need her to hear him out. 'Right through to the end,' he adds.

Kent slowly nods. That's the kind of thing people say when they're going to say something batshit crazy. 'You have my attention.'

'James has created a different world.'

'You've already lost me.'

'I did say you're going to need to hear me out.'

'You're right, I'm sorry. Please, go ahead.'

'James has created a world where his parents didn't die, which he calls "Coma World",' he says, putting Coma World in air quotes as he says it. Then, for the next ten minutes, he explains that James has been writing in notebooks, and how they detail that world, how they're broken down into days like a diary. He explains how things from The Real World have been absorbed by James and used as material in Coma World. He tells her about *Lord of the Flies*, and *The Day of the Triffids*, and the weather, and James's grandmother dying, and how the dates line up. None of it makes sense.

When he's done telling, he adds, 'Before you say he's making it up, I will say making it up is as impossible as ... well ... as Coma World itself. I know how it sounds, and I can tell you that if you put a hundred experts on comas into a room and asked if this were possible, one hundred coma experts would shake their heads. And yet here we are.'

She isn't sure what to say next, and comes up with, 'I take it that means there are no other cases like it?'

'Not that I know of,' he says, then tells her a story of a man who created an entire rugby division in his head. 'I think part of why James has this ability is to do with the fact he has an eidetic memory.'

'Isn't that like a photographic memory?'

'Depends on who you ask. Photographic memory is very hard to prove, and some would say has never been proven. A photographic memory suggests you can recall something in detail years down the line, whether it's a photo, or text, or a phrase, or a number. Our eidetic memory hangs onto a visual, before storing it in our short-term memory, or discarding it. We all have one. But where yours and mine will store or delete it within a few seconds, for others that process can take months, potentially even years, making that visual readily accessible. It's possible this is connected to the world James has created, but I'm only guessing. The truth is I don't know.'

'Is this where you tell me there's something in this Coma World that can point me toward the men who killed his parents?'

'Sadly no, or at least, not yet.'

'Then what?'

'Do you remember who Georgia Perry was?'

'No.'

'She was a coma patient. Six years ago she came into our care after falling from a balcony while on holiday in Queenstown. She was flown here, and we saved her life, but she slipped into a coma she never woke up from. Four years ago she died.'

'I'm sorry to hear that.'

'James has written about her,' he says, tapping the notebooks. 'Four books covering four years, with five more to go. He writes about her accident on the same day it happened.'

It's crazy, all crazy, but she decides to play along. 'Maybe he saw it online? Or somebody told him.'

'He hasn't had any access to a computer or tablet, and there's zero reason for anybody to have told him. In The Real World Georgia was a web designer, but James has her in Coma World as his high-school teacher. I believe James overheard her family speaking to her in the coma ward, and he turned her into a character.'

'But changed her occupation?'

'Yes. It's not like the conversation in the coma ward would have been "so, what do you do for a living?" James has heard her name, and created a person around it. We've known for a long time that coma patients can hear, and they can dream. It's why we encourage people to talk to them.'

'To this extent?'

Wolfgang shakes head. 'No, but James got Georgia Perry's name from somewhere, and I think it was from when he was in a coma. I think James not only heard things, but has an acute sense of time and a memory good enough to recall it.'

'How does he explain it?'

'He won't tell me anything until he's completed all nine books.'

'Why?'

'He's so focused he'll barely talk to us.'

Kent takes a moment with that, but can't play along for much longer. 'I don't know, Doctor, it's a leap, and I sense you still haven't gotten to the point.'

'Georgia Perry.'

'Who fell off a balcony.'

'Her husband, Nathaniel Perry, confessed to pushing his wife off the balcony one year after it happened, and was arrested for attempted murder, but only in Coma World. In this world, Detective, an arrest was never made. Here it was only ever ruled an accident.'

Kent takes a few moments with that too. 'Okay. I see where your head is at, Doctor, but like you said, James has heard things in the coma ward around him, and used that as material. The difference between her husband being a killer is the same as Georgia being a school teacher instead of a web designer.'

He ticks points off on his fingers. 'Georgia comes into our care. Roughly one year later in Coma World, her husband is arrested for attempted murder. And roughly one year after that, she dies – and soon we'll know if it was the same day in both worlds. Nathaniel came in here often that first year, but never again over the second, not until Georgia died and he came to collect her possessions.'

'Coma patients have possessions?'

'Photographs on the table, or a teddy bear, or a book being read to them. Jewellery too, often wedding rings.'

'Nathaniel moved on,' Kent says. 'Some people do that better than others. What is it you want me to do here, Doctor? Open a murder investigation?'

'I wanted to lay it out for you, because maybe there were questions at the time. Maybe it got ruled an accident, but the detectives always had doubts. Or maybe Nathaniel confessed to his wife in the coma ward and James heard every word of it. Whatever it is, I thought it best to share it, and you can decide what to do next.'

Silence as Kent stares at the window for a few moments as she gathers her thoughts. Then, 'Can I see the notebooks?'

He slides them across the desk. 'I've marked the relevant pages.'

She reads through the bookmarked sections. He described them earlier as a diary, but really it reads like a novel. He told her they were detailed, but she wasn't expecting them to be as detailed as they are. She reads the pages leading into and out of the entries he marked.

She looks up when she's done. 'You make a compelling case.'

'So you'll look into it?'

'I'll look into it.'

Chapter Forty-Two

The re-enactment reminds Tate of doing renovations around the house, how as a rule of thumb everything takes twice as long as you think, how you never have the right tool or the parts don't fit. It's the same now, with what in theory should only take an hour now entering its third. The crew is small – one to hold a camera, another a boom microphone, another taking care of the lighting, while a fourth directs the scenes. Tate has worked with them before, and the actors too. The guy playing Copy Joe has played other criminals since Tate has been involved in the show, including Joe Middleton. The woman playing Denise Laughton has played two of Middleton's victims, as well as a nurse who was assaulted on her way to her car earlier this year, a mother who was car jacked and a prostitute whose body was found in the Botanical Gardens. The actors treat the job seriously, as if this is the break they need to get noticed – as if one day you're playing a real killer, and the next you're on the silver screen playing a fictional one.

The actors are put through their paces. They film, they reset, they film again, trying to get each take better. They film Copy Joe using a key, and picking a lock, and climbing through a window. At least it's not raining.

As expected – and hoped – an audience has shown up. Officers watch and blend into the crowd. Others walk the neighbourhood, writing down licence plates. These onlookers will be cross-referenced against the onlookers who showed up after Denise Laughton was killed. There will be multiple hits, but maybe one of them has a criminal record. Maybe one has been reported for some seriously dodgy shit. Is Copy Joe out there right now, looking back at them?

After three hours, filming comes to an end. The actors and the crew wade through the crowd to their cars, all instructed to ignore any questions that come their way. Kent and Tate wait for the crowd to die down, then do the same. Like the actors and crew, their cars are parked beyond the barriers, so they're out of frame for any exterior shots. Questions come at them and no answers are given. Kent puts a hand on his arm when they reach her car. There is an envelope hooked under the windshield wiper.

They study the remaining crowd, the other cars, the street. Has Middleton been here, missed by the police? Kent approaches the car slowly, as if the envelope is thick enough to carry a bomb.

'We should wait for forensics,' Tate says.

'I want to see what the sick son of a bitch has to say this time.'

She pulls on a pair of latex gloves, snapping the ends against her wrists. She reaches into her car and pulls out a folder, empties the contents onto the passenger seat, then opens the folder onto the hood of the car. She places the envelope into the middle and carefully opens it. Inside is a single sheet of paper. She unfolds it slowly, as if the paper were brittle, revealing the message:

Go back to the kitchen, you scar-faced uggo.

She balls up the note.

'I'm sorry,' Tate says.

'Yeah? What for?'

'Sorry somebody here would say that to you.'

'I've had worse.'

He stands in the street and watches her drive away.

Chapter Forty-Three

The crowd is rugged up in thick jackets and scarfs and woollen hats, making them all harder to identify. The police are going to spend how many hours sifting through photographs and footage, tracking them all? They've been pointing their cameras outwards when they should have been pointing them inwards.

Copy Joe watches as Detective Kent screws up whatever was in the envelope before driving away. Can't be a parking ticket. Can't be a tip from somebody in the crowd. Maybe a takeaway menu, or a local church selling Jesus. The crowd is drifting off in search of another real-life tragedy. It's after midnight. And so cold he's shivering. The nerves from the last two days have gone. He was silly to be fearful that his colleagues were on to him. What do they know? Tonight has confirmed the answer to that is nothing. They don't even know how he got inside. And they sure as hell don't know what he's going to do next. He overheard Kent telling Tate that they have all the other Carver locations under watch in case Copy Joe has those on his list too. Which he doesn't, because of course they were going to be watching every place Middleton left a dead body.

A man bumps into him, and before he can say anything, the man tells him to watch where the hell he is going. He wonders if the guy would have had the balls to say this to him if he'd been wearing his police uniform. Probably not. Which means the guy has the ability to control himself, which means he's choosing not to. If he didn't already have plans, he could follow him home and bash his skull in with a hammer. He imagines the headlines – 'Arsehole Butchered by Copy Joe'. He likes it. Likes the idea it would confuse the police. But it's convoluted. And risky. He has to stick with the plan.

He focuses on Theodore Tate, who is getting into his car. 'Ex-Detective Killed by Copy Joe'. Not as thrilling, but still one hell of a shock. Imagine the public waking up, discovering the people once tasked to keep them safe were now the very targets. Actually – strike that. Half the public would celebrate. Either way, this also isn't part of the plan.

He turns his attention to the woman who played Denise Laughton. Somebody has approached her, asking for an autograph. What the hell is wrong with people? She smiles at the guy, and he can tell she's reluctant to sign the piece of paper he's jammed at her, but she does. The guy says something else to her, and she slowly shakes her head. He points aggressively at her before tossing the signed piece of paper into the gutter and walking away. Best guess – he asked her out, and she said no, and now he's pissed off.

He watches her get into her car.

Watches her pull out from the curb.

'Actors Targeted after Playing Copy Joe and Murder Victim' – now that's a headline worth seeing.

Chapter Forty-Four

Callum Hayes isn't worried about Hazel Garrett spotting him –
he's followed people before, and does it well, and he's been following her all day without her giving as much as a glance his way.
What he *is* worried about is the problem the others will have when
they realise his plan now includes some alone time with Hazel
before he puts that bullet through her brain. She was a wee cutie
when he first saw her nine years ago, but these days she's hot. Full-
blown hot, the kind of hot that turns killing her into a crime. It
won't just be him thinking that too – the public can stomach
many things, but what they can't stomach is a pretty woman's life
being snuffed out. Maybe a park bench will pop up somewhere in
her honour with her name stamped into it.

Today has been boring, and he figures this is her routine.
Home. Hospital. Work. Earlier she swapped cars with a friend,
which led to a moment of paranoia before he realised the swap
had nothing to do with him and everything to do with a wheelchair not fitting into her two-door coupé. The wheelchair thing
is interesting – he's seen movies where people have been wheeled
into swimming pools, and he's always wanted to do that to somebody. Hopefully the Garretts have one in their backyard. And, on
that subject, just how crazy is it that the hot sister is still living
there? Hot doesn't mean smart, and in his experience with
women, it often means the opposite.

Right now, Little Miss Hotstuff is at a bar, not to drink away
the reality of having to live with her gimpy brother, as he first
thought, but to serve drinks and wait tables. Rather than watch
her through the window all afternoon, he's left her alone, coming
back later in the evening, figuring she'll leave when the bar closes
up. For the last hour there's been no foot traffic. Not long after
midnight, half the bar lights are turned off and a handful of people

spill out onto the sidewalk. He can see her in there, cashing up, laughing with another bar tender, and it's stupid, so damn stupid, but he feels a pang of jealousy that makes him want to kill them both.

When they leave together fifteen minutes later, that pang red-lines, but dials back when he sees it's nothing more than the bar tender walking Miss Hotstuff to her car before heading to his own. She lets the engine warm up for a minute, and he doesn't start following her until she's through the first intersection.

The chances of her going to the hospital to pick up her idiot brother this late are zero, but he follows just the same. He sticks with her as she drives home. She parks in the driveway and he drives past, the house dark, the wheelchair ramp complete. When he drives back a minute later the car is inside the garage and the door is rolling down.

He keeps on driving.

Tomorrow night he'll be back.

Chapter Forty-Five

The physical therapist is the prettiest woman James has ever seen. She has short dark hair, and blue eyes, and a killer smile, and he wishes he could say things to make her laugh. She's two years older than him, at least physically. Sometimes he feels like he's eleven, other times twenty, other times he has no idea at all. His tastes still haven't changed, and his Coma Life may have played out for nine years, but his education level didn't advance any. Working through the filing cabinets in the warehouse, he has become aware that in school he was learning the same thing over and over, or variations of the same thing. The lecture halls at university were halls from various TV shows, and one of his lecturers was Han

Solo. Coma World, it seemed, was populated with people he's taken from this world. They may not have had the personalities of those characters, but they shared the attributes. There were blind spots in Coma World, and his education was one of those things that fell into it, along with new music, new movies, and fashion. Computers, phones, cars – there is a long list of things that stalled the year he was shot.

'You're doing really well,' Fiona tells him, as he bends one leg, bringing his knee to his body without any help. It hurts less than usual, and he thinks that's because today is Thursday – the day he can go home. Even his breakfast earlier tasted better than ever.

He nods. He doesn't try to say 'thank you', even though he knows he can do a half decent job of it. He doesn't want to sound silly, even though Fiona – or anybody here for that matter – would never think such a thing. When Fiona tells him they're done for the day, and despite the fact he is keen to get back to the notebooks, he writes, *More.*

'Are you sure?'

He nods. He's sure. She seems pleased, and he likes that he's pleased her. So they do more, and it hurts, and it's difficult, but he keeps going, thinking about his house, his bedroom, about getting home, about what might be next, about his parents, how he misses them, how scared they must have been their final night. He finds he is as scared of returning home as he is excited. Will it still feel like home? Coma World felt so real to him, and he can't shake the idea that when he passes through the front door, his mum and dad will be waiting there for him.

Maybe they will be. As ghosts. He has always been on the fence as to whether ghosts were real. Perhaps he'll get to find out. If Mum and Dad are ghosts, they'll be the good kind, won't they?

The therapy finishes, and Fiona wheels him back to his room, and despite having gained some strength, she still has to help him onto his bed. In the process he can smell her shampoo. He likes it. A lot. She tells him she's going to be the one coming to his house daily to help him, and he smiles. Hopefully she can stay for dinner on occasion. He has no idea if Hazel can cook, or if she lives on bread – something James thinks he could do. Bread is the best.

He picks up the sixth notebook. He made a start on it last night before falling asleep, getting only a few pages in. He wants to finish it before lunch and start on the seventh. At this rate it's possible he could finish them all today. He turns on the TV, preferring the background noise from cartoons rather than the hospital. Cartoons are different from when he used to watch them at home – something else that has fallen into Coma World's blind spot. The animation has evolved, and the storylines have more humour, and some are darker, but he is enjoying them. While he writes, he keeps the remote control by his side. If Fiona were to walk back in, he'd switch it off. After all, what kind of twenty-year-old man watches cartoons?

Chapter Forty-Six

The motel the department have paid for is uncomfortable, the curtains so thin the parking-lot lights burn through, the walls so flimsy they vibrate from the snoring in the next room, keeping Kent awake. She tries to get a few more hours once that guy is gone, but the traffic outside has the same effect. The shower has bad water pressure and the towels are scratchy, and when she goes to boil the jug and make a coffee, she finds the jug doesn't work. Maybe she should just go back home, stay armed and upgrade the security system. Could be the only way they'll catch Middleton. God she feels like a zombie.

She packs her gear and checks out. She'll get the department to find her somewhere nicer, or get them to put a guard on her house. The guy behind the counter wishes her a pleasant day, and points to a feedback box if she has any suggestions. The pen next to it has been stolen.

The note from last night is still on the floor of her car. It shouldn't have, but it's gotten under her skin. She almost died in the car explosion that scarred her. Her chest was pierced by a piece of metal, narrowly missing her heart. Her hands were burned, the side of her face torn open, her arms fractured. She almost died protecting the people of Christchurch, and in return they treat her like garbage.

She puts on one of the podcasts she downloaded yesterday. She listened to a few last night, and carries on from where she left off. She hits a drive-through on her way to work, then eats her breakfast in the parking lot beneath the station. She has been giving a lot of thought to how convincing McCoy was yesterday. Maybe he was just that kind of guy. Maybe all brain surgeons are. After all, that is what people compare themselves to if they've just done something stupid. He left her a message last night confirming Georgia Perry died in James's fifth notebook the same day she died in real life.

The first thing she does when she gets to work is check on Vega, who's taking the lead on the photographs of last nights' crowd. They're being checked off against criminal-record databases, but so far there are no matches. They're also being compared to the night of the murder to see how many people came back – of which there are many.

'We should run the photos against the original crime scene too,' Kent says. 'Could be our guy was hanging around in the crowds back then. Also compare them to the re-enactment shot back then.'

'Will do.'

She goes to her desk and spends the next hour familiarising herself with Georgia Perry's case. The first thing she learns is the lead detectives on that case were Wilson Hutton, who died last year of a heart attack, and Eric Wilson. She groans when she sees Eric Wilson's name. The two men often worked together, and were first coined The Wilson Twins, then their names were combined to 'Twilson'. Twilson visited the hotel in Queenstown where Georgia fell. They interviewed guests and staff at the restaurants and tourist destinations the Perrys had visited. In Christchurch they interviewed everybody who knew the couple. They found no evidence of foul play. Nathaniel and Georgia Perry were known for their ability to drink and have a good time, and that good time ended when Georgia, whose autopsy showed was five times over the legal limit to drive, toppled from the balcony while using her phone to take a selfie. According to the husband, she dropped her phone, leaned over to grab it, and just kept on leaning.

Kent's phone pings with a message from Tate. The first edit of last night's re-enactment is ready to be checked. She texts him back to say she'll be there in twenty.

She finds Wilson in his office. He's clicking at something on his computer, and, without looking up, he asks her how last night went.

'It went well,' she says. 'I'm about to head into the studio to check it out.'

'Good,' he says, but yesterday when she ran the idea past him, he was reluctant. She had convinced him by saying Copy Joe – and perhaps Joe Middleton too – might be in the crowd of onlookers.

'And the footage from the crowds?' he asks.

'Being combed through as we speak. Let me ask you something.

You and Hutton worked a case a few years back where a woman fell off a balcony in Queenstown.'

'Georgia Perry,' he says. 'How is this related to Copy Joe?'

'It isn't. It was ruled an accident, but did you ever suspect the husband?'

He looks confused. 'I don't understand why you're asking about this.'

'I had a conversation with Doctor McCoy yesterday about—'

'James Garrett's doctor?'

'Yes. While in his coma, James…' she begins, and every time she's pictured this conversation with Wilson, this was where she's got stuck. She never did figure it out. 'You know how doctors encourage people to talk to coma patients?'

'I thought that was only a TV thing.'

'It's real. Anyway, McCoy thinks James Garrett was a sponge, that he heard everything going on around him.'

'Okay.'

'And Georgia Perry was a patient in the same room as him.'

Wilson slowly shakes his head. 'Where is this going, Detective?'

'McCoy thinks James heard Nathaniel Perry confessing to Georgia that he tried to kill her.'

'You want to run through that again for me?'

She does. Coma World. The notebooks. James using names of people he couldn't have possibly known. The books, the weather, the dates lining up. Georgia and Nathaniel Perry. When she finishes, she wonders if the look of disbelief on Wilson's face is the same she showed McCoy yesterday. Part of her feels embarrassed at even mentioning this.

'Let me get this straight,' Wilson says. 'You think Nathaniel Perry tried to kill his wife, because of a diary a coma patient wrote?'

'I know it sounds a bit out there, but—'

'Not just a bit, Detective. You're entering *Twilight Zone* territory here.'

'I don't think so. Coma patients hear things, and James didn't just make up those names. McCoy wouldn't have brought this to me if he didn't think it were possible. He's a brain surgeon, Eric, and that makes him one of the smartest people you'll ever meet.'

'Not that smart, apparently.'

'I think there's something here.'

'Don't you want to catch this Joe Copy arsehole?'

'Of course I do. But that doesn't mean—'

'Then you need to start acting like it and stop wasting your time on this Perry thing, otherwise I'll find somebody who is up to the job.'

Chapter Forty-Seven

The TV studio is a brand-new four-storey building on the edge of Christchurch Central City that still smells like fresh carpet and glue. The bottom three floors have floor-to-ceiling windows on all sides, one end looking over a brothel, the other a church, the folks working here often joking it is the perfect place for a TV studio – right between sin and redemption. It's early afternoon when Tate meets Kent in the lobby. She looks like she hasn't slept since last night.

'Hey,' he says.

'Hey,' she answers. She's carrying a cardboard file box.

'First time here?'

'It is,' she says, looking around the ground-floor foyer, where there's a reception area, a waiting area and a coffee bar. 'How's the coffee?'

'Depends on what you're comparing it to.'

'The station.'

'Then you're going to love it. You want me to carry the box for you?'

'I'm fine.'

They get coffee, then he carries the box anyway so she can carry the drinks.

'So what's in here?' he asks, shaking the file box when they're in the elevator.

'Let's wait till you're sitting down.'

He leads Kent into an editing suite on the third floor filled with tables, computers, audio equipment, mixers, other people at work. He finds a free desk and puts the box on the floor. They get comfortable around a large monitor and watch a cut from last night's footage while sipping at the coffees. Kent makes some suggestions, and he makes some notes.

'What about the script?' she asks.

They watch the same thing again, only this time with him reading out the script he's come up with. He makes more notes.

'It'll all be ready by tonight?'

'Within the hour. I can send you a link,' he says.

They've both finished their coffees. Kent is tapping her foot against the box. 'What's your impression of Doctor McCoy?'

A line from an old comedy comes to mind, where a guy asked that question says, 'I don't do impressions.' He doesn't think Kent would appreciate the joke. 'If it weren't for McCoy, James would have died that night. I think he's smart. Skilled. Compassionate. I like him.'

'You don't think he's prone to flights of fancy?'

A question like that, he wonders where she's going. 'I wouldn't have thought so.'

'I'm going to tell you a story he told me,' she says, 'and I'd ask you to defer any comments until the end.'

Over the next fifteen minutes, she uses logic to bring something impossible to life. James, his Coma World, Georgia Perry, dates James couldn't know lining up with his notebooks. A couple of years back Tate took such a heavy blow to his head that he was put into an induced coma. He didn't live out another life while he was under, or if he did, he has no memory of it. For him it was like falling asleep one day and waking up the next, only to find that two months had passed.

McCoy and Kent – he's not sure he'd believe any of this if it weren't coming from them. He wonders if Wilson might be reluctant to look any further into the case for fear he may look bad dropping the ball on this thing two years ago – if indeed a ball was dropped. To be fair, Tate isn't sure he wouldn't make the same decision if he were in Wilson's shoes.

'Which brings us to you,' she says. 'Since I can't look into it, I'm thinking...'

'I don't know, Rebecca. I don't do that stuff anymore.'

'If not you, then who? If McCoy is right, then Nathaniel Perry is getting away with murder. Look, at the very least, take a look at it.'

'McCoy won't be thrilled that you've chosen me.'

'Why would you say that?'

'Because I never solved who shot the Garretts. Why would he think I'd be any better at figuring out what Nathaniel Perry did or didn't do?'

'Some cases don't get closed, Tate, the same way doctors can't save everybody.'

It's a fair point, but doesn't make him feel any better about it. 'Even if I agree to look at this, what are you expecting me to do here? Rock on up to Nathaniel Perry's house and ask him to be honest with me?'

'If you think that will do it.'

'Any authority I had ended when I left the force.'

'When has that ever stopped you?'

'And nobody has any reason to talk to me.'

'They will. Georgia's parents never suspected anything at the time, but they came into the station after she died to say they had grown suspicious of Nathaniel, but were unable to provide anything. Talk to them. Get them to hire you as a private investigator, and you make it official.'

'And what? Look like a vulture?'

'They'll jump at the offer to have somebody look into it. But talk to McCoy first, and if you're convinced, then look at the files,' she says, tapping the box with her foot. 'He's expecting your call. Take him with you to go see the parents, let him explain what's happening, and how the concept is too thin for the police to look at.'

'Honestly, Rebecca, I don't know about this.'

'If you don't think there's anything here after you've spoken with McCoy, then I'll let it go.'

Chapter Forty-Eight

Tate spreads the files from the cardboard box across the conference-room table. He picks up a photograph of Georgia and Nathaniel Perry. They have their arms around each other, smiling at the camera, each with a drink in their hand, an ocean behind them, a dark future ahead. Georgia is easy on the eye, relaxed, blonde hair flowing over a long summer dress. Nathaniel is tall, lean, dark hair, dark stubble, a fit-looking guy in a buttoned-up polo. A good-looking couple.

It doesn't take long to see why Twilson signed off on the fall as an accident. People fall from things without having been pushed, and he knows there's always a temptation to see more than there really is. The investigation focused on the marriage, whether there was motive, whether either or both the Perrys were quick to anger. All marriages have arguments, and the Perrys had their share, but there was no record of domestic abuse, no record of Georgia or Nathaniel walking into doors, no voiced concern from friends or family. Their life-insurance policies were the type you spent the bare minimum on to get the bare minimum back. They entered the relationship on an even footing, and there were no prenups. Neither came into money in the years that followed. Tate doesn't see money being a motive. Maybe it's the other big one – love. Was one of them having an affair?

The trip to Queenstown was prepaid on Nathaniel's credit card. He had phoned the hotel to make the booking because, despite being in his thirties, Nathaniel had somewhat of an aversion to modern-day devices – which went nicely with his job: he owned and operated an antique store. The calls were all made on a land-line since his affinity with the old meant he didn't even own a cellphone. Part of his job was to visit auction houses to find pieces of furniture he could restore. It's how he met Georgia – her father, an appraiser for an auction house Nathaniel frequented, intro-duced them when she had popped in to see him at work while Nathaniel was there. So, Nathaniel called the hotel and asked for a room on the top floor for the best view, and he got it. But on the day of check-in, a family staying in that room were forced to stay longer because of a sick child, making it unavailable. They were given a room on the floor below.

Did Georgia Perry really die from dropping her phone while trying to take a selfie?

Or did Nathaniel try booking a room not for the view, but for the height?

He calls McCoy, and after a brief hello, he gets right to the point. 'You really think there's something here with this Perry thing?'

'It's not just the way the dates line up,' McCoy says, 'but it's the speed at which James is recalling everything that convinces me this is real. I don't know at what pace people write novels, but it can't be this fast. Watching him, you'd think he was copying everything directly from another book. People who write novels have to invent, and it's hard and takes time.'

Tate doesn't doubt it. He's had to be creative over the years with what he's told the police when he's gotten in the way of an investigation, and he imagines if he had to account for nine years of it, it would be impossible.

'Don't you want to know for sure?' Wolfgang asks.

'I'll pick you up in an hour.'

Chapter Forty-Nine

Kent goes back to the list of names she was calling yesterday before Doctor McCoy interrupted her. Six for six calls she has no luck – nobody has any recollection of their houses being broken into, but she keeps reminding herself these are folks caught up in the grief of having a loved one murdered and may not have noticed, or that whatever was stolen may be something they thought they had lost elsewhere. But that changes on her seventh and final call when she talks to Harvey McMurry. He starts by telling her that after his wife was murdered by Joe Middleton, he moved out, and the house sat unoccupied for three months before he put it on the market.

'I'm sure somebody broke into the house during that time,' he says. 'Some of the stuff had been put into storage, but not all. I didn't really see it as much of a priority. Fact is, back then, if somebody had burned the place down it would have annoyed the hell out of me, but only because I didn't have the courage to do it myself.'

His words remind her of Matthew Durry. 'What did they take?'

'All of Susan's jewellery. It was never expensive to begin with. They took CDs and DVDs, and Susan's iPad. They raided the pantry and took bottles of whiskey and wine, and...' His voice catches, and he says, 'I'm sorry. I'm sorry. Give me a ... a moment.' He disappears, and she hears a tap run and some splashing, and she taps a pen against the desk as she waits, *tap, tap*, and she stares out over the floor and to the windows beyond where it's gotten dark.

McMurry comes back. 'Even now I keep expecting you to tell me there's been a mistake. Every time the phone rings and I don't recognise the number I think it's going to be the police, or the hospital, to tell me there's been a wonderful screw-up. I fantasise about it. I pretend the woman who died wasn't my wife, that somebody else died in her place, somebody who looked like her. I never saw her body, so there's always a maybe, right? Not much of one, but it's something, and sometimes small maybes can keep you from blowing your brains out. The fact this guy is still out there, the Carver, it makes me sick. How am I supposed to find any peace when this monster is free?'

'We're going to get him,' she says.

'And maybe you will, but he's already inspired others who want to be him. Or be better than him.'

'Were there any signs of forced entry?'

'Nothing.'

'No open windows?'

'The back door was open,' he says, the words exactly what she was hoping to hear.

'You left it open?'

'Under any other circumstances, I'd guarantee I didn't, but back then, I guess it's possible.'

'Was there a key in the door?'

'On the inside, sure, it's always there so we could go into the backyard easily.'

'Was there a spare?'

'There would have been one in the kitchen drawer.'

'Was it still there?'

'I don't know, I never checked.'

'Did the real-estate agent have a copy?'

'It was before I listed.'

'You didn't report it?'

'I tried.'

'You tried?'

'I went into the station to file a report, and when I asked the officer what the chances were of getting any of it back, he said they were next to none, so I didn't bother.'

It's a frustrating thing to hear, and she's heard it before. The truth is stolen items are incredibly difficult to get back, but that doesn't mean police should put people off making a report.

'It's not like the police department was going to lock down the city for some missing stuff I no longer cared about. See, that's what happens – stuff that used to be important becomes valueless when the one thing that matters most is taken away.'

'Do you know the exact date of the break-in?'

He does, and she writes it down. It was a month before the house was listed.

She thanks McMurry for his time and hangs up. If Copy Joe is Matthew Durry's pain tourist, then he's shown up at two scenes. The things he's taken could be souvenirs, but they also have something else in common – they are all things that can easily be turned into cash in pawn shops and the backrooms of bars. Was this guy breaking into these houses because he needed the money? When he broke into the Laughton house, did he go in there to burgle it, only Denise came home and caught him? No. She thinks he went there with intent – the photographs and the video playing on the TV show that.

She calls back the owner who didn't sell the house, choosing to change the locks and buy a gun instead. 'When you were changing the locks, did you throw out all the spare keys too?'

'I did. You know how it is, your drawer fills up with them.'

'Were there any missing?'

He doesn't answer right away, then, 'You know, I think there was a key missing for the garage door. All the spares were kept on the same loop, but that one was missing. I just figured we must have loaned it to one of our friends to look after the place whenever we were away … but I couldn't remember who at the time, and it didn't matter since I was replacing the locks anyway. Why do you ask?'

She thanks him for his time. If he hadn't replaced the locks and got an alarm, would Copy Joe have broken into his house too? She thinks so. He was taking keys from the scenes where he could find them. And where are spare keys kept? Junk drawers in kitchens and living rooms. Not difficult to find. Take a key, come back weeks or months later and take what you want.

She stares at the computer, where she has paused an image from the footage Tate sent yesterday from the re-enactment filmed after Angela Durry was murdered. The image is from the raw footage that wasn't used. She can see the bed and the bedside table, along with the knick-knacks of life … an alarm clock, a book, a lamp, a box of tissues. But what she can't see is what she's looking for. She closes the image down and puts on another podcast, then starts trawling through the Internet, looking for crime-scene photos that made it into the public domain.

Chapter Fifty

Wolfgang hasn't seen Tate since the days following the Garrett shooting. In the nine years that have passed, Tate has gone from a man of thirty to a man of fifty. His hair is shorter and is greying at the temples, and his stubble is sprinkled with grey around the chin, and the wrinkles around his eyes and forehead have deepened, as though he spent those nine years in a permanent state of frustration. Wolfgang knows he has been through a lot – from the loss of his daughter, to his wife's injury, to the loss of his job and the loss of Schroder.

They shake hands, and Wolfgang says, 'It's good to see you again, Theo.'

'Likewise.'

It's dark out, and drive-home traffic is in full swing. Seeing the beaten-up Toyota that Tate climbed out of, Wolfgang offers to drive them in his car, and Tate is happy to let him – probably in part because Wolfgang owns a year-old Porsche.

'Nice car,' Tate says, when they get in.

And it is a nice car, and Wolfgang loves how it feels powerful enough to get him to the moon if he floored it. Getting in and out of it, however, is a younger man's game.

It takes five minutes to escape the hospital parking lot and merge into traffic. While Wolfgang drives, Tate looks through the notebooks.

'Rebecca told me they were detailed, but even so...' Tate says, trailing off.

'Even so?'

'I see what you mean about it being impossible to write something at this pace if you were making it up. But I would add that when authors make things up, they're finding a way to get pieces to fit. Nothing that James says has to go anywhere. There doesn't have to be a reason for this or that, and nothing has to have a conclusion.'

'True,' Wolfgang says, and the thought has occurred to him. 'But even so, I don't think that's what has happened here.'

It's the only conversation they make, as Tate reads the rest of the way, a ten-minute drive that takes an hour in these conditions. The rain picks up, and by the time they reach Georgia Perry's parents' house, it's falling heavily enough that he grabs an umbrella from the trunk for them to share. They walk quickly up the path and get under cover on the porch. The house is single-storey white weatherboard, narrow in the front and rolling deep into the yard. The door is dark red and has two stickers on the window, one saying *No Salesmen,* and the other *No Bible Thumpers.*

Wolfgang knocks on the door. 'Let me do the talking.'

Ross Jensen answers. He's tall, grey hair on the sides, bald on top, deep wrinkles and a chin that disappears into his neck. He's wearing a shirt and tie, the tie loosened.

'Hello, Ross,' Wolfgang says.

'Doctor McCoy,' Ross says, clearly surprised to see him on his doorstep at seven o'clock in the evening – or any time of any evening for that matter. He extends his hand, and they shake. 'I can only imagine this has something to do with Georgia?'

'It does.'

He leads them through to a lounge, passing family photos on the way. There are photos of Georgia covering her too-short life, and there are photos of Tabitha, her younger sister, who Wolfgang chatted with a handful of times while Georgia was in hospital. There are none of Nathaniel Perry.

They are led through to the lounge, where Kylie Jensen is on the couch reading a newspaper. She replicates the look of surprise her husband gave at the door. Like Ross, she's late fifties, but looks older, aged from the loss of their daughter.

'Doctor McCoy?'

'Hello, Kylie,' McCoy says.

She stands up, and they fall into a brief hug.

'He has some news about Georgia,' Ross says, as they're separating.

She looks from Ross back to Wolfgang. 'Is that true?'

'It is,' Wolfgang says, then introduces Tate.

'Is this about Nathaniel? About what we told the police?' Kylie asks.

'It is,' Wolfgang says, 'but first I need to tell you about James Garrett.'

Kylie looks at Ross, then at Wolfgang. 'Isn't that the boy in the coma ward in the bed along from Georgia's?'

'That's him,' Wolfgang says.

'What could he possibly have to do with Georgia?' Ross asks.

'That's why we're here. It's quite a story, but I would ask that you hear me out before you ask any questions.'

Chapter Fifty-One

The pen is no longer a pen, but a medieval device designed to elicit pain. His fingertips are raw, the joints stiff, the muscles are being held over a fire. Finishing the notebooks will be at the expense of never straightening his hand again. And yet James continues, driven forward by sheer willpower, the knowledge he is almost finished, and that soon he will go home.

This afternoon he wrote the penultimate year – the gap year between school and university where he spent his days working on his novel; a story about a guy who gives up his soul to the devil for the promise of being a wicked guitar player, only to have a stalker cut his hands off the evening before his first stage performance. That year he also worked odd jobs for his parents, took driving lessons from his dad and saved up for a car. Mum sold her first piece of art – a landscape, mountains in the background, a boat in the water in the foreground, a storm on the horizon. Hazel had her engagement party, when the weather was bad all day but cleared in the evening, his dad gave a speech and his mum cried. The biggest news came late in the eighth year when his parents left the real-estate firm to go out on their own. Any attempts to develop the warehouse failed.

After finishing that notebook, James started on the last, pausing briefly to pick at the dinner a nurse had brought in for him. In that time Doctor Wolfgang came in to say he had an errand to run and possibly wouldn't be back before James was discharged, but would see him tomorrow when Hazel brought him to the hospital.

And now the finish line is approaching, and the final few pages of the notebook are being filled. He hopes Hazel can find comfort from them, and he certainly feels a sense of relief knowing the contents of the warehouse are now written down, so if for any reason he's locked out, he has a backup of what is most important.

Year nine, and it's his first year at CWU – Coma World University – but he doesn't write it down as that. He won't complete his studies. His mum is selling more of her art. She paints a landscape of a woman carrying a dog leash, staring out at a lake, but there's no dog. The painting makes people sad. It gets featured in an art magazine where she is profiled as one of New Zealand's up-and-coming talents. *The Missing Dog* sells for $30,000. It doesn't exist – yet James can see every detail, every brushstroke, and he wishes he could bring it out of Coma World with him. If he could do that, then he would bring out the painting, his parents, his missing childhood.

The real-estate firm Mum and Dad started is going well.

They've been getting expensive listings, and Dad is up for an award for top realtor of the year. The awards, just like the Friday they will be on, will never happen.

One of the blisters on his fingers pops. He wipes it on his shirt. He writes, and he writes.

It's time to say goodbye to his parents.

After breakfast, his mum leaves for a meeting at an art gallery, hugging him first, and he will never see her again. His dad leaves to show a listing. He tells James to have a good day, snatches his keys off the counter, and disappears forever. He has breakfast with Hazel, they say goodbye, and she leaves that world to wait for him in this one.

He doesn't know he is crying until a tear hits the page. He can hear Hazel show up in The Real World, ready to take him home. She asks what's wrong, but he doesn't answer. He goes to university. He spends the day with his friends, and when he comes home, his parents aren't there. He makes dinner. He watches cartoons in the evening. He goes to bed.

The alien spacecraft dream returns, but he doesn't write it into the notebook. He's hungry. And tired. He is no longer in the warehouse, but in the hospital room. Hazel is in the chair next to the bed, watching closely. He puts the pen down. He smiles at her, and she hugs him, and he hugs her back, and he doesn't know why, but they both end up crying. When they let go, he wipes at his eyes, picks up the pen, and on the pad he's been using to communicate, he writes, *How about we get out of here?*

Chapter Fifty-Two

Tate figured it could go either way with Georgia's parents, but when McCoy is done, Ross and Kylie, who have been holding hands the entire time, look at each other, then back to McCoy, and Ross says, 'So what do we do now?'

'You believe us?' McCoy asks.

Ross looks as though he's been asked a trick question. 'I can't imagine you would be here if you weren't convinced.'

'I'm convinced about Coma World,' McCoy says, 'but as to the parallels with Georgia, that's what we're trying to figure out.'

'The same way you're convinced about James is the same way we're convinced Nathaniel killed our daughter,' Ross says. He looks at Tate. 'We went to the police, but they didn't want to hear it, and the fact you're here and not them tells me they still don't want to.'

'It was too big a leap for them to make,' Tate says, 'but I would like to follow up on your behalf, and it will be easier if I can tell people you hired me to do so.'

'Whatever you need,' Kylie says.

'Whatever it costs,' Ross says.

'It was the wedding photos,' Kylie says.

'Excuse me?'

'That's what you're getting ready to ask us, isn't it? What made us suspicious?'

'Yes,' Tate says.

Kylie carries on. 'Six weeks after the funeral, we asked Nathaniel for copies of their wedding photos. We were trying to get everything we could of Georgia. The more of her we have with us, the more ... well ... it's hard to explain.'

'I understand,' Tate says.

'With all due respect,' Ross says, 'unless you've—'

He doesn't get to finish before Kylie puts a hand on his knee. 'He understands,' she says. 'Don't you,' she adds, looking at Tate.

'Yes.'

'I remember you from the news. I remember what happened to your daughter. What was her name?'

'Emily.'

'I'm sorry for your loss,' she says.

'I'm ... I'm sorry too,' Ross says. 'Then you know, every photo, every blurry video on a cellphone, we wanted everything. Georgia had no future, and all we could do was live in her past. When she was in the coma, we didn't hunt all that stuff down, because to do that would be...' He turns to Kylie. 'Help me out here.'

'It would have been an admission Georgia wasn't going to come out of the coma. That we would jinx her somehow. We stayed positive, and the way to stay positive is to cast aside any doubt she wasn't going to pull through.'

'Then she died,' Ross says.

'After the funeral we went through everything, salvaging as much of her past as we could. We asked Nathaniel for copies of the wedding photos...'

'Only to find he'd thrown them out,' Ross finishes.

'What kind of person does that?' Kylie asks. 'People throw photos out if you get divorced, but not when your loved one dies, and not within six weeks. We asked Nathaniel for any photos he had of her...'

'And he had none,' Ross says. 'I remember thinking, the way we hadn't pooled stuff together because we were afraid of jinxing Georgia, well, he jinxed her by throwing everything away. He jinxed her, and she died.'

Tate hopes this isn't their reason for thinking Nathaniel killed Georgia – a reason built on nothing more than superstition. Before he can ask if they have anything more tangible, Ross carries on.

'A year after Georgia went into the coma, Nathaniel stopped coming to visit. It was like one day he just decided to move on,' he says, which is what McCoy told him earlier. 'We rang him and we left messages, and sometimes he'd get back to us and say he was busy, and that he would get to the hospital, but he never did. In the end he stopped taking our calls.'

'The only time we saw him after that first year was at Georgia's funeral,' Kylie says, 'and to be honest, we weren't even sure he was going to show up to that.' She looks at her husband. 'Remember you went to see him, not long before Georgia passed?'

Ross nods. 'Back then I had thought he was keeping his distance because he was hurting so much he couldn't deal with it. I would have been annoyed at that, but I would have understood. I drove to their house. He'd sold it, and moved on without telling us. I was going to drive to his store the next day, but I knew if I did I would have strangled him. I was that angry.'

Tate doesn't think it's enough. There's no doubt Perry sounds like an A-grade arsehole, but that doesn't mean he killed his wife.

'You don't look convinced,' Ross says.

'I'm thinking it through.'

Ross carries on. 'If he had loved our daughter, he never would have abandoned her, which means their entire marriage was based on a lie. And if that's a lie, then everything he's said and done is a lie, including everything he said about her falling off the balcony.'

'Then there's Tabby's wedding,' Kylie says, 'which was two weeks before Georgia fell. We don't know what happened, only that Georgia and Tabby didn't talk again after it. Of course that wasn't unusual for them – they were never the closest of sisters growing up – but still, it's odd they didn't talk in that time. Whatever it was, it led to Tabby walking out of the hospital if Nathaniel showed up anytime she was visiting.'

'Something happened, that's for sure,' Ross says. 'They were all stressed right after it. It's one of the reasons Georgia and Nathaniel were going to Queenstown. Georgia was keen to unwind. I knew they'd drink a lot while they were away, because that's what they did. That's why the police think it was so easy for her to have fallen. But after everything you've told us about James and what he overheard, I'd say the drinking is what made it easier for her to be pushed.'

Chapter Fifty-Three

James pulls the tags off the new jeans and T-shirt Hazel has bought for him, and she pulls the tags from the jacket. He's able to dress himself easily these days. He's relieved. It's eight o'clock, and he has been worried either Hazel or Doctor Wolfgang would decide it would be best to keep him one more night now that it's getting late.

Eight o'clock isn't late. It used to be, when you were eleven and it was a school night. But it's not late anymore.

He wonders what is considered late these days.

'There are more clothes in the car,' Hazel says. 'We can exchange them if you don't like them. I didn't buy too many things on account you'll put on weight soon enough, but when you do I can take you shopping.'

He nods. He's not a big fan of shopping. Coma Mum took him Coma Shopping every year until he was thirteen before she let him shop by himself.

He manoeuvres to the edge of the bed and into the wheelchair, with Hazel holding it so it doesn't roll from beneath him. There is fifteen minutes of paperwork to fill out, during which a nurse finds some band-aids for his blisters. If he ever has to write the Coma World opus again, he'll type it.

That same nurse wheels him to the parking lot – procedure, she says, rather than letting Hazel push him. It's cold out and raining, and he's thankful for the new jacket. Hazel has borrowed a station wagon. Over the month, he's been wheeled out for fresh air often, and on those occasions he has seen how much sleeker and sportier cars have become. Hazel puts the bag of notebooks into the backseat while the nurse helps him into the front. Then he's waving goodbye to her as they drive away. His life was saved here, but he's not going to miss the place. Anyway, he'll be back tomorrow. He's excited to get home.

He writes, *Can I drive?*

'You never used to be this funny,' Hazel says.

He has never seen Hazel drive – at least not in The Real World. She drives the same way Dad did – cautiously, like every intersection has a truck about to barrel through it. He likes the sound of the window wipers as they scoot back and forth, clearing the view of town over and over. Most of the buildings in the Central City were old to begin with, and have only got older. Some have new licks of paint, some have more exhaust fumes soaked into the brick, most have lichen and bird crap caked onto the windowsills. His excitement is waning. They pass bookshops, office buildings, clothing stores, pharmacies, music stores and gaming stores and malls. Soon they're in the suburbs. His excitement is gone. They pass his old school, a church, a park, another park. Something is turning inside his stomach. He fights the temptation to ask Hazel to pull over because his fear is unfounded – the horror that happened is in the past, and if he doesn't go home tonight, then when will he? In another nine years?

Hazel takes the final turn. The house comes into view – only it's not just the house, it's *two* houses. There's the house from his childhood, only different, the walls painted, the guttering new, the trees grown and cut back, a wheelchair ramp leading to the front door. Then there's Coma House, and Coma House got Coma Renovated – the roof replaced after a tree fell through it, a porch swing got hung beneath the veranda in the middle of a hot summer, an extension got added for a music room, where his dad tried learning the guitar.

They pull into the driveway. He's cold. His skin is tingling. He has the irresistible urge to flee, and would, if he were able. Hazel buzzes the garage door remote and soon they're inside. He closes his eyes. He's in the lounge, on his knees, the gun against the back of his head, his parents dead in front of him. He should never have busted the lock on that filing cabinet. He runs his fingers through his hair, feeling the scars and the lumps where pieces of skull were patched and cemented back into place. The life he had here is gone. So are his parents, so is his childhood. Are there bloodstains in the lounge? Bullet holes? Are there shell casings on the—

'Are you okay?'

He opens his eyes and looks at Hazel.

'We can go somewhere else.'

He shakes his head.

'Are you sure?'

He nods.

'Then let's go in.'

Chapter Fifty-Four

Copy Joe is imagining it's Jess tied up on the couch in front of the TV and not the actress from last night. He has put her into a weird situation – one where she knows she is in the process of being murdered, all while holding out hope that the opposite is true. He knows what hope is like. He tried hanging on to it even when things were falling apart with Jess. Even if he told the actress there was no surviving this, she wouldn't believe him. She's the type to be blessed with a sense of eternal optimism, which is an attractive quality and one soon to be put to the test. He wishes there were a way to kill her and possess that optimism.

It's almost eight-thirty. A reality show where women shout 'Don't pretend you know me' at each other while trying not to spill their wine is wrapping up.

'Excited?' he asks.

The duct tape wrapped across the actress's mouth goes around the back of her head and once more around the front. It stops her from answering. Even if he didn't have her tied up in front of the TV, she'd be sitting here anyway. After all, the next show coming on is the one she was part of last night. She looks a little like the victim she pretended to be, but not enough to mistake her on the street for the real thing.

'Just think, the same way you played Denise Laughton, somebody might play you. That's some weird-arse symmetry, isn't it?'

She stares at him. She's crying. He can't tell if she gets the symmetry or not. He can't imagine any actors in the country wanting to play her, or him. Makeup has smeared down her face. She has what Jess used to call panda eyes.

There are ads, including one for the late-night news, where they mention Matthew Durry was arrested yesterday morning for trying to set fire to his old house. If he'd been a betting man, he'd have put money on Durry putting a shotgun in his mouth a couple of years ago. Looks like he'd have lost that bet. But the arrest might be a small hiccup in the way Copy Joe wants all this to play out. Hopefully the police will cut him a break and send him back home.

The ads finish, then they're looking at a man in a suit in front of Denise Laughton's house. 'Tonight, on *New Zealand Crime Busters*, we're looking at the murder of Denise Laughton, the young woman who was brutally killed in her suburban home.'

He wasn't expecting it, but he's becoming lightheaded with excitement. Laughton was his first. The woman who pretended to be her his second. It's like getting to kill Jess over and over and over. The man on the TV sets the scene: a woman at home alone at night, her husband at work, a stranger gains entry to the house – the very house in which Joe Middleton killed another woman three years ago. Then the opening credits roll.

'How many people do you think are tuning in?' he asks.

The actress groans and shakes her head, and cries some more.

The credits end, then an opening shot of the house. Copy Joe is walking through the backyard. The lighting is hazy, and there's a slight angle to the camera, and the whole thing has the quality of one of those horrible infomercials where some arsehole can't come to terms with how to paint a wall. Copy Joe reaches the patio doors.

'I like to think the entire country is tuning in,' Copy Joe says, turning from the TV to the actress. 'Five million sets of eyes. After they find your body, it will go global. Hundreds of millions will see it. You always wanted to be famous, didn't you? Now you're going to be.'

He likes talking to her. Sometimes you just need to get things off your chest.

On TV, Copy Joe is pushing Denise Laughton onto the bed.

'You know what police hope for when they can't solve a murder?'

She shakes her head. Tears are streaming down her face.

'They hope for another one. It gives them a second crack at it. More evidence and another chance of snagging a witness. You thought you were helping that woman when you filmed this? Well, now you're going to get to help her in an entirely different way.'

Chapter Fifty-Five

They wrap up with the parents. Wolfgang thinks things have gone well and that Tate is more convinced Georgia's fall may not have been an accident. The parents certainly are. Kylie writes down Tabitha's details for Tate and says she'll ring her daughter to let her know he'll be in touch.

'The husband was at the hospital a lot over that first year, right?' Tate asks, once they're back on the road.

'Almost every night in the beginning, then it became a few times a week, then every few weeks. That isn't uncommon. What is uncommon is for somebody to stop coming completely.'

'You have much of an opinion about him?'

'It's difficult, because it's been coloured by him abandoning Georgia. But if I'm being honest, I liked him well enough. He seemed genuinely distraught that his wife was in a coma. Now I wonder if maybe he was just upset she hadn't died.'

As on the drive in, the conversation quickly dries up, and Tate returns to the notebooks, not looking away from them until they're almost back at the hospital – a journey much quicker now that the roads have emptied out.

'I've been thinking about something,' Tate says. 'In the beginning, Nathaniel is in the hospital most days, but James only mentions him in the notebooks once, right? The day he was arrested for attempted murder?'

'That's right.'

'Which begs the question, did James not notice him any of those other times? Or did he notice him and not mention it?'

'I had the same thought,' Wolfgang says. 'I think James wrote in these books the same way we would have written in a diary, by choosing what will and what won't make the cut. People don't always mention every detail of everyday life.'

'So you think he's only mentioning the highlights.'

'Otherwise it would take another nine years to write.'

Up ahead a bus pulls out from the side of the road just as he's turning into the hospital entrance, and he has to hit the brakes hard to stop in time. The bus goes by, revealing an ad across the back for a car insurance company, which makes Wolfgang think the bus cutting him off was no accident.

'If you're right,' Tate says, 'then it means he might remember more about Nathaniel that he hasn't mentioned. We should ask him if there's anything else that isn't in the notebooks.'

Wolfgang pulls up next to Tate's car. 'He'll have finished all the notebooks by morning and will hopefully be in a better mood for talking then. Perhaps he can give us a better understanding of how his mind works.'

Chapter Fifty-Six

James hugs the bag of notebooks to his chest as if it's a talisman that will protect him from the dark memories of this place as Hazel wheels him into the hallway. How is it that one five-minute period can poison the eleven years preceding it? He looks at the family photographs that were always here; they've now been added to with pictures of Hazel and their grandparents. He points at a photograph of a cat.

'I was keeping him as a surprise,' she says. 'I got him when I moved back here. He'll be hiding upstairs because he's shy around people he hasn't met, but you'll get to meet him soon enough. Probably when he gets hungry.'

He uses his pad. *Name?*

'Instead.'

He doesn't think he's heard her right, and he frowns, then draws a question mark on his pad.

'You heard right.'

Why would you name a cat Instead?

She smiles. 'Because I originally wanted a dog.'

He shrugs.

'I got a cat instead.'

He nods. He writes, *You're kidding?*

'You don't like it?'

He imagines Hazel on the street calling out, *Instead! Instead!* Even the cat would feel embarrassed. But he likes it. It's different. He gives her the thumbs-up, and he smiles, and he can't wait to meet Instead.

That smile disappears when she wheels him into the lounge and switches on the light. His parents with pillowcases over their heads are kneeling on the floor. There are monsters with guns. His heart stops. He closes his eyes, counts to five, opens them back up. His parents are gone. The monsters, too. His heart goes from a hard stop to a fast beat, making him woozy. It doesn't help when he looks quickly around the room. It's the same experience as he had seeing the house from the street – with old fighting new. The carpet is different, the furniture is different, the curtains different. The TV is bigger, and thinner – thinner than he thought TVs could ever get. A bed has been set up in here for him, and there's a desk with a computer on it, along with some of his favourite books.

It's wrong.

All wrong.

This is his home, but at the same time it isn't. He stares at the floor where his parents were killed, where he was shot, where The Real World hit pause for 106 months.

It's too much for him. All too much.

He closes his eyes. He steps into the warehouse and locks the door.

Chapter Fifty-Seven

They're in an abandoned farmhouse beyond the edge of the city, where a year ago a farmer grew tired of slaughtering animals and moved onto his family, before throwing himself into a piece of farming equipment, which scattered him across the barn. The place has been on the market since then, but so far no takers. Its isolation is good for them, and particularly good for Callum Hayes, who plans to return with Hazel Garrett who, earlier, he followed home. It is the first time the three men have been in the same room since the night things went to shit.

He lays out the plan. They will drive to the Garrett house, and he will sneak in while the others keep watch. He will put two shots into the back of the boy's head and a third into his heart. The plan doesn't need three of them going into the house to do what one person can do alone. There are any number of options for subduing the girl, who he will bring out to the farm before burying her in the field.

The two men stare at him when he's done talking. He's seen that look before, and he doesn't like it. They have made it no secret they think he's an animal, and he's betting he's about to get a reminder. Lance Burrows shakes his head, and so does Damien Keith. Both men are bald, and hard-looking. Not huge, but built well from years of lugging heavy shit around. Burrows has grown a beard to balance out the baldness and hide his weak chin, and has a flat nose from the beatings his dad used to give him as a kid. Callum heard a rumour the dad once kicked him so hard he lost one of his testicles from it. Keith is clean-shaven, thin lips, his eyebrows angled down, giving him a permanent scowl, the way a kid would draw the eyes of a bank robber with a sack of cash over his shoulder.

'It's a stupid plan,' Burrows says. Burrows pulled the trigger on the parents last time, and will no doubt be happy to pull it again. Too happy, even. He's the reason things got so messy nine years ago. They didn't need to kill that family. They could have just tied them up, but once Burrows took that first shot, there was only one way things could go. Not that Callum had a problem with it.

Keith picks up where Burrows left off. 'The girl is a liability. You go in there, and it's kill shots for them both. You bring her out here, for all we know you get pulled over on the way for speeding, or you have a tail light out. This weather, hell, maybe you go off the side of the road, and somebody finds you in a ditch with her in the trunk. Or she gets away somehow, she—'

'None of that shit is going to happen,' he says.

'You can't know that,' Keith says. 'Bringing her back puts you at risk, and when you're at risk, we're all at risk. And for what? A few hours of fun?'

Callum stays calm when he says, 'I can handle it, and when I'm done, nobody will ever find her.'

'You're not getting it,' Burrows says. 'If you get caught with—'

'I won't.'

'But if you are, we're all done.'

Callum knows they're right. But after following Hazel he's been fantasising about what he will do to her, and he doesn't like the idea of a good fantasy going to waste. Perhaps he could tie her up, tell the others he killed her and go back for her later.

'Whatever you're thinking,' Burrows says, 'let it go.'

'She's the reason all of this fell apart,' Callum says. 'Shooting her in the head lets her off easy.'

'The reason this fell apart is because we got the wrong damn address,' Burrows says. 'You can't blame the girl for running when thousands of years of evolution were telling her to. It's your fault for letting her get out the window.'

Callum wants to punch him.

'We go in there, we put her down, we never look back,' Keith says.

Callum wants to punch him too.

'Keeping her alive one second longer than we need to is a risk,' Burrows says. 'And let's not forget Kent is looking for you.'

'Fine,' he says.

'Then we're in agreement,' Keith says.

'We are,' he says, but they're not. The girl is coming with him.

'Good,' Burrows says. 'Let's not mess it up like last time.'

Chapter Fifty-Eight

Tabitha Munroe lives twenty minutes west of the city in a two-year-old subdivision where cookie-cutter houses cover the colour palette all the way from beige to dark brown. Tate parks outside a two-storey house with a swing ball set pounded into the middle of the front yard. He rings the doorbell. The woman who answers is full of sharp angles, with short dark hair and a small nose piercing. Even if he hadn't just seen a photograph of Tabitha, he'd know right away she was Georgia Perry's sister.

'Tabitha, my name is—'

'My parents already told me,' she says. She doesn't look happy about seeing him on her doorstep, and sounds even less happy when she adds, 'I just didn't think I'd be seeing you tonight.'

If what happened to Georgia Perry was deliberate, wouldn't Tabitha want to know? Of course she would. Which means what he is seeing is her frustration with her parents, who she thinks have got something into their heads they can't let go.

'Do you mind if I come in? It's freezing out here.'

'Fine,' she says, exhaling the word more than saying it, letting him know it's not fine at all.

She leads him to a lounge that is clean and messy at the same time – with the room tidy but with toys piled into a corner and smears on the wall where crayon and felt-tip have been cleaned away. They sit on opposite couches, a coffee table loaded up with remote controls and colouring books between them.

'First things first,' she says. 'We need to keep our voices down. Herschel is upstairs trying to get the kids back to sleep – kids you woke up a minute ago by coming here.'

'I'm sorry.'

'I'm sure you are. Now, if you're here because of the wedding photographs, I can tell you you're wasting your time. I've heard Mum and Dad's theory, but people throw out photos all the time. It doesn't mean much. You've never thrown out a photo?'

'Not wedding photos, and those photos mean a lot to your parents,' he says. He wasn't sure if he would mention James or Coma World, but now knows he won't, not unless her parents already have. 'Your parents did mention you and Georgia had a falling-out at your wedding.'

'We didn't have a falling-out.'

'You didn't talk before Georgia and Nathaniel's trip to Queenstown, is that right?'

'There was nothing unusual about that. Trust me, Mr Tate, not speaking to my sister during that time is the biggest regret of my life, and if I'd known our time was limited, I'd have spent every moment with her.'

'Your parents said whenever you were at the hospital at the same time as Nathaniel, you found a reason to leave.'

'My parents are remembering everything through a lens of suspicion – a suspicion you're not helping with, by the way. I left because it was difficult. Mum and Dad, Nathaniel, myself, all sitting around George at the same time, it's hard to make idle chit-chat when your sister is lying there, and harder still to sit there in silence. That's probably why Nathaniel didn't go so much in the end.'

'He didn't visit Georgia at all in the second year,' he says.

'People deal with things differently. Maybe it just hurt too much.'

'Maybe.'

'Even I didn't go as often in that second year.'

'But you still went.'

'Her doctor said it was good for George if I talked to her, and it was good for me too. Here's the thing, Mr Tate. My parents, they're logical people, and logical people need to find reasons in things when sometimes there just aren't any. I loved my sister, and Nathaniel loved her too. I know you came here wanting me to give you something that would help find what they're looking for, but you're not going to find it, because it simply isn't there.'

Chapter Fifty-Nine

The house tells the world whoever lives here can't afford anything else. It's cold, dark, uninviting, the kind of house that even on a summer's day would have a raincloud over it. 'A struggling actor's house,' Copy Joe says, because that's exactly what it is.

The street is devoid of life, and the rain is steady. He walks over the front yard, his feet sinking into the lawn, water soaking into his shoes. He should have worn gumboots. He opens a side gate, his glove absorbing water from the latch. He makes his way to the back door. His fingers are so cold he's worried about dropping the prybar. The high from killing the actress isn't matching the high from two nights ago. It's possible this is what drug addicts experience when they chase that first-ever hit. It's also possible the thrill of killing the actress was dulled when her boyfriend showed up.

He pauses when the neighbour's backdoor light comes on and spreads out over the fence. He ducks into the shadows. The door opens, there's a muffled voice, then a dog's paws are hitting the ground as it runs. Jesus, is the dog coming for him? He holds his breath and doesn't move. The light stays on. He can see out over the overgrown backyard and weed-choked garden. There's a dead tree leaning in the corner, looking ready to fall through the fence.

'Hurry up!' the man next door yells out.

The dog must hear him, heads back for the door, but stops on the other side of the fence close to where Copy Joe is waiting. It growls.

'Come on!'

The growling gets louder. Jesus, is the stupid thing going to jump the fence? What will he do if it does?

'I said come on,' the man says again, and this time the growling stops. The door closes, and the light goes off.

He counts to sixty, then moves quickly to the house. He wedges the tip of the prybar into the seam between the backdoor and the doorjamb. It doesn't go far, but it makes a small dent that expands when he stabs it in a second time. A third stab and the prybar gets in good. He's worried the wood will crack like a gunshot, his hope being the wind and rain will hide it, but it turns out the frame is rotten and it splinters away noiselessly. The house probably has lost so much of its weight to wood mites he's probably lucky the whole thing didn't just collapse.

He steps inside.

Chapter Sixty

Wolfgang is guided by a GPS with an English accent that they have to crank the volume up on to be heard over the storm. A shopping trolley, lost from the herd parked by the supermarket a kilometre back, rolls out from the sidewalk and forces him to swerve as his window wipers struggle to outpace the rain.

He reaches the house and parks up the driveway, grabs his bag and dashes through the rain to the temporary wheelchair ramp. Hazel flings the front door open and ushers him inside before he's even had the chance to knock.

'How is he?' he asks, handing her his medical kit so he can take off his jacket and hang it by the door. Fifteen minutes ago he'd been lying on the couch in his office at home while Caroline had been at book club – though Caroline would be the first to admit they ought to change the name to wine club. He does some of his best thinking on his couch while listening to rock concerts from the seventies – The Doors, Creedence, Pink Floyd, Springsteen – all while smoking a cigar and feeling nostalgic for his youth. Tonight he'd been listening to a Neil Young concert while rolling over the idea of asking Hazel and James for their permission to write a research paper on James, before coming to the conclusion it could be a book. Millions would be fascinated. Pages from the notebooks could be included, or perhaps James could write out other things in even more detail. Wolfgang wouldn't want any of the royalties, but the money for James and Hazel would be life-changing, and God knows they could do with it.

Then Hazel had called.

'He's the same,' Hazel says. He follows her into the lounge, where he's greeted by a silent James Garrett and the acidic smell of urine. 'It only just happened,' Hazel says. On the phone she sounded upset, but now she sounds distraught. 'I need to change him, but ... but I can't. I can't manage to move him by myself.'

The lounge has been set up as a bedroom, with the couch pushed in from the wall to make room for a single bed. Everything has been spaced out for the wheelchair that James is sitting in, his eyes closed even though he doesn't appear to be asleep.

'Hi, James, I thought I'd drop by to see how you're doing,' he says, and he waits for a few moments, but James gives no indication he's heard.

'He's been like this from the moment we came into the lounge,' Hazel says. 'As we got closer to the house he seemed ... off, and it got worse when we arrived. He said he was fine, but I should have turned around anyway. What was I thinking?'

'This was the room where it all happened?' Wolfgang asks.

Nothing for a few moments, then, 'It is.'

'And this is the room James is going to be sleeping in, and spending most of his time in while he's in the wheelchair.'

'It is,' she says. 'I should have known better than to bring him back here, but he was so keen to come home. I was stupid to think the good here would outweigh the bad. I always thought if I sold the house before he woke, it would hurt him even more, but now I wish I had.'

This isn't on her, it's on him. He should have known better. Worse, he did. 'This isn't your fault, but mine. I should have foreseen this.'

'I should never have told you how desperate he was to come home.'

'James had already made that clear.'

'First thing tomorrow I'll call a real-estate agent and talk about getting the house listed.'

'Let's not make any rash decisions, but let's get him out of this room and cleaned up, then decide from there if we go back to the hospital,' Wolfgang says. He turns back to James. 'How about you let us change you into your pyjamas now that it's night time, huh?'

Nothing.

'James?'

Nothing.

'What are we going to do?' Hazel asks.

'Let's change him, and decide from there.'

Chapter Sixty-One

Plastic bottles float in the gutters along the side of the road, coming to a stop in the soup of chip bags and fallen leaves blocking the drains. From the van parked at the end of the block, Callum's and Burrows' view of the Garrett house is limited to the letterbox and part of the front yard. Keith, parked at the other end of the block, will have the opposite view. At the moment the idiot boy's idiot doctor is in the house, the idiot doctor recognisable by his Porsche. It's almost ten o'clock, and they don't know how long the doctor has been in there since they have only just arrived. Callum hopes he's not in there banging the sister. If he is, he's going to stuff him into the trunk of his stupid Porsche and send him off a cliff.

'I don't like this,' Burrows says.

None of them do. They're exposed, waiting here like this. The bad weather is keeping people inside, minding their own business, but even so, they are monitoring police frequencies with scanners in case somebody reports them, or the stolen vehicles they're using.

'We should go and come back,' Burrows adds.

'Or I go in there now and kill the doctor too,' Callum says.

'You can't kill the doctor. What if you need him one day to save your life?'

'I just want to get this done,' Callum says.

'And we will, once the doctor is gone.'

Burrows uses a burner cellphone to call Keith's burner cellphone. He puts it on speaker. 'How's it looking at your end?'

'Same as it looked two minutes ago,' Keith says. 'I don't like sitting here. We should leave and come back in a few hours.'

'Agreed. Let's go back to the farmhouse.'

'This is bullshit,' Callum says. 'I say we do the doctor.'

Burrows shakes his head. 'No.'

'What if he's here right now because the kid has started remembering stuff?'

'Then it would be the police showing up, not the doctor.'

'For all we know the kid has something to say, and the doctor is helping him say it, and they're getting ready to call the police. We have a chance right here to tie up all the loose ends.'

Burrows doesn't say anything, and Callum can tell he just needs a little push.

He gives it: 'Nobody wants to go around killing doctors, but sometimes you have to do shit you don't want to do.'

The phone line is still open, and Burrows says, 'What do you think?'

'I don't like it, but he has a point,' Keith says.

'The plan doesn't have to change,' Callum says. 'I go in there, and you guys keep an eye out.'

Silence from Burrows, silence from Keith on the phone.

'Well?'

'I say let him do it,' Keith says.

Burrows takes a few more seconds, then he agrees. It pisses Callum off that these guys think there's a hierarchy here, but at least they've come around to his way of thinking.

But not quite, because Burrows then adds, 'In, and back out. No messing around with the girl.'

'It'll take a few minutes to get in,' Callum says.

'Just get it done.'

He climbs out of the van and into the rain.

Chapter Sixty-Two

James unlocks the warehouse door and steps out. *Where are you? This looks like your bedroom, but is it?* He thinks it might be, but the walls have been painted, and what happened to all his posters?

Doctor Wolfgang and Hazel are standing beside the bed. He knew Doctor Wolfgang was here, had heard him earlier through the warehouse door. They must have carried him upstairs.

'How are you feeling?' Doctor Wolfgang asks.

Now that he's out of the room where his parents died, better. He isn't sure if that feeling will remain if he goes back downstairs, but he does know he doesn't want to go back to the hospital. He gives them the thumbs-up, then signals for a pen.

'We were worried about you,' Doctor Wolfgang says, as Hazel slips out of the bedroom. 'I made a mistake by letting you come home so early. I think it's best if' – James shakes his head – 'you return to the hospital in the morning. Or perhaps even tonight.'

James keeps shaking his head. Hazel returns and hands him a pen and a pad. He writes, *I'm okay. I don't want to go to the hospital.*

'I'm glad you're okay,' Doctor Wolfgang says, 'but I think it's for the best.'

It was a shock coming home that's all but <u>I'm okay now</u>. He underlines the last three words, then adds, *I know you want to know about Coma World I'll tell you everything you want to know that will show you I'm okay.*

Both Hazel and Doctor Wolfgang look unsure.

Please.

'I don't know, James,' Hazel says. 'I guess ... well ... We could stay here tonight, and tomorrow we move in with our grandparents until we find somewhere else. I'll sell the house and...'

She stops talking when she sees him scribbling on the notepad: *We don't need to sell the house.*

'He does seem better,' Hazel says.

'I agree. But still...'

Do you want to know about Coma World?

'Of course,' Doctor Wolfgang says, 'but I won't let you use that as a bargaining chip to convince me you should stay here.'

James thinks on it, then he writes, *But isn't the decision mine? After all I'm twenty years old I'm an adult.*

He watches as Doctor Wolfgang and Hazel share a look.

'I appreciate your viewpoint, James,' Doctor Wolfgang says, then turns to Hazel, and adds, 'but ultimately the decision is Hazel's.'

Hazel weighs it up. Then, 'He's upstairs, he's comfortable. Let him stay tonight, and we'll reassess in the morning.'

Doctor Wolfgang nods and he smiles at James. 'You get your way on this one, James, but if there's any change, or any concerns,' he says, turning to Hazel, 'you'll call me, okay?'

James nods, and Hazel says, 'I promise.'

Chapter Sixty-Three

From the bushes next door, Callum watches the doctor drive away. He hates him for saving the kid's life nine years ago, hates him for coming here to see the sister, hates him for owning a nice car. That thing he said earlier about nobody wanting to kill doctors, he didn't mean it. He shifts from foot to foot. Water is pooling in the garden and soaking his shoes. No doubt he's in danger of leaving footprints everywhere. He'll throw the shoes out before cops start interviewing people with size fourteens. They knew his size would be a factor last time – so they used that to his advantage and set up the hardware-store robbery as a backup. He's cold. He's wearing a soft jacket that absorbs the rain rather than repels it. It seems a small thing, but best not to risk anybody hearing the drops bouncing off his clothes.

He's eager to get out of the rain and into the girl, but stays where he is in case the doctor comes back for his cellphone, or his wallet, or his jacket, or whatever the hell else it is that old fucks forget. As he waits, the downstairs lights in the Garrett house start going out. Half a minute later a light is turned on in a bedroom upstairs – the same bedroom the girl escaped out of last time he was here.

He has waited long enough.

He holds his hand to his earpiece. It's connected via Bluetooth to the phone in his pocket. On other occasions he's had earpieces in both ears, each connected to different phones so both Burrows and Keith can talk to him. But only one is necessary tonight – the phone is an open line to Burrows, who has a separate open line to Keith.

'I'm going in.'

'Just get it done,' Burrows says.

He moves quickly. Last time he knocked on the front door while Burrows and Keith hid out of sight. One hand held a rag to his face splashed with red food colouring, and the other held out a stolen police ID towards the door. He said he was an officer in urgent need of help. Who wouldn't open the door to that? Certainly not Frank Garrett, because he swung it open and said a doctor lived opposite.

If he were a betting man, he'd put money on Hazel Garrett having an aversion to opening doors to strangers at night, no matter what the story.

He races across the front lawn and through a gate into the back-yard. He gets under the eaves by the side door to the garage. He says nothing into the earpiece – it's been agreed that once he is at the house, the only communication will either be him asking for help, or them warning somebody is coming. He checks the door and confirms it isn't already unlocked – that's a mistake you only make once – then goes to work.

Chapter Sixty-Four

The shortcut through the smaller streets of Tate's neighbourhood becomes a good decision turned bad when the road ahead is blocked by a fallen tree and downed powerlines. The streetlights are out, but the road is lit up with safety lights. Maintenance workers are cutting up the tree and shifting it to the sidewalk for tomorrow's woodchipper. A cherry picker is being raised into position, a couple of guys loaded up with tools hoping to restore power to a lot of unhappy people.

He does a U-turn made tighter than it needs to be as he makes room for a wheelie bin blown into the street. He still hasn't had dinner, and the chicken kebab he bought on the way home is cooling quickly on the passenger seat. His stomach is rumbling. He pulls over and unwraps the kebab and takes a bite, then another, then carries on driving. He's still chewing when his phone goes. It's McCoy. He puts him on speaker.

'Hope I'm not calling too late?'

He swallows down the kebab. 'I'm still on my way home.'

'As am I. I wanted to see how it went with Tabitha.'

He gives McCoy a short version of the conversation, which is easy considering there isn't a long one. 'I'll keep looking, but my hope is James can give us more of a direction – that is if there is a direction.'

'Let's pencil him in for the morning, but there are no promises,' McCoy says. 'He took a little bit of a turn earlier.'

Tate's stomach drops, and before he can ask what happened, McCoy carries on.

'It's nothing serious, and he's okay now, but I don't want to push him tomorrow if he's not up for it.'

'Agreed,' Tate says. 'I'm sorry to hear he's not well. What happened?'

'It's hard to say exactly,' McCoy says. 'I suspect it was a panic attack, brought on by being back home for the—'

'James is back home?' Tate asks, his pulse quickening.

'He is.'

'Since when?'

'Since an hour or two.'

'Just him and Hazel?'

'That's right.'

'Why didn't you tell me earlier?'

'I ... I don't know. I guess I didn't think about it. What's wrong?'

'Does Kent know?'

'I'm not sure. Why?'

'I'll call you back,' Tate says, and he hangs up before Wolfgang can say another word.

Chapter Sixty-Five

Kent uses the remote to kill the loop of *Crime Busters,* turning the TV into a dark mirror that reflects the lounge lights and the body of Simone Clark. The house is quiet, the silence only broken by soft footsteps and the occasional cough. She is keeping her thoughts to herself, as is Wilson. Vega and Travers are at the other end of the house, Vega going through the master bedroom, and Travers going through the home office. The storm has got worse since her arrival, as if what happened here has made Mother Nature angry. It sure as hell has made Kent angry – she wants to get her hands on the person who did this and put them down. Perhaps tomorrow she'll feel differently – but she doesn't think so. Less than twenty-four hours ago she was talking to Simone Clarke, and now this. It's taking all her strength not to scream.

Simone is upright on the couch, her head slumped forward, her chin close to her chest. Her hands are bound behind her, her feet tied together. She's dressed in a faded pair of jeans and a white T-shirt. There are drops of blood around the collar of that T-shirt. There is a clear plastic bag over her head that was torn open by the paramedics who arrived. Her eyes are wide, haemorrhaged, pained.

Simone's on-again, off-again boyfriend, Edgar Burton, called it in. Burton had come by to watch *Crime Busters* with her. He had been running late, and had texted her to say so. He had let himself in using a key and had found her on the couch with the bag over her head. At that stage she was still alive. He had been carrying a bottle of wine, and says he doesn't know if he dropped it from the surprise or from the blow to his head. One moment he's looking at Simone, the next he's waking up with an incredible headache and tied to a chair.

Copy Joe suffocated Simone while Burton watched, put Burton's phone on the floor where he could get to it, then left. Burton tipped the chair, and over time wiggled himself to the phone. He used his nose to punch in his pin code, then dial the police. Because there was duct tape over his mouth, all he could do was groan. The call was traced, and the police came. Burton is in hospital with a concussion, being monitored. He is a suspect, but Kent doesn't think a viable one. Everything here, from the choice of victim, to *Crime Busters* playing on a loop, to the photographs from around the house being pooled into the lounge, screams Copy Joe.

'Why keep the boyfriend alive?' Wilson asks, breaking the silence.

'The photographs suggest he wants an audience, and I guess the boyfriend became an audience who lived to tell the story.'

'That makes sense,' Wilson says. 'Here's what also makes sense.

Copy Joe was waiting for the re-enactment to be made so he could do this very thing, and you played right into his hands.'

She wasn't expecting him to say that, and it hurts. She knows she's a link in the chain that got Simone killed, and it makes her feel sick. Was she played? Before she figures out how to respond, her cellphone rings. It's Tate, probably calling about the case she gave him earlier. Tate was another link in the chain, and she knows he's going to take this as hard as she's taking it. She isn't sure how to tell him, but it will have to wait. She doesn't want to take the call in front of Wilson.

She drops the phone into her pocket.

Chapter Sixty-Six

Tate leaves a message for Kent to call back, saying it's urgent. He's five minutes from home. He has a gun there, but does he have time to get it? That depends on whether or not he's overreacting. Which he's sure he is.

But what if he isn't?

He calls Kent again. The same deal, only this time he adds, 'James Garrett went home tonight. Call me.'

He doesn't want to do it, but he calls Eric Wilson.

Wilson doesn't sound thrilled to hear from him, and says he needs a moment. That moment is thirty seconds, and then, 'What do you want, Theo?'

'Did you know that James Garrett went—'

'James Garrett is no longer your concern.'

'But—'

'I'm going to hang up now, Theo.'

'Please, listen to me,' he says, as he picks up speed through the wet streets to the Garrett house, hoping there will be no more downed trees and powerlines. 'James Garrett went home tonight.'

'I didn't think that was happening for a few more weeks.'

'Exactly. What if the people from nine years ago come after him?'

'Why would they come after him?'

Kent wouldn't have to ask that question. Probably no other cop would have. 'Because they're worried he might remember something that's useful.'

Wilson sighs heavily, like he's had a day of dealing with children, and here comes another one. 'Then they would have come after him at the hospital years ago.'

'It might have been too risky, or maybe they never thought he would wake up.'

'And most likely they still don't know. For all we know these men are dead, or in the wind, or in jail, or have forgotten all about it. They're not going to risk killing a kid who can't talk and who has no memory of that night. James Garrett stopped being your concern the day you left the force. You go poking around, and I'll arrest you for interfering with an ongoing investigation. Others have warned you in the past for this kind of bullshit, but the difference between them and me is they liked you and I don't.'

'You might be right, and I hope you are, but at least send somebody to keep an eye on them until we know for sure.'

'Where my people need to be is right here where I am, which is at a crime scene you helped create.'

Wilson's words don't make any sense. 'What are you talking about?'

'Your great idea about shooting a re-enactment for TV is what I'm talking about. Simone Clarke was killed tonight, and so far things point to Copy Joe.'

Despite being desperate to get to the Garrett house, he has to pull over. His ears are ringing and his chest is tightening and his vision is blurring. He opens the window, the cold air and rain coming in.

'You still there?' Wilson asks.

His breath is labouring. Is he having a heart attack? 'Simone ... is dead?'

'Freshly so, thanks to you. I told Kent your show was a waste of time, and—'

'I—'

'And now a woman is dead because of it.'

Tate rests his forehead against the steering wheel and closes his eyes. He pictures Simone. Smart, fun, engaging, young, wanting to help, eager to work – everything she would go on to do in life taken away. He pictures himself going to a bottle store. Going home, opening it, having a drink, only one wouldn't be enough. Hell, one bottle wouldn't be enough.

'What's wrong? You got nothing to say?' Wilson asks.

'I—' he says again, but can't get anything else out. His chest hurts bad, his heart is in a vice, and even if he could find the words he's not sure he could say them. He needs to get himself under control. Needs to get his voice back.

But it doesn't matter, because Wilson is already gone.

Chapter Sixty-Seven

The station wagon is in the middle of the garage, covered in beads of water. The air is no warmer in here than outside. His fingers ache. He had to remove his gloves to pick the lock. Picking the lock isn't like it is in the movies. It takes longer – but a movie or a TV show wouldn't be a lot of fun if it took five minutes, as this one did.

Callum breathes into his hands to warm them up. He imagines the girl reading a book until she gets sleepy, and with the storm raging outside, she won't hear a creak on the stairs. He puts his gloves back on. They're wet and cold.

He slowly opens the internal door, and just as slowly closes it behind him. He confirms his cable ties are still in his pocket and not in the neighbour's garden. The same goes for the duct tape. He's bringing the girl with him, despite all the shit the others gave him earlier. Unless they're willing to shoot her in the street, they'll get her quickly into the van and be on their way. He removes his gun from the waistband of his jeans. He likes wearing it that way, Hollywood style, even though Burrows has warned him one day he's going to shoot his dick off.

The events of nine years ago seared the layout of the house into his memory. The bedrooms are all on the second floor, the living areas down here. He heads for the lounge, figuring that's where the cripple will be sleeping – doubtful the sister will want to lug him up and down the stairs. The only light in the lounge is from a small red dot on a TV set and a clock on a stereo. They don't offer enough to make the furniture look anything other than boxy caves. One of those caves he sees just as he walks into it – the goddamn wheelchair. His knee smacks the frame, it rattles and rolls away, and he reaches out and stops it. He lowers into a crouch, waiting for somebody to react to the noise. Did they hear him? Are they calling the police? He counts off thirty seconds. Nothing. He pulls a small penlight from his pocket and switches it on. He points it from the wheelchair to the armchairs to the couch. Nothing except for a cat sitting on its haunches staring back at him. So the kid was lugged up to his bedroom after all, which is just as well, otherwise walking into the wheelchair would have woken him. Perhaps the plan is for him to live his days up there, staring out of the window and jerking off to the neighbourhood kids.

He'll certainly live out the rest of his life up there now.

He heads for the stairs.

Chapter Sixty-Eight

Kent follows Copy Joe's muddy footprints from the lounge to the front door, careful not to step on them. The front door is open, and directly outside, a gazebo has been set up to keep rain off the porch and the immediate yard and path beyond. Any footprints potentially left in the garden or the lawn have been destroyed by the rain. Even in this weather people are watching her from footpaths and driveways. A twenty-something spectator has her umbrella torn from her grip by the wind and hurled into the lounge window of the house behind her; the impact is loud enough to be heard over the rain.

Kent turns into a guest bedroom and finds herself alone. Her head is spinning. She crosses the room and gets out of sight of the corridor then turns her back to the wall and drops to her haunches, her jacket snagging as she does so. She hadn't noticed until now, but the walls are gritty, like the paint had sand poured through it before it was applied. She hangs her head and rides out the urge to throw up. Wilson was right. When Copy Joe killed Denise Laughton, he was hoping *Crime Busters* would do a show. He pulled photographs from other rooms in each of the houses and put them around his victims. He played the videos for each of them for the same reason. He kept the boyfriend alive so he could tell the story around campfires till his end of days. There are many questions spinning in her head, but whether or not Copy Joe is done is an easy one to answer.

'This wasn't your fault,' Vega says, stepping into the room.

'Wasn't it?'

'No. But I have some news. It's not worst-case scenario, but it's not good either.'

Kent isn't sure she can handle worst case right now.

'The officers we sent to check on Martin Thomas,' she says, Thomas being the man who played Copy Joe in the re-enactment last night, 'well, they just called in. They say his backdoor has been busted wide open, and there are footprints all through his house. We don't know if Copy Joe has taken him or if he wasn't home. His car is gone, but it could be he's in the trunk. Either way, Simone Clarke wasn't the only person this psychopath was after.'

Chapter Sixty-Nine

Tate rings the bell and stays close to the door to shelter from the rain. It's not working as the wind brings it in sideways. It occurs to him he never called McCoy back. He's about to ring the bell again when an interior light comes on. A moment later the outdoor light joins it, and then Hazel is looking at him through the narrow window beside the door. She recognises him and opens it. He saw her a lot in the months that followed her parents' murders, then less so as the years went by and the case grew colder. She would come into the station for updates, and he was embarrassed not to have any, yet she never accused him of letting her or her family down.

Before she can say anything, he says, 'I know it's late, Hazel, but it's important. I need to talk to you and James.'

'You've found them? The men who killed Mum and Dad?'

'No, but it's possible if they find out James is awake, they might try to hurt him. We don't know if they've been keeping tabs on you and James, but—'

'You think we're in danger?'

He knows he's overreacting. 'It's possible.'

'I didn't see anything back then,' she says, letting him in. 'And James didn't see anything either. He's proven that. So there's no reason for them to—'

'But they don't know that,' he says, rain dripping off his jacket onto the floor. 'They're cold-blooded killers, Hazel. And right now they think their freedom is at risk. There should be police officers watching your house.'

'Why aren't there? If the police thought we were at risk, then—'

'Because they didn't know you were coming home today.'

'Oh.'

'And the detective looking after your case—'

'Detective Kent.'

'I can't get hold of her.'

'Can't you call somebody else?'

'I can, and I did, and they don't agree. Look, there's every chance I'm being paranoid, and if it turns out that's the case, then what's the harm? If I'm right, and you stay here, then...'

'I get it.'

'We need to find you a hotel for tonight.'

'I can't afford a hotel. I ... I just can't.'

'I'll pay for it.'

'We can stay with my grandparents,' she says.

He shakes his head. 'If they're looking for you, they may go there. Can James go back into the hospital?'

She doesn't answer right away, then, 'I guess.'

'He doesn't like the hospital?'

'He doesn't, but it's not that. I can't afford the hospital either. His medical bills, I...'

'You're covering his medical bills?'

'Insurance stopped once he woke up.'

He knows what that's like. He is barely covering the mortgage by the time he covers all of Bridget's medical bills. Insurance stopped covering her last year and are arguing her relapse might be unconnected to the original accident. The problem is the legal bills to fight it would very quickly look like the medical ones.

'Then you stay at my house. Tomorrow we speak to Kent, and we form a plan and see if we can find you somewhere more permanent. Pack some things together, and let's get out of here.'

Chapter Seventy

Callum is still holding the cushion he grabbed from the couch after Burrows told him to get out. He used it to wipe his footprints from the hallway floor before retreating into the garage, and is now trying to hear the conversation on the other side of the internal door. But he can't – the main garage door is intensifying the sound of the storm rather than blocking it. Who does the other voice belong to? It's not the doctor, otherwise Burrows would have said that. Could be a boyfriend, or maybe a priest, to give the kid his last rights or to pray the brain damage away.

Or it could be a cop.

He slips outside and moves along the house, bringing the driveway into view. Definitely not the doctor's car, but not a cop car either – an old Toyota that looks like it should have been put out of its misery years ago. He's still carrying the cushion. He tosses it into the garden, crouches, and into his earpiece, he whispers, 'I'm outside. I'll wait it out.'

'Understood.'

He's tempted to go back in and let the stranger become collateral damage, but the stranger brings an uncertainty to proceedings. What if it is a cop who just has a cheap car? What if

he's armed? Bad luck can always win out over good preparation –
hell, look what happened last time he was here.

The garage door slowly opens, a shaft of light growing over the
driveway as it does. He moves to the garage window. The view
inside is blurred by the rain, but he can see the sister putting the
wheelchair into the back of the station wagon. So she and the kid
are going somewhere, and the stranger might be going with them.
Back to the hospital? Another figure appears, two, actually, as one
is carrying the other. The boy who is no longer a boy but a man,
and a skinny one at that. He's put into the backseat of the car.
Callum can't get a clear look at the man doing the putting, but
then that man is walking to his own car. He turns to get in...

Callum can't believe it. 'Shit.'

'What?'

He doesn't answer. He stares at the goddamn cop from all those
years ago.

'You okay?'

'Wait,' he whispers.

The ex-cop gets into his piece-of-shit car and backs out of the
driveway, followed by the sister in the borrowed station wagon.
He watches as the garage door rolls down and kills the view.

'It's Theodore Tate,' Callum says. 'He's figured out the kid's a
target. We need to follow him. If we're lucky, they're heading back
to his place.'

Chapter Seventy-One

Tate leaves his car parked outside the Garrett house and rides with
Hazel and James. The rain keeps coming. Any heavier and people's
houses are going to become unmoored from their foundations
and float into the street. He gives directions to Hazel, at the same

time answering questions about how far he and Schroder got with the case. At one point during the ride Hazel offers her condolences about his daughter. James sits in the back staring out of the window, not writing anything to add to the conversation. He took the news of why they had to leave well. It's the first time Tate has seen him since the week of the shooting.

When they get to his house, he uses a fob hanging from his keys to trigger the garage door and deactivate the alarm. A while back a crazy man broke into his house and killed his cat, and ever since he's been more security conscious. Hazel pulls up inside, and he hits the fob to close the door behind them.

James looks around as Tate wheels him into the house. It's left to the bedrooms and the front door, and right to the living areas and kitchen. He wheels James through to the lounge, and while Hazel stays with him, he hangs his dripping jacket on a coat rack by the front door and goes about getting the rooms ready, putting fresh sheets on his bed and on Emily's. Then he wheels James into Emily's room and, while James gets himself into the bed, Tate shows Hazel where everything is, insisting she take the bed while he takes the couch. He checks in on James one last time, feeling a little weird to see somebody sleeping in Emily's bed that isn't Emily.

Tate goes to the lounge to make up the couch. He still hasn't reached out to McCoy, so sends a quick text message saying everything is fine, and he'll call tomorrow. McCoy texts back to say he's glad to hear it. He switches off the lights and lays down in his clothes, but isn't tired. With James and Hazel safe, and only the storm and his thoughts to listen to, his thoughts quickly turn to Simone Clarke. The guilt can no longer be contained to a lump in his stomach and floods his system. The room sways, and the couch with it. He rushes to the bathroom, a feat made difficult by the house becoming a boat in a storm. He throws up, the few bites of kebab he had earlier showing up. He doesn't know how Simone was killed, but he imagines a dozen scenarios, then a dozen more. He tries to picture her as he last saw her, but all he can see is her, bloody and discarded on the floor of a lounge.

Hazel knocks on the bathroom door. 'You okay?'

'Just something I ate,' he says. 'I'll be fine.'

'You sure?'

'Completely.'

'Okay. Goodnight, Theo.'

'Goodnight, Hazel.'

The re-enactment wasn't the first time he worked with Simone Clarke. Over the last few months they often struck up a conversation on set. Recently she played a corpse on *The Cleaner,* first playing the body as it was found in a park, then under the harsh lights of a studio morgue. He knows the way she looked in that fake morgue will be similar to the way she'll look in the real one. She told him she had always wanted to be an actor since she starred in plays as a kid in school.

The earlier urge to drive to a bottle store is still with him. Would he, if he were alone? He doesn't know. When they put together the re-enactment, he had been part of the team to choose who would play the roles. The guy was easy. They used the same guy that played Middleton a couple of times. For Denise Laughton, they wanted somebody who would match her physically. He had to choose from a list of four women, and he chose Simone. And why? It's not like it mattered. It's not like there was going to be any detail anyway, but it made sense to do it that way – you're not going to recreate a scene with actors twice the size or a different sex. But he chose Simone because he thought she was a nice person. That's all it was. They all could have matched. They all could have done the job. Last night he told her about a movie he's consulting on that starts shooting next week. The crew were short of a couple of extras for a new scene being added, and he suggested she tell her agent to get in touch with somebody. She said she would. He had wished her luck.

And now she's dead, and Tate can't shake the feeling it's as if Copy Joe handed him a catalogue and asked him to pick out his next victim.

Chapter Seventy-Two

It's the same set-up – Callum and Burrows at one end of the block, and Keith at the other. The wind rocks the van. Callum wishes they had stolen something with seat warmers. The street is so quiet it's as though a bomb has made the neighbourhood unhabitable.

His legs jiggle as he waits. He should have been out at the farm-house by now with the girl. The appetite he's had all day for her has been blunted, and now he just wants this over. He wants to get into the house, put a few bullets into everybody in there and put all of them into the rear-view mirror of life. Even the girl. Well, maybe even the girl. He knows he can be fickle when he's cold and grumpy, and when he sees her, there's every chance he'll want to bring her with him. He's annoyed for not acting earlier, for not backing himself against an unknown and getting the job done. It's not like he's shy when it comes to shooting people. It's a missed opportunity, even more so now that he knows who the other person is.

'I'm going in,' he says.

'The lights have only been off for five minutes,' Burrows says.

'I don't care.'

'Well I do. It's not like the kid is in there spilling his guts. He's asleep. We have time. Let's give it another thirty minutes.'

The thoughts he had earlier about the doctor banging the sister come back, only now he switches out the doctor for Tate. The idea, like before, makes his stomach turn. If that's what's happening, then the girl definitely isn't coming out to the farmhouse. He'll shoot her in the face instead.

Fifteen minutes into the thirty and he can't wait any longer. 'I'm going in.'

'Fine. Remember, the girl isn't coming with us.'

'She won't be,' he says, unsure if he means it.

'And be careful. Nothing is ever easy with this guy,' Burrows adds.

'He won't be a problem.'

'You go in there thinking that, and he will be.'

A minute later he's at the corner of the house, his clothes and gloves even wetter than before. Tate's house is ground floor only, which means no creaky stairs, but it also means less distance between the bedrooms and him sneaking around outside. The storm is as frustrating as hell, but at least it will mask his approach. Better to be wet and safe than dry and in jail. The gate down the side of the house is locked. He's always been good at climbing, something that served him well as a kid when he used to climb trees for fun, and then as a teenager when he climbed through windows for a different kind of fun. He hoists himself up and over where the gate joins the fence, finding himself a few metres from the side door to the garage. He goes to work with the lock pick, worried his cold hands are going to make this impossible, and a minute in that's exactly what is happening. He wonders if he could do what he did to the Garrett's years ago and knock on the front door, flashing a stolen badge and faking an injury.

Would Tate fall for something like that?

If he can't get this door open, he might have to try.

Chapter Seventy-Three

The knocking sounds to Tate like somebody thinks the world is ending, and the only safe place is on this side of the door. He jumps to his feet and picks up his gun. The men who killed the Garretts, have they figured out James is here? Are they knocking at one door while readying to breach another? He is hitting the hallway when his phone goes off. The person knocking knocks again. Tate goes back for the phone. It's more likely somebody would ring to warn him not to open the door than knock and tell him not to answer his phone. It's Kent, and he quickly answers it.

'Is that you at my door?'

'Not me, but two officers,' she says.

He relaxes. 'So Wilson finally agreed.'

'Agreed to what?'

'Hang on.'

He heads down the hallway and flicks on the light. The knocking stops. 'Who is that?' Hazel asks, coming out of the bedroom.

'It's the police,' he says. 'Wait with James and I'll talk to them.'

She disappears into Emily's bedroom, and he calls out to the officers he'll be a moment.

'When I couldn't get hold of you earlier, I called Wilson,' Tate says.

'I hope you didn't call him about Georgia Perry,' Kent says. 'He wasn't on board with—'

'I called him about James Garrett.'

'What about him?'

'You don't know?'

'Know what?'

His head is spinning more from this conversation than from rushing to the door. 'Hazel took James home tonight.'

'What? We should get a patrol car to their house right—'

'They're here, at my place.'

'That was Hazel you were just talking to?'

'It was, but if you're not ringing about them, then I guess you're ringing about Simone Clarke. I honestly don't know what to say.'

'Copy Joe went after Martin Thomas too. We don't know where he is, but we do know Copy Joe broke into his house. We don't know yet if Copy Joe has him, or if he just wasn't home. But if he went after both actors, it stands to reason he may go after anybody else who worked on the show. We're putting eyes on everybody involved. I know you have questions, but don't bother the officers with them as they don't know the answers. Let them in and let them do their job. I'll be in touch when I can.'

Kent hangs up, and Tate tucks the gun into the back of his pants and heads for the door.

Chapter Seventy-Four

The way Callum sees it, they're losing two-nil. Two houses, two attempts and the same damn thing each time. It's like he thought earlier – bad luck can beat out good planning any day of the goddamn week. He was almost in when Burrows told him to abort, that the police scanner picked up chatter that officers were on their way to the house. The only way out of there at that point was to jump the back fence and run through the neighbour's yard, which he did, meeting Burrows on the next block over.

'We should go back,' he says, in the van now and out of the rain.

'And what?' Burrows asks.

'You know what.'

'We're not killing cops.'

'It's just two of them.'

'I said we're not killing cops,' Burrows says, keeping his eyes on the road. 'And you need to calm down. Look, they're not there for the kid, but to protect Tate from whatever is going on with this Copy Joe idiot. And don't forget they're armed. They think—'

'With tasers, not guns.'

'You want to take a taser to the balls? Or the face? Because it'll happen. They think Copy Joe might be dropping by, so what do you think they're going to do if they glimpse somebody sneaking around the house?'

'It'd be three on two. They wouldn't stand a chance.'

'There are more officers on their way, and the detective too. There's no going back there tonight.'

Callum knows he's right, but damn it, he just wants this done. 'Then when?'

'Tomorrow.'

'And if the kid remembers something by then?'

'We both know this is about tying up a loose end that probably isn't even loose to begin with.'

'We don't know that.'

'Then you better pray I'm right. Listen, I get what you're saying, but going back isn't going to end well for any of us. The way I see it, there are two risks. We risk getting caught, which is almost a definite, or we risk the kid remembering something, which is almost an impossibility. But, if you really think I'm wrong, then go back there by yourself and see how it plays out, but you better make damn sure you get the job done or die trying. So what's it to be?'

Burrows is right. Callum hates him for it, and hates himself for not having done more earlier, when he had the chance, but most of all he hates Copy Joe – he doesn't know what it is that psychopath did tonight, but whatever it was, it's the only reason the Garretts and Tate are still breathing.

'Let's wait for tomorrow.'

Chapter Seventy-Five

When he's not acting, Martin Thomas stacks groceries at night at a local supermarket, often finishing up around midnight. It's from here he has driven home to find his house lit up, with patrol cars out front and some very relieved police officers inside.

'I'm kind of that cliché,' he tells Kent. Despite being the same height and build as Joe Middleton, there are few other similarities between the two. Thomas is mid-thirties, thin, good-looking, dark hair that is combed to the side and puffed up at the front. He's paler than when she met him last night, the blood having drained from his features at the idea somebody came to his house to kill him. He is staring at his hands wrapped around a hot cup of tea to stop them from shaking. 'When I'm not acting, I'm thinking about acting, and while doing that thinking I'm unloading boxes of cereal onto shelves so I can pay the bills. It was either that or wait tables.'

As well as the busted open door and muddy footprints that fade the deeper Copy Joe went into the house – a single plastic bag identical to the one used to suffocate Simone Clarke has been stabbed into the dining table with a knife from the kitchen. The footprints left behind match the footprints from Simone's house.

'How well did you know Simone?'

He breaks eye contact with the tea and looks up at her. 'Is she really dead? I mean, I know you wouldn't be here telling me she was if she wasn't, or saying she was if you weren't really sure, but … I don't know. I don't really know what I'm saying. It just doesn't make sense. None of it does.'

She pictures Simone Clarke on the couch, her head slumped forward, the plastic bag identical to the one stabbed into the table here around her neck. 'It never does.'

'Do you think he came here first? Then went to her house when I wasn't home?'

'What time did you leave here?'

'Right after *Crime Busters* ended. I started work at six, but came home before eight-thirty to see the show. I went back to work right after it, then came home after my shift to find you guys here.'

'Then he didn't come here first,' she says. 'If you hadn't noticed the back door, you would at least have noticed the bag and the footprints.'

He bites his bottom lip and slowly nods. 'I guess you're right. I don't know if that makes it better or worse. If he'd come here first and I'd been here, maybe there was something I could have done to have stopped him.'

She thinks that's unlikely. She gets him talking about last night. His car had been parked behind Simone's on the other side of the crowd. People had approached and asked questions, but he didn't stop to answer any. Simone had signed an autograph for somebody. Did he get a good look at the guy? Not really. Had anybody stood out? Not really. What did he chat about with Simone during and around the shoot? Acting, what else was there? They had left, and they had shared the same direction for two blocks, then she had gone one way and he'd gone another. Their paths had crossed a few times on sets over the last five years, including both having worked on the same episodes of *Crime Busters*, but he knew nothing about her. No he didn't see anybody following her, and didn't notice anybody following him. He tells her there have been no weird phone calls, no weird messages online, no weird people hanging about. Until twenty minutes ago, he had no idea anybody would want to hurt him.

'You could use me as bait,' he says, after she's told him he's going to need to pack a bag as he can't stay here tonight, and perhaps not for the next few nights either. 'Simone was cool. You know, what we do, it's a weird job. We recreate people's last moments and we get paid for it, but it doesn't sit well with us, you know? It's like our job depends on people getting hurt.'

Kent can relate.

'I try to think that we're helping. Not like you guys help, but I like to think we're a small cog in the machine. We take it seriously. We respect it. We understand somebody died, that they left a hole in the world, and that we pay our rent by playing out their last moments. If there is a way to help Simone and stop the man who killed her, I'll do it. Even if it means filming some kind of re-enactment.'

'I appreciate the offer, but—'

'I'm happy to do it. What's the alternative? Stay at a hotel until this maniac is captured?'

She doesn't know what the alternative is, but creating another re-enactment or using him as bait isn't it. 'I'll think about it.'

Chapter Seventy-Six

It's three in the morning on Friday when Kent gets to Tate's house. The rain has stopped, and the wind has died down, and she tries to convince herself this is the turning point, where things start to get better. There are officers guarding the house, and more inside. She finds Tate on the couch, going through the files she gave him … when? Only half a day ago, but it feels like a week.

They fall into an embrace and hold on tight, and she holds her breath and focuses on not crying. She feels stupid for having the urge, but goddamn it's been a tough day. She doesn't know what to say, and Tate must be the same because neither of them say anything until they let go.

'You'll get him, Rebecca, I know you will.'

'I just have to hope it's before he hurts anybody else.'

'Want some coffee?'

'Please,' she says, knowing she's so tired she doubts it'll stop her from sleeping. She can see Tate has made up the couch to sleep on, while Hazel and James used the bedrooms. It reminds her she hasn't decided where she's going to stay tonight. Most likely she'll go back home, and get some armed protection to go with her.

They go into the kitchen. Tate puts on a fresh pot of coffee while she sits at the breakfast bar.

'Is Wilson going to put a couple of people on James and Hazel?' he asks.

'I'll talk to Wilson, but you know what he's going to say.'

'I do, because he's already said it to me.'

'I don't like it, but he has a point. The thing is we don't know anything about these men, or if they'll come after James. And how long do we keep officers on watch? A week? A month? A year? Is it a lifetime assignment?'

'Let's start with a week, and go from there.'

'Like I said, I'll talk to Wilson.'

Tate pulls a couple of cups from the cupboard.

'I keep seeing her. Every time I close my eyes she's dead on the couch, and we put her there.'

'It's not your fault,' Tate says. 'I'm the one who called you. I'm the one who pitched the idea. I'm the one who chose Simone.'

'It's my job to have anticipated something like this. Seeing her dead, it broke me,' she says. 'I've thought about throwing it all in before, you know? There are always ups and downs, but this – this broke me.'

'It's not your fault, Rebecca.'

'And it could have been worse. You know, despite everything, Martin Thomas offered himself up as bait.'

'I assume you said no?'

'I did, but that doesn't mean it was a bad idea. I'm thinking we could try with the men who shot James. We could put a news story out there, say James has woken up and is getting some memories back, then we get a couple of officers to pretend they're James and Hazel, and we go fishing.'

'We considered it nine years ago,' Tate says. 'We ran the idea up the food chain, but it was risky. It meant lying to the public, and once you do that it's hard to get that trust back, even if the intentions are good. On top of that it would put friends and family of the Garretts through an emotional roller-coaster, reading the news that James was okay only to find out it had been a ploy. I still thought it was worth a shot, but there was a third problem. The news had reported in detail what had happened to James, and we figured those who had shot him would know it was a trap. The idea ran out of steam. But you're right in that we could try it now.'

'I'll talk to Wilson about it, but I think he'll go for it. Did you contact Georgia Perry's parents?'

'I went to see them with McCoy. They have a lot of suspicion, but not much to back it up. I spoke to Tabitha Perry, Georgia's sister, and she thinks her parents are looking for a reason for Georgia's death that doesn't involve an accident.'

'What do you think?'

He pours the coffees. She wraps her hands around her cup, enjoying the warmth.

'McCoy is going to talk to James in the morning to get a better idea of how Coma World works. Maybe there's something there, I don't know.'

'What does your gut tell you?'

'To keep looking. And what about Copy Joe? You getting anywhere?'

'The guy's a ghost. When I went to the hospital to interview James, I spoke to Hazel before meeting him. She said something to me about you that stuck.'

'Which was?'

'The night her parents died, she asked you if it was your job to stop monsters. You said it was.'

Tate slowly nods. 'I remember.'

'Do you still believe that?'

'More than ever.'

'I believe that too. Yet all we did was serve this monster up his next victim.'

Chapter Seventy-Seven

Hazel drives Tate back to the Garrett house after breakfast so he can get his car and so she can feed the cat. Then she takes James to the hospital for his morning therapy, Tate following them, a patrol car following him, his car smelling of the unfinished kebab left in it overnight. There is no protection detail for Hazel and James, but he is hopeful that will change today.

The officers follow him beyond the hospital once he's seen Hazel and James inside, then north and out of the city. Houses and shops become paddocks and farms. Ditches filled with overnight rain line the motorway. He hits a patch of roadworks two kilometres long that until this week had seen no progression since Christmas, the city council rich with intentions but low in funds, the surface of the road hard-packed gravel for six months, now hard-packed gravel ready to be paved. Heavy equipment lines the shoulder, along with a shipping container full of tools. He phones McCoy and explains what happened last night, and is still explaining it when he hits the turnoff to the care home fifteen minutes out of the city. He takes it, and tells McCoy he has to go.

Winter has stripped the life from the trees and leeched the colour from the gardens lining the driveway to a forty-year-old, grey-brick, two-storey building that stretches fifty metres across and fifty metres back. It has a low-angle roof with multiple down-pipes and satellite dishes. Scaffolding lines one side, where windows are being switched out for energy-efficient ones. There are half a dozen cars out front belonging to other folks visiting loved ones. He parks, and he tries to put Simone Clarke out of his mind, not wanting the darkness to follow him inside in case it finds a way to stick. The patrol car parks behind him, but the officers don't get out.

He heads in. The furniture and décor is dated, but the foyer warm and inviting, drenched with light and littered with pot plants and paintings of landscapes. To the left there's a large room where residents can sit with family while looking out over the gardens. There is a similar area for eating further along on the ground floor, as well as areas behind the building where folks can eat meals and watch the setting sun bring them one day closer to leaving. It's a care home, not a retirement home. The people here aren't well. Some never have been. It breaks Tate's heart every time he comes here.

He heads to the reception area. Nurse Hamilton is behind a desk reading *A Christmas Murder,* a crime novel written by a local author who now lives in this very care home after Alzheimer's stole his identity. In her early sixties, Tate has always thought Carol Hamilton could crush a bear in a hug if the occasion called for it. She has the same hairstyle his grandmother had – black and grey, and in a tight bun, and the same smile too – a big one that warms people up when it's pointed in their direction. She lowers the book and her reading glasses and turns that smile on for him.

'Theo, how are you?'

'The usual. How is Bridget doing?'

'She wasn't responding earlier, but she's been good for the last hour. I think you've arrived at a good time.'

He signs the visitors' book. Over a dozen people have already been out here today, which makes him feel better about the world.

Nurse Hamilton carries on. 'She's been saying she can't wait for the baby to arrive, but she followed that up by saying it will be exciting for Emily to have a little baby brother or a baby sister.'

A few months ago they decided if Bridget believed Emily was still alive, there was no reason to tell her otherwise. Not when she was forgetting things at a slightly faster rate than she was remembering them. There are days when he envies her that.

He heads upstairs, passing rooms where people are talking, some are crying, some are laughing, some are rocking back and forth as they sit on the edges of beds or chairs or couches. Bridget has the same room she had when she was first here, with a view over the scaffolding and the parking lot, and the gardens beyond. Her door is open. He heads in. She's lying on the bed with a cross-word-puzzle book.

'Hey,' he says.

'Hey,' she says, smiling up at him. She looks pale, with the bags under her eyes suggesting she hasn't been sleeping well. Her hair is longer than it's ever been, hanging in a limp pony tail that she fiddles with while getting to her feet. She wraps her arms around him, which these days is a difficult fit, given she's eight months pregnant. It's a very bittersweet thing for him. He's excited about the baby, but at the same time Bridget is retreating into her own world. He wonders if it can be similar to the world James has, and hopes she can find Emily there and be happy.

'Thank God you're here. I'm bored out of my mind. I was getting ready to plan my escape and take everybody with me.'

'What stopped you?'

'Apart from having a brain injury that means I can switch off at—' She stops and stares blankly at him, and his heart sinks a little, and then she smiles and laughs. 'Got you.'

His heart bounces back. 'You did.'

'The real reason is it's winter, and I'm fat, and I doubt I'd get far, and even if I could get far, where would I go? Other than coming back home, and then you'd just bring me back.'

'Bridget…'

She smiles again, but it's a sad smile, and it hurts seeing it. 'I know, I know, this is the best place for me, but sometimes – sometimes I just think, how did life get like this, you know?'

They sit on a couch that faces the window. They hold hands, and she puts on a brave smile, and soon she won't even be able to do that. She puts her other hand on her stomach, and they talk for a little while. She tells him what she's been up to since he saw her yesterday morning, and she asks if he's consulting on any exciting TV or movie projects, and he tells her the same things he told her yesterday that she's forgotten.

'Have you gotten a cat yet?'

'Not yet,' he says. The man that killed Daxter two years ago dug him back up after Tate buried him, and hung him from the roof. He told Bridget the cat had been hit by a car.

'You should. Emily would love it. I hate winter,' she says, looking out the window. 'It looks like the world is dying, and with it being so cold and dull I keep thinking Emily is never going to want to come and visit. Did you pick her up from school already?'

'School hasn't finished for the day.'

'Of course. I should have known that. Can you bring her tomorrow?'

'She's studying hard, but I'll try.'

'Try hard, Teddy. Please, I can't remember the last time I—'

She stops talking, and this time it's not a joke. Her face becomes expressionless as she stares out at the gardens, only she's not looking at them anymore, she's looking beyond them, possibly out to nowhere, or maybe into her past for the last memory she has of Emily, which isn't a pleasant one, because that memory would be of them bouncing off the front of a four-door sedan. He keeps hold of her hand, and he watches her face, and the light drains from her eyes as the gears that keep her running become loose. He wishes he had come here last night, and earlier this morning, but instead he's been pulled into a rabbit hole with James Garrett and his Coma World, and now Copy Joe too. He has failed to leave them out in the parking lot like he wanted.

He lets go of her hand and picks up the crossword-puzzle book. She's written E in the first box, M in the second, I in the third, and so on, spelling out Emily over and over all the way through the puzzle, just like she has done every day over the last month.

He tells her everything is going to be okay, that she's going to be okay, that the baby is going to be okay, hoping she can believe all of it. Then he tells her he has to go, that the rabbit hole is waiting. He squeezes her hand and tells her he loves her, and she doesn't say anything, doesn't respond, doesn't notice him leaving.

When he gets into the car, he looks up at the window of Bridget's room. She's sitting, staring out through the scaffolding. He waves, but she doesn't wave back.

Chapter Seventy-Eight

The hospital, home, the warehouse, going to the former detective's house because he thought they were in danger, and now the hospital again – James is struggling to catch his breath from it all. *Is life ever going to get back to normal?*

While Hazel studies in the hospital café downstairs, he spends an hour with Fiona, only he can't lift his legs as high or for as long as yesterday. She tells him it's fatigue. She tells him there will be days when it might feel like he's going backward with his rehab. 'I'm sorry you're so down today,' she adds, 'but maybe this will cheer you up.'

She tap dances for him. It's bad, and he can't help but laugh. She's wearing soft-soled shoes, so there's no real tapping, but he appreciates the effort. It only lasts ten seconds, and she finishes off with jazz hands. It confirms she's the coolest person he's ever met. He writes, *Next time I'm filming it.*

She shakes her head. 'Next time you're the one doing it.'

She wheels him to Doctor Wolfgang's office. Hazel is already in there. They look happy to see him, and he's happy to see that the notebooks, which Hazel brought with her, are stacked in the right order with the spines facing outward. He used a sharpie to write a single letter on each spine that, when the books are side by side, spell out *COMAWORLD*.

'I'll see you later today for another session, okay?' Fiona asks.

James nods. He looks at Hazel, who looks at Fiona, then back at him, then smiles. There is no doubt his sister knows he has a crush, and he hopes she doesn't mention it.

'How are you feeling?' Doctor Wolfgang asks.

It's a tough question. But he gives a simple answer: *Better.*

'I hear you had quite a night.'

He nods.

'I'm glad you're okay, but we should look at finding you somewhere else to stay, at least for a little bit.'

He nods. He wants to go back home, but he knows that's not going to happen any time soon.

'Are you still happy to talk about Coma World this morning?'

He is. He knows Doctor Wolfgang is keen to learn more, and the truth is he's keen to understand how it works too.

'Before we start,' Hazel says, 'there are some things you need to know. Grandma dying in Coma World at the same time she died in The Real World isn't the only example of the two worlds over-lapping.'

He listens patiently as she explains the books she used to read to him were books he gave her as gifts in Coma World. She explains names and dates, and the weather and other connections. He can't say why, but it doesn't surprise him.

'This,' Doctor Wolfgang says, putting his hands on the note-books, 'and what we've just told you, is completely unprecedented.'

James doesn't know if it is or not. He's never met anybody who's come out of a coma. He thinks it's pretty cool, but he also thinks it might mean people won't believe him.

He writes, *What do you want to know?*

Doctor Wolfgang and Hazel share a look, then Doctor Wolfgang picks up the top notebook, and says, 'I want to start by giving you some dates from your notebooks to see if your memory is consistent.'

Okay.

'Well then, if you're ready, let's begin.'

Chapter Seventy-Nine

The cinderblock walls are made thicker by a heavy coat of cream paint that's easy to wipe down. The blue linoleum floor is stained with the streaks from the gurneys that have brought folks down here for a day or two of cold storage and vivisection. Kent's foot-steps echo as she makes her way to the double doors, and continue to echo as she passes through them into the morgue. In here the cinderblocks are tiled over and the light gleams off a thousand polished surfaces. There's a row of boxy-looking refrigerator doors where folks who have met their end can be slid in and out to see how that end was met. There are trays of tools on display across various surfaces. Kent hates coming down here. Hates it even more today. This place is a serial killer's wet dream.

The body of Simone Clarke is on a table in the middle of the room, a sheet pulled up to her neck. The bright light makes her pale skin even paler. There is a nasty-looking graze across her right cheek. Tracey Walter sees her through the window of the office in the corner and comes out. She walks over and gives Kent a hug. It's unexpected.

'You look like hell,' Tracey says, pulling back.

'I feel worse,' she says. She opted to sleep at the station last night, and didn't get to take a shower this morning, so she knows she doesn't just look like hell, but smells like it too. Half the clothes she was wearing yesterday she's wearing today, the rest stuffed into a suitcase in the back of her car.

'I can't imagine what you're going through,' Tracey says. 'I heard Wilson said this was your fault. You don't really think that, do you?'

'He has a point.'

'You can't be blamed for the actions of a psychopath.' When Kent says nothing, Tracey carries on. 'Come on, Rebecca, you know that.'

She does know it, but still … It's like Tate told Hazel all those years ago: it's their job to stop monsters. Not feed them.

Tracey gives her the run-down, and Kent listens quietly, her hands balled into fists. Simone was asphyxiated, and Tracey explains what that would have felt like, and Kent balls her hands even tighter. Tracey points out the bruising around Simone's right wrist and the back of her neck, along with inflammation and bruising around her shoulder. 'It's possible he wrenched one arm up behind her back,' Tracey says, taking Kent's arm and mimicking the gesture, albeit softly. 'Then he forced her onto the couch. It hurts to imagine what she must have been thinking.'

Kent can imagine it too, the same way she thinks any woman could. 'And the graze on her cheek?'

'It's like she fell off a bike. She was wearing makeup, so whatever caused this will have her makeup on it too, as well as skin cells.'

There are no signs of sexual assault, and a toxicology report will be back in two days. There are thin lines around Simone's feet and hands where she was bound with cable ties.

'They were pulled as tight as possible,' Tracey adds.

Tracey fetches the evidence bags from the examination that contain the duct tape and the cable ties and Simone's clothes. The plastic bag used to suffocate Simone was removed at the scene last night and has already been printed, with no results. Tracey has also included a sample of the makeup.

Tracey puts it all into a box, Kent signs the paperwork for it and heads back to the elevator, eager to get out of there.

Chapter Eighty

James writes, *It was a Tuesday Dad made us pancakes for breakfast and Mum left early to meet a client. It was raining and on the way to school a Phil's Plumbing van sped through a large puddle and soaked Hazel and she had to return home to change and she got into trouble for being late.*

James hands the page to Doctor Wolfgang, then goes back to the cabinet in the warehouse to read more files. The next one says, *Geography. Boring,* and the one after that, *Science. Boring.* He doesn't write either of those down, but he does for the next file where, because of the rain, they stayed in the classrooms for lunch. *Aaron Mackenzie shoved John Willis and he fell back smashing the window with his elbow.*

Doctor Wolfgang reads it, and he nods, and James thinks

there's a flicker of a smile there. He seems impressed. So does Hazel, who mentions that both Aaron and John were real students from James's class.

'Let's try another,' Doctor Wolfgang says, and he picks up a different notebook and opens a page at random and lands on a date.

James walks through the warehouse, this time to where the dust is thicker, and finds the date Doctor Wolfgang has given him. It was the time he got an A+ in math, and his parents celebrated by buying him ice cream. He writes it down.

'Same as in the notebook,' Doctor Wolfgang says, clearly happy with where this is going. 'Let's try it backward. I want to give you an event, and I want you to tell me what date it is. Is that something you can do?'

James doesn't know, but is happy to try.

'Do you remember when your next-door neighbour got a dog?'

He remembers the dog, but not when they got it. He closes his eyes, and he looks at all the cabinets, but all he sees are dates. There are no references to dogs anywhere. So it's not going to work—

Click.

He looks over to where the sound came from, and sees a drawer slowly rolling open. He goes to it, both surprised and happy by this development. Sure enough, the files inside cover the day Mr and Mrs Simon came home with a Golden Retriever puppy.

He writes the date down and shows it to Doctor Wolfgang, who nods, and sounds excitable when he says, 'That's correct. There's an entry where your dad was popping a cork on a bottle of champagne and it smashed a light in the ceiling.'

Click. Wheels rolling against metal, and a drawer opens. He writes down the date.

'Right again,' Doctor Wolfgang says. 'If I mention a name, can you tell me where you know it from?'

He writes, *There will be lots of times people get mentioned.*

'How about the first time?'

What is the name?

'Nicholas Childs.'

He remembers Nicholas was a new student whose family moved down from Wellington ... when? He closes his eyes. *Click.* A drawer opens, and there's his answer. He writes down the date, and Doctor Wolfgang nods.

'There are missing days in your notebooks. Do you remember what happened those days too?'

Every day is in the warehouse, but not every day is in the notebooks. Some things just weren't that interesting. He nods.

'Can I give you an example?'

He nods again.

Doctor Wolfgang gives him a date. He trails his fingers over the cabinets, watching the dust pool onto his skin. He finds the drawer and reads the contents. It was a Thursday. He got up, he had breakfast, he went to school, he came home, he did homework. The highlight of the day was they had pizza for dinner, but that didn't make it a highlight worth mentioning. He writes it down. Doctor Wolfgang reads it, then asks, 'Do you remember Georgia Perry?'

Click. He searches the open drawer, then writes, *The teacher who fell off the balcony.*

'That's right,' Doctor Wolfgang says. 'Georgia Perry is an example of the two worlds combining. She was my patient, and like in Coma World, she also fell off a balcony. You wrote that her husband was arrested for murder.'

He slowly nods, wondering where Doctor Wolfgang is going with this.

'In this world, she died, but her husband was never charged.'

Now he gets it. He writes, *You think her husband killed her in this world?*

'That's what we're going to try and find out.'

Chapter Eighty-One

Peak visiting hours mean the closest park Tate can find to the hospital leaves him with a ten-minute walk that starts in light drizzle and ends with him soaked to the bone. A nurse who recognises him offers to get him a towel. He dries his hair and face as he walks to McCoy's office, and ends up running into him at a vending machine on the way. McCoy is flattening out a five-dollar note, trying to get the machine to take it.

'I tested James's memory, from naming dates, or events, or names, and everything he said lined up with what he had written,' McCoy says, sliding the note back in. 'He's like a walking almanac.'

'So it's real.'

'I don't doubt it.'

The machine swallows the five-dollar note, and Wolfgang punches at the keypad and a can of Coke rolls into the dispensing tray. He picks it up and taps the top the way Tate has seen people do on TV, before grabbing his change.

'I've read people can wake up from comas speaking different languages,' Tate says, as they walk to James's room. The view out of the windows shows a darkening skyline. 'Is this something like that?'

'No, because that's not a real thing,' McCoy says. 'There are always anecdotes when it comes to comas, and that's a common one. But the evidence shows these people were exposed to those languages, usually in their childhood ... but, I guess with everything James has shown us, I should reassess that conclusion. For all we know they were overhearing conversations in other languages.'

'In Coma World, James was meeting new people?'

'He was.'

'Who are they based on? People he's met before?'

'He said people in Coma World are people he's seen. He's taken movie characters and turned them into teachers. Years ago Hazel told me he had an incredible memory for books and movies and was an avid story-teller. I guess it came in handy.'

'You told him about Georgia Perry?'

'Briefly, but not the details, but I did tell Hazel.' They stop short of James's room. 'You really think these men could come for him?'

Tate thinks of Simone Clarke. He thinks of the night James's parents were killed. 'I think anything is possible.'

They head into James's room. He's sitting up with pillows between him and the wall, watching TV, while Hazel is on the couch going through a textbook.

'As requested,' McCoy says, handing James the Coke.

James smiles and quickly opens it. He takes a sip, then closes his eyes and swallows. Tate imagines doing the same thing with a bottle of whiskey. James takes another sip then puts the can on the bedside table. He holds his pad and shows it to Tate. *Doctor Wolfgang says you have some questions for me about Mrs Perry.*

'Is that okay?'

James nods.

'She was one of your teachers, right?'

James nods, then, *But I never met her. Or her husband.*

It's not lost on Tate they're starting a conversation about somebody who both exists and doesn't at the same time. It makes him think of the cat-in-the-box paradox. 'You don't mention Nathaniel Perry until the day he is arrested for attempted murder. Can you recall other dates he was in Coma World?'

James takes a moment to think about it, then, *He is in Coma World twice. Once when he confessed and was arrested, and again when the charge is upgraded to murder.*

'Who did he confess to?'

The police.

'Do you know why he hurt Mrs Perry?'

He said he wished she had died when he pushed her that if she had kept her nose out of his business it wouldn't have come to this.

The hairs on Tate's neck bristle. 'Do you think you overheard him saying that in real life? Or did you take bits and pieces you've heard, and constructed that narrative?'

James thinks on it, then writes, *I don't know.*

'Nathaniel Perry came in here for a year after Georgia fell. You would have heard him some of or all of those times, correct?'

He nods.

'And yet Nathaniel doesn't show up in your notebooks until the day of his arrest.'

James closes his eyes. He looks like he's hunting through his memories, then he shakes his head, opens his eyes, and writes, *I don't remember him from before that day.*

'Others have come and gone in the ward during that time,' Hazel says. 'Other patients, family members, other doctors and nurses. I didn't see any of them in the notebooks, but of course I don't know them all by name.'

'Yet Nathaniel Perry stuck with him,' McCoy says.

None of this is helping Tate.

James writes, *He was in the news.*

'Nathaniel? In Coma World?'

James nods.

'What did the news say?'

The news said before he confessed he gave Mrs Perry a necklace while she was in the coma.

'A necklace?'

James nods. Tate can't see how this helps either.

But then McCoy ties it together when he says, 'Tabitha gave Georgia a necklace while she was in the coma. Maybe it's one of those details James overheard and used.'

'James, can you remember why they mentioned the necklace?' Tate asks.

James nods, then writes, *It belonged to a woman who went missing.*

Chapter Eighty-Two

The block where Simone Clarke lived and died is still cordoned off. Last night's crowd has been replaced by a few diehards milling about in the hope of glimpsing something to tell their friends about. Inside, Kent pulls her gloves on and runs her hand along the wall beside the front door, feeling the texture she felt last night when her jacket snagged against it in the bedroom. Her sister had paint like this in her house on a feature wall. She had it stripped back when she had her first child, worried the kid would fall against it and tear half her face off.

Even though the house is lit up, she highlights the area near the doorway with a flashlight, then moves further into the entrance-way. She doesn't have to move far before finding a smudge of makeup at head height, transferred to the wall where Simone was pushed against it. The paint is red, so if there's any blood in there she can't see it. She'll get a forensic technician to confirm it. She shines her flashlight at the bottom of the door. There are a few scuff marks, along with the wear and tear that comes with front doors, but one of those marks has flakes of dirt stuck to it.

She plays it out in her mind. There are no signs of forced entry, and having a key ahead of time would have required pre-planning that wasn't possible. Which means Simone responded to some-body at the door. Copy Joe says something that convinces her to open it. He pushes his way in, spins her round, wrenches one hand up her back, and shoves her against the wall. He tells her if she makes a sound, he's going to kill her. While holding her there, he kicks the door to close it. He puts the cable ties on her wrists either before or after he frog-marches her into the lounge. He pushes her into the couch, puts duct tape around her mouth, and a set of cable ties around her ankles. The show comes on. He puts the plastic bag over her head, and that's when the boyfriend shows up. He subdues the boyfriend rather than kill him, because he wants to kill Simone in front of him. Then he goes to Martin Thomas's house.

Friends and family have said Simone would never open the door for a stranger at night, and yet she opened it for somebody. Who?

It's time to share her theory with the others.

Chapter Eighty-Three

If Tabitha Munroe didn't look happy to see Tate last night, today she looks downright furious to find him on her doorstep.

'This is harassment.'

'I only have one question, then I'll be out of your hair.'

'Just the one?'

'You gave Georgia a necklace when she was in hospital,' he says. She flinches, and all his doubts disappear.

'Is that your question?'

'My question is, where did you get it from?'

She doesn't answer.

'I wouldn't be here if I didn't think this was important. Please, Tabitha, can you tell me where the necklace came from?'

She closes her eyes and massages the centre of her forehead. It looks like she's talking into her wrist when she says, 'I wasn't the one to give it to George. Whoever told you that was wrong.'

'It's Doctor McCoy's recollection the necklace came from you.'

'Well, it didn't.'

'He seemed sure.'

'You can't blame me for what other people are sure about.'

'Then clear it up for me. Who gave Georgia the necklace?'

She says nothing, the hand away from her face now. She looks angry, but then that anger fades as her eyes focus on something a hundred kilometres away. She's thinking hard, figuring out whether to open the door the rest of the way or close it forever.

She sighs and says, 'Mum and Dad, they were right about the wedding. George said I kept looking at Nathaniel like he was a piece of shit. I said I didn't know what she was talking about. We got angry at each other. It was stupid. That's why we weren't talking.'

'Was there something to it?'

Still looking at something on the horizon, she doesn't answer.

'Can you tell me why you left the hospital whenever Nathaniel showed up?'

She sighs again, and he's sure she's about to tell him he's well past his one question, but instead she says, 'I always knew this day was going to come.'

'I need your help, Tabitha. Georgia needs your help.'

She says nothing.

'Whatever it is, I can try to keep it between us. I promise.'

She glares at him, the anger back. 'And if it's something you can't keep between us? What if it's something that destroys my life?'

'Then I would say you have a very difficult decision to make.'

Back to the horizon, and to her thoughts. She nods a little, then shakes her head a little, as if testing different versions of the immediate future and figuring which one to shoot for. She balances things up, and whatever she can see out there tells her to invite him in.

He's taken into a dining room warmed by a log burner, where she can keep an eye on two small boys playing in the lounge in front of the TV. One must be between four and five, the other half that. Neither turns to look at them, each engrossed in their own world.

Tate and Tabitha sit at right angles at the dining table, and she says, 'There isn't a day goes by that I don't think about it, and there are days where I think about picking up the phone and calling somebody about it, but then I remember what I have.' She looks at her children. 'And what I have to lose.'

He's getting an idea where this might be leading. He needs to be careful.

'I don't know why I thought I could do nothing. One way or the other, the truth always comes out.'

Not in his experience, but he says nothing.

'I need a drink,' she says. 'You want something?'

Two years ago he would have brought his own with him. 'No, thank you.'

She comes back a minute later with a large glass of white wine, sits back down, and has a long sip before resting it on the table, her fingers around the stem. He doesn't like the idea of her drinking before lunch while looking after her kids, but there's not much he can do about it.

'There are some things,' she says, 'that I didn't tell the police. I mean, when George fell, I never believed it was anything other than an accident. She liked to drink,' she says, then looks at the wine, and laughs. She takes another long sip, and a quarter of the glass disappears. 'Both George and Nath did. She was always taking photographs of herself too. Like, all the time, the way people do these days. But hers were stupid, like, her on the edge of something, a roof, a cliff, a bridge, a building, whatever, always chasing the perfect shot. I warned her one day she was going to fall.'

Another sip, and the level is down to halfway. This is what they should do in interrogation rooms – provide alcohol to tight-lipped people.

She keeps spinning the stem of the glass. 'It's been four years since she died, can you believe that?'

He can. It's been four years since Emily died. There are days where the past feels so close he could reach back and touch it, and then there are days where his old life feels like it belonged to some-body else. When Emily died, part of him wanted to die along with her. In the end getting revenge gave him purpose. It kept him alive. And when he got that revenge, he started to heal. Or tried to.

'The time, it goes by fast,' he says. 'What happened, Tabitha?'

'What happened is I'm a horrible person who loves her husband and kids so much she doesn't want to hurt them. Do you have children?'

'My wife and I have one on the way.'

'Then you know every decision you make is no longer about you, but about them. Four years,' she says, and she closes her eyes and keeps them closed when she adds, 'Six since George fell. We were having an affair, Nath and me. It started after they got married, and before you ask, yes, I was seeing Herschel then too.' She opens her eyes and looks at Tate. 'You must think I'm awful.'

'No,' he says. 'People have affairs. Relationships are compli-cated. People fall in love with other people. It's how life works.'

'You make it sounds so ... pedestrian.'

'I don't mean to.'

'You ever cheat on your wife?'

'No.'

'So that gives you a position in which you can judge from.'

'I'm not judging.'

'You should.'

'When did it end?'

'A year before I got married.'

'Georgia knew?'

She shakes her head.

'Who ended it?'

'I did.'

'How did Nathaniel take it?'

She slides the rest of her wine away without finishing it. 'He took it well, or so I thought. We barely spoke over the year that followed, then he called me a few days before my wedding, wanting to meet. He insisted. What we had, our history, well, it's like how countries don't nuke each other because they know what they send out will come right back. Mutual assured destruction they call it. With Nat, there's something beneath the surface I found attractive, something dangerous, but that same something told me if I didn't meet him he'd launch those nukes. So I met him for coffee. He had a gift for me.' She clutches at her chest even though there's nothing there. 'It was the necklace you were asking about. It was an antique gold heart that had come into his store. I told him I couldn't accept it. He took my hand, and when I tried to pull away he held on tight,' she says, massaging the hand she must have grabbed. 'He told me I had to wear the necklace all the time so I could remember him. He said if I didn't, he would tell Herschel everything.' She wipes at her eyes. 'That's when he told me he had filmed us in bed. He said he knew how much I wanted to have kids. He said if he ever saw me without the necklace he would show the video to any future children I had.'

She reaches back for the wine glass.

'Did he show you the video?'

'No. He had filmed it on a hidden camera because he doesn't own a cellphone. I had no choice but to believe him. I wore the necklace. I had to. It's in every one of our wedding photos. I told Herschel I had found it while browsing through a jewellery store.'

'How did Georgia end up with it?'

She gulps down the rest of the wine. He wishes Kent were here. He is sure this is going to head into some very dark territory, and that Tabitha might find it easier to talk to a woman.

'There is a police detective I can...'

'No,' she says. 'I don't want the police knowing, because I have to have hope, right? Hope there might be a way you can keep this to yourself and still do the right thing. Hope that my life doesn't have to fall apart, and Herschel never has to find out. Promise me you'll try.'

'I promise.'

'For all that I've told you, it only gets worse.'

He figured it would.

Chapter Eighty-Four

Wilson glances at his watch when Kent enters the task-force room, just so she sees that he knows she's late. Vega gives her a wry smile, and Travers does the same. Photographs of Denise Laughton and Simone Clarke have been taped to a large white-board, pictures of them in the prime of life next to photos of them in death. Denise's side of the whiteboard is heavy with details, but Simone's side is light – it will be their job today to add to it. She adds to it now by writing up the time and cause of death.

'I think he came through the front door,' Kent says, turning to face the others before going on to explain the graze on Simone's cheek, the corresponding makeup on the textured wall and the scuff mark across the bottom of the door. 'I got one of the forensic guys looking at it, but I'm confident the marks will match.'

'That's why you were late?' Wilson asks.

'It was.'

'It's good work,' Wilson says. 'So either she opened her door to somebody she knew, or a stranger convinced her to do so, despite what Simone's friends and family have said. What about Martin Thomas?'

'I have a few thoughts on that,' Vega says. 'Copy Joe shows up when Thomas is at work. Maybe he knocks on the front door, and when nobody answers, he goes around the back and finds a way in. He was probably there when the first patrol car showed up, then bolted the back fence.'

'It's also possible Copy Joe was confident he could overpower Simone, but not Thomas,' Travers says. 'The frame around Thomas's back door had a lot of rot in it, so even if he had been home he might not have heard it being prised open over the rain. We've spoken to neighbours, and nobody saw anything, but the next-door neighbour said his dog started barking at the fence, but couldn't be sure what time that was, just that it had to be around nine or ten. It's possible that's when Copy Joe was making his way in.'

'So in a nutshell, Denise Laughton was chosen because of her house, and Simone Clarke and Martin Thomas were chosen because of their role in the TV show,' Kent says.

The other three nod.

'I've been working on something. It started with the keys,' she says, then explains the series of phone calls she made about the spare keys, before going on to suggest Copy Joe may have gained access to Angela Durry's house not long after she was killed there. 'There's more too. I've been looking at the crime-scene photos from back then, and looking at what photos made their way into the public. I've also been looking at the documentaries about Middleton, and also the re-enactments made, and on top of that I've been listening to podcast after podcast about Middleton, and still I've barely scratched the surface.'

'I assume there is a point to all of this?' Wilson asks.

'The beer bottles,' Kent says.

'What about them?'

'They're in the original crime-scene photos, but they're not in the re-enactment, and they're not in any of the crime-scene photos that have made it into the public domain, and so far I've heard no mention of them in any podcast. As best as I can tell, Joe Middleton drinking beers at the scenes and leaving the bottles behind is a well-guarded secret, and probably for no real reason than it wasn't interesting enough to get out there. It's not like the eggs that were put into the victims' mouths to suffocate them – that was so sensational it would have been impossible to keep under wraps. But the bottles are interesting now, because Copy Joe knew to stage it that way, and not just with the one upstairs, but the one downstairs too.'

'If you're going where I think you're going with this...' Wilson says.

'It's not just the beer bottles he knew about. He also had access to the keys at this and other crime scenes. And we know Simone Clarke wouldn't open the door to a stranger, but we do know who she would open the door to – the same kind of person who would know about the beer bottles, and the same kind of person who had access to the original scenes. I think Copy Joe might be a cop.'

Chapter Eighty-Five

'Sometimes Herschel's work has him away overnight,' Tabitha says, 'which was the case when ... back when it happened.' She runs a finger around the rim of her glass, staring at it closely while looking into the past. 'I was home alone, and I was having a glass of wine with dinner. The next thing I know...'

She trails off when the oldest of her two boys comes into the dining room.

'What's wrong, Mummy?'

'Nothing is wrong, Honey,' she says, barely looking at him.

'Is this man a bad man?' the boy asks, looking at Tate.

'No. He's trying to help Mummy,' she says. 'Go back and play with your toys.'

Suddenly Tate hates himself for being here. He hates himself for making Tabitha relive the most painful moments of her life. Hates himself for knowing he has to stay.

'But—'

'I said go,' she says, without raising her voice.

The kid throws one more stare at Tate, then turns and walks away.

'My kids are my life. Without them...' she pauses, but then doesn't say what. Instead, she says, 'I came home that night, I had a glass of wine, and the next thing I knew I was waking up on top of my bed. I was naked, and I knew what had happened to me. I could feel it.'

'It was Nathaniel?'

'At the time I could only suspect, but the necklace was gone, so yeah, I was sure it was him. I wanted to report what had happened, but how could I, without admitting to the affair? And once the police found out I had been lying to my family about it, then they would think I was lying about being raped. Or a defence lawyer would. When you're a woman, you only need two seconds to figure all of that out. So no, I didn't report it. Instead I stayed in bed for the next few days, and when Herschel came home I put on a brave face and pretended nothing had happened. A week later I went back to the hospital to see George, and there it was, my necklace. It was around her neck. It confirmed what I already knew. A month after that I found out I was pregnant.'

Tate looks at the boy in the lounge, the one who came to check on her.

'Exactly,' she says. 'He took away the necklace, but left me something else. I love my son, I do, but there are times where I can barely stand to look at him.'

'You never told anybody?'

'How could I, with that video tape out there he could ruin my life with? You have to find it, and destroy it.'

'I promise to do my best.'

'If he can do that to me, then it only stands to reason he could have hurt George.'

'Do you have a photograph of the necklace?'

'Boxed up somewhere, yes. Even our wedding photos. I had to make up an excuse to Herschel that I didn't want them on display because I looked fat in the face, my hair looked stupid, and I looked frumpy. The truth was I didn't want to see it even in a photo. If it were up to me, I'd burn them all, but that would be harder to explain. But yes, I can find you one.'

'Did Nathaniel ever tell you who brought the necklace into his shop?'

'The way he took it from me and put it on George like it was a trophy ... I don't think anybody sold it to him. I think he's done this before.'

'That's what I'm thinking too.'

She sits on that for a few moments, then asks, 'How many women might there be?'

'I don't know.'

'Do you think he's hurt others since? If I had come forward, if I had said something—'

'It's not your fault, and what he's done since then isn't on you. This is on him. Don't have him let you take the blame for his actions.'

'That's easier said than done.'

'There are people who can help you. I can put you in touch with somebody.'

'That's the last thing I want.'

'I'm sorry I had to bring all of this up,' he says.

'You didn't. I have a son who reminds me every day. Did you mean it, what you said before? That you promise you'll do everything to find that footage and destroy it?'

'Yes.'

She stares at him, and after a few moments, she says, 'I believe you.'

Chapter Eighty-Six

The room has been quiet for the last thirty seconds as Wilson and Vega and Travers stare at her. She knew they weren't going to like her theory, but hopefully they can see the merit in it.

'I still have more footage and podcasts to get through,' she adds, 'so it's possible there's mention of the beer bottle somewhere, but if I have to hunt this hard to find it, then it means Copy Joe had to have hunted hard for it too, or he was at the scene at some point.'

'You really think we're looking for a cop,' Wilson says.

'I think it's possible,' she says.

Again silence, but this time it's not as long. 'We need to keep this theory to ourselves,' Wilson says, 'which means it's going to be hard to allocate resources to you for looking into it. The fact you're telling us means you've already ruled us out as suspects. I don't know whether we should be flattered, or annoyed you could think any of us did it.'

'All three of you were here when Simone was killed last night,' she says. 'It was that simple.'

'That simple,' Wilson says. 'Just so we're clear here, I'm not saying I agree with your theory, but then again, Middleton is proof we can't be afraid to look within. I take it you have a plan?'

'We need to go through the Middleton crime scenes to see who had access to the key. I'm hoping to get more details of the items stolen from the other two addresses that were burgled after Middleton had been there: one was four weeks after, and the other was six. It's possible we might be able to track some stolen items back to the source. Durry can hopefully provide a list too. There's always a chance there is a coincidence at play here, but if not, we have three locations where people were murdered where some-body returned to the scene weeks later.'

'Do you know how many people went through the Durry house two years ago?' Vega asks.

She does. People can't just come and go – they're signed in. Everyone who entered the Durry house during the investigation is listed, from the husband to the responding officers to the de-tectives to the coroner to the forensic technicians. There were five pages of sign-in sheets, with several of the names appearing more than once as the same people came back over the days. Schroder's name was in there the most. She misses him.

'Twenty-four people entered the house, but then you have the officers who guarded the scene during the day and night, which was a rotating shift, so that's another thirty who shouldn't have gone inside, but could have, which makes this more complicated than just cross-checking lists.'

'What about crime-scene cleaners?' Wilson asks. 'Are they on the list?'

'I doubt any were used,' Vega says. 'The crime was violent, but contained to the bedroom and bathroom, and there was no blood.'

'I'll double-check anyway,' Kent says.

'Okay. Try and make the list shorter,' Wilson says. 'We don't rule out the women, but I think we can all agree we focus first on the men.' He pauses for somebody to object, and when nobody does, he carries on. 'Some would have been working last night, and others the night Laughton was killed. But we can't throw all our eggs in one basket here, because this theory is nothing more than a theory.'

Wilson hands out the next steps. Vega will continue to go through footage and photos taken from the crowds at the re-enactments and crime scenes. Travers is tasked with interviewing Edgar Burton, Simone's on-again, off-again boyfriend, who is coming into the station soon with his lawyer. He is also tasked with speaking to those involved with the re-enactment – including Tate – to see if Simone said anything to give them pause, or if they noticed anything out of the ordinary. It's possible one of them may also have been targeted. Kent will start going through the lists of people who had access to the crime scene to see if she can rule people out or find some commonalities. While doing this, they will continue to listen to podcasts made about Middleton that Kent will divide up between the four of them. When the meeting is over, Vega and Travers disappear. Kent stays.

'Is there something else, Detective?'

'James Garrett.'

'I know where this is going. Tate still thinks this is his case, that they're in danger, but before you ask, no, we don't have the manpower to put a guard on them. Tate is being paranoid.'

'That's not what I'm going to say. We have an idea how we can put an end to this once and for all.'

'We?'

'Tate and myself.'

'Damn it, Rebecca, I—'

'Please, Eric, just listen,' she says, and she knows how to win him over. 'The plan is good, and if it works out how we hope, then this time tomorrow you can be the guy giving a press conference saying you brought these men to justice.'

Chapter Eighty-Seven

The missing-persons website is one heartbreaking story after another. People from all walks of life disappearing off the face of the earth, some under their own volition, others under somebody else's. Tate starts backward from a month after the wedding at which Tabitha Jensen became Tabitha Munroe, the month to allow for the time it can take for people to be reported missing or to enter the system. He writes down the names of women who have disappeared. Over the following hour, he makes his way through ten years of missing-persons records, coming up with six potentials. He plugs their names into social-media platforms – none of them have accounts, but all of them show up on the accounts of friends and family, especially around birthdays and the anniversaries of when they disappeared. He finds several photographs of them, but in none are any wearing the gold heart necklace.

He moves on from missing persons to news articles, focusing on the years leading up to and just beyond the time where Nathaniel gave Tabitha the necklace. It came from somewhere, and perhaps not from somebody who only disappeared, but somebody who disappeared and was found dead sometime later, in which case they'd have been removed from the missing-persons website. He finds six more names. So far he has spent two hours down the rabbit hole, and each minute has been a reminder of how dark humanity can be – as if he needed one.

His eyes get sore from all the reading as the afternoon stretches on. He could call Kent. She'd be able to determine quickly if the necklace has been identified as a missing piece of property from either a homicide or an abduction, but he doesn't want to involve her. Not yet. He intends to keep the promise he made Tabitha.

He searches through online articles, moving forward from a month before the wedding, thinking the woman who owned the necklace before Tabitha might have disappeared around then. It doesn't take long to find a possible candidate – Scarlett McVicar, who went missing a week before Tabitha Munroe's wedding, and who three years later was found in a steel drum in marshland. The husband, Bevin McVicar, was found guilty of her murder, the verdict based on circumstantial evidence, including the fact friends of Scarlett suspected she was having an affair and Bevin had found out. It didn't help that the police had been called to their house a week before she disappeared after neighbours reported a screaming match.

He taps his fingers over his desk. He remembers Scarlett's case. The detectives working on it felt they had a slam dunk. The husband hadn't reported her missing for three days – he said they had fought, she had stormed off for a run, and when she didn't come home, he figured she was staying with a friend. He goes back onto Facebook. It doesn't take long to find friends and family posting photographs of Scarlett on the anniversary of her disappearing, but none of the photographs have her wearing the necklace.

He needs to talk to Bevin McVicar.

Chapter Eighty-Eight

Despite the night being a frustrating disaster, Callum has managed to sleep long into the afternoon. It's an ability he has always had, being able to sleep anywhere through anything no matter how stressed he is. It's a skill he has had since childhood, possibly since the night he slept through his father pushing his mum's head through the bedroom wall and into a wheelchair for life.

But despite sleeping well, he's angry. He goes through to the kitchen and makes breakfast, which, at this time in the afternoon, is a late lunch. All his actions are heavy, shoving the bread in the toaster, banging the pantry door closed, smacking his coffee cup onto the bench. He is tempting things to break, knowing he won't care if they do, almost wanting it. Even his footsteps are heavy when he walks. He needs an outlet for his anger, and not having one till tonight only serves to make him angrier.

He goes online and reads the news. He makes it a point to stay up to date with what's happening in the city in case it relates to him. Today it does. The man he dropped into the ocean has been reported missing. Police are investigating, but unless they're in scuba gear, they won't get far. Not that they'll try too hard – the dead man is an ex-felon who once sold a bad batch of drugs to high-school students who fried their brains on them. Plus they're busy with this Copy Joe shit anyway, who last night took out the actress who played the dead woman, which gives him a good chuckle and goes a small way to repairing his bad mood. He can see the dead actress becoming a mindfuck over time, a repetitive do-over of Copy Joe killing the person who played the person who played the person, a snake eating its tail until the country is out of actresses.

He goes cold as he reads the next story, his jaw grinding so tight that it clicks when he answers his burner cellphone moments later.

'You've seen the news?' Burrows asks.

'I'm reading it now, but I was right,' Callum says, and knows he was right because he's always right. He wants that etched on his gravestone so nobody can ever forget. He ought to etch it into

Burrows' gravestone too – *Callum is always right.* 'We should have finished it off last night, even if it meant killing a dozen doctors and cops. The article says the kid is regaining his memories, that the police are going to talk to him tomorrow.'

'I know what it says,' Burrows says. 'You checked social media?'

'Why the hell would I have social media?'

'James Garrett is trending. Hashtag Comakid. There are photographs of him at the hospital. He's there right now. There are journalists there too, wanting to interview him. Even if we went to the hospital right now to finish him off, we wouldn't get anywhere near him. Following him will be difficult.'

'He's probably going back to Tate's house,' Callum says.

'We don't know that, but we need to figure it out. One way or another, this ends tonight.'

Chapter Eighty-Nine

Christchurch Men's Prison is a little under ten kilometres from the edge of the city, a distance the fittest of those escaping could cover in under forty minutes. That forty minutes would see them jogging along roads, surrounded mostly by farms, offering access to four-wheel drives and quad bikes and tractors if they wanted to speed that journey up, even horses if they were up for it. This time of the day, those farms have folks working the land as they deal with the onslaught of the rain over the last few days. To Tate, being a farmer looks like the toughest job in the world.

He takes the turnoff to the prison and stops at the guard post. He shows a guard his identification, and that guard compares it against a log then waves him through. Up ahead there's a new wing being assembled that, over the last few years, has been in various stages of development. The biggest delay was when the original contractors blew out the budget, and the project manager got caught embezzling his employer's money – meaning he now sees the project from the inside of the concrete walls. There are no cars in the parking lot, and he figures he might be the last visitor for the day. When he's inside he hands his ID over to a guard behind a Plexiglas window and tells her who he is here to see.

'Take a seat,' she says, and he does, in a lifeless room with uncomfortable chairs and the air conditioning set to chill, as if the prison authorities are trying to dissuade folks from coming here to visit. That dissuasion continues for thirty minutes, and in that time five o'clock rolls around, darkening the evening sky, and the early spots of rain against the windows become a steady pour.

A guard leads him to a room similar to an interrogation room at the police station. Bevin McVicar is sitting on the other side of a metal desk. He's cuffed, the chain looping through a metal bar welded to it. McVicar is forty, hippy-length dark hair, gaunt, like he hunger-strikes every second day in the hope of slipping through the bars one night. Tate is thankful he's agreed to see him. The guard that escorted Tate waits outside.

'I asked around about you,' McVicar says.

'And?'

'People say you'll burn anybody who gets in the way of you finding the truth.'

Tate doesn't like that description of himself. It's not always that black and white. 'Sometimes you just have to do whatever it takes.'

'And now you're here about Scarlett,' McVicar says. 'Only reason I can think why a whatever-it-takes guy like you would be here is if you've figured out what I've been telling people all along, and that's that I didn't kill her.'

'Which makes me the only friend you have at the moment,' Tate says, 'and I'm hoping it also means you're willing to talk to me.'

'I'm here, ain't I?'

'I have some questions, and you're not going to like some of them.'

'There ain't much I have liked as of late. Me and Scarlett, we had our problems, but she didn't deserve what happened to her, and I didn't deserve to end up here.'

'There were reports she was having an affair. Is that true?'

He shrugs. 'That affair story, I don't know where it started, but once it was out there it really took hold. Was she? I don't know. I wouldn't be surprised if one of the detectives started the rumour just to make me look bad. People hate to think cops do shit like that, but cops do dodgy shit all the time to get what they want – it's why I'm in here. It's why some folks get freed from jail after years inside when DNA clears them.'

'You ever suspect Scarlett of seeing anybody?' Tate asks, wanting to get McVicar back on track.

'No, and before you ask, no, I wasn't seeing anybody either.'

Tate opens the folder he's brought in with him and slides out a photograph of Nathaniel Perry. 'You recognise him?'

McVicar leans over the photo and studies it. 'Should I?'

'His name is Nathaniel Perry.'

'You think he killed Scarlett?'

'I don't know. You're sure you don't recognise him?'

'Positive.'

He shows him photographs of Georgia Perry and Tabitha Munroe. 'How about them?'

'No.'

'Take a closer look at this one,' he says, tapping Tabitha's photograph.

'I said I don't recognise her.'

'Humour me,' he says.

McVicar leans closer to the photo, shaking his head, then his head stops shaking and he touches the necklace in the photo, and Tate's breath catches.

'This necklace,' McVicar says.

'What about it?'

'This looks like the same one Scarlett had.'

Tate shows him a close-up photo of the necklace.

McVicar nods, his mouth turning down at the edges. 'You're sure of it too, huh? I call it the argument necklace.'

'Argument necklace?'

'Scarlett bought it from a jeweller in town and was really cagey about it when a friend asked where it came from. It led to a stupid argument, and her friend said she was sorry she had asked, and Scarlett made the mistake of telling her she didn't want her to go and buy something similar, which made no sense because the necklace was old and a one-off. It took a few days for them to get over it.'

'Can you remember when this was?'

'Was close enough to the wedding that we weren't sure if Adrianna – that's the friend – was going to show up, but she did.'

Another wedding, and another connection. 'Did the police ever ask you about it?'

'Never.'

'Did Scarlett wear it much?'

'Funny you ask that.'

'Why's that?'

'She never wore it at home, but she made sure to never leave the house without it, and if she did, she'd go back and get it.'

'I couldn't find her wearing it in any photographs.'

'She didn't like having her picture taken much after the wedding. She even went as far as deleting all her social-media accounts. She said it was messing with her wellbeing, and she could live cleaner without any of it.'

Tate knows the real reason why. She suspected that even though Nathaniel Perry didn't own a cellphone or use a computer, he still might have found a way to monitor her social-media pages and the pages of her friends.

'What about when she went jogging?'

'She even wore it when...' he says, then stops. 'You know, thinking about it, after Scarlett was found and before I was arrested, they returned her wedding ring to me, but not the necklace.'

'You're sure about that?'

'Positive.'

'Did the police know she would have been wearing it?'

He shrugs. 'I don't remember. All I know is she would have been.' He taps the photograph of Nathaniel. 'This guy. He killed her and took it, didn't he.' Not a question, but a statement.

'I'm going to find out for sure.'

Chapter Ninety

Tate hits the missing-persons website when he's back home, scrolling backward from today, looking for more potential victims of Nathaniel Perry. It doesn't take long before he finds one: April Gilmore. He recognises her from the news but hasn't followed the case. April Gilmore, twenty-eight years old, married, a gym trainer, disappeared biking to her 5.00am shift on a Monday six weeks ago. Her husband, Trent Gilmore, said she would often leave without waking him up. Which is exactly what happened the day she disappeared, meaning he last spoke to her the night before. Her bike and bag were found along a quiet stretch of road outside a park. The media fall marginally short of calling Trent, who she had married six months earlier, the primary suspect.

Her Facebook is still active. It's full of comments from friends and family all praying for her to come home, as if her disappearance is something she has control over. It isn't until he scrolls through their profiles that he finds a photograph of April wearing the gold heart. There can be little doubt now that she fell into Perry's orbit.

He carries on scrolling back through time, but doesn't find any other potential victims. He goes through articles of homicides – both solved and unsolved – and finds nothing there either. If he's right about Nathaniel Perry, then hopefully his victims are contained to the four he knows of – Georgia, Tabitha, Scarlett and April. The list of women he has hurt could be considerably longer. Is there somebody else out there right now wearing the necklace? It was given back to Perry at the hospital after Georgia died – did it go to April next, and now on to somebody else?

He leans back in his chair. He can draw a line directly from Scarlett McVicar, to Tabitha Munroe, to Georgia Perry, and now to April Gilmore. He can call Kent. She has the resources to see if that straight line can be extended in other directions. But he made a promise to Tabitha Munroe that he would find the footage Perry took of her and destroy it, and he still intends to do that. Yes, he will bring Kent onboard, but not yet.

Chapter Ninety-One

Callum clocks them from across the road from the hospital, Hot Stuff pushing Brother Gimpy in the wheelchair, Detective Scarface walking alongside them. They're all bundled up because of the weather, Scarface with an umbrella that bobs about as the wind catches it. There are no journalists, the rain having pushed them inside, or perhaps the story has been put to bed for the day, ready for a fresh start tomorrow when the kid spills his guts to the police. Not that he'll get the chance.

Traffic is always thick on a Friday evening, and this evening it's made even thicker as the rain gets heavier. His view of the trio is broken up as cars come and go. It will be difficult to tail them, but also difficult for them to notice him. Plus they won't be looking. He loses sight of them, but knows both Kent's car and the station wagon the Garretts were using last night. He stays calm, and a few minutes later they come out of the parking lot in Scarface's car, the cop driving, with Hot Stuff in the passenger seat, and Gimpy rolling around somewhere in the back.

He follows.

He hates traffic. He avoids going anywhere at this time of the day unless it's a matter of life or death, which this is. Christchurch is renowned for drivers who speed up to stop others changing lanes, people taking it as a personal slight if somebody gets ahead of them. He experiences that now, getting stuck in a lane, unable to move across. If he wasn't worried about drawing attention to himself, he'd be driving with his hand on the horn, ready to pull over and punch anybody who dared to flip him a finger. Up ahead, Scarface hangs a left. He gives the car some gas so he can follow her through a space up ahead. A driver lurches forward to close the gap, but Callum keeps going, forcing the guy to brake hard, and rightly so, because the kind of mood Callum is in would have him writing the dude's licence plate down with a plan to visit him one night. There is no collision, and Callum gets the spot, only to get stuck at the next red light. Luckily traffic is so backed up that cross traffic can't come through the intersection, meaning the trio are still only a few car lengths around the corner.

For the next thirty minutes it's rinse and repeat as the rain falls and the red lights grind traffic to a halt over and over. They eventually clear the city and hit the suburbs, and it's obvious where they're going. When they turn down the Garretts' street, he doesn't make the turn, heading straight ahead and making his way out of the neighbourhood.

Chapter Ninety-Two

James's last time in an ambulance had him strapped to a gurney while a paramedic staunched the flow of blood, his vitals scattered in all directions, the expectation of his survival zero. He knows that on the operating table that expectation was met and defied four times.

'Are you okay?' Hazel asks.

While two police officers dressed as paramedics ride up front in the ambulance, James rides in the back with Hazel. He's on a gurney, a strap across his body acting like a seatbelt, while Hazel sits on a small bench opposite. Thirty minutes ago they had swapped places with two constables in the bathrooms downstairs at the hospital, undressing and swapping clothes too – along with the wheelchair. One of the constables had cut and styled her hair to match Hazel's, and a constable who barely looked twenty had done the same with James. Jackets on and hoodies up, those two had gone with Kent, while he had waited in the bathroom for another twenty minutes with Hazel. Earlier, Hazel had given Detective Kent the house key so four armed officers could wait inside. Kent was unclear how many nights this would go on for, and had said hopefully only the one – which was a good answer if she was right, but a bad one if she wasn't.

He nods. He gives Hazel the thumbs-up, but can't find the strength to smile. Sometimes out of nowhere the melancholy will strike. He misses his parents. He misses his friends from Coma World. He repurposed people, both fictional and real, to fill that world, and having gone through all the cabinets in the warehouse, he has been keenly reminded of his loss. In a way, it's as though everybody in his life since the night of the shooting has died, and in some cases, twice.

'It's okay if you're not okay,' Hazel says. 'With everything that's happened, you're allowed to be sad.'

He knows. He wants her to let it go, and she does. He looks around at all the lifesaving pieces of equipment that look like they've come from the future. There is so much packed in here he comes to the conclusion ambulances must work on the same principal as Doctor Who's TARDIS. With that thought comes the realisation that in Coma World, a range of Doctor Whos worked the checkouts at the local supermarket, with the one in the long scarf often pushing the trolleys.

After ten minutes the ambulance comes to a stop. The officers get out and the back door opens. They've pulled up on an empty stretch of road with open fields on one side and a forest on the other. There is one other car in sight, and it's parked right behind them. The door opens, and Mr Tate steps out, holding up an umbrella as the police pretending to be paramedics help James out of the ambulance. It may be over the top, but he feels like he's in a spy novel as they get into Mr Tate's car. Nothing like this happened in Coma World, but next time...

He almost laughs at the thought of there being a next time.

Chapter Ninety-Three

It's Kent's first time at the Garrett house, but she has seen enough crime-scene photos to recognise that it's been renovated since that night. The constable pretending to be Hazel pushes the constable pretending to be James into the lounge. Neither are armed, but

Kent is, as are the four officers who entered the house earlier. The house opposite, still owned by Mr and Mrs Mann, has two more armed officers ready and waiting. The decision has been made not to have any undercover officers in unmarked cars anywhere nearby in case it spooks the potential attackers.

To complete the illusion, if they have been followed here, she can't stay. She wishes everybody good luck and rushes through the rain to her car. All up, heading to the hospital and coming here has taken longer than she hoped, mostly because of the traffic. She puts a podcast on as she drives and listens to people give their theories on Joe Middleton. She hadn't realised how much of this kind of content was available until Matthew Durry lamented it. In this particular podcast a man is saying that none of the women would have been murdered if they'd made better efforts to lock their doors or had married men who could look after them better. He says ever since New Zealand started voting in women prime ministers, the country has gone to shit. Then he goes on to explain what the victims could have done differently, how the objects at hand could have saved their lives. He doesn't mention any beer bottles, though Kent sure as hell feels like smashing a few over his head.

She pauses it and calls Vega, who took over from Kent cross-referencing who had access to the locations so Kent could leave for the hospital. Together they've managed to narrow down the list of officers who were posted outside the same scenes to twelve. As for who entered the scenes, the list is at fifteen.

'So twenty-seven possibilities,' Kent says.

'Eighteen of whom are men,' Vega says.

'We're getting closer.'

'I'll email you a list. I've been going through their records too, but nothing stands out. You going home or coming back to the station?'

'Neither. I have something else I need to follow up on.'

'You need some sleep, Rebecca. I know you're taking a beating on this, and if you don't—'

'I'm fine, Audrey, but I appreciate the sentiment. Keep looking through those records, and I'll see you in the morning.'

Chapter Ninety-Four

Kent shows up just before eight o'clock with a welcome bag of Indian food. Immediately the dining room fills with the smells of butter chicken and tikka masala, making Tate's stomach grumble. Kent's does the same. It reminds him of the dualling banjos scene from *Deliverance*. Hopefully the four of them will survive the spicy food in better condition than the four who went rafting through hillbilly country.

They keep the conversation light. James has his pad by his side, but doesn't use it, seemingly happy to eat while listening in. After dinner, Hazel and James watch TV in the lounge, Hazel doing her best to catch James up on some of the greatest shows he's missed over the last decade, which is a list that starts small but quickly expands as she thinks of more and more titles. Most Tate has never heard of, and some he did hear about he never got around to seeing. Ever since Emily died, he's hardly had time for TV, instead throwing himself into work, revenge or drinking, or a combination of the three – with the hope two of those are now fully in the past.

Staying at the table, and keeping their voices low so they can't be heard, Tate and Kent talk about Nathaniel Perry. 'I'm confident McCoy was right, and Perry pushed Georgia off that balcony,' he says.

Kent is soaking sauce from her plate with garlic naan. Before she pops it into her mouth, she asks, 'How confident?'

'You remember Scarlett McVicar?'

She eats while thinking, then nods. 'Is this where you tell me we got the wrong guy?'

'Yes,' he says, already knowing from the newspaper articles it wasn't her case. 'And she isn't the only one. I think he's behind April Gilmore's disappearance too.'

'You want to tell me how you got there?'

'Some I can tell Rebecca the detective, and then there's some I can tell Rebecca the friend.'

'Oh geez,' she says, looking exactly as unimpressed as he knew she would. 'Don't do this to me.'

'You brought this to me, Rebecca. You need to choose.'

'That doesn't mean I want you going all vigilante on me. I brought this to you to see what you could find, then give me everything you have.'

'It's not that simple.'

'So what are you saying? That you want to be able to tell me stuff I can't act on?'

He glances at the bulge in her jacket. 'I'm saying that since you're here, and armed, and since there's a car outside with two officers keeping an eye out for Copy Joe, then I can leave you here to keep an eye on Hazel and James while I go and check out Nathaniel Perry.'

'Check out how?'

'I just want to ask him a few questions, that's all.'

'That's all? If you're planning on killing him, Theo, then—'

'It's nothing like that, I promise. There's a link in the chain here I promised to protect, and when I've done that, I'll bring every-thing to you, and you can make the arrest.'

'This person you have to protect...'

'I can't say.'

'But I can make a pretty good guess. Here's what I think. I think if you're honest with yourself, you want this. You want the rush of closing a case because it's been a while. You've put things together, and you could lay it all out for me, but you won't, and you're using this promise as an excuse.'

'Maybe,' he says, but he knows there is no maybe about it. 'I can give all of it to you now as Rebecca the friend, but if you want to hear it as the cop, you'll have to wait a little longer. This guy, he's a monster, Rebecca. He's as bad as they get.'

'And that's what you do, isn't it? You stop monsters.'

'Let me do what I'm good at.'

Chapter Ninety-Five

Earlier, Tate had opened the garage door so Kent could park inside and keep out of the rain. Now he takes her car, hoping the police will think it's her and not follow. He wants those officers protecting the house on the slim chance Copy Joe does show up.

It works, the officers staying their ground.

At 10.30pm, the only shops open in town are a handful of twenty-four-hour convenience stores. He buys the cheapest pair of smartphones he can find, and adds a pair of sim cards along with a voucher so he can purchase some apps. The guy behind the counter is indifferent to the purchase, as if he's seen it a hundred times already this week. Back in his car he slots in the sim cards and powers the phones up. Both have eighty-percent charge, more than enough for what he needs. He uses one to access a website he's familiar with to create a fake email address full of random numbers and letters, and uses it to set up accounts for the phones, using the same fake password he always uses. He programs the number of the first phone into the second, and downloads spyware on the first so he can track its location. After testing them, he puts them on the passenger seat next to a roll of duct tape and a small pair of binoculars. The gun, which he has brought with him, is buried deep inside his jacket pocket.

It's a fifteen-minute drive to Nathaniel Perry's last known address, which he hopes is still current. It's a single-storey brick townhouse with a low-pitch roof and bay windows that stretch a metre out over the garden. The lights are on inside. After doing a U-turn, he parks halfway down the next block, then peels off two strips of duct tape and sticks them loosely to his jacket before climbing into the rain. He walks quickly to Perry's house and uses a handkerchief to wipe water from the bay window, then uses the duct tape in a cross shape to secure the phone to it. He crosses the road and heads three houses closer to his car and hides behind a neighbour's Griselinia hedge, where he has a viewing angle through to the duct-taped phone. He dials.

Over the rain, he can't hear it, but he knows it will be loud as it rings and vibrates against the window. He watches through the binoculars as the phone shifts back and forth. Will it shake itself free? He is suddenly worried it might. But before it can, the curtain opens, then closes. If he's wrong about Nathaniel Perry living here, then he's wasted a hundred bucks on a phone. But if he's right...

He's not wrong, because Nathaniel Perry steps out of the front door. He's in a pair of pyjamas with a yellow slicker over the top. He looks around, aware there's every chance he's being watched, but no idea from where. He steps into the rain and walks over to the phone but doesn't touch it. He knows it can't be there for a good reason. He's faced with a decision. Bury his head in the sand or accept things are going to get bad for him.

Really, there's only one choice. He peels the lower part of the tape away and grabs the phone. He stares at it, and Tate is reminded the guy doesn't own a phone, and is probably figuring out what button to press.

He figures it out, turns to face the street, and answers the call. 'Who is this?'

'This is the man who knows you killed your wife,' Tate says.

'What the—?'

'And the man who knows you killed Scarlett McVicar.'

'I have no idea what—'

'I'm talking about? Then hang up and we'll let the police figure it out. Or you listen to what I have to say.'

Perry says nothing. He paces the front yard, looking in all directions. He looks over at Tate, but looks past him. 'What do you want?'

'Fifty-thousand dollars.'

'Now I know you're full of shit. I don't have that kind of money.'

'Then I suggest you figure out how to find it, because if you don't I'm going to give the police everything. You have twenty-four hours.'

'You have the wrong guy.'

'I know what you did with April Gilmore.'

A pause, and then, 'I don't know what you're talking about.'

'Then you have nothing to worry about. You have twenty-four hours, arsehole,' Tate says, and before Perry can respond, he hangs up and switches off the phone.

Chapter Ninety-Six

James, having overindulged on the online news about his family, turns his attention to Theodore Tate. There is plenty about him on the Internet covering his days on the police force, and also a lot that covers the death of Emily, his daughter, who was run down by a car in the parking lot outside a cinema. The man who ran Emily down disappeared, having done a runner to escape what would have been jail time. He reads up about Detective Schroder, the other detective who tried to solve his parents' murders. Schroder left the police force but it doesn't say why, and months later was wounded in a shooting, the same way James was, only the eventual outcomes were different.

When he's done reading, he finds himself drawn back into the warehouse. Something here has changed, and it isn't until he walks to the far end that he sees a gap in the wall the size of a double garage door, a plastic sheet hanging over the opening. He pulls back the plastic.

There's a new room here. Power tools, wooden and metal beams, paint and nails and drop saws and skill saws and table saws and handsaws. Ladders, bolts, clamps, chisels, glues – all of it in aid of the brand-new extension. New floors, new rafters, new walls, all to be painted. New windows too, larger and thicker than the ones in the original part of the warehouse. There are electrical wires hanging from the ceiling. There's a metal skip in the corner with beams of old wood and drywall. This new room is a tenth of the size of the warehouse.

But it's not the room that surprises him the most, it's the filing cabinets, two or three hundred of them, all of them brand new. The closest one has today's date on it. He opens it. It's full of empty files. He goes to the next one. Empty. But waiting to be filled with what? He walks to the far end, watching as the dates go back in time, back to the first cabinet.

The date on it gives him the answer.

It's the day after Mr Tate's daughter was killed. He gets it now. The same way he created an alternate world for himself, he can create one for somebody else. He leaves the warehouse, and he goes online and finds several articles back from when she died that include testimonials from friends, from family, from school teachers. He will need to read it all. He will need to talk to Tate and find out everything he can about her, and when he does he'll be able to fill those cabinets and give her the same thing he gave his parents – a life she never had.

Chapter Ninety-Seven

Tate's confidence in the plan remains high for thirty minutes, then circles the drain for the thirty that follow. His eyes grow sore from the binoculars, and he has to keep switching hands to stop his forearms from cramping. He could be here all night, and even then there's every chance it's all for nothing. Will Perry's paranoia kick in? At what point will he no longer be able to help himself?

That point is ten minutes into the second hour, when Perry backs out of his driveway in a large curvy car that looks fifty years old but lovingly restored. Tate isn't a car guy, so can't tell what it is, only that it must handle like a tank when taking corners. He gets a good look at Perry through the binoculars, seeing him as he angles his car onto the road. He ducks down as Perry comes toward him, then pops back up when the car turns at the intersection rather than coming through.

Tate opens up the app on the phone and watches the blue dot that is the other phone moving across a map. He waits for the gap to reach two blocks before following. As he drives, he imagines this going to court, and Perry's lawyer standing up and saying, 'Is the prosecution really asking the court to believe the police – and not even the police, but an ex-detective – were led to my client's house because of a dream a teenager had?'

Then again, it won't matter what the hell his lawyer says if this goes the way Tate thinks it's going to go.

Perry heads south, and it reminds him that Scarlett McVicar's body was found thirty minutes in that direction out of the city. He is settling in for the ride when Perry changes course, and soon comes to a stop. A minute later Tate catches up, figuring Perry's car is parked in behind the block of shops up ahead. He doesn't know this side of the city well, but assumes there'll be a pharmacy and a fish-and-chip shop, a hairdresser, maybe a bar, maybe a real-estate agent, maybe a dairy. He pulls over and uses his binoculars. He's wrong about the bar and real-estate agent, but right about the rest, with a picture framer and antique store to boot. He focuses on the antique store. It must be the one Nathaniel Perry owns. Perry restores old furniture too, which might mean the store has a workshop attached – a workshop full of power tools for cutting. Did April Gilmore meet her fate in there? Is she still there, stored in a freezer?

The blue dot starts moving again. He lies down and waits for it to move well past him before sitting back up. Perry heads north, and Tate follows. After ten minutes the suburbs peter out as roads turn to motorways and houses become farms. The distance between lampposts doubles, then quadruples, then they're football fields apart. Off the side of the motorway, trees stand like giants and paddocks roll into the dark. The rain keeps coming, as it will tomorrow, and the day after, perhaps now until the end of time. They pass the roadworks and the heavy equipment and shipping container he had to slow down for when he came to visit Bridget earlier, and then they pass the turnoff to the care home. He hopes Bridget is asleep and dreaming of better times.

Perry hangs a right off the motorway, and less than a minute later Tate makes the same turn onto a road that's nothing but trees either side. The blue dot hangs a left then comes to a complete stop. On the GPS there is no road up there, so perhaps he's turned into a driveway, or a road that doesn't count as a road. It leaves

Tate with a tricky decision. If he drives there, and Perry is parked only a few metres around the corner, he'll be spotted. There is also no hiding his car. If Perry is up there doing a U-turn and on his way back, there'd be nothing Tate could do about it. But if he's right, Perry won't be coming back. Not right away. And he is sure he's right, because the dot is moving again, only this time incredibly slowly. Perry is on foot.

He parks up two hundred metres short, grabs his gear and hugs the tree line on his way to the turnoff. There's a narrow dirt road heading into the trees and no sign of Perry or his car. The trees are tall and thick and block any view, and the road is lumpy, with deep ruts, like the kind a tractor would make. All he can see is the next twenty metres. He walks them, his shoes already soaked. The dot, a hundred metres away, becomes ninety, then eighty, then seventy. Up ahead there's a curve, and then the car. He pauses next to it. He holds his breath and listens, but all he can hear is the rain. He continues forward, into the trees now, closing the distance on the dot. Fifty metres. Forty. Thirty.

He keeps going.

Chapter Ninety-Eight

There are differences from last night's setup. Instead of Callum being in the van with Burrows, he's in the van by himself, and Burrows and Keith are together in the sedan. In addition to that, while the sedan has a clear line of sight of the house, Callum has the van one street over, parked a few doors down from the neighbour who lives in the house directly behind. They've also left it much later in the evening. It's 1.00am, Friday night now having spilled over into Saturday. Over the evening he's made peace with the fact that Thursday night didn't fall under the umbrella of bad luck, because when you're dealing with guys like Theodore Tate, bad luck can see you in jail, or in a grave, but tonight will go better. He has also made a decision on Hazel Garrett. He's bringing her with him. He deserves it. He's earned it.

The wind from last night hasn't returned, but the rain has, and again he's worn clothes that absorb the rain rather than repel it. When his watch hits one, he gets out of the van. There are no lights on in any of the houses. His job is made easier by the fact the house he needs to sneak past has a detached garage he can keep between himself and whatever arseholes live here. He walks through the vegetable garden at the back, not knowing what can be grown this time of the year and not giving a damn, nor giving one when he stomps through it all with his size fourteens. His shoes will be melted down into blobs of leather and plastic when all this is done.

He climbs the fence in the corner and drops into a garden so thick with weeds he doesn't think he could leave a footprint behind even if he tried. There are two more differences between last night and tonight. The first is he's worn waterproof gloves to keep his hands warm, which will make picking the lock easier. The second is last night nobody was in the mood for killing cops or doctors, but those niceties have been left in the past. He's going to put a bullet into anybody who gets in his way.

There is a third difference too – an all-important one. Tonight they're not wasting time at the Garrett house. Right now that place is full of officers in wait. He hates to admit it, but the move almost worked. But they'd learned they'd been duped – that he had followed Kent and a couple of decoys there, that the news article had been planted to draw him and the other two out. Right now he would have been walking into a trap. But instead he's going into Theodore Tate's house, where the kid and his sister are hiding out, and he's going to do what he should have done last night: not just put a couple of bullets into James Garrett, but a couple into the ex-detective too.

Chapter Ninety-Nine

Branches scrape and snag at Tate as he tries not to roll an ankle on the clumpy roots and mossy pinecones. He once saw a documentary about how easy it is to get lost in the woods and how hard it is to walk in a straight line, but he didn't think it would happen this fast – barely a minute in and he knows the only way out of here is with the GPS on his own phone. Given it's unlikely Perry will own a GPS, Tate figures the guy is either using a compass or has drawn a map. With close to forty percent of New Zealand being covered in forest, there is a lot of real estate to hide a body. It's possible he's already passed one.

He slows down, then comes to a stop a few paces short of a small rectangular clearing the size of a bus. In the middle of that clearing, with his back toward Tate and a flashlight on the ground lighting it up, is Perry in his yellow slicker kicking a shovel into the earth. Tate's assumption all along was that April was dead and buried, and the hope was he could bluff Perry into revealing her location. It's worked. April Gilmore is in that clearing, and by finding her Tate hopes to bring her family some closure. If he shot Perry where he stood, he figures he could find them even more.

He steps out from the trees. He points his gun at Perry, who continues to dig, and not that well. He's struggling with ground that seems more solid than it ought to be for dirt that was turned over within the last six weeks. It doesn't make sense. The rain hammers off Perry's slicker and hat.

'Stop,' Tate says, loud enough to be heard.

Perry flinches, then stops, one foot and both hands on the shovel.

'I have a gun. You try anything, and I'm shooting. Hands out to your side.'

Perry straightens up and puts his arms out to the side. The jacket is too big for him, swallowing up his hands. Tate's phone in his pocket vibrates.

'Now turn around.'

Perry turns around.

Only it's not Perry.

'What the—?'

'I'm sorry,' Tabitha Munroe says.

Before he can react, something hits him hard in the back of the head, and a moment later he's face down in the dirt.

Chapter One Hundred

Tate's dead cat is going to save her life. Her life, and Hazel's, and James's too. Kent knows the story, about how Daxter was killed, buried, then dug back up and left swinging from the roof. After that Tate had an alarm installed in the house, along with sensors on the doorways and windows. Though the alarm isn't currently active, the sensors are, and right now an alert has been sent to her phone – a safety precaution Tate set up before leaving. And right now, her phone is telling her the door leading into the garage has just been opened.

The lights are off in the lounge, but the TV is on, providing light that bounces from here into the dining room. It ought to draw Copy Joe this way first. She gets to her feet and moves to the corner of the lounge. There isn't time to head to the bedrooms to warn Hazel and James, and she hopes they won't wake up to the sound.

A door opening – the one between the garage and the hallway. She holds her breath. She could use her phone to call for help, but the screen will light up, and she doesn't want to risk Copy Joe walking in and seeing that. Or hearing her talk. What if Tate calls right now? He might, because he will have gotten the alert too. She reaches into her pocket and holds down the power button, feeling a slight vibration as it shuts down. Then she puts both hands on the gun. She's a police detective, she is armed, she will be fine.

A pair of hands extend into the lounge. In those hands is a gun. Copy Joe. Will she be right? Will he be a cop? She wills him to keep coming, wills him and screams in her mind for him to do so, knowing it's unlikely as he can see the couch, can see it's empty, meaning...

Hands and now arms on display, the gun pointing ahead, the front half of the body, a leg, and now the rest of him, and it's a *lot* of him, a big guy not in a police uniform, but in dark clothes and a ski mask. She can't think of anybody on the force as big as this guy. Her mind flashes to Denise Laughton, then to Simone Clarke. How could they have had a chance against somebody so huge?

Before Copy Joe can decide the lounge is empty and head for the bedrooms, her finger on the trigger in case he spins toward her, she says, 'I'm armed. Don't move.'

The man doesn't move. He continues to face the couch.

'Hands out to your sides.'

He puts them out to his sides.

'Drop the gun.'

He drops it.

'Step to the couch and keep facing it.'

He does exactly that.

'Put your fingers behind your head.'

Copy Joe does it, and she is surprised – she would have thought Copy Joe would have resisted. Looking at the size of him, she is reminded of Callum Hayes. Has she gotten this wrong? Is she looking at one of the men who killed the Garretts, and not Copy Joe? It would explain why he's calmly complying, as he won't be here alone.

'Where are your friends?'

'I don't have any friends,' Big Man says, and his voice is low and gravely, like a smoker whose last cigarette got stuck down his throat.

'Get on your knees.'

Big Man gets on his knees. She moves out from the corner and flicks the nearest light switch. He doesn't move. She circles the room so she can face him, purposely kicking the dropped gun under the other couch in the process. 'Pull the mask off.'

Big Man pulls the mask off, and damn, it really is Callum Hayes. How the hell did he know to come here? His hair is greyer than his mugshot, and shorter, and there are more lines on his face. There is a mess of overlapping tattoos on his neck that she can't decipher and that weren't in the mugshot.

'Where are they?' Kent asks.

'Where are who?'

'Your two partners. Where are they?'

'I want a lawyer.'

'Where are they, Callum?'

'I. Want. A lawyer.'

She moves behind him at a safe distance should he try something. She's concerned for the two police officers parked out front. Are they still alive? She's at the wrong end of the house to open the curtains, turn on the lights and wave them in, and even if she was at the right end, she's not sure it would be a good option. She has no idea what's going on out there. She turns her phone on.

THE PAIN TOURIST 263

There are no missed calls or texts from Tate. She calls Wilson. He answers right away.

'I'm looking at Callum Hayes,' she says. She sees cable ties sticking out of his back pocket. Ties equal restraint. Ties mean Hayes was coming here to do more than just kill them.

'Who the hell is Callum Hayes?'

'He's one of the three men who killed the Garretts. I'm at Tate's house, and he snuck in with—'

'You're at Tate's?'

'I don't have time to explain, but I need backup right away,' she says.

'Aren't there officers parked outside the house?'

'Please, just call it in. I have Hayes in custody, but there may be two more armed offenders on the scene.'

Chapter One Hundred and One

Hazel is pulled from her sleep by Detective Kent calling out to her. She is out of bed within seconds, and she approaches the lounge cautiously, where a big man is on his knees with his back to the doorway, and Kent is covering him with a gun. Kent and Tate said earlier there was a slim chance Copy Joe would come here, and that if he did there were officers who—

'It's not Copy Joe,' Kent says, breaking her chain of thought. 'His name is Callum Hayes. He's one of the men who killed your parents.'

Hazel's world drops so quickly she has to grab hold of the wall to stay balanced, and even then she ends up sliding down it to the floor. The man that shot her mum and dad? Right here in front of her? How can that be?

Detective Kent carries on. 'I don't know how he's figured out you and James are here, but we'll know for sure soon. Right now I need you to go to the end bedroom and watch out of the window. Stay to the side and keep your head down. There's an un-marked patrol car parked outside. In a few seconds you're going to see two officers in uniform get out of it. When they do, I want you to unlock the front door for them, okay?'

She wants to answer, but finds that she can't.

'Hazel?'

'I ... okay.'

'If nobody gets out, tell me.'

'Okay.'

'You see anybody else out there, you tell me.'

'Okay.'

'Now go. Quickly.'

She pushes herself off the ground and gets to her feet. The hallway sways as she makes her way down it, but is steady by the time she reaches James's room. Her brother is awake and looking confused. She goes into the master, and stands to the side of the window and pushes the curtains enough to get a view. There's a car parked opposite, and as she watches, the doors open and two men in uniforms get out. They look around as they rush across the road, as if they're expecting people to jump out of the bushes. They don't have guns. She wishes they did. She steps into the hallway and halfway toward the lounge. 'The two officers from the car are here,' she calls out, and a moment later they're knocking on the front door.

'Answer it,' Kent says. 'Make sure to tell them I have a gun, and that it's trained on the man who broke in.'

'Okay.'

Back past the bedrooms, to the front door with the coat rack and the jackets that are no longer dripping. She answers the door. The two officers on the doorstep are soaking wet, one with his shoulders hunched up, the other with his hands clasped together.

'Miss Garrett?' the one with the hunched-up shoulders asks.

'That's me.'

'I'm Officer Lance Burrows and this is my partner, Officer Damien Keith. We just got a call you need some assistance.'

Chapter One Hundred and Two

Tate is pulled off the ground and forced onto his knees. His own cuffs and gun are now being used against him. He lost consciousness from whatever hit him, but can't tell if it was for a few seconds or a few minutes. His head is pounding, and there is a heaviness to his thoughts that is one part from the blow and one part from the realisation he's not getting out of here alive. He's taken a few heavy hits like this over the last couple of years, with his doctor warning him the next one could be his last.

Nathaniel Perry and Tabitha Munroe are staring at him, Perry with a sneer and, to her credit, Tabitha with a look of shame. Perry isn't in the yellow slicker but a black one. Tate sees how it went. It wasn't a *what* that was being picked up at the antique store, but a *who*. He follows them out here, Tabitha lying down in the backseat because they know Tate is watching. Maybe they have eyes on him the whole time. They switch jackets. Tate follows Tabitha into the trees and Perry follows him. What he doesn't understand is *why*. Why would Tabitha do this? And how did they figure out he was trying to draw Perry out here?

'The police know everything,' he says.

Perry's sneer turns into a full-blown smile, and Tate wants to hit him.

'If that were true, they'd have been the ones following me tonight, not you, and they wouldn't have tried some game with a cellphone, they'd have barged into my house with a warrant.

You're out here on your own. You had your chance, and you blew it.'

'You're wrong. It was a police officer who gave me the case. She knows I'm here.'

'Here? In the middle of nowhere?'

'I called her and gave her the location.'

'You called her.'

'I did.'

'On this,' he says, and holds up Tate's phone in his other hand. It seems everything he brought out here is now being used against him. Maybe they'll finish him off by running him over with Kent's car. 'We can see what the last number was called on these things, is that right?'

Tate shakes his head and immediately wishes he hadn't as the world sways. 'I used the burner phone.'

Perry tosses the phone onto the ground, then reaches into his pocket and pulls out Tate's burner. 'You mean from this one?'

The headache, the pounding, it's making it difficult to come up with something believable.

'Well?'

'Her boss doesn't like me, so we figured it best to keep my name out of it. That way she can say she was contacted by an anonymous source. So after I made the call, I deleted any record of it from that phone.'

'You have an answer for everything, don't you?'

'It's the truth.'

Perry tosses the phone onto the ground next to the other one. 'Let me tell you what the truth is. The first thing Tabitha did after you visited her this morning was call me. See, she understands what's best for me is best for her. She wants to keep her family together and her reputation intact. What I want is for you to fill in the blanks. You and Doctor McCoy approached her parents yesterday. Why?'

Tate looks at Tabitha, but she won't meet his gaze. Perry's question tells him the parents didn't tell Tabitha about James. Tate sure can't mention him, otherwise James will end up in the forest next to him. 'There are people in the police department who think you killed Georgia and the file should never have been closed. One of them asked me to look into it. I approached McCoy to ask what he thought, as he knew you and the family. We decided to talk to the parents, which led to me talking to Tabitha.'

'Which led to you asking about the necklace. Why is that?'

'McCoy said the only time you came to the hospital after that first year was to claim her belongings. I thought that was suspicious.'

'Are you saying if I had kept visiting her, we wouldn't be here right now?'

'Yes,' Tate says, hoping the story is convincing.

Perry goes from being motionless to slowly nodding. 'It was the wedding photos, wasn't it? I shouldn't have thrown them out. That's why they were so eager to talk to you. What happened after you knew about the necklace?'

Tate does the math, and no matter how he adds things up, there's no way he can get to his feet before Perry puts a few bullets into him. The shovel is stabbed into the ground a metre away, and the fact Tate's hands are cuffed ahead of him and not behind tells him in a few moments he's going to be told to dig. He looks back at Tabitha. She's staring at the ground, her arms hanging limply to her sides, her hands invisible inside the sleeves.

'What happened next?' Perry asks.

'What happened next is I connected that necklace to Scarlett McVicar and April Gilmore, and everything I know the police know too,' he says, then looks at the ground where Tabitha had been digging.

'She's not here,' Perry says.

'Where is she?'

'Who are we talking about?' Tabitha asks, looking at Perry.

'April is somewhere nobody will ever find her,' Perry says.

Tabitha flinches at his words.

'The police know I was following you. They'll find me. The best thing you can do is let me go and turn yourself in.'

'I don't believe you. I've seen you in the newspapers. I know who you really are deep down inside. You came here alone because you wanted to kill me. It's why you came here with a gun. It's why you haven't told the police any of this. This all started with Doctor Wolfgang. He said something to you, and after we're done here, I'm going to make it so he can't say anything to anybody ever again.'

'He doesn't know anything, and you're wrong about the police not knowing.'

'Tabitha made you promise her you were going to find the tape I have of her, and you were prepared to do whatever it took to get it. Am I wrong about that too?'

Tate says nothing.

'That's what I thought.' Perry nods at the shovel. 'You weren't smart enough to figure out where this was going, but you're smart enough to know what's coming next. It's time to dig.'

Chapter One Hundred and Three

Kent hears the officers introduce themselves and recognises their names. From where? Well, she's been a cop for some time, it only makes sense she'd have run into them in the past. Hazel tells them everything Kent told her to tell them.

'Show us,' one of the officers says.

They come down the hallway. Hazel enters the lounge first,

which is a little odd, given the circumstances of there being a threat. Neither officer has a firearm, but both have their hands hovering over batons and pepper spray, which is what she would expect to see, and neither of them relaxes when they see her holding a gun. She recognises them too, but can't place it, but knows Keith is the shorter of the two. Keith nods at Burrows, and Burrows steps forward, and, careful not to get into the line of fire, removes a set of plastic zip cuffs from his gear belt. 'Put your hands behind your back,' he says to Hayes, and Hayes does so. A moment later his hands are zipped up, and Burrows steps back in line with his partner.

Kent holsters the gun. 'It's possible his two accomplices are—'

Everything happens too fast for Kent to fully understand – it's a movie being fast forwarded, blurring the plot beyond understanding. Hayes gets to his feet, saying, 'About time,' and as he does, a gun appears in Keith's hand and is turned toward her, and, as if the movement is rehearsed, one appears in Burrows' hand at the same time, only his one points at Hazel. Both guns have silencers on them.

'Wh—' she says, not understanding the what, or the why, only understanding that she is in some seriously deep shit.

'Don't,' Keith says, as Kent's hand inches toward her holster.

She doesn't. She puts both palms up to shoulder height. She looks from Hayes to Hazel, whose mouth is hanging open as if wanting to ask the same whys and whats Kent wants to ask. That's when it comes to her, who Keith and Burrows are – they're the police officers who arrested Hayes at the hardware-store break-in the night the Garretts were killed.

Burrows shoves his gun into Hazel's stomach while jerking her head back with a handful of hair. Keith keeps his gun on Kent, and tells her to slowly take her gun out of the holster and put it on the floor.

She weighs up her chances. If she tries anything, they'll gun her down. She also knows they're not going to let her out of here alive. But reaching for the gun is sudden death, that she knows for sure. Every second longer she lives is a second to try and make something happen.

Just not with the gun.

'Carefully,' Keith says, as she reaches for it. She slowly takes it out of the holster, bends down, and lowers it to the floor.

'Kick it over,' Keith says.

She kicks it. It travels halfway and comes to a stop. Where is backup? And Tate, he would have gotten the alert on his phone, is he on his way back?

'Shoot them and let's get out of here,' Hayes says.

'It's not that easy,' Burrows says.

'What do you mean it's not that easy?'

'She used your name.'

'What?'

'The call came in over the radio. She,' Burrows says, nodding towards Kent, 'used your name when she called it in. Everybody knows who you are.'

Hayes' face scrunches up as he tightens his jaw. 'There has to be a way out of this.'

'There is,' Burrows says, and he pulls the gun away from Hazel and shoots Hayes in the centre of his face. Hayes drops and Kent jumps and Hazel screams.

'Shut it,' Burrows says, digging the gun back into her.

Hazel stops screaming. She stares at the dead man on the ground, a hole in the centre of his face, his eyes open, blood leaking out.

Stalling them is all Kent can do, so she says, 'The police are on their way.'

'We're already here,' Keith says.

She glances toward her gun. There's no chance of getting to it. But Hayes' gun is still under the couch from earlier. Can she get to it?

Burrows adds, 'We got here in time to stop the suspect, but sadly we didn't make it in time to save either of you.'

Chapter One Hundred and Four

The math comes back as Tate gets to his feet. It's no longer a matter of *if* he can get the shovel, it's a question of *what* he can do with it. For now that *what* doesn't extend beyond digging a hole, and even that's going to be a struggle. The ground is hard, and he's going to have to stomp on the shovel to get any penetration, which will kill his feet. It's not going to be like in the movies, where he'll have a tidy rectangle carved out in half an hour. It's going to be messy, and it's going to take all night, the entire job to be made harder and slower because of the handcuffs. Which, of course, he's okay with – he wants this taking as long as possible. Hopefully Perry will fall asleep in the process.

His thoughts go back four years to when Emily was run down. The man who did that running down was Quentin James, a guy who was unable to learn from his multiple convictions for drinking and driving, a man that society and the courts just kept giving another chance. He used one of those chances to get liquored up in the middle of the afternoon and get behind the wheel of a car, his journey ending after he ran into Emily and Bridget, and for this he would finally face serious jail time – only between being charged and showing up to court, Tate stuffed the guy into the trunk of his car and drove him out to a place very similar to this. He handed him a shovel, and while the guy dug his own grave, he said over and over how sorry he was, how he would take it back if he could. The problem was he couldn't. All he could do was say he was going to get better, but how was that going to help Bridget? How was that going to bring Emily back? 'The drinking is a disease,' he had said, then followed it with, 'I'm a different person when it happens. I'm no longer me.'

Tate knew what he meant, because he was no longer himself in that moment either. His family had been taken away from him, his world torn open. He shot Quentin James and buried him in the grave he fell into, and now it's his turn on the other side of that equation. Will the doctors and nurses ever tell Bridget he disappeared off the face of the earth? Even if they do, the following day she'll stare out the window waiting for him to arrive, and soon she won't even remember him at all.

'Dig,' Perry says.

He digs.

Chapter One Hundred and Five

Hazel is going to die. Detective Kent first, then her, then James. She imagines how they're going to look when the police arrive, laid on the floor, eyes open and vacant and staring into the distance, blood everywhere, the way she thinks her parents must have looked back when...

Kent dives for the couch. The Keith arsehole fires at her, and at the same time the Burrows arsehole lets go of Hazel's hair to do the same. Both men miss as Kent disappears behind the couch, and in that same moment Hazel tells herself she isn't going to die, not here, not now, screw that. She isn't the fourteen-year-old Hazel from the night of the attack. She's the Hazel who has spent two nights a week since then taking self-defence classes.

She slams her elbow into Burrows' stomach, kicks her foot into his shin, spins, and, before he even knows what is happening, drives the full impact of her palm into his nose, envisioning her palm coming out the back of his skull like her instructor taught her. There's a crack as his nose explodes. His head whips back, and when it rocks forward there is blood all over his face and a look on it that suggests he's not sure where he is. She can hear her self-defence coach screaming at her, yelling the job is only half done.

She drives her knee into his balls, and when he folds in half, she rams her knee into his chin, slamming his mouth closed, the tip of his tongue protruding beyond his teeth – one moment that piece of tongue is there, the next it's hitting the floor. He gets one hand onto his balls, and the other he uses to turn the gun toward her. Fully expecting a bullet at any moment from Keith, she gets both hands onto Burrows' wrist and bites the side of his thumb as hard as she can. If chewing this guy's thumb off is the last thing she ever does, then—

He takes his hand off his balls, and swings his fist at her, getting her in the jaw. She lets go of his thumb and rolls away, trying to wrench the gun from his grip. She can now see back into the lounge. Kent has tipped the couch up, and Keith is firing into it.

Burrows gets in another blow, this one to the side of her head. She holds on to consciousness, but can't hold on to the gun. She rolls out of the lounge and into the dining room and scrambles on all fours toward the hallway. From there she can ... she doesn't know. Something. Anything. The wooden frame of the hallway door explodes into splinters as Burrows opens fire. She keeps going, the angle taking her away from his line of fire. She gets to her feet and races down the hallway and isn't sure why there is no more gunfire coming her way as she reaches the front door. She has her hand on the handle – then lets it go, choosing instead to strip the jackets from the coat rack. The rack is long, wooden, heavy. She picks it up, one hand near the base, the other near the top. She hugs the wall as she makes her way back to the dining room. She reaches the lounge. Burrows is advancing towards the couch, firing into it, but Keith is down, face to the ground. It explains why Burrows didn't come after her.

Burrows doesn't see her when she steps into the lounge.

Doesn't see her when she raises the coat rack.

She punches it forward rather than swing it, the base of the rack hitting the base of his skull.

He stops shooting, falls straight down, and it's all over.

Chapter One Hundred and Six

'He's down,' Hazel says. 'Both of them are.'

Bullets have come through the back of the couch, while others lodged into it. Kent doesn't think she's been hit.

'I think I killed him,' Hazel adds.

Kent pokes her head around the end of the couch. Hazel is standing in the middle of the room holding a coat rack. Both men are flat on the ground. She gets to her feet and points the gun at them. Keith – who she shot twice in the chest – has landed face forward. She checks him for a pulse, not expecting one, and not finding one. She doesn't check Hayes – the gunshot in the centre of his face tells her everything she needs to know. She checks Burrows. The guy is still breathing.

'Keep an eye on him,' she says. 'If he moves, hit him again.'

'Okay.'

She holsters her gun, then pats herself down. No blood. No holes. How close was that to being a different story? She doesn't want to think about it, not right now. Hayes is a struggle to roll over, but she turns enough of him to reach the cable ties in his back pocket. She uses them to secure Burrows' hands behind his back.

Hazel puts down the coat rack. 'Fake cops.'

'Real cops,' Kent says. She points at Keith and Burrows. 'These two anyway.' Then she points at Hayes. 'But not him.'

Hazel chews on that, then asks, 'Is this why you were never able to figure out who killed my parents?'

'The big guy, his name is Callum Hayes, he was a suspect, but these other two alibied him.' There is knocking at the door. 'Backup is here.'

'I'm going to check on James,' Hazel says.

Before they go anywhere, Hazel steps over to Kent and puts her arms around her. 'Thank you,' she says. 'You saved our lives.'

'The way you dealt with Burrows, I'm not sure you needed me here at all.'

Hazel goes into the bedroom, and Kent to the door. There are three patrol cars in the street and two officers on her doorstep and others on the sidewalk. She explains the situation, and two officers come inside to secure the scene. She calls the officers at the Garrett house and briefs them. She asks them to look around to see if there are any signs that somebody might have broken in last night.

'Callum Hayes had a lock-pick set on him,' she adds, 'and might have come through the garage door.'

They promise to call her back. She calls Wilson and updates him. He says he's a few minutes out. She calls Tate. He doesn't answer. More cars show up on the street. An ambulance arrives, and the paramedics take Burrows away. She hopes Burrows makes it. The world would be better off if he didn't, but Hazel deserves to see a trial. She makes a few more calls, then goes and checks on Hazel and James. James is awake, Hazel explaining everything to him.

She goes to the master bedroom and watches from the window as Wilson arrives. Media are arriving too. There isn't much yet, but there will be. A story like this, neither rain nor the late hour will keep them away. All the houses in the street have lights on. Some folks are standing on porches, watching, others are at the end of their driveways under umbrellas. Wilson hunches his jacket up around his neck and runs from the car to the house. He knows what he's walking into – two dead men, including a police officer. A third person, another officer, rushed to hospital.

She leads Wilson to the lounge. The couch has been tipped up and is riddled with bullet holes. There are more in the walls. This time tomorrow every inch of the lounge will have been examined, and every bullet tracked back to where it was fired. There is blood on the carpet, and something she can't at first identify, then realises is a piece of Burrows' tongue.

Her phone goes. It's the officer she called earlier at the Garrett house. She stares at Wilson while she listens. Wilson is paler than usual, and she knows why. He misread the situation. Hayes, Burrows and Keith were always going to come after James. She suspects he's going to go even paler when she tells him what she just learned on the phone, but first she needs to confirm it. She goes back down to the bedroom where Hazel and James are waiting. Both have dressed over the last few minutes, and both are sitting on the edge of the bed.

'I called the officers at your house,' Kent says. 'They're looking around to see if there are any indications these men went there last night.'

'And?' Hazel asks.

'Is there any reason one of the couch cushions would be outside beside the garage?'

Hazel shakes her head. She looks confused. 'A couch cushion?'

Kent checks her phone. The officer said he would text her a picture, and he has. She shows it to Hazel.

'It's definitely ours,' Hazel says, 'but I don't understand why it would be outside.'

'Was it on your couch last night?'

'Yes. I mean, I can't be sure, but there's no reason it shouldn't have been, let alone end up outside.'

Back in the lounge she updates Wilson. She was right – he does go paler as he realises how badly this could have gone, and how easily he could have prevented it. She had wanted Hazel and James put into protective custody, and he had said leaving them with Tate was good enough, but really what he meant was leaving them with Tate was free.

'And where is Tate?' Wilson asks.

'He's out working on something.'

'Don't tell me he's looking into this Nathaniel Perry thing.'

'He is.'

'I told you to drop it.'

'You also told me you didn't want Hazel and James under protection,' she says, spreading her arms out to encompass the scene.

He looks like he wants to say something but can't figure out what. Today's trap was never going to work because Keith and Burrows would have known about it. She bets they volunteered for the assignment of watching the house. She looks at the two dead men and knows it could easily have been her on the floor, along with Hazel and James.

She's killed a man, but she's pretty sure she's not going to lose much sleep over it.

Chapter One Hundred and Seven

It takes Tate an hour to dig a hole that could have been dug with a digger in thirty seconds, or perhaps in thirty minutes by a man whose head wasn't still spinning from being struck. He doesn't think the grave four years ago took this long, but maybe it did. He wasn't focusing on the clock back then, because he wasn't the one running out of time. This time it's different.

Every attempt to get Perry talking is met with a demand to shut up. Perry stands on the edge of the clearing to one side, and Tabitha on the other. When he tries to get her talking, again Perry tells him to shut up. Perry seems content with the lack of conversation – at least that is until the grave is knee deep, and Perry tells him to stop.

This is it.

'Toss the shovel,' Perry adds.

The shovel is the only weapon he has, but it's no good against a gun. Nothing is, except another gun. Or distance. And he has neither. He's standing in the grave. He's not as afraid as he thought he would be, and he thinks that's because he hasn't fully accepted what's about to happen. He has hope. Hope that a serial killer will have a change of heart.

'Toss it,' Perry says.

'You won't get away with this,' Tate says. One way or the other, he will never listen again to somebody who's just come out of a coma.

'Yes, I will.'

'You won't. The police will—'

'I know. You said already. Even if they do, it will be too late for you. I'll get caught, or I won't, but either way you end up in the hole. Toss the shovel.'

Tate launches the shovel at Perry, but it's in vain as Perry steps aside, letting it crash harmlessly onto the ground. Desperation replaces the hope when Perry raises the gun, and says, 'Goodbye, asshole.'

Tate's body tightens as he waits for the bullet. Will he bleed out slowly, or will it be lights off? Will Perry aim for—?

'Oh shit, his phone!' Tabitha says.

Perry relaxes his aim. 'What?'

'His phone,' Tabitha says, walking over to Perry, giving the grave a wide berth on the way. 'Is his phone turned off?'

'Why the hell would that matter?' Perry asks, but Tate knows why, and he should have thought of it earlier. Kent will be able to trace where he's been. She'll know he came out here. Not to where exactly, but she'll figure out what part of the woods, and a corpse dog will do the rest.

'The police will track it. They'll know he was out here,' Tabitha says.

'The police can do that?'

'Yes,' Tabitha says.

'And you're only telling me this now?'

'I only just thought of it.'

'This is why I hate technology,' Perry says. He stomps on Tate's phone. In the process it lights up, and he can see there's been an intruder alert at his house. Is Kent okay? James and Hazel? Jesus, did Copy Joe go there? A second stomp and the screen cracks and the phone sinks into the ground.

'She's right,' Tate says, putting thoughts of Kent and James and Hazel aside. Whatever happened there has happened, and there's nothing he can do about it. 'The police are going to come here.'

Two more stomps and the phone is a bent and twisted clump of glass and plastic. Then Perry moves onto the burner phone. 'Not anymore.'

'They'll still know the phone's last location before it was switched off,' Tate says.

Perry looks at Tabitha. 'Is this true?'

'They do it on TV all the time,' Tabitha says.

Perry tightens his jaw and puts his free hand on the back of his neck as he paces back and forth. Then: 'We can't leave him here.'

'Run. That's your only option,' Tate says.

'Shut up.' He hooks his foot under the shovel and kicks it toward Tate. 'Fill the grave back in.'

'And then?'

'I'm working on it,' he says, but Tate knows the *and then* will see him in the trunk of that big ol' car. 'Pick up the shovel.'

He picks it up. He leans on it as he climbs out of the hole that is no longer a grave.

Both Perry and Tabitha take a step back, and Tate steps on the other side of the mound and starts scooping. When he looks down, he feels lightheaded. When he looks up, he sees Tabitha inching closer to Perry. Her hands are still hidden inside the sleeves, but something hanging beneath the cuff catches the light from the flashlight. He looks at the shovel, at the dirt, then steals another glance. The unknown something is no longer unknown, but is the blade of a knife. Tabitha sees that he's noticed, and she slowly shakes her head.

It all comes to him then. It started this morning with that moment on her doorstep where she stared off into the distance, hesitating. Only it wasn't hesitation. It was planning. She wasn't questioning whether to turn him away, but was mapping out a path of revenge she's been wanting from the day she figured exactly who Nathaniel Perry was. And who can blame her? Tate sure as hell can't. It's why she called Perry. It's why she agreed to help. Tate came here thinking he was laying a trap, only to find out it was Perry who was setting it, and to discover now that Tabitha was using him as bait.

'Hurry up,' Perry says.

It's the last thing he will ever get to say.

Tabitha swings the knife, and at the same time Tate drops behind the mound of dirt. The knife gets Perry in the neck, the gun goes off, and the bullet sails through the space Tate had been standing in a moment earlier and buries itself into a tree.

281 TEH PAIN TOURIST

Chapter One Hundred and Eight

While the police are doing whatever it is they need to do, Hazel stays in the bedroom with James, telling him in detail what happened. 'You're the one with the great imagination, what's your take on the cushion?' she asks him.

He thinks about it, and after a while shakes his head, then nods, and writes, *Maybe as a silencer for the gun?*

'The guns had silencers.'

Maybe last night they didn't?

'Maybe,' she says. 'You sure you're feeling okay?'

He nods. She's worried everything that's happened tonight will send him back into Coma World for good. But he says he's fine, and she believes him. Even so ... 'We can't stay here tonight, and I know you want to go home, but I'm going to call Doctor Wolfgang and get you into the hospital, just to keep an eye on you. Okay?'

He nods, but he doesn't look thrilled about it. She makes the call. Doctor Wolfgang sounds both tired and concerned when he answers the phone, immediately asking if everything is okay.

'I think so,' she says, then tells him what has happened. He doesn't interrupt, but he does say 'Oh my God' a few times, and at one point she hears him snap off a muffled explanation to his wife who must have been woken by the call.

'If something had happened to you both, I...'

He can't finish the sentence, and she makes it so he won't have to. 'We're okay. Both of us are okay, and the men who did this are never going to hurt anybody again.'

Doctor Wolfgang says he will arrange an ambulance to pick them up, and he'll meet them at the hospital. She realises she doesn't know Tate's address, and says she'll find it out and text it to him. She has just hung up when Kent comes back into the room.

'How are you holding up?'

'We're okay,' she says, but she really isn't sure. 'The man I hit with the coat rack, is he going to live?'

'He will.'

'James is going to stay at the hospital tonight, and I'll go stay with my grandparents. They don't know about any of this yet, and it's best I tell them in person.'

Kent nods. 'It's over. It's been a long time, but it's finally over. You and James will never have to worry about those monsters again.'

Chapter One Hundred and Nine

Tabitha lets go of the knife and Perry lets go of the gun and Tate lets go of the shovel. Perry falls to his knees and clutches at the blade sticking out of the side of his neck. He gets hold of it too, and he does the thing everybody from a young age is told not to do – he pulls it out. Tate doubts it really makes much of a difference in this case, other than bringing the inevitable forward by thirty seconds. Blood jets out like somebody has stomped on a plastic tomato sauce bottle. It hits Tabitha's jacket. Perry drops the knife and claps his hand onto the wound, then makes the same mistake again – this time taking his hand away to see what he already knows he's going to see. He puts it back. He watches Tate get to his feet, but can't do anything about it as he topples back, his legs bent under him. Tabitha picks up the gun and points it at Tate.

'I had no choice,' Tabitha says, even though she did. She's made several choices today to get to this point, and now she has one more big one to make. She's pale, and shaking, and the blood on her jacket mixes with the rain and drips off the bottom.

'I know,' Tate says, his hands in the air.

'He was going to kill you.'

'You had no choice,' he says. 'You can put the gun down now.'

'What are you going to do?'

'I'm going to check on Nathaniel.'

She shakes her head. 'We're not saving him.'

He keeps his hands in an 'easy does it' gesture. 'We need him to tell us where April Gilmore is. She's—'

'I know who she is, just not that ... I didn't know Nathaniel took her. He told me there was nobody out here, but that you would think there was. But she's somewhere, isn't she?'

'Her family deserve closure. We have to return her to them.'

She hesitates the same way she did on the doorstep. Then she nods, and she steps back and lowers the gun. Tate steps over to Perry, but it's already too late. Was too late from the moment the knife went into his neck. His eyes are open, rain landing in them, his hand limp next to his neck. A minute ago he looked shocked to have been stabbed. Now he looks shocked to be dead.

'I'm sorry,' Tabitha says. 'I couldn't risk not doing everything I could.'

'You did the right thing,' he says, and she did. If she had stabbed him anywhere else he might have gotten more than one shot off.

'There will be other ways of finding her,' she says, her words more hopeful than a statement.

'There will be,' he says, his words the same. He picks up his phone. It's completely dead. He wonders how long ago the alert came through, and who triggered it. Kent, stepping outside? Or Copy Joe, stepping in?

'Can they really trace where your phone was?' she asks.

'To a point.'

'To this point?'

'If we were in the city, then yes. But out here? It'll have pinged single cellphone towers on the way, but there's not enough of them to triangulate the location. They'll know the last one we passed, and they might be able to figure out distance but not accuracy. Finding this spot would be like finding a needle in a haystack. You did good convincing Nathaniel otherwise. Do you have your phone?'

She points the gun at him again. 'It's not going to happen.'

He immediately regrets everything he just said. 'We have to call the police.'

She shakes her head. 'There's a reason I waited for you to dig that grave before killing him.'

'You planned all of this, didn't you? From the moment I asked about the necklace.'

She nods and says, 'I couldn't let him get away with what he did to George, or to me. I couldn't risk my family finding out and losing them. I didn't know there were other women, if I had ... well, maybe it would have gone differently, but I can't say that for sure. I don't know if Nathaniel was going to let me walk out of here alive, but you were definitely going in the ground, and that means you owe me.'

Tate doesn't know if she's right or wrong. Doesn't know if his original plan would have worked or not. 'You want to bury him.'

'I do.'

'You're turning this from self-defence into murder.'

'We both know it was premeditated murder all day long. I could have called the police this morning, and didn't. I could have called you, and didn't. If this makes it into a courtroom, they're going to say it was a revenge killing, and they'd be right. If we call the police, my life is over and Nathaniel wins. Or we leave him here. Nobody will ever find him. The police will have no reason to try and track you, and even if they do, it's like you said – they can't find the body. He just disappears off the face of the earth.

You can say you spoke to him. That he knew you were on to him. That he ran. We can go to his house and pack a suitcase and make it look like he left.'

'You've thought this through.'

'I have.'

'It's a lot of work, Tabitha.'

'Don't you think I know that?'

'And if I say no are you going to shoot me?'

She looks at the gun as if unaware she has been pointing it at him. She shakes her head and lowers it. 'Here,' she says, and hands it to him. 'My fate is in your hands. The question is, what are you going to do?'

Chapter One Hundred and Ten

The handcuff key is still inside Tate's own pocket, only now he can get to it without getting shot. He removes the cuffs, then they drag the body into the grave, patting Perry down first for his keys and for the other cellphone, the one that Tate followed to get here. He's tempted to leave Tabitha here to clean up the mess and come back for her after he's checked on Kent, but again he reminds himself that whatever has happened there has happened, and anyway, he has faith that Kent can handle anything that comes her way. Anything beyond that can be picked up by the cops watching the house. Tabitha picks up the broken burner and is about to toss it into the grave when Tate tells her not to.

'Having him found would be bad enough, but worse if the phone is on him.'

'But it's broken.'

'Techs might still be able to get something from it.'

She drops it into her pocket instead.

He's getting ready to start covering the body when Tabitha picks up the shovel.

'I want to do it,' she says.

She first skims the ground where Perry bled out, slinging the dirt into the grave. Then she works away at the mound of dirt. It takes fifteen minutes, and there's still dirt left over that together they kick around the floor of the clearing. He doesn't like any of this. Burying a body a few feet deep in the woods isn't foolproof, and of course when Kent realises Perry has disappeared, she might track Tate's phone and ask why it was in the middle of nowhere. What will he say to that? The truth? No, because the truth would see both him and Tabitha doing time.

With his own phone broken, it makes leaving the woods difficult. It's 3.00am and still dark, and he's not even sure daylight would help even if they waited for it.

Tabitha picks up the flashlight and nods to the trees behind him. 'We came in from that direction.'

'You're sure?'

She shines the flashlight at her other hand – she's holding a compass – another sign she was well prepared. 'Positive.'

She leads the way, and two minutes later they're at Perry's car. He puts the shovel in the trunk and Tabitha gets in behind the wheel and starts turning the car, a move that will require a bit of back and forth. Tate walks to his car. He has a headache from the blow he took earlier, and he still feels lightheaded. He pops the glovebox and is relieved to find Kent has some painkillers in there. He takes two.

They drive toward the city in separate cars. There's still no traffic. He turns the radio on for the news, and learns there has been an incident at a former detective's house – believed to be Theodore Tate – and that two people have been killed. He tightens his grip on the wheel and is wondering if he should scream now or pull over first, then has to do neither when the reporter adds the men killed are possibly responsible for the deaths of Frank and Avah Garrett nine years ago. Hopefully that means Kent and James and Hazel are okay.

They pull over at the roadworks near the care home. He pounds the shovel into the gravel and digs a hole deep enough to hide the knife in. He fills the hole in and stomps it down. In the next few days this whole stretch of road will be paved over. If he thought they could have gotten Perry under there too, he would have suggested it, but it would have taken longer digging up compacted shingle than the forest floor. He breaks the lock on the shipping container with the shovel. He searches for a fuel canister, and finds a ten litre one that's three quarters full. He leaves the shovel in there among other shovels.

Tate leads the way again for the next part of the journey. They make a turn short of the city limits ten minutes later, taking a road that leads them to the beach and away from houses and any signs of life. They park up on the sand. He wipes down the steering wheel and the door handles of Perry's car, then pours petrol through the insides of it.

He uses a road flare he swiped from the storage container to light the car up. Tabitha balls up the yellow slicker and tosses it in, and the moment it's out of her hands he remembers the burner phone is still in it. Techs getting information from a broken phone is one thing, but getting it from one turned into a crisp another entirely, but even so it's evidence he'd rather the police not have. He looks around and spots a long piece of washed-up driftwood, and uses it to hook the jacket back out. He puts it into the edge of the water. A moment later he's pulling out a glob of melted plastic that he drops into his pocket. He tosses the jacket back into the flames.

They drive into town, and keep going south. They don't make

any conversation. It's after four when they reach Perry's antique store. The alleyway leading to the parking lot out back has weeds pushing through the pavement, and cracks and potholes filling with rain. The walls are cinderblock, patched paintjobs used to cover graffiti. Tabitha's car is the only car around. He pulls up next to it.

'What are you going to tell Herschel?' he asks.

'Nothing.'

'Won't he ask?'

'He won't know. He will have slept through me leaving, and he'll be asleep through me coming back. I've made sure of it.'

'How?'

'Do you really want to know?'

He doesn't. 'Was the knife part of a set?'

'No.'

'Will Herschel notice it's missing?'

'I only bought it today.'

Her words are a reminder that if they had called the police the question wasn't going to be if she would go to prison, but for how long. 'You must really have had faith I was going to help you.'

'I looked you up. I knew you'd do the right thing.'

It bothers him that she thinks this is what the right thing is. And yet here they are.

'We should check the store since we're here anyway,' she says. 'Maybe Nathaniel keeps the tapes here.'

'There's more than one?'

'If he's filmed me, then he's filmed others.'

'The shop will be locked.'

She holds up Perry's keys. 'I took them from his car.'

'There'll be an—'

'Alarm, I know, but the code will be the same for the shop as for his house. George once told me Nathaniel's as useless with alarms as he is with computers, so they made it simple. They used his birthday so he'd never forget. We're here, we're alone, and there are no security cameras. I say we take a look.'

He is desperate to get home and check on the others. Desperate to lie down, because the pills haven't helped. He just wants to fall asleep in the hope his headache will be gone when he wakes up. He pops the glove compartment and grabs the box of latex gloves he saw in there earlier. He pulls out two pairs and hands one to her. There's a small flashlight too that he takes. 'Don't make a mess,' he says.

There are three locks on the door, one high, one in the middle, one low, all accessed by the same key. Tabitha gets the door open, and they remove their muddy shoes and step in, and Tate closes it behind them. He was expecting the back door to lead into an office or the workshop, but it goes directly into the store. He can see through to the front and the streetlights outside. He flicks on the flashlight. There are chairs and couches. There are tables full of lamps and books and goblets that will all land loudly if he bumps into them. There are mirrors and clocks in all directions reflecting the light. The walls are lined with framed photographs and the floors lined with rugs. There are racks of clothes against the righthand wall. Tate has never been an antique guy. There isn't anything in here he wouldn't toss into a bin if he found it in his garage. They move through it, following the beeping to the alarm pad. When they get past a large bookcase full of plates on stands, the view opens up, and he can see the counter with the cash register, and behind it a doorway that must lead into the office or the workshop. The control panel for the alarm is just inside the doorway. If Tabitha is wrong about this, they'll have to get out of here quick. She taps in four numbers and the beeping stops. The only sound left is the rain on the roof.

He points the flashlight around the room. It's an office. A

desk on a large rug in the middle of the floor and a filing cabinet in the corner and one window looking into the parking lot. Tabitha switches on the desk lamp and goes through the drawers. He can't remember the last time he saw an office that didn't have a computer. The rug theme throughout the shop and office extends through a doorway to the right and into the workshop. He goes in. There are tools hanging from the walls, tables full of different types of saws and shelves full of varnishes and paints. There are a hundred pieces of equipment he can't name and a thousand places you could hide a video tape. Tabitha is swearing as she moves from the desk to the filing cabinet. He hopes she isn't ransacking the place. There are no windows in the workshop, so he flicks on the light. The tapes could be hidden inside a wall or under a floorboard. He looks at the cans of paint and varnish. Could one of them be hiding what they're looking for? Even if the tapes are here, it could take all day to find them. How long do they have before anybody notices Perry missing?

'There's no money in the cash register,' Tabitha says, joining him in the workshop.

'Meaning there has to be a safe somewhere,' he says. He looks around the workshop. 'How good is Perry with this stuff?'

'Very.'

'So maybe he's made a fake wall to hide the safe.' He looks at the rug he's standing on; it takes up most of the space between the benches. 'You know what's weird? That a guy making a mess with woodchips and sawdust would have a rug in here rather than just the wooden floor where he could easily sweep up.'

'Let's check it.'

The corners are pinned down on the left by the legs of a bench, and weighed down on the right by an empty shelving unit. He lifts them and kicks the rug free. Tabitha crouches and rolls it up.

In the middle of the floor is a locked door. Tabitha pulls Perry's keys from her pocket. It doesn't take long to find the one that fits.

Chapter One Hundred and Eleven

The scene has wound down for the night. Wilson has gone home. Hayes and Keith have been taken to the morgue, Hayes' removal almost comical, with it taking four people to lift him. The close neighbours have been interviewed but nobody saw anything – which, tonight, isn't a problem. With nothing left to see, even the media have left. Kent is tired. She wants to go home, but with the way things have panned out, she figures Copy Joe or even Original Joe could be waiting there for her. It's too late – or too early – to find a motel room. Best bet is to drive to the station and get a few hours' sleep, but she doesn't even have her car.

An officer guarding the street radios her to say Tate has arrived, and she's grateful to hear it. She tells the officer to let him through. She stands in the doorway and watches him pull up in her car. He parks opposite and runs over. He's soaking wet, clothes stuck to him, hair stuck to his face.

'Where in the hell have you been?' she asks.

'Thank God you're okay,' he says, and before she knows it he's hugging her. Her arms hang to her sides for a few moments, then she wraps them around him. 'I'm so sorry,' he says. 'I heard it on the news. How are James and Hazel?'

'James was in his room while it all unfolded, but Hazel kicked arse. If it wasn't for her, things might not have turned out how they did. One of them was Hayes. And you remember Officers Damien Keith and Lance Burrows?'

He shakes his head, then winces. 'No. Maybe. Should I?'

'You okay?'

'Just tired. Tell me about Keith and Burrows.'

'They were the officers who arrested Hayes at the hardware store nine years ago. They were all in on it.'

He looks like he's going to fall over when she says that. 'Jesus. It's why we never got anywhere.'

He's about to step inside when she stops him. 'You can't.'

'What?'

'I'm sorry, Theo. It's a crime scene, you know how it is.'

'Can I at least get a change of clothes?'

'I'm sorry.'

'My car?'

'Of course.'

'And no sign of Copy Joe?'

'None. How did you get on with Nathaniel Perry?'

'Can I see Hazel and James?'

'They're not here. How did you get on with Perry?'

'Not well,' he says.

'Not well?'

He looks around, and, seeing nobody can hear them, he says, 'I went to his house. I asked him some questions about Georgia. He was happy to talk. I asked him some questions about Scarlett McVicar, and he clammed up. Then I left, only I didn't leave. I waited out front, and a few hours later he left. I followed him for a bit but lost him.'

'And?'

'And that's it.'

'That's what you've been doing all night?'

'I drove back to his house to wait for him, but he never showed.'

She looks him up and down. 'You look like you did more than just wait for him.'

'I looked around his yard a little bit, that's all.'

'Jesus, Theo.'

'I didn't touch him, I swear.'

Her cellphone goes. It's Wilson. Hopefully it's not more Copy Joe stuff. She takes the call. It's not Copy Joe stuff at all. Sixty seconds later she's off the phone.

'You're coming with me,' she says.

'Coming where?' Tate asks, crossing the road with her to her car.

'You'll see when we get there,' she says, but she's pretty sure he already knows.

Chapter One Hundred and Twelve

Kent doesn't mention Perry as they drive, not wanting to talk about him until she's seen what she knows Tate has put into motion. He'll deny it, because that's what Tate does. Then she has a big decision to make: push him, or let it go? She tells him more about the night, about the alarm going off on her phone, capturing Hayes, Burrows and Keith showing up, the shitshow it turned into when the bullets started flying. She tells him the reason she got out of there alive is because Hazel has been learning self-defence over the years.

'I should have figured out Burrows and Keith were in on it back then,' he says.

'Were the pieces there?'

'Maybe I just didn't look in the right places.'

She's not so sure about that.

They reach Perry's antique store. A tarp has been hung over the window to block the view from the media that will soon show up. She turns down the alleyway and they park among a smattering of vehicles out back.

'Wait here,' she says.

The rain has finally stopped. She reaches the back door. It's been forced open, the edges all twisted and broken. It's what triggered the alarm, which brought the security guards. The lights are all on inside. She makes her way through a pathway of furniture, many of the pieces originally owned by people who are now dust. She's always thought if anywhere in the world was haunted, it wouldn't be castles and cemeteries, but places like this. Wilson is over by the cash register, his fingers tapping out a message on his phone. It's been a tough night for her, but an even tougher one for him, made tough by a bunch of shitty decisions.

'She's in there,' Wilson says, nodding toward a doorway that leads into an office.

She goes through the office and then into a workshop. It reminds her of the workshop her grandfather spent his retirement in – except her grandfather didn't have a trapdoor leading into a basement. Like the back door of the shop, it has also been prised open, the edge of the door and flooring ripped from the lock. The smell almost sends her back into the store. She can't blame Wilson for not having warned her – she should have figured it out from the phone call. Bodies smell. Bodies kept in tiny rooms smell even more. There's a light on down there. She can hear voices.

She takes the stairs, bringing the two paramedics into view. April Gilmore is sitting on the side of the bed staring beyond them and at the wall. She is pale, gaunt, a rash around her neck, her hair flat and dirty. Her fingernails are chipped and ragged, her eyes bloodshot. Her lips are chapped. Kent can't tell if the marks under her eyes are bruises or something else. Kent's chest tightens and her stomach tightens and she takes a deep breath to hold on, and the deep breath smells of stale air and sweat and from whatever chemicals are in the chemical toilet in the corner. She has to sit on the stairs to stop herself passing out. She suspects Nathaniel

Perry is dead, and that Tate killed him, and she can't rightly say how much of that she hopes is true.

She takes in the rest of the surroundings. They're in a concrete box, between four and five metres square, with a ceiling she can touch with the palm of her hand. A pullcord hangs from a bulb in the centre of it. There is a bed pushed against one wall. There's a bookcase adjacent to it. A thick chain runs from April's ankle to a metal eyelet pounded into the wall. They can't find a key for it; lying on the ground are a pair of bolt cutters that weren't strong enough to cut through the chain or the lock. A larger set of bolt cutters are on the way.

'It's going to be okay, April,' she says, but she's not sure she says it out loud, and if she does, she doesn't say it loud enough to be heard. Maybe that's because she doesn't believe it. April is alive, but she may never be okay again.

One of the paramedics turns around. She wasn't aware of it till now, but it's the same two who wheeled Burrows out of Tate's house a few hours ago. He comes over.

'You okay?'

'I will be,' she says. 'How about April?'

'I don't even know if she knows that we're here. The restraint on her leg, you could remove it and she'd probably keep on sitting here.'

'Is there any chance of asking her what happened?'

'None. She hasn't said a word since we got here. If we hadn't sat her up she'd still be lying down. He's probably had her here the entire time.' He shakes his head. 'What in the hell is wrong with people?'

She isn't sure how to answer.

A workshop full of tools above, surely there's something up there that can cut through the lock or the chain? Or remove the eyelet from the wall? She gets to her feet. Only now does she notice the TV adjacent to the stairs. It's a boxy fourteen-inch screen only seen these days clogging up landfills. On the shelf next to it is a video camera that takes the pocket-sized video tapes that bridged the gap between VHS and digital. A line of those tapes is stacked neatly next to the camera. There are twelve with names and dates going back fifteen years. She recognises some of the names. She knows what is going to be on them.

There's a gap in the middle where one has been removed.

Chapter One Hundred and Thirteen

Tate watches as an officer removes a large set of bolt cutters from the trunk of a patrol car that's just pulled up. An hour ago, when he and Tabitha found April, everything changed. At first, he thought she was dead. She looked it. And smelled it. But then he had seen the pulse in her waxy throat and had heard her breathing. She was asleep. Tabitha was seeing the same thing. He's seen a lot of fear and horror on her face over the last twenty-four hours, but nothing like that. He thought she was going to throw up. As it was, she slipped off the bottom stair and twisted an ankle. He helped her to her feet, and that's when they saw the TV and the tapes. They were labelled. Tabitha's one had two dates on it. One from during the affair. Another from the night Perry broke into her house.

By then his headache had faded, and he was no longer feeling lightheaded. They staged the store to look like a break-in, rather than somebody who entered with the keys. He has little doubt the bread crumbs lead directly to him, but that doesn't mean he shouldn't try to sweep them up. When Tabitha removed the video tape, he didn't slide the rest together to conceal the gap. It suggested the possibility of another victim being out there who had taken their revenge – which is actually what happened. By now that tape is either a smouldering piece of plastic in the log burner in Tabitha's dining room, or about to be. Perry disappearing does mean that there's no closure for Tabitha's parents, or for other victims and their families, but he thinks they'll come to believe Perry met a very bad end. It won't be enough – nothing ever can be – but it's something. Unless Perry claws his way out of his grave, or somebody claws their way in, he's hoping never to see Tabitha again. If he does, it will be because they're sitting in court together with lawyers.

The adrenaline that has gotten him through the night has almost completely faded. His body feels heavy, his thoughts too, which is a concern. He needs to stay sharp for what's ahead, and if he can't stay sharp, then he needs to stay quiet. How easy it would be to say the wrong thing, especially now that he's starting to feel woozy again, probably because he's finally slowed down.

He lowers the seat and leans back. His clothes are wet, and he's uncomfortable and cold, and these things give more weight to his exhaustion, his body now heavy enough to fall through the floor of the car and the ground beneath it too. He wants nothing more than to go home, but he suspects that won't be tonight – and even if he doesn't end up in custody, his house is a crime scene. He still has his gun on him, which is a problem, since it's illegal to carry one. Plus the gun is illegal too. If he gets taken to the station for questioning – and he thinks he will – it will be a problem. He should have dumped it on the way home earlier – somewhere he could have retrieved it from later. It was a mistake. He tucks it into the pouch behind the driver seat. He adds the handcuffs too, and the surviving burner phone, which is now locked with a PIN number he set up earlier. The other burner – the one that actually burned – is in a dumpster, along with the cardboard boxes they came in. In somebody's roadside bin he added the torn-up receipts and the duct tape he removed from Perry's window, having swung past to remove it before walking through a water-filled gutter to get the mud off the bottom of his shoes and pants. He closes his eyes and links his hands over his stomach and gives in to the exhaustion.

He doesn't know how long it is until the passenger door is opened by a burly officer with the kind of beard found on flannel-wearing cabin builders. Could have been seconds, or five minutes, or an hour. 'Get out,' the officer says.

Tate gets the seat back into the upright position. 'Why?'

'I said get out.'

So this is how it's going to go. Tate gets out, and the officer spins him so he's against the car. The ambulance is gone, so he's gotten at least a few minutes sleep. He doesn't feel any better for it. His hands are cuffed behind him, and then he's escorted through the shop. He feels like he's walking through thick soup. He looks around like it's his first time here. All the lights are on. Between the last time and now, his opinion on antiques hasn't changed.

Wilson is in the workshop and gets straight to the point when he says, 'You want to tell me how you found her?'

He looks at Wilson, looks around the workshop and at the trapdoor, then back at Wilson. He manages to swallow down a yawn, then realises he's starting to zone out.

'Are you listening to me?' Wilson asks.

'Of course I am.'

'Good. Then tell me how you found her.'

'Found who?'

Wilson sighs. 'I thought you said you were listening.'

'I'm listening, I just don't understand what I'm listening to.'

Another sigh from Wilson, then: 'How about we just have a straight conversation.'

'I can do that, once you tell me why I'm here.'

'You know why you're here. How did you find her?'

Tate shakes his head. Normally he could do this all day, but given how tired he is, he doubts he can last much longer. 'Find who?'

'April Gilmore.'

'April Gilmore?' He nods toward the trapdoor. 'Her body was down there?'

'You know damn well she was down there and still alive.'

'What are you talking about?'

Wilson sighs again. 'Where is Nathaniel Perry?'

'Back up a moment here. April Gilmore is alive?'

Wilson sucks in a deep breath and lets it out heavy. 'I thought we were going to have a straight conversation.'

Before Tate can say anything, Kent comes up from the basement. She sees the cuffs on him. 'Take those off,' she says to the officer.

'They stay on,' Wilson says.

'There's no reas—'

'I said they stay,' Wilson says.

'You found her?' Tate says, looking at Kent. 'You found April?'

'We did.'

'And she's alive?'

'She is.'

'How is she?'

Kent takes a moment with that, then says, 'I'm not sure that's a question anybody will be able to answer for a long time. You want to tell us what led you here?'

Now it's Tate's turn to take a moment. 'You brought me here.'

'You going to tell us where Perry is?' Wilson asks.

He swallows down another yawn, then, 'Like I told Kent earlier, I followed him from his house but lost him. He was heading north, and he looked to be in a hurry.'

'Yeah? Did he come by here?'

'If he did, I didn't see him.'

'We know you staged it to look like somebody broke in,' Wilson says. 'The problem you have is that records show the alarm was deactivated a little over an hour ago, and reset seven minutes later, then set off a minute after that.'

'Perry must have set it. He must have come here for something.'

'And what would that be?'

'You'd have to ask him.'

'Only we can't do that, can we. Last chance, Theo. Where is he?'

'I don't know.'

Wilson takes in another deep breath, followed by another long exhale. 'If that's the way you want to play this then I have no option but to place you under arrest. You have the right to refrain from making a statement and to remain silent. We'll pick this up back at the station.'

Chapter One Hundred and Fourteen

Tate is tossed into an interrogation room and the handcuffs left on. It's a bullshit move. He has been on the other side of these walls enough times to know how this goes. They'll make him wait in the hope it'll throw him off balance. He sits on the floor and tries to bring his cuffs down his body and up in front of his feet. He can't do it. His wrists are sore, and his shoulders are tight. He gets up and sits at the table. He rests his forehead against it. He's feeling lightheaded again. He has come to the conclusion that ever getting dry clothes again is an unattainable fantasy. He closes his eyes and gets to stop thinking about it.

He's woken up thirty minutes later when Wilson comes in and

sits opposite. There is one of those moments – just a second – where he isn't sure where he is, before it all comes back to him, plus his shoulders and back hurt like hell. At least he's feeling sharper. Wilson looks tired. And stressed. Tate doesn't doubt he's had a rough night, with a rough few days ahead.

He straightens up. 'You gonna remove these cuffs?'

'You're still wearing them? Ah, geez, that's an oversight,' Wilson says, and he stands up to remove them. He drops them into his jacket pocket. Tate knows it isn't an oversight, but says nothing. Wilson sits back down. 'You're in a—'

'What? A world of shit? We wouldn't be if you had listened to Kent about Perry. You'd have found April before whoever else did.'

Wilson looks angry. 'You're—'

'And you almost got Hazel and James Garrett killed. I warned you they were targets, and now it looks like Hayes and these other arseholes went there last night too to kill them, and the only reason they didn't is because I got there first.'

'The same way you got to April Gilmore first?'

The thirty minutes of sleep has been short, but helpful enough that he should be able to get through this without tripping over himself. 'I didn't get to her first. In a moment I'm going to ask for my lawyer, and then they're going to get here and I'm going to tell them everything, and they're going to tell the media everything, and you're going to be eviscerated. Your job is to protect people, Eric, not put them in harm's way.'

'Don't tell me what my job is, Theo.'

'Somebody has to. You're lucky you're not facing a bunch of cameras right now, explaining how you got James and Hazel killed.'

Wilson, who was leaning forward, now leans back. He lowers his voice when he says, 'There's no way I could have known there were cops involved.'

'That won't save you. How's it going to look when the public find out you were warned and did nothing? That those men tried to kill them two nights in a row? How will it look when they learn that you shut down any investigation into Nathaniel Perry, despite there being overwhelming evidence that—'

'There was no evidence that he was anything.'

'There was, only you never saw it, and when Kent came to you—'

'She came to me with nothing but a bullshit theory with no weight to it.'

'And I ran with it, and I linked it to Scarlett McVicar, whose husband is in prison, by the way, and I spoke to Perry about it, and when I told him what I knew he fled. He's out there probably driving as far away as he can—'

'He's not driving anywhere, Tate. We found his car. It's burned to a crisp.'

'So he knows the police are after him, and is hiding his tracks.'

'We found his wallet at home. If he was running, he'd have taken it.'

'Not if he didn't want his credit cards tracked.'

'There was cash in it.'

Tate shrugs. 'I'm not going to pretend I know what he was thinking.'

'No, you're just going to pretend the guy is still alive and that you're not the one who set fire to his car or found April Gilmore.'

'If I found April, I'd be a goddamn hero, and my lawyer would lead with it just for the goodwill alone.'

'Bullshit. You found her because you tortured it out of Perry.'

'I want my lawyer.'

Wilson taps his fingers on the table and holds Tate's stare. The anger is still there. But there is fear too. Tate knows it's coming – a way out of this for both of them.

'When you think about it,' Wilson says, 'if I had sent officers to the Garrett house when you first asked, there's every chance it would have been Burrows and Keith who responded since they were already making their way there. And if not, they at least would have heard the call and known not to show up. They would have waited it out. It's not like we could have kept the guards there forever. We only know in hindsight it wasn't a matter of if, but when.'

'You're saying things worked out for the best,' Tate says.

'Yes.'

'Let's hear it.'

'Excuse me?'

'There's no camera in here. No recording devices. You want a way out where you get to keep your job, so let's hear it.'

Wilson says nothing for several moments. Then: 'We suspected there may have been one, possibly two police officers involved with the Garrett killings. We concocted a sting. We set up a fake trap at the Garrett house and let officers in the department know Hazel and James weren't really there, but were at the house of a former detective. That's where the real trap was, but only Kent and myself and one former detective – you – knew about it. It's why Kent was there, and armed. We just couldn't have known the two officers we used at the scene would end up being the very two we were meant to catch. There was no way we could have known that.'

Tate lets that hang for a few moments. Then says, 'I can see people buying that. And Hazel?'

'Hazel has medical expenses for James the department can help her with, and she wants this over. She'll say whatever we need her to say. She's a team player.'

'I've been thinking about Perry,' Tate says. 'The police are understaffed and underbudgeted. Georgia Perry's parents hire a former detective to poke around because the police don't have the resources to open a closed case. The former detective finds something, and he brings it to the police. The police are putting it together and are about to get a warrant, only Perry is spooked. He goes on the run. He'll show up, but we may never find out who broke into Perry's store.'

Now it's Wilson's turn to let the idea hang, before saying, 'I can see people buying that. You saw the video tapes?'

'I was never there.'

Wilson nods. 'There was a gap. Whoever was there took one. Like a victim who figured him out. If Perry has been dropped into a hole somewhere, it could be connected to that missing tape.'

'Makes sense, and means there's no reason to drag my name into it. No reason for me to need a lawyer. No reason for either of us to go to the media and point out any mistakes, because there were no mistakes.'

'Then we have an understanding,' Wilson says.

'We do. Only there's one more thing.'

'Yeah? And what's that?'

'I hear my lounge got shot to shit. You're going to buy me a new couch.'

Chapter One Hundred and Fifteen

An exhausted-looking Tate is leaning against the wall by the elevator when Kent sees him. The fact he's walking out by himself is a good sign. Even so, he looks frustrated, and she figures he has many reasons to be. The doors open, he steps in, and she follows. It's six in the morning, after a long night in a long week with no end in sight.

'You still can't go home,' she says.

'I know, but I need my car.'

'Where are you going to go?'

'I haven't decided.'

She reaches into her pocket and hands him a key. 'Hazel knew you wouldn't be able to stay at your place, so she said you can stay at hers. James is in the hospital for routine observation, and she's staying at her grandparents.'

He takes the key. 'What about you? You want to stay there too?'

'I'll come back here and get a few hours' sleep upstairs, then I'm back at it.'

The conversation stops, and she figures neither of them have the energy to make any more. The elevator doors open into the parking lot under the building. They make their way to Kent's car. Kent drives up a ramp and hits a button to get the gate open to the street.

'How's Burrows doing?' he asks.

'He's got a busted nose and cheek, a cracked orbital socket, a severe concussion. Plus he bit off the tip of his tongue, but he'll be okay.' She makes the turn into the traffic. It always surprises her to see this many cars on the road at such an early hour. 'When Burrows and Keith turned their guns on us, I thought we were done. Hazel, James, myself.'

'I should have been there.'

'If you had been, then April would still be in a basement.'

'It wasn't me who—'

'Sure it wasn't. Tell me something: why do you think Burrows and Keith didn't file the time of the original arrest nine years ago as the exact same time of the shooting? Having it a few minutes later created doubt. It's what got under your skin.'

'Can we do this tomorrow?'

'You'd rather just ride in silence?'

'I'm tired, I'm cold, my clothes are wet, I just want this night to be over.'

She lets it go. Tate cracks the window open a few inches and puts his face into the stream of cold air to help keep him awake. Then he winds the window back up and turns toward her. 'My guess is they needed leeway in case there was something found at the house that proved Hayes was there. It would have put Burrows' and Keith's story at risk. Is Burrows talking?'

'Not yet, but when he does, the first thing he'll do is ask for a lawyer,' she says.

They get a string of green lights and make it to the edge of town before she restarts the conversation. 'You going to tell me what happened with Perry?'

'I went to his house and spoke to him. He was spooked, and—'

'And he ran. You said that. How'd you break your cellphone?'

'I dropped it.'

'And if I were to get a warrant to see where it last was before you dropped it, what would I find?'

'I'm not sure.'

'And if I were to check the GPS on my car to see where it's been tonight? What would I find then?'

He says nothing. She looks over at him, and for the first time he looks panicked.

'The GPS is new,' she says, looking back at the road. 'A few months ago they started getting installed in the fleet. You'd think it would have been done years ago, but as you know, it never was. But the department is finally catching up.'

He still says nothing.

'My guess is my car has been on quite the journey, and if I were to recreate it in reverse order, it would take me to Perry's store, then to his burned-out car, then to wherever he's buried.'

'I didn't kill him. I give you my word.'

'I want to believe you.'

'I swear, Rebecca. I didn't kill him.'

'Is he dead?'

He doesn't answer.

'You asked me before who you were talking to, Rebecca the cop or Rebecca the friend. Right now it's the friend, and if you want to keep me as one, you'll tell me the truth. Is he dead?'

'He is.'

'And you didn't kill him.'

'I didn't.'

'But you know who did.'

'I do.'

'I told you about Matthew Durry's "pain tourist" theory?'

'You did.'

'Nathaniel Perry was one too. He filmed his victims so he could relive the moments. I bet he'd watch those tapes the same way people look at holiday photos to remember being there. Every time he looked at them, it would be like he was going back on a tour through the misery he had caused. The person on that missing tape would have known that too. She would have known that every now and then he would watch the worst moment of her life.' She takes a deep breath. God she's tired. 'I guess what I'm saying is that the woman on that missing tape, I wouldn't blame her for killing him.'

'I didn't say it was a woman.'

They drive in silence for a few more moments, and now it's Tate's turn to restart the conversation. 'Perry made me dig a grave. I was standing in it. He was—'

'Jesus,' she says.

'He was going to shoot me. Same way you thought you were done when Burrows and Keith tried to kill you, I thought the same thing with Perry. Only this person saved me, and they saved April, and they saved whoever would have been next. I swear I was only ever going to take him into custody.'

'What happened?'

'He tricked me.'

'And then what? This woman tricked both of you?'

'I didn't say it was a woman.'

'It sounds premeditated.'

'I'm not saying who it was, Rebecca.'

'You don't need to. He probably called her after you called him. You do know we'll be checking his phone records.'

'And you'll get nowhere with them. He was a bad guy, Rebecca. The tapes will show that.'

'Why did Wilson let you go?'

He explains Wilson's mistakes. His reputation, and the reputation of the department. The cover-up. She knows it will take others who were at Tate's house tonight to keep the secret. But they will. The department protects its own. She should be angry, but she's not. The things she's seen over the last few days ... maybe Perry is where he deserves to be.

'Will he ever be found?'

'Not if you delete the GPS data,' he says.

'I was lying about the GPS,' she says. 'My car doesn't get done till next month.'

Chapter One Hundred and Sixteen

Tate falls asleep for the last few minutes of the car ride, waking when Kent gives him a shake. Rather than driving him home, she's driven him directly to the Garrett house. He makes his way up the wheelchair ramp and unlocks the front door. The house is empty. And cold. By how much did he beat Callum, Burrows and Keith here the other night? Minutes? Hours? Why take the cushion outside? They may never know.

He's sluggish as he finds sheets and blankets in the linen cupboard and makes up the couch. How many movies has he seen where people have been hit on the head, then told not to fall asleep? Is that a real thing? He's too tired to care either way. He turns the heating on and spreads his clothes out to dry. His wallet and broken phone were taken off him when he was brought into custody, but given back before he left the station. He puts them on the coffee table, then remembers the burner phone and gun and handcuffs hidden in Kent's car. He's annoyed at himself for something so stupid. The burner can direct Kent within walking distance of Nathaniel Perry. Would she look for him? He doesn't know. Yesterday's Kent would have, but today's Kent is a different person, and either way, this is to-morrow's problem. He stares at the spot where Frank and Avah Garrett were killed.

'I'm sorry it took so long to find who did this to you,' he says. He doesn't believe in ghosts, but he feels better for having said it.

The next thing he knows he's waking up at ten in the morning with the sun coming in through the lounge window. The same sense of not knowing where he is waking up that happened at the police station happens again now. This happened a whole bunch back when he'd drink so much that drinking more made perfect sense to him. Mostly he'd wake up at home, on the couch, or in bed, or on the floor, or on occasion in the empty bathtub. His head would throb, the world would spin, nothing would focus, his joints would hurt. He kept the cure-all for such things at hand; the only question was whether he wanted to add ice.

Now he's waking the same way, the hangover meaning a back-slide into a life he doesn't want, before everything rushes back to him – James, Hazel, Perry, digging his own grave. He isn't drunk, he's just feeling old and sore. He has lost track of time. Is it Thursday? Yes. Wait, no, it's Friday. He sits up and rubs the back of his neck and waits for the room to stop spinning, which it does, but the headaches from last night are still there – not bad, but not gone either. It isn't until he's in the shower that he realises it's Saturday. Freshened up, and in clothes that are finally dry, he goes through the house, tidying up the fast-food bags left behind by the officers. He loads all their dirty coffee cups into the dishwasher and starts a cycle. He folds up the sheet and blanket he used and leaves it on the end of the couch. He knows there's a cat here, but hasn't seen it. He finds its bowls and fills them with food and water. He rummages through the bathroom and finds some pain-killers and swallows a couple down.

He gets a taxi to a nearby strip mall and heads into a phone store. He's greeted by a tech guy with a patchy beard and a pimply chin. Despite the fact his phone is broken, the guy is confident he can transfer the data across to a new one. 'Just depends on how much on the inside we can retrieve. Give me an hour to see what I can do.'

Tate spends that hour at a diner a few doors down. He reads a newspaper while eating an all-day breakfast, but like they say, it's yesterday's news – and yesterday's news is mostly about Copy Joe and Simone Clarke, and the only story about James Garrett is the one Kent planted.

When he gets back to the phone store, the guy proudly tells him where most tech guys would have given up, he was able to switch out a circuit board and transfer all the data onto a new phone. He has switched the SIM card over too. Tate pays for it and checks his messages. There's one from Kent. He wasn't sure she'd be working the weekend, but she must be. The police are done with his house.

He can go back home.

Chapter One Hundred and Seventeen

The story continues to grow, and the only reason Hazel's cell-phone isn't ringing off the hook is because the media don't have her number. She doesn't have any social-media accounts either, so there's no way for journalists to contact her, other than doing what they're doing now – which is waiting outside her grandparents' house. Right now those journalists are getting louder, and a moment later there's knocking at the door. A glance through the window and she can see it's Doctor Wolfgang.

'As you both know,' he says, once they're settled in the lounge, 'James's story is unique, but what he did with Nathaniel and Georgia Perry takes it to a whole new level. I was getting ready to ask for your permission to write a research paper, but now I'm thinking there is enough material here for a book. I would like to be the one to write that book, with all the proceeds going to you, to do with what you see fit.'

Hazel and James stare at each other for a few moments, then she looks back at Wolfgang. 'That's very generous, but I'm not sure we want that kind of attention. The media already have a million questions about what happened last night, and if they find out about Coma World, we'll never get a moment's peace again.'

'I understand that,' Doctor Wolfgang says, 'but their focus on you would be just for a few days until they move on. It's completely your choice, of course, but I have some connections in publishing. I can reach out and see what they think.'

James writes, *We could do with the money.*

'I know,' Hazel says. 'But you know what people are like. Some people are going to call him a freak, and others are going to call him a liar.'

'The proof is conclusive.'

'These days proof is subjective. Proof is what you want it to be.

Half the population will believe and sympathise with James, and the other half will accuse him of making it up for the publicity, and then there'll be some who will argue James was never shot to begin with, while others will say he deserved it.'

'You're right,' Doctor Wolfgang says. 'There is always going to be an element of that, and that's whether we write a book or not, but there is a lot of good here. It gives people hope for loved ones who are in comas. It gives them comfort they might be having a similar experience. James's story can bring more money into coma research. It can help.'

'And it might scare people too. James had a good nine years, but that doesn't mean others will. What happens if you think your loved one is locked inside a nightmare? Because I bet that's the first thing people will start saying online.'

'But it can be good too. We know coma patients listen, and now we know it's possible they can do more than that. It will encourage their families to visit them more. It will encourage people to be more like you were with James.'

She looks over at James. He is holding up his pad: *At least see what the publishers have to say?*

'Something like this,' Wolfgang says, 'it's not just a New Zealand story, this is global. Publishers from different countries will pay advances. I'll take time off work, and I think I could put something together within a month, I really do, and we can include a lot of what James has written. And it needs to be soon, because right now there is a lot of free publicity.'

'It does all sound good,' Hazel admits.

'Give it some thought. If it's a direction you want to take, then we sit you down with a journalist and tell more of the story. At the moment people don't know anything about what really happened last night. But we talk about Coma World, we get the police to verify how James's notebooks led to April Gilmore being found, and we see if we can get some offers. It can mean moving into a new house. It can mean helping James with his education.'

She looks at James. He's nodding. He writes *Please,* and underlines it.

'Make some calls,' she says. 'Let's see what we can do.'

Chapter One Hundred and Eighteen

A full-scale manhunt is in progress for Nathaniel Perry – with everybody thinking he's either on the run, or is a victim of foul play; Kent, on the other hand, knows which one is true. There were ten other women found on the tapes, eight of whom they've contacted, and one of whom disappeared six years ago. And then there is Alana Foley, who might be Nathaniel's first victim. Alana would have been fourteen years old according to the time stamp on the video tape, recorded fifteen years ago. Two months after the video was made, Alana took her own life. They don't know at this stage if she confided in any friends or family about what happened to her, but they do know she didn't report it to the police. Kent hasn't – nor will she – watch the video Perry recorded of his sexual assault on her. She can't bring herself to do so, and thankfully there are others here who are trained and counselled for such a thing. Instead, Kent has been provided with a screenshot from the video – a close-up image of the necklace around her neck that Perry had given to each subsequent victim. Earlier Vega spoke to Alana's parents, who were able to confirm the necklace was a gift from Alana's grandmother. Their family had lived on the same street where Nathaniel Perry was raised. Eleven tapes – plus the one that was missing, which she assumes belongs to Tabitha Munroe. Phone records show two calls were made between Tabitha Munroe and Perry yesterday. When questioned about the call, Tabitha said, after speaking to a private detective, she had some questions she wanted answered, so called Perry at his shop. He was busy, and returned her call last night. What was their conversation about? It was about her asking for the truth and still not getting it.

Some of those women willing to talk openly to the police have said they knew Perry intimately, and the breakups were amicable – that was, at least, until they moved on with their lives and got married. It was then that he showed up again, this time to punish them with threats of showing soon-to-be husbands videos he had secretly filmed. There were multiple stories of the women waking up knowing they had been raped, and the necklace taken. None considered going to the police. The police still don't know what led to Georgia's death, but it's possible she saw or heard something that led him to throwing her from the balcony. It's likely they will never know for sure.

All of this has meant the foot has been taken off the Copy Joe investigation, which is why she's here working the weekend instead of heading off, and watching her niece's netball game like she promised. She is tired and irritable, having only gotten an hour's sleep this morning back at her house, sleeping with a knife under her pillow and a chair wedged under the door handle while an officer sat in the lounge. There is a real danger she will crash and burn during the day. Her irritation grows as, for the next hour, she has to sit in an interview room answering questions about last night. She feels like a criminal as she goes over, in detail, what is an officer-involved shooting. Her story stays the same each time she tells it, and despite now seeing things that she could have done better, shooting Keith isn't one of them. It was him or her, and all things considered, she likes to think that the two detectives tasked with interviewing her are happy she's the one they're talking to, and not Hayes, or Keith or Burrows.

Now she returns to a desk full of messages, including a text from Tate asking if she can give him a ride. She texts him back and says she's not a goddamn taxi service, then immediately regrets it. She could have helped him out. Her phone pings a moment later, Tate telling her it's no problem, and asking if he can catch up with her later today. She texts him back that she'll be in touch.

She checks in on Burrows' condition. She learns he woke up two hours ago, and with his first breath and the tip of his tongue missing, he asked for a lawyer, and with his second said he has no memory of last night due to the blow to his head. Having seen the result of that blow, it might be the only honest thing Burrows has said his entire life.

Her next call is to the doctor treating April Gilmore. She is expecting to find that April was malnourished, beaten, physically abused and sexually assaulted, and her expectations are met. Physically she will recover, but mentally and emotionally – there's no way to tell.

'She has a long road ahead of her, likely paved with therapy and pills,' the doctor says, before saying she will let Kent know when April is in a state to be interviewed. 'I hope you catch the bastard who did this and put him in a hole somewhere.'

'We will,' Kent says, knowing the catching part won't happen, but the hole part already has.

She tries to focus on the win. They got the men who killed Frank and Avah Garrett. They got April Gilmore back, Scarlett McVicar's husband will be set free, and a guilty man has disappeared off the face of the earth. And yet when she closes her eyes, all she can see is Simone Clarke, the plastic bag over her head, her eyes open, *New Zealand Crime Busters* on repeat on the TV in front of her.

It's only a matter of time before Copy Joe kills again.

Chapter One Hundred and Nineteen

Tate's car is a mess from having been searched, and the inside of the trunk is wet because that search happened in the rain. In the house there is no new couch. Blood has dried on the carpet, and there are holes in the wall. Nothing some patching and repainting won't take care of. He takes a knife to the carpet and drags it into the backyard, knowing no amount of cleaning will convince him bits and pieces of skull and brain aren't still mixed into the fibres. He goes about dragging the ruined couch out there too. The second couch has fared well, but it does look lonely.

He still has to find a way to get into Kent's car to retrieve his gear since she's refused to come and pick him up, but for now he wants to go and see Bridget. He's grabbing his keys when his phone goes. It's Hazel.

'How are you?' he asks.

'We're okay,' she says. 'We're at our grandparents' place. James is going to stay here for a few days, and then we're going to introduce him to the house again. Maybe it won't be such a shock the second time, and maybe there's some closure there now too. Anyway, I just wanted to say thanks for everything you did for us. If you hadn't come to our house two nights ago, we'd be dead.'

'From what Kent has told me, I very much doubt that would be the case.'

'I appreciate the sentiment, but we both know that's not true. We owe you. I know we can never repay you, but if there's anything you ever need, all you have to do is ask.'

'I appreciate that,' Tate says, 'but all I care about is that you guys are okay.'

'I wanted to ask you something. Doctor Wolfgang wants to write a book about James's experiences. He thinks it could help coma research, as well as provide for James and myself. What do you think?'

'I think the world owes you, and if you can get something back from it, you should.'

'We could definitely do with the money it could bring. But Doctor Wolfgang thinks we should go public with James's story, and that includes talking about Nathaniel Perry. Are you okay about that? I don't have to mention your involvement at all, but won't mention any of it if you don't want us to.'

He thinks on it for a moment, and can't really see how it can hurt. If anything, it makes the scenario he and Wilson came up with make even more sense – of course the police wouldn't reopen the case on the word of a coma patient. 'It's fine,' he says.

'There's a TV journalist we can talk to as soon as tomorrow morning if we want to, with the piece going to air tomorrow night. I think we're going to do it.'

'Just batten down the hatches once you do, because there'll be an onslaught of people asking questions.'

'Will do. Maybe we'll even get a hotel somewhere, or leave the city for a few days. But before we do, James wants to see you. I'm not sure why, but he said it's important.'

'He's remembered more?'

'He won't say, only that he wants to come to your house. Is it okay if we come by tonight? We can bring dinner. Do you like Thai food?'

'It's my favourite, and tonight is fine.'

'I'll pick some up on the way.'

Chapter One Hundred and Twenty

Yesterday:

Yesterday he was on every front page, he led every news bulletin, he dominated watercooler talk in every office around the country. He doesn't take personally all the things being said about him; after all, Copy Joe is only an image, a persona, a tool used on the road to becoming famous. For some he is a monster, for others a fraud for imitating a monster. He doesn't care how people see it, as long as they see it. Yesterday he was a celebrity. He saw 'I survived Copy Joe' T-shirts selling online. He saw a meme of Simone Clarke captioned with 'I gave a killer performance'. Another was a silhouetted Copy Joe next to Joe Middleton with the line, 'I did it his way'. As if sensing his new celebrity status, Jessica has called four times, probably having figured out she'd made a mistake and wanted him back. He didn't answer. Yesterday he had a big future ahead of him that didn't include her.

Today:

Today he's a nobody, the guy mentioned on the TV news after the first ad break. Today he is a small asterisk, he is a footnote relegated to the gutter, his story buried by the ton of shit that went down last night, from a serial killer on the run, to a home invasion where people died. But that's not even the most newsworthy part. No, it turns out James Garrett, the person who survived getting killed last night, is the one who pointed the police in the direction of the serial killer. And how? Because he dreamed it in a goddamn coma.

What. The. Hell.

Story after story has been coming out this afternoon about James Garrett and some *Forrest Gump* gibberish about a coma he survived that led him to solving a murder, and people are going to lap it up, and it's unfair. He's going to be famous. And why?

For taking a bullet to the back of the head and making shit up? Jesus, anybody could do that. Some people just get everything handed to them. He sees an interview with Detective Eric Wilson, who's asking the media to respect James Garrett's privacy, but that isn't going to happen now, is it? The media are going to be all over him like white on rice, and Wilson knows it. Wilson adds that the poor kid hasn't even had the chance to mourn his family, hasn't had the chance to visit their graves, hasn't had the chance to ground himself in his new reality.

He reads story after story, thinking...

Thinking...

Thinking fuck James Garrett, and fuck the wheelchair he rode in on.

Once he was delusional, thinking he could be the one to figure out who Joe Middleton was. Delusional to think he could do what the detectives couldn't. He couldn't be a hero back then, but he sure as shit can be one now. He was always going to be the man to stop Copy Joe. Stop him, revel in the adulation that follows, then star in the movie written about him. He has already picked out who he's going to pin everything on – a husband lost to grief and gone insane, who even tried to burn down his old house a few nights ago. Copy Copy Joe, he thinks, and smiles at the thought.

But unless he tosses James Garrett into the mix, nobody is going to give a damn. The problem is there's no getting within a mile of James Garrett before hitting a wall of media. He needs a way to draw the kid out.

He just has to figure out how.

Chapter One Hundred and Twenty-One

The three of them have dinner, and whatever important thing that James has to say ends up waiting as Hazel tells the story of last night's experiences, before Tate gives her a version of his own that is fifty percent truth and fifty percent fiction; but he does tell her what kind of man Nathaniel Perry turned out to be.

When they're done, James puts a pad on the table. He writes, *Can I look around your house?*

It's not what Tate is expecting. He looks at Hazel, and it doesn't seem to be what Hazel was expecting either, because she shrugs.

He's about to ask why when James writes, *Please.*

'Sure. Want me to help you?'

Hazel can help.

They both look at Hazel, then Hazel looks back at Tate and shrugs again. 'You want Theo to wait here?' she asks James.

Is that okay?

'I guess so,' Tate says. 'I'll tidy up.'

'I didn't know he was going to do this,' she says to Tate.

'It's okay. Take your time.'

Hazel wheels James into the lounge. He looks around, pointing where he wants her to go. Tate tidies up then goes into his office to catch up on work. For the next hour he loses himself in making notes for the next episode of *The Cleaner*, and jumps when Hazel knocks on the open office door.

'You're done?'

'He's done looking,' Hazel says, 'but he's not done. He wants to talk to you.'

'About?'

'He won't say.'

They head to the lounge. James stays in the wheelchair, Hazel takes the couch, and Tate takes the armchair. James has his pad on his knee, and he writes on it, then shows it to Tate.

I want you to tell me everything you can about Emily.

Chapter One Hundred and Twenty-Two

Hazel and James do the interview the following morning, with the hope being that once one large story is done, the media's appetite will be satisfied. The interview is with Cassandra Ripley, a well-known host of a well-known Sunday-night current affairs show James has never seen. She's flying down from Auckland for the piece, then flying back in the afternoon to work with the editing team to prepare it for air tonight. James will share the interview with Hazel, with him writing down his answers. The segment will be edited to show his responses are more instant, with the words being shown on the screen and dubbed over by a voice actor. The entire thing will be made to fit in a forty-minute time slot, with anything left over made available online from tomorrow.

Cassandra shows up at the house with a small crew, a collective and audible groan coming from the journalists outside as they each become aware they've been scooped. Hopefully this will mean they'll all leave soon. This evening Hazel is taking James to the cemetery to see where their parents are buried, and it'd be nice not to be followed. After seeing Detective Wilson's comments on TV last night about James still not having been to his parents' graves, Father Richardson, a priest from the church connected to the cemetery where they are buried, called Hazel to offer them sole use of the church and grounds this evening, saying he can lock the gates and doors so no media or onlookers can join them. He also offered to accompany them to the grave and say some words, which Hazel agreed to.

Cameras are set up in the lounge, and James's grandmother hands out cookies she has baked for the occasion. His grandfather, an avid photographer in his youth, asks the cameraman a lot of questions about f-stops and lighting. The woman operating the boom has tattoos starting from her wrists and disappearing under her rolled-up shirt sleeves and keeps calling him 'Champ'. Cassandra is in her thirties, long dark hair, flawless complexion, a smile that makes him feel warm inside. He used to think people in their thirties were old. Now he's not so sure.

'Remember,' Cassandra says, when they're about to begin, 'we can stop at any time. I just want to make sure you're comfortable, okay?'

He gives her the thumbs-up. They're sitting in the lounge. He's in an armchair rather than the wheelchair. Hazel gave him a haircut earlier, and styled his hair, and gave him pointers when he shaved. It was his first time shaving, but not his first time being shaved.

The interview starts. Earlier they had gone through some of the bigger questions, and Cassandra pulls them out again now, getting quickly to Coma World and how, for nine years, his parents were alive there, and how it felt to wake up to discover they were gone. He tells them his reaction to Doctor Wolfgang saying he may have overheard the aftermath of a crime, and his reaction to learning the man he overheard was now a murder suspect on the run, and how it led to a young woman being found who had disappeared weeks earlier. They talk about the men who killed his family, and how they were stopped when they came back to finish the job.

'I'm curious,' Cassandra asks, now heading away from the questions he knew were coming, 'this ability to fill in the blanks of somebody's life after they have died, can you do this with other people?'

He nods, and he holds up a card that says *yes*. He also has one that says *no*. Easier that way than writing the same thing over and over.

'You've done this?'

He hesitates, then holds the *yes* card up again.

'With who?'

Silence, then, 'He won't want to say,' Hazel says, 'but he's doing it for somebody who lost a family member. Somebody we both owe a lot to.'

To James, Cassandra asks, 'You're saying you're writing an ... an equivalent of Coma World?'

He nods.

'You're writing this by hand too?'

He shakes his head.

'He's typing it this time,' Hazel says.

'Have you read any of it?' Cassandra asks Hazel.

'It's not for me.'

Back to James, and, 'Is it as detailed as the world your parents were in?'

James nods, then writes, *Yes. It's in the same world, but a separate story.*

'This is incredible,' Cassandra says. 'Can people in those separate stories interact? Can one story impact another?'

It's a good question, and one he hasn't thought about. *It's possible, but it hasn't happened yet.* He suspects it will if he were to write about more people, the same way you run into people you know at the mall.

'And you can do this for anybody?'

I haven't tried.

'But it's possible you can take somebody who has passed away and bring them to life again? Not technically, but in a ... well ... an almost virtual way?'

'It's not like that,' Hazel says. 'He's not a supercomputer that can process a person's past in order to give them a future. He's a story-teller. He always has been. It's not like he's saying this is what would have happened, it's more like he's saying here's a potential, almost like a parallel world.'

'Yes, but he told a story that led to Nathaniel Perry's arrest warrant,' Cassandra says. 'That's more than just a story.'

'No. That was him overhearing Nathaniel Perry confessing to his wife, and then using it.'

'But even so,' Cassandra says, 'don't you see the potential here?'

'No,' Hazel says, and James doesn't see it either.

'James has the ability to bring comfort to people who have lost loved ones. What he has is a gift that can help many people.'

Now James gets it. The media are no longer waiting outside his house, but he can picture others arriving soon, the same way they arrive outside a tent with a healer who can fix broken spines and take away cancers. He doesn't want that kind of attention, and perhaps this interview was a bad idea after all.

But ... if he can help people, then shouldn't he?

'I can tell you from experience it may be a comfort, but it won't bring closure,' Hazel says. 'It's a Pandora's box that, once opened, you can't close again. I miss my parents every day, and now I miss a version of them I never had. James has taken the abstract of the people they could have been and turned it into a reality. You call it a gift, but I wouldn't be so sure.'

Chapter One Hundred and Twenty-Three

Tate has been watching the story play out over the afternoon ever since the news of James's connection to Nathaniel Perry was released. The question is being asked – if James can catch one murderer, can he catch others? The story is blowing up online, and there are promos already playing for tonight's interview, which James and Hazel recorded this morning. He wonders how Hazel and James are holding up. Last night they were awake until one in the morning talking about Emily. James's request was so left-field he didn't know what to make of it, but as he started talking, he found himself remembering things he hadn't thought of in a long time as he showed photo after photo of his daughter. He thought James was going to take notes, but he didn't. Occasionally James would write questions, and Tate would answer them. James didn't say what he was doing, but Tate got the sense he was creating an alternate world for Emily, the same way he created one for his family, for which he needed as much information as he could gather. Tate didn't know last night how he felt about that, and today he's no closer to figuring it out. Even so, it didn't stop him from bringing Emily to life for people who had never met her.

His theory is confirmed that afternoon when Hazel shows up by herself and hands him a USB drive. 'I wanted to bring this to you, rather than email it.'

He stares at the drive, as if what's on it can be seen on its plastic surface.

'You know what this is, don't you,' she says.

'This is if Emily had lived?'

Hazel nods. 'The first two years after the accident. I haven't looked through any of it, so I don't know what's in there. But James, he's done this because he thinks he's helping. He's typing out the third year at the moment. But it can be like ripping open a wound. Part of me wishes he didn't have this ability. He explained more of it to me earlier. He said he can imagine what people's lives are like up till this very day, but not tomorrow. He said if somebody in Coma World bought a lotto ticket for tomorrow, he wouldn't know if that ticket was a winner until tomorrow.

With our parents, he said he said goodbye to them in that world, but with your daughter he said there's always going to be a tomorrow. I can see how that would become addictive.'

Tate can see the same thing.

'The TV station is already forwarding on requests for James to write worlds for their loved ones too. They're offering money. James wants to help. He thinks if he can bring comfort to people, then he should. But once people see you making money from this, their perspective will change. They will see you as somebody trying to cash in on the pain of others. I'm starting to regret going down this road, but Doctor Wolfgang rang before and said he spoke to a literary agent who thinks he can get us a six-figure deal, more, maybe, so maybe it'll be worth it. I don't know. James laughed at that. He said it was ironic that in Coma World he couldn't get published, and now he's getting published without even writing a book. So, you'll take a look?' she asks, nodding towards the USB drive.

'How can I not?'

Chapter One Hundred and Twenty-Four

The police station is almost deserted – Kent is on the fourth floor, watching the only other person up here with her, a janitor who is dragging a vacuum cleaner behind him. It makes her think of Joe Middleton, and how he flew under the radar here, all those years vacuuming the same floors. The thought of him coming to her house once again gives her the chills. Maybe she should give Matthew Durry a box of matches and her address.

She's tired. Another long day in another long week and all that, and with Monday only hours away, she doesn't see next week being any better. The janitor senses he's being watched and looks over at her. He cocks his head and points at himself. She smiles and shakes her head, and thinks they should check the guy's alibi – after all, what better way to replicate the Carver than work a forty-hour week in his shoes? And hell, maybe it is the janitor, because her theory that Copy Joe could be a cop has hit a dead end. They have gone through the lists of those who attended the scenes and ruled everybody out – twice. They've gone through photographs of the crowds and found nobody of interest. It's been a day full of failures, and now she's doubting her theory. Who had access to the crime scene three years ago? Plenty of people – not just then, but in the years ahead and the months that followed. Who knew about the beer bottles? Well, cops are pretty careful about what they say, but it's easy to imagine a detective or a patrol officer who saw the scene mention it as an aside, something along the lines of 'the bastard even had a couple of beers while killing her'. Of course Matthew Durry was drinking a lot back then too, so who's to say his memory from those days is accurate? Who's to say it was nothing more than a burglary, nothing more than somebody driving past and seeing an open window? And even if he's right about his pain-tourist theory, it doesn't mean the person who broke into the house back then is the same person who broke into it this week. There are a hundred different possibilities. A thousand. Including Matthew forgetting to lock the door, and Simone Clarke and Denise Laughton opening theirs to a stranger. Sure, it wouldn't be hard for a police officer to figure out where the actors worked and lived, but it wouldn't be hard for others to figure that same thing. Perhaps only Martin Thomas was followed home, and Copy Joe already knew where Simone lived. Or vice versa. Or he's followed them from previous re-enactments as he planned all this out.

And now people are asking, could Nathaniel Perry be Copy Joe? DNA from Perry's house is currently being compared against

DNA found at the crime scenes. The answer isn't in yet – the results are due within days. If it is him, then they have to figure out where he is. She knows Perry is out there somewhere, dead and buried, and though she hasn't had that conversation with Wilson, she's pretty sure he knows it too. If it is Perry, they'll have to put pressure on Tate to reveal where the body is.

But she doesn't think it is him. Perry's thing is a very different thing from Copy Joe's thing. Even so, Tate's actions mean there can be no closure for the families of Perry's victims. How can there be, when they think he jumped onto a cargo ship and is halfway across the Pacific?

Their only respite has been Copy Joe not striking again. It's possible whoever his next target is may have been somebody on the list of those under surveillance for their own protection – but that protection ended this morning, Wilson pulling the pin on it, saying there wasn't the budget to watch these folks indefinitely. He's right, of course, but she would have expected at least a few weeks of round-the-clock surveillance. She can't shake the idea that tomorrow morning she'll be heading to another crime scene. At least those they were guarding will be taking measures to protect themselves.

It's getting late. The interview with James Garrett is airing soon. She'll watch it – at the very least it will remind her to accept the small victories. Then she's going to visit Martin Thomas. She thinks of all the people Copy Joe might target, it will be him. He told her he'd be willing to help out in any way he could – an offer that has stuck with her. A story put into the news brought Frank and Avah Garrett's killers out of the shadows, and despite what Wilson thinks, she believes they can get that to happen again.

After watching the interview, she'll go and see him.

Chapter One Hundred and Twenty-Five

First, there will be the serial killer – in this case Copy Joe has picked out a grieving husband gone mad – Matthew Durry. Second is James Garrett, a victim to make one of the biggest stories even bigger – Garrett complicates what was originally a risk-free finale, but he believes the risk is worth it. And third is Martin Thomas – the other half of the acting team that recreated his attack on Denise Laughton. A lot of moving parts, but nothing he can't handle.

Things are already in motion – the guy bound and sedated on the living-room floor is proof of that – and even though there is much more to do tonight, he finds himself pacing the room, distracted by the TV. James Garrett is on there talking about Coma World. The stuff they say he can do in this interview, it's like magic. But magic isn't really magic, is it – it's illusion. It's sleight of hand.

Really, magic is lying.

And that means James Garrett, with his dumb-fuck notebook, is lying, and his dumb-fuck sister is too. They want the world to think he's some kind of Rain Man, but he's actually a conman – has to be, otherwise it alters the entire world's perspective on comas. Medical science would change – doctors would bring guns into coma wards and shoot their patients in the head to give them their own make-believe fantasies. Given how the interview is going, he wouldn't be surprised if by this time tomorrow half of the country will have reached out to Garrett, asking for alternative lives for those they've lost. His own parents died a few years back, and personally he couldn't think of anything worse than pretending they were still alive.

The idiot sister starts talking: 'He's not telling you what would have happened, he's telling what could have happened. He gave our parents alternative lives. How much of that would have played out the same way if they hadn't died? I don't know. I'd say somewhere between none and some, and there's no way to prove that one way or the other. But when you read it in the diaries, you'd swear it was all true. You'd swear they were lives lived. That's the power of it, but it's also the pain. Their lives end when the diaries end. He can only—'

He switches off the TV with the remote rather than throwing it at the screen. He walks into the dining room and stares at the knife mark he left the other night when he stabbed a plastic bag onto it. He takes deep, calming breaths and tells himself there is enough fame to go around, and what's good for James Garrett is, ultimately, good for himself too. He imagines his own inevitable interview, where he'll sit with a journalist ten times sexier than Jess and she'll ask questions ten times smarter than anything Jess ever asked, including what it feels like to be the man who caught Copy Joe. He'll tell her he was just doing what anybody would under the circumstances, that all he cares about is the world being a safer place. Is he a hero? Well, that's her word, not his. He's just an average guy who stopped a serial killer and, sure, if people want to make a big deal out of that, and make a movie out of that, then he's fine with it. Finer still if they want him in it. She sure as hell won't nag him about the way he uses the washing machine.

It's time to pick up the night's second victim.

Chapter One Hundred and Twenty-Six

The wind is cold, and the ground damp, and his daughter's gravestone looks like a small, dark cave on a horizon full of small, dark caves. It's been a while since Tate came out here so late – not that nine o'clock is late, but it does seem that way when you're hanging out with the dead in the dark. He used to come out here often after dark a few years back – sometimes with a bottle in hand – but has since outgrown both those habits.

Reading the diary James wrote out earlier has thrown him. He printed it out and read it on the couch over and over, putting James's words into a fantasy and watching his daughter grow up. And in those fantasies Bridget was there too. Emily's days were full of slice-of-life moments – restaurants, movies, school, play, grandparents, pets. All the things that make life a life.

He has brought a blanket to the cemetery to sit on to stay dry. He really can't tell one way or the other if he should be here, should be reading these diaries to Emily. Truth is, he doesn't believe in any kind of afterlife. His daughter is gone, there is no heaven, and yet here he is anyway, hoping he's wrong while reading to her a life she could have had. Hazel had told him James was working on another two years, and having read the two he already has, he's desperate for them. As he read about Emily's life, he recognised within himself the same addiction he first had to revenge, then had to alcohol, and now has to atonement. He has done bad things for good reasons, but bad things nonetheless, and despite not believing in a higher power, he still wants to make sure the scales are tipping in his direction when he dies. He has what he never knew he had until Emma died – and that's an addictive personality. And now it's there again – the desire, the pull, the need. Why did James have to give him this incredible gift? He understands better now the warning Hazel attached to it. For others, perhaps, a couple of extra years with memories that aren't real may be enough, but for Tate, it's not, and he's struggling – he's addicted to something that isn't real, that is impossible to obtain.

So he sits on the blanket on the damp ground by his daughter's grave, wearing a headlamp to light up the pages, and he reads to her, knowing she's in a place where she can't hear, a place where nothing exists. But he can only read so much – he doesn't know if it's because he's tired, or if it's a combination of the cold and the hit he took to the head two nights ago, but a third of the way in the words look like they're swimming on the page, and the headache he's been keeping at bay with painkillers is back. He carries everything back to the parking lot next to the church, where his is the only car around. The church is an old stone building that needs a good water-blasting, especially on the south side, where moss and lichen blend into the ferns and flaxes. Lining the upper walls are stained-glass windows in which Jesus does Jesus stuff: turning water into wine, turning one fish into ten, turning sick people into healthy ones. He imagines Carpenter Jesus wouldn't have had any problems turning a three-bedroom house into a four.

He's getting into his car when the church doors open and Father Jacob steps out. Jacob is sixties, tall, thin, thick grey hair parted to one side. They make small talk, Father Jacob asking how Bridget is, and Tate telling him she is as well as could be expected, before the priest goes on to ask if Tate was involved in any of the recent stories in the news, to which Tate says no – more just so he can get out of the conversation and go home. It works, but Father Jacob does get to add that somebody broke into the church last night and smashed apart the donation box, stealing around thirty dollars in change. A few years back somebody broke into the church and murdered the priest here, so Tate sees the petty theft as a sign the world is getting better.

By the time he gets home, a feeling of light-headedness has joined the headache. He reminds himself that this is the part in the movie where the person begs the other person to stay awake. Once again he's too tired to care. All he wants now is to sleep for the next twenty-four hours. He puts his phone on mute and heads to bed.

Chapter One Hundred and Twenty-Seven

Matthew Durry can't finish things at home. Not when his kids might be the ones to find him. They've been through so much, with so much more to go, but where he first thought his suicide would hinder them, he now realises it will free them. The only way he can be a good dad now that Angela is gone is to step out of his kids' lives in a way that makes it impossible to step back in.

For the last hour he's been hunched over the coffee table in the lounge, working on the goodbye note, while the TV plays in the background. Mostly he's been able to tune it out, the nightly news merging into an hour-long reality show about farming before merging into a current-events show. Misery, sheep, misery – and now some interview about a kid whose parents were executed in front of him: misery, misery, misery.

The kids are in bed asleep, and his mum has gone to bed too. How quickly she has stepped into the parental role Angela left behind, and how quickly her burden is about to double. He feels guilty about that, but he can't change his mindset. He can't explain it, but if somebody could offer him a pill to make him feel better he would turn it down. He wants the misery. Perhaps the reason he didn't kill himself three years ago is because he deserves the pain. Angela suffered, and isn't it only right he suffers too? He hurts, and he wants to hurt, and he doesn't want the cure to be anything other than sitting on a beach with a bottle of whiskey and a bottle of pills.

The goodbye note complete, he writes his mother's name on it and the address, as if he's off to the post office to send it. He tucks it into his pocket, along with his driver's licence, so the police can quickly identify him. He quietly checks in on the two kids, and watching them sleep only confirms he has made the right decision in leaving.

His shoulders immediately ache from the cold when he steps outside. His car is out on the road – he left it there earlier so he wouldn't wake his family by starting it in the garage. He was told this morning that the police would no longer be guarding his house, but there's an officer parked opposite in an undercover car. What in the hell is the point of being in an undercover car when you're still in your uniform like this guy is? They nod at each other.

He's unlocking his car when the officer steps out of his and crosses the road. He looks familiar, but Matthew can't place him. Was he one of the officers who worked the scene after Angela died? Maybe. It's going to bother him.

'Mr Durry?'

'I'd appreciate being left alone,' he says.

'I'm sure you would,' the officer says, his eyes going to the bottle in Matthew's hand. 'Have you been drinking tonight?'

'Any other night it'd be a yes by now, but not tonight. Truth is I'm planning on it.'

'So you're planning on drinking, and you're planning on driving too?'

'First the driving, and then the drinking.'

'And then?'

'I haven't done anything wrong. Look, shouldn't you be keeping an eye out for Copy Joe rather than hassling me? Isn't that your job?'

'It's my job to make sure everybody is safe,' the officer says, then he sighs, rubs his hand across the back of his neck, and adds, 'Look, I guess ... well ... given the circumstances I can give you a lift.'

'Excuse me?'

'If you've got somewhere to be, I'd be a lot happier making sure you get there in one piece without a car to drive back home in.'

'You'd do that?'

'Only this once, but it stays between us. I don't want to get chewed out over it.' The officer walks back to his car, makes it halfway, then turns back. 'You coming?'

Police aren't usually this helpful, are they? And where does he know him from? If he takes his own car, the guy is going to follow him anyway. Perhaps this way he can get dropped off at a bar and duck out a back door and get a taxi. It's not like he needs to save his money. He crosses the road to a twenty-year-old Toyota that hasn't seen a car wash in the last nineteen of those. He gets in, and he's doing up his seatbelt when it comes to him who the officer is – only ... only he's not a police officer at all.

'Hang on, aren't you—' he begins, but he doesn't get to say the rest, because by then the syringe is already in his leg and the sedative flowing into his bloodstream. He swings the bottle of whiskey at the guy but doesn't get to find out if it hits.

Chapter One Hundred and Twenty-Eight

By ten o'clock the Christchurch population is hunkered down behind drawn curtains and locked doors, leaving the bars and restaurants shuttered up and the streets empty. The only good thing about a Sunday night, Kent thinks, is people seem too depressed to be out killing or robbing each other, more so as the winter kicks in. Perhaps the same is true for Copy Joe – he's not biding his time until the police protections lift so he can target somebody involved in the case.

She calls Tate. After a few rings it goes to voice mail. She leaves a message saying she's heading to Martin Thomas's house in the hope she can convince him to be part of a trap similar to the one that flushed out the Garretts' killers. She hangs up and realises she's relieved he didn't answer. Bringing Tate into this would be bringing in more cons than pros – the biggest con potentially seeing her burying Copy Joe out in the woods. Not that that would be her intent – it's just when you're dealing with Tate, that's the way things can go.

When he rings back, she'll say she has it sorted.

But it also means this is on her. She needs Martin Thomas to do something or say something that will engage with Copy Joe. It needs to be something that sounds like a throwaway line, and not something that could incite Copy Joe's rage and prompt him to kill the person closest to him. She doesn't doubt Copy Joe will see the news too. His actions at the crime scenes suggest he's desperate for an audience. The guy probably has scrapbooks filled to the brim with articles about himself. For Copy Joe, his victims may be nothing more than tools to become famous.

She pulls into Thomas's street. There's a fifty-fifty split between houses with lights on and those in darkness. Usually at this time of night in her own house the only light is coming from the TV set as she falls asleep in front of some old science-fiction movie – a tradition she started with her dad after begging him to stay up late to watch *Alien* when she was ten years old. She parks outside Thomas's house, where half the lights are on. She walks the cracked footpath to the front door and rings the bell and, when she doesn't hear it ringing, she knocks. No extra lights come on. No sound. No signs of life. She knocks again. No answer, which is odd, because before she left the station she called and though he was at work, he confirmed he would be home by the time she got here. Perhaps he was delayed. Or fell asleep when he got home.

Or...

Or maybe Copy Joe has paid him a visit.

She uses the light from her phone to navigate her way around the house. She reaches the garage and can see Thomas's car parked in there. Okay, so he did make it home. She keeps going. The back door hasn't been repaired since Copy Joe prised it open, instead it's been reluctantly jammed back into the frame. The areas damaged from the break-in have swollen as the exposed wood sucked in the wet weather. She knocks. Nobody answers. She pushes at it. It grunts and grinds against the frame, then shudders open. She can't hear a shower running. Can't hear a TV. Can't hear a thing other than the wind swirling around the house.

'Hello?'

Nothing. The only sound is her footsteps as she steps inside.

'Hello?'

She reaches the hallway. No Martin. No signs of life. Just left-over pieces of drywall from the patched-up ceiling leaning against the wall. The joins in the ceiling haven't been plastered over yet, and the draft coming through the gaps makes her shiver. Thomas explained the other night that a broken roof tile led to all the damage, and that he was fixing it up himself.

She doesn't like this. And Thomas won't like it either, if he's home and asleep.

'Hello?'

Still no answer.

She makes her way to the dining room. A dark suit is hanging over the back of a dining-room chair, the white clerical collar making it stand out. For a moment she wonders why a priest would be here, let alone one who left his outfit behind, before real-ising it's probably something Martin is wearing for a role he is playing. Perhaps he has a wardrobe full of costumes for different parts he plays, or for photoshoots...

'Shit.'

It all comes to her then – an actor with uniforms, an actor who's played Joe Middleton, an actor who would have overheard police conversations at crime scenes, an actor who would have access to keys at each of the crime scenes, an actor who could have followed Simone Clarke home then broken into his own house to make it look as though he was followed too, an actor who is so desperate for fame and attention that an audience of one isn't enough, so he brings photographs into the room to pretend they're watching. She was wrong. She has made a fundamental mistake, and the problem with fundamental mistakes is you often don't realise until it's too late.

Which is the case here.

An arm gets her around the throat from behind and squeezes. She struggles against it, she stomps her foot back and rakes at Martin Thomas's / Copy Joe's arms but he has too-good a hold, and the speed at which she's losing control makes her think perhaps she's just been drugged too.

She doesn't get to think anything else.

Chapter One Hundred and Twenty-Nine

A pounding headache and a world that stubbornly refuses to come into focus makes it impossible for Hazel to know where she is, or even when. Only thing she knows for sure – other than the headache – is she's wet and she's cold. She can feel lawn beneath her, but can't see it that clearly – a sea of grey, occupied by small black boats. She rubs at her eyes and the sea stays a sea, but the boats sharpen up to become gravestones. A moment later the sea sharpens up too.

She is lying on the ground in the cemetery, dizzy, clothes heavy and sticking to her, her teeth chattering, her—

Where is James?

She tries and fails to pull herself into an upright position. She doesn't know what has happened, but knows it must be bad –

there's no other reason for her to still be out here. The cemetery is mostly dark, with only a little light bleeding in from the street running parallel. It's a miracle she hasn't frozen to death, but given her proximity to the church, perhaps a miracle is exactly what she has gotten.

'James?'

No answer.

She pats down her pockets; her phone is gone. She uses a grave to brace herself and get to her feet. Her legs are stiff, sore, and after a few paces they are soft, jelly, and she grabs gravestone after gravestone for balance. To her right more graves, to the left the fence that stops the dead from mingling with the living, and ahead is the caretaker's cottage where they met Father Richardson in the parking lot out front. Beyond the cottage, the church where she parks when she comes to see her parents. The details are fuzzy, but things are coming back to her. They arrived at the cottage where Father Richardson said he would meet them, as the main gates to the church would be locked. He was waiting outside for them, jigging back and forth trying to stay warm. He introduced himself and they had shaken hands, and even though he looked sixty, there was something about him that seemed much younger. He was telling her it was going to be tough rolling James across long stretches of lawn after all the rain they'd been getting, and she was saying she appreciated the effort he was going to, and was asking where Father Jacob was when...

There's nothing else, until two minutes ago.

She reaches the cottage. Her car is where she left it. She pats down her pockets again, but her keys are gone too. She hobbles toward the caretaker's cottage, the street lights highlighting the long tentacles of ivy trying to pull it into the ground. The cottage looks abandoned, and her unanswered knocks only confirm her suspicions. Maybe there's somebody in the church. She heads toward it, then changes her mind. She'd be better off walking out to the road and flagging down traffic. She passes her car. It's unlocked. Her keys and phone are on the front seat. Did she leave them there? She doesn't think so, but that would mean they were left here for her to find. Why would that be? Her phone tells her it's almost five in the morning.

She calls Detective Kent, and Detective Kent doesn't answer.

She calls Theodore Tate, and Theodore Tate doesn't answer either.

Then she calls 111.

Chapter One Hundred and Thirty

James isn't alone. He can hear grunting as somebody skids and rocks something back and forth, making him think whoever else is here – Hazel, he's guessing – is in the same predicament that he's in: blindfolded, gagged, with hands tied to the top of a chair. He's not in his wheelchair – maybe an office chair. His legs aren't tied, not that that's going to do him much good, because what could he do? Stand and fall over? The last thing he remembers is being helped out of the car at the cemetery by Father Richardson. Maybe he's in that small cottage he saw. Or the church.

He wiggles in his chair, pushing his weight from left to right. The chair makes a sound similar to one coming from nearby. Is Hazel trying the same thing? Both of them stop when footsteps approach. A dragging sound – a chair being pulled across the floor toward him perhaps – then a sigh as somebody sits down. Is it Lance Burrows, escaped from police custody and wanting revenge?

'Is … is it … true?' a man asks.

James waits for somebody else to answer, and when nobody does, the man carries on.

'This thing that ... umm ... that you say you can do. Is it true?'

The question is for him, about Coma World. He nods, then immediately regrets it. What if he's just answered something that's going to get him and Hazel killed?

'So umm...'

James waits for the rest, but nothing comes right away. The guy sounds nervous. Maybe this wasn't planned. Maybe he's worried somebody is about to catch them.

Thirty seconds go by, then: 'If I told you everything there was to know about my wife, you could tell me what she would be doing now if she were alive?'

Hazel was right. They should never have gone public with his story.

'You can't talk, can you?'

He can talk – it's not the best, but it's getting better. But he doesn't want to talk now. Especially with this guy. He shakes his head. His hands are cut free from the bindings, and something is put onto his lap. He reaches down. It's a laptop with the screen open. So this is where things are going.

'You ... don't need to be able to see to be able to type, correct?'

No, but it helps. Even so, his fingers find the small key bumps on the F and J, and he types, *Where is Hazel?*

Nothing for thirty seconds, then, 'Hazel is in a very bad place right now unless you do as I ask,' the man says. 'I want you to tell me what my wife would be up to if she were alive.'

Not until I—

The slap is hard, twisting his head painfully to the side. He's never been slapped before, and it's loud, and it stings, and he feels humiliated. The laptop slides halfway off his lap but something stops it from falling. A moment later it's pushed back into place.

'I will kill you and Hazel if you don't do what I ask. Do you understand?'

He understands, and he's angry, and he wishes he could defend himself, only he can't, all he can do is sit and nod and hope those two things will get them out of here alive. His fingers go back to the key bumps, and he types, *I need to know everything about your wife.* Or at least he thinks he does. There must be plenty of typos.

It must be clear enough, because the man says, 'Her name was Angela,' and that's how it starts, and he suspects it's how it will always start if he is to do this for more people in the future. The man no longer sounds nervous as he tells James the story of his wife, and while he does, James walks through the recently constructed room of the warehouse while he listens.

Chapter One Hundred and Thirty-One

Tate's consciousness has laced up a pair of boxing gloves and is right now using them to beat against the walls of his skull. He knew there might be problems with his head, and this is his punishment for not going to the hospital. The folks in movies telling folks with head injuries to stay awake were probably saying it for a reason.

The pounding continues, bringing him further out of sleep, and he realises the majority of the pounding isn't inside his head, but is coming from the front door … at – he checks his watch – six in the morning.

He switches on the lights, and they seem brighter than normal. The walls aren't straight. He reaches the front door just as whoever is on the other side of it knocks again, that whoever turning out to be Detective Inspector Eric Wilson, which can't be good, because Wilson sure as hell wouldn't be here at 6.00am to deliver good news.

'Kent is missing,' Wilson says, pushing his way past.

'What?'

'I said—'

'I know what you said,' Tate says, following him into the lounge. The walls continue to sway, and he grabs onto them for balance. Kent ... missing. Middleton? Or Copy Joe? 'What happened?'

'Where in the hell is the light switch in here?'

Tate flicks it on. 'What happ—'

'Phone records say she called you.'

'When?'

'Six hours ago.'

'My phone is off.'

'Well turn it the fuck on.'

He gets his phone from his bedroom and comes back. It wasn't off, but on mute. There are eight missed calls from Wilson, one from Hazel, and one from Kent. His hands are shaking as he taps at the phone to retrieve the messages. He plays the one from Kent on speakerphone. She says she's heading to visit Martin Thomas.

Tate hangs up. 'You need to speak to Thomas.'

'I was hoping she'd said more.'

'You've spoken to Thomas?'

'No.'

'Then you need—'

'Kent's phone led us right to his house. There were signs of a struggle, including blood on the floor in the lounge, but we didn't find anybody.'

'Her blood?'

'We don't know yet.'

'How much?'

'Not enough to kill anybody.'

'You thinking they got into a struggle with each other, or are sharing the same fate?'

Wilson doesn't respond right away, then slowly nods, then reaches into his pocket for his phone. He tilts the screen so Tate can see it. 'These images were found on her phone. We think she snapped them when she was attacked.'

There's a photograph of James Garrett lying on the floor, his arm beneath him, his face turned toward the camera. Dead or alive, it's impossible to tell. Wilson slides to the next photo: this one of Martin Thomas, also in a similar position, but definitely alive – his eyes open and panicked, duct tape across his mouth.

Wilson tucks the phone back into his pocket.

'There isn't one of Kent?'

'No. At this stage we're working on the assumption that she's still alive.'

Tate staggers to the couch and sits down. Could Rebecca be dead? And James? And Martin Thomas? 'Where is Hazel?'

'Hazel is the one who reported James missing an hour ago,' Wilson says, 'before we knew about Kent. She had gone with James to visit the cemetery last night. They had a meeting with Father Richardson. He said he'd seen in the news that—'

'You mean Father Jacob?'

'No, and that's the problem. There is no Father Richardson, but it was a Father Richardson who reached out after seeing in the news that James still hadn't visited his parents' graves. He offered to show him, as well as conduct a small kind of service. They met him there, and the next thing Hazel knows, she's waking up among the graves. We assume he drugged her, but at this stage we don't know with what.'

'Was Hazel hurt?'

'Unharmed, as best as we can tell.'

'I was at the cemetery last night, visiting Emily's grave.'

'What time?'

'I don't know. Nine or ten I guess.'

'They arrived earlier than that. You didn't see anything?'

'You think I'd have done nothing if I had?'

'That's not what I meant. You see anything odd? Any other people around? Cars?'

'Was just me. How can I help?'

'You misunderstand, Tate. I'm not here to get your help, I'm here to see if Kent left you a message that was useful, and she didn't, and now I'm leaving.'

'Kent thought maybe a cop was involved, have you—?'

'Can you hear anything I'm saying?'

'Goddamn it, Eric, have you looked at people within the department or not?'

'Of course we have, and there's nothing to suggest anybody there is behind this. Kent was barking up the wrong tree.'

'Was she? Or do you just want that to be the case?'

'Do I need to put an officer on you to make sure you don't do anything stupid?'

Tate doesn't answer. He plays last night's journey backward. Did he see anything? He left the cemetery, before that he spoke to Father Jacob, before that he read the notebooks to Emily, before that he visited his wife and told her some of the things Emily had been up to, unsure if she heard any of it. He rocks the memory forward. What was Father Jacob telling him about? A break-in. Somebody stole donation money.

'Tate?'

'I'm inclined to agree.'

'Great. I'll have somebody babysit you until—'

'Not with that, but with Copy Joe not being a cop.'

'Hell, Tate, that's damn magnanimous of you.'

'You spoke to Father Jacob?'

'Of course we did.'

'And he told you about the break-in?'

'He did. Some kids, probably, you know what it's like.'

'What if it was Copy Joe?'

'You think he's moved on from rape and murder to stealing petty cash?'

'What if stealing the money was a cover? This phone call to Hazel, was it to her, or to her grandparents?'

Wilson doesn't answer right away, and Tate can see him trying to get to wherever Tate is going by himself. Only he can't. 'Her grandparents. Why?'

'I remember their phone number was unlisted. Is that still the case?'

'It is.'

'But their number would be on file at the church. If Copy Joe was a cop, he would have had access to that number easily enough. But he's not, so he—'

'So he broke into the church, got their number, then rang Hazel to offer his services. That's a lot of work to go to.'

'There's no way he could have got to them at their house with all the media around, so he drew them somewhere quiet. James was the target, and he had to get their number without asking somebody for it. He call from a burner?'

'He did. So let's say for a moment you're right, then why James?'

'This was always about notoriety. Killing James is as big a splash as anybody could make.'

'And Kent? And Thomas? Why take them too?'

'Maybe for the same reason. But they're together, and that means Copy Joe has a plan. We just have to find them before he can enact it.'

Chapter One Hundred and Thirty-Two

Kent is woozy from whatever drug Thomas used. She doesn't know how long ago she was sedated. It's still dark out. Do her colleagues know she's missing yet? What were her last actions? She called Tate. Did she leave him a message? Did she tell him where she was going? She isn't sure.

Of all the places she could have woken up in, from abandoned slaughterhouses with hooks hanging from worn and crooked beams, to hillbilly huts out in the middle of nowhere, it makes sense to be waking up here. Of course it's here, and she should have had an officer posted on the door here since day one.

And now she's going to die here.

The room is lit up by a camping lantern. James Garrett is duct-taped around his waist to a kitchen chair across the room. He has duct tape over his eyes and a laptop on his knees. Instead of typing, he's listening. Talking to him is Matthew Durry. He's telling James about his wife. Standing near the window is Martin Thomas, who is pointing a gun at Durry while keeping an eye on his phone. Martin Thomas, who went from scene to scene years ago while the police told him where to stand and what to do while telling him all that had happened there. Martin Thomas, a pain tourist who pocketed keys so he could come back when the desire hit, then one day the desire was for so much more. Martin Thomas, who could dress and act like a cop, could dress and act like a priest, could dress and act like anybody he wanted to.

He notices Kent is awake, but turns his attention back to Durry and James. She has a good idea why James has duct tape over his eyes when neither Durry or herself do. It means James is getting out of here alive, but not Durry, and not her. The duct tape around her wrists won't budge. Nor will the tape around her chair.

Thomas picks up a pad from the windowsill, writes something down, then shows it to Durry. Durry takes a moment to read it, then turns back to James, and asks, 'Aren't you going to write any of this down?'

James types at the laptop, then turns it so Durry can see, and of course Thomas can see it too. Thomas writes back on the pad and hands it to Durry.

'What? You're just going to remember it all?' Durry asks.

James types something else, then turns it back.

'You're sure?' Durry asks.

James nods.

Thomas peels the page from the pad, folds it into a small square, then pops it into his mouth. He's telling Durry what to say, and because James can't see anything, he thinks what he is hearing are Durry's words. When this is over, James will be the witness who said Matthew Durry attacked him, that he wanted a coma history of his wife.

She gets it now, the next role that Martin Thomas will be playing – that of the hero. It won't just be James who's a witness, but Thomas too, and Thomas will say everything he needs to say to prove that Durry is Copy Joe, and of course he'll be the one to have stopped him, saving James in the process. Only he won't have been able to save Kent. That's why he didn't bother putting duct tape over her eyes. She's never going to get the chance to tell anybody what she saw – plus he probably likes having the audience. She thinks back to when she met him the other night. He was scared, charming, eager to help. Her radar was off reading the guy. Because he's an actor? Or because she's shit at her job?

She twists her arms, tightens and loosens her hands, and works at trying to free herself as she listens to Durry tell his wife's life story.

Chapter One Hundred and Thirty-Three

Martin Thomas is an affable guy, and Tate doesn't doubt he'd have been willing to help Kent with any plan she had. She gets to his house, and instead of finding him willing to help, she finds him gagged and bound on the floor, along with James. Was she killed there and then? No, because then there'd be no reason to take her. Her car isn't at the scene, so Copy Joe moved it or used it. Wilson confirmed Kent's car didn't have GPS installed, but if it did, Tate thinks it'd lead them to a burned-out shell along an abandoned stretch of coastline.

Question: why take James to Thomas's house in the first place, only then to have to leave with him?

It takes a few laps of his lounge before the answer comes to him. Kent. Whatever Copy Joe was planning on doing, his plan changed when Kent showed up at the actor's house. He'd have known the police could track her with her phone, but he wouldn't have known when they'd start looking. So he had to get out of there. He left in Kent's car and not the one he arrived in. Why the switch? Was his own car too small? He might have a two-seater. Room for one in the front and one in the trunk, but not for a third, now that he has Kent to add to it. So he drives his car a few blocks away and walks back. He drives his victims to wherever they are now, dumps Kent's car and comes back for his own. Does he walk? Taxi? Is he still using Kent's car? Could Copy Joe's own car still be parked a few blocks away from the house?

A minute later he's backing out of his garage, relieved there isn't a patrol car blocking his exit. He makes his way toward the actor's house, having looked up the address. Driving the surrounding blocks looking for two-seater cars isn't the best plan, but it's all he has. The police have probably already thought of it, but even so he'll make a list and call Wilson with the details. And if Copy Joe parked a kilometre away? Or two? How far would he have been willing to walk back?

The very thing that saved Kent from figuring out where he buried Nathaniel Perry is the very thing that could save her – the

GPS. How the hell is it not a standard thing in police vehicles? Money, probably. Just like money is the same reason Martin Thomas and everybody else linked to the case were left to fend for themselves. And now Kent and James and others could end up dead so the department could save, what, a hundred bucks? Five hundred? A...

'Wait.'

He pulls over, his breath catching as he remembers he still hasn't gotten the burner phone out of Kent's car yet. The other phone went into the fire, then went into a dumpster, but if he can find it, it's possible enough data can be retrieved that still links it to the phone hidden in Kent's car. He can't log in with a different device, because the email address he used was randomly generated, and he doesn't know what it was – only that it had a long string of numbers and letters.

Will the dumpster have been emptied? And even if he can find the phone, will enough of the circuitry have survived? And even if those two things fall in his favour, the phone in the back of Kent's car still needs to have enough juice to tell him where it is.

He pulls away from the kerb and puts his foot down.

Chapter One Hundred and Thirty-Four

The alleyway stinks of piss and vomit, and the air, despite the early morning being cold, manages to feel even colder. The dumpster is one of two servicing the nearby shops, the back doors and walls of which are covered in spraypainted swastikas and penises. His fear the dumpster may have been emptied already is almost coming true, a truck currently in the alleyway levering it up to dump the contents into the back. He runs to the driver's door. The guy behind the wheel is dressed in a grey pair of overalls that look as though they came out of the last dumpster he emptied. He takes a large drag on the cigarette he's working at before lowering the window.

'Help you?'

'There's something in that dumpster I need.'

'And what would that be?'

'Something I accidentally threw out. Look, can you do me a—'

'Favour? Look, buddy, I have a schedule to keep. My advice is not to throw things out you want to keep.'

'Please, it's important. It's a—'

'Matter of life or death?'

'Yes.'

The driver flicks the stub of his cigarette out the window past Tate, then goes about lighting another. 'It always is, and I'm going to tell you what I tell everybody else. If it's that important, it's going to cost you.'

'I could just call the police.'

'You could, but by the time they arrive whatever is in this dumpster will be in the back of my truck, mixed and crushed in with the contents of two dozen other dumpsters. Or you give me a thousand dollars right now and I lower this thing back down.'

Tate knows he could call the police. He could spend a few minutes convincing Wilson of why he needs the phone, and then maybe Wilson sends somebody to this alleyway, and of course by then it's all too late.

'There's an ATM around the corner. I'll give you five minutes.'

It takes Tate four. He hands the money over as the guy lights another cigarette. Maybe the guy can use the cash for chemo.

'You got an hour.'

Tate figures that ought to do it. The truck backs out, and Tate gets to work. The other night the dumpster was three quarters full, but now rubbish is up to the brim. He hauls out bags of cut hair, of food scraps, old newspapers, coffee cups and tea bags and cardboard and polystyrene and food wrapping and milk containers, and a thousand other things, the ground behind him filling up with bags that stay intact and others that don't. He wishes he had brought gloves and a facemask. Gumboots too. After ten minutes he's wondering if he wouldn't be better off calling Wilson for help. But twenty minutes in and, with the morning finally beginning to lighten, he finds the phone wedged between a dead rat and a hypodermic syringe.

He feels like an arsehole leaving all the bags of trash scattered across the alleyway as he rushes back to his car. The slot for the sim card has melted shut, and he uses a pocket knife to pry it open. The card comes out and looks to be in good condition, but doesn't have its phone number printed on the side. He slots it into his own phone only to be greeted by an error message. He wipes the card down and tries again and gets the same result.

Strike one.

The phone store he came to on Saturday morning is in the process of opening when he arrives. The same guy who helped him then helps him now. He seems happy with the challenge when Tate explains that he either needs this phone to pick up the location of the one it's connected to, or for the email address he used.

'Leave it with me for a few hours and I'll see what I can do.'

'Can you do it now?' Tate asks, hearing the desperation in his own voice.

'I've got a few others I have to look at first. Even then I'm not sure I'm going to be able to look at it today, and even then it might not actually work.'

Strike two.

Tate pulls out five hundred dollars and slides it across the counter. He'd gotten it earlier when he drew out the other thousand. People are a lot more helpful when there is something in it for them.

'This is to look at it now, and there's another five hundred if you're successful.'

'It's that important to you, huh?'

'It is,' Tate says, wondering if the guy will now want two thousand, or five thousand. In which case that might be strike three, because he doesn't have that kind of cash.

But instead of taking the money, the guy slides it back toward Tate. 'If that's the case, I can look at it right away. I'm not making any promises, but I'll see what I can do.'

Chapter One Hundred and Thirty-Five

Matthew Durry has finished talking, and James Garrett is writing, but even so Copy Joe is finding his patience waning. He's exhausted. It's been a long night, and one he hasn't been able to speed up due to having to wait for people to wake up after being drugged. His back is still sore from getting people onto the top floor of the building. James having wasted away in a coma made him easy to carry – which was a good thing considering there were three flights of stairs. Kent was heavier, and Matthew Durry heavier still. Without the hand truck – something he purchased a year ago to move paving stones across his yard that he never ended up moving – he never would have gotten them past the first floor.

Soon Martin Thomas will stop being Copy Joe and will hand that mantle to Matthew Durry, which then frees Martin up to be the hero who stopped him. He'll go on TV, and he'll charm sexy breakfast hosts and make late-night hosts laugh, and Jess will beg for him to come back – and he won't even give her the time of day, because nothing hurts more than being ignored. And then there will be calls to play roles that are worth his time until somebody pitches the idea that all of this should be turned into a movie. And James ... well he's unsure about James. The whole point of having Durry do all the talking was so when all is said and done, James will verify that Durry kidnapped him, Durry asked him to write up a history for his dead wife, and that Durry is an insane person, all with Martin saying the same thing. But he's not so sure he really needs James to survive this. They will forever be linked coming out of this, and as James's story grows, so will his own. But as the days turn into weeks into months, he will find himself growing jealous of James's attention – especially if the movie makers of the world show more interest in James than in himself. If life takes that path, he'll always regret not killing him, and isn't there a line about that? That on your deathbed, you regret more the things you didn't do than the things you did? He let Hazel live because he liked the idea of a pretty woman being indebted to him, and perhaps she won't feel that way if James doesn't get out of this alive.

There will be other pretty women.

Then there is Kent. She was never part of the final equation. He was already on his way here with Martin sedated in the front seat and James in the trunk when she called to ask if she could swing by. He considered telling her he was busy, then thought about how much better the movie would be with a good police-detective sacrifice at the end. So he drove home and pulled Matthew out of the car and hid him on the floor in case Kent looked through the garage window on her way to the back door. He'd been watching her from the moment she pulled up alone. He knew she would come around to the back of the house if he didn't answer the door.

He had to work on the assumption Kent's colleagues knew where she was going and were waiting to hear from her. He dragged James into the lounge and took a photo on her phone after he had subdued her. Then he staged a second photo of himself gagged and bound. There wouldn't be time for two trips in his car since he couldn't fit them all in there, so he used hers. It was perfect, because her car would come in handy in leading the police to where they were. It's only a matter of time before they start looking, if not because they were expecting Kent to report back in, then at least because Hazel will have woken by now. It's only a matter of time before they figure to look for Kent, or before somebody spots her car parked outside.

Anyway, it is all coming to an end now. James, typing away at the laptop Copy Joe stole from Simone Clarke's house the other night, has already constructed enough material to suggest why he was needed here. Which means it's almost time to make a decision on what James's fate will be. Matthew Durry and Detective Kent's fates are already set in stone.

He stands by the window and looks down at Kent's car parked opposite, then at his phone. First thing he did when he arrived tonight was plant a small surveillance camera on the building opposite and connect it to his phone. The police will show up soon. He just has to be patient until they do.

Chapter One Hundred and Thirty-Six

The insides of the old phone are now the insides of a new phone, and the IT guy has been able to jigsaw enough of the components together to get it up and running.

'It's not pretty, but it'll let you get from it what you need.'

'What do I owe you?'

'Just the price of the new phone. Everything else is on the house.'

Tate pays the bill and tips the guy an extra hundred. He goes into the phone's menu and finds not only the number of the other burner phone, but also finds that the spyware software he installed is still up and running. It goes about orientating itself for thirty seconds before locking in on the location of the other phone. If it is still in the back of Kent's car, then her car is parked across town. He knows the area a little, and knows some of the rougher buildings are being pulled down to make way for new office blocks, the folks who could barely afford to pay rent there now having to find somewhere more expensive.

He needs to call the police, but he also needs to get to Kent's car before they do. He needs that phone back. It's a tricky balance. He cares deeply for Kent, but he also cares deeply about his own freedom, especially with a child on the way. He can't take the chance that the deal he made with Wilson won't fall apart if they know exactly where Perry is buried, and of course he has Tabitha Munroe to consider too. A minute into driving toward the blue dot he phones Wilson – after all, the most important thing here is getting Kent and James and Martin Thomas back alive. Wilson doesn't answer. He leaves a message saying he knows where Kent's car is. Then he calls Detective Travers and does the same, and then Detective Vega. Could be they're busy, but he'd put money on them dodging his calls.

He scoots around corners where there are red lights, and he swerves past cars, forcing others to pull over. He keeps the burner phone open and glances at the map as he gets closer to the blue dot, reaching the neighbourhood ten minutes later, where buildings are boarded up and busted windows and streetlights litter the pavement. A minute later he's driving past Kent's car. There's something familiar about the building it's parked opposite. The lower windows have bars over them. He doesn't think he's been here before, but he knows this place. He continues past and parks around the corner, then walks back, carrying a tyre iron with him. He tries the doors on Kent's car – locked. Is Copy Joe in one of these buildings, or did he just dump the car here? He can see an alarm light blinking. Smashing the window might be Copy Joe's early warning system. He could be watching from any one of these windows.

He swings the tyre iron at the rear side window of the car. It bounces off on the first attempt, but smashes it on the second. The alarm is instant. His gun and phone are where he left them. He grabs them then runs up the street, away from the car and the building, hoping that if Copy Joe is watching he'll just be thinking the car was broken into and stuff stolen from it. He gets around the corner, and keeps running. His phone goes. It's Wilson.

'Where is she?'

'I don't know, all I know is where her car is.'

'You're sure?'

'I'm sure.'

'Jesus Christ, Tate, I told you—'

'You want me to tell you where it is or not?'

'Where?'

Tate gives him the address as he reaches the next corner. He goes right.

'Why are you puffing?'

'Look, Kent's car has already been broken into,' he says. 'The side window is shattered.'

'We're on our – oh damn.'

'What?' he asks, switching off the two burner phones and dumping them into a trash can.

'That address. That's – look, just wait there.'

'What is the address?'

'It's nothing. Don't go in there.'

He reaches the next corner and goes right again. He is willing his memory to make the connection to the building he was outside a few moments ago. He's seen it on TV, he's sure of it. Several times. Why is that? 'I'm heading in there.'

'You'll do no such thing, Tate. I have officers two minutes out.'

'And Kent might not have two minutes, and even then the officers aren't going to do a thing until you have an assault team here.'

He reaches the next corner and makes the final right, coming back to where he started. The car alarm is still going off, but there's nobody around to pay it any attention. He crosses the road.

'Tate, don't. I'm—'

'Are you going to tell me what's in there or not?'

'It's where Joe Middleton used to live.'

Of course that's it. The guy is pretending to be Middleton, only makes sense he'd come here at some point. Only it's looking like he's come here to make a big scene. Is he still in there, or has he fled already, mayhem and death left in his wake? Tate thinks he's still in there, and the car alarm has started a timer. Hopefully running from the scene has done the trick.

'Don't—'

Tate doesn't hear the rest. He hangs up as he reaches the building. When the officers arrive, they won't arrive with sirens blaring. They might enter the building, but he thinks they won't – he thinks they'll hold back and gather around the corner until they have a plan.

That means for the next few minutes he's on his own.

Chapter One Hundred and Thirty-Seven

From the window of Joe Middleton's apartment, Copy Joe stares at Kent's car where, moments ago, some arsehole smashed the window and stole something. Probably the car stereo – or so he first thought, because now that same person is being streamed from the hidden camera across the street to his phone as he approaches the apartment building door. Copy Joe watches as the man – he's not a hundred percent sure, but he thinks it's Theodore Tate – uses a tyre iron to pry the door open.

It's time to get this party started.

He looks at Kent. She's still struggling against the tape.

He looks at James. He's still writing.

He looks at Matthew Durry. He read the suicide note he found in his pocket earlier, and figures he's doing the guy a favour by helping him get to where he seems keen to go. He's still sitting patiently with his hands in his lap as he waits for the inevitable. Ideally those hands would be bound, but he doesn't want there to be any evidence of that. He told the guy he'd kill his kids if he tried anything, but that was bullshit. He's not a monster.

Kent stops struggling as he steps around behind her, where he can keep his eye on Durry sitting on the couch. Will he try something? Get up and rush him? He's ready for him if he does. All Kent has managed to do is wrinkle up and twist the edges of the duct tape binding her. Maybe if she had another hour she might have had some success, but she doesn't have another hour. Before leaving his house, he stuffed some plastic bags into Kent's pocket. Now he pulls them out and shakes one open. What was good enough for Simone Clarke will be good enough for Rebecca Kent.

He barely has it over her head before her panic sets in. She shakes back and forth so much it's a struggle securing it around her neck with a length of duct tape, but he gets it there. He steps back and watches the struggle. Matthew Durry stays where he is.

Then Copy Joe figures what's good enough for Rebeca Kent is good enough for James Garrett.

He shakes open a second plastic bag.

Chapter One Hundred and Thirty-Eight

Kent can't breathe. Can't see anything beyond the bag. The plastic pulls tighter against her face as she tries sucking in the last few bits of air through her nose. She thrashes back and forth, then rocks the chair until the chair falls over ... She lands heavily and her head whiplashes into the floor but the bag doesn't break, nor does the chair. The world is exactly the way it was five seconds earlier except she's horizontal instead of vertical. She has survived men with guns and a car explosion, and she's going to be taken out by a layer of plastic less than a millimetre thick.

People say drowning is peaceful. Maybe this will get there, but right now all it is, is pain, a tight burning in her chest and throat. She has seen documentaries of people free diving past a hundred metres on a single breath. They'd be able to survive in a plastic bag for four or five minutes. How long can she last?

She writhes on the floor, the chair banging and bouncing along with her. She can't straighten her body. She tries to drag her face against the floor hoping to break the bag, but the way she's tied into the chair, she can't get enough pressure against it. And still she keeps trying to draw in that breath – all she needs is one, one to get her lungs full and then perhaps another so she can reassess, so she can think clearly, because right now her thoughts feel ... warm ... if that's even possible. She suddenly realises she isn't trying to break the bag anymore. She's not even bouncing around on the floor. She has seen news stories about free drivers who can hold their breath for ... wait ... didn't she just think that? What has that got to do with Copy Joe? She thinks about the man she shot, and about April Gilmore, and she's so tired and perhaps it's best she isn't struggling anymore and her thoughts are warm and free drivers can hold their breath for five minutes or longer and everything is going to be okay will be okay will. Be. Oka—

Chapter One Hundred and Thirty-Nine

The foyer is cold, and the stairwell discoloured from various stains from over the years. Take-away flyers, band aids, rotten fruit – it all lines the sides of the stairs along with other trash, more at the bottom, less as Tate climbs, as if it's all rolled downhill. A rat runs out from a bag of trash, stares at him defiantly, then runs back in. He pauses at the first floor to listen for any sounds – there are none – then carries on to the second. He pauses there and does the same. Nothing. At the third floor he hears a bang from somewhere above.

He keeps going, reaching the top, where the corridor is free of trash but has walls covered with graffiti. The graffiti points him in the right direction, getting congested down the corridor and peaking around a door covered with notes pinned to it: *Marry me Joe. The Carver kicks arse. Make my wife famous by killing her. All those bitches were asking for it.* Hundreds of them, probably written by hundreds of similarly minded people. It reminds him of what Kent said about the pain tourists. People have flocked here since Joe's arrest to see touch feel smell taste the atmosphere, to wrap themselves in it, to rubberneck at where the worst of humanity once lived. He's glad they're pulling this building down. But the people who wrote all these messages will find another place to be drawn to – perhaps Copy Joe's house, when all is said and done.

There's another bang, this one similar to the first, but louder since the source of the sound is coming from the other side of the door. He points his gun at the door as he reaches out and carefully tries the handle. It's locked. Wait for help? If he pries it open with the tyre iron he could be walking into a hail of bullets, or even putting others into further danger. But to do nothing could be worse. He gets down onto the floor, but the gap under the door is barely a centimetre high, and he can't see a thing. The door doesn't have one of those old keyholes to peer through either, and the only way to see through the windows is if he abseiled off the roof. He steps back from the door and grabs his phone and—

'GET OFF ME!'

He doesn't recognise the voice, but it doesn't matter. He drops his phone into his pocket, forgoes the tyre iron and kicks the door next to the lock. It rattles in the frame, but a second kick gets that frame splintering apart. The door swings open so hard it hits the wall and comes back, just as Tate is falling through it. He's able to get his arm up to stop it from hitting him in the nose. He gets the gun up too.

He takes only a split second to understand what he's looking at. A chair on its side, somebody unmoving and tied to it with a plastic bag over their head. Kent? Another person in a chair, this one also tipped over, hands bound to it, a plastic bag over their head too, only this person is still wriggling back and forth, the bag being pulled into their mouth as they struggle for air. James? Martin Thomas and Matthew Durry struggling in the centre of the room, Martin Thomas has a torn plastic bag over his head, taped to his neck, and torn duct tape hanging from his wrists, another piece hanging from his mouth. Thomas must have been bound to a chair like the others, but managed to free himself. There's blood on his shirt. Some of that is from a long slice running down his arm, and some is from Matthew Durry, who has a knife sticking out from the centre of his chest. Durry is still standing, a look on his face of complete confusion as if he can't believe what he's seeing is real. His hands go to the knife, and whether he'll try to pull it free like Nathaniel Perry did, or not, Tate doesn't stand around to find out.

The threat eliminated, Tate drops the gun into his pocket and the tyre iron onto the floor, covers the distance to Kent in three long strides and tears the plastic bag open. Her skin is blue, her eyes open. He doesn't have time to check for a pulse because he has to get that bag off James. He gets up and turns at the same time Durry drops to his knees, the dumbfounded look on his face softening.

'I'll get him,' Thomas says, as if reading his thoughts, and now it's his turn to take large steps, his to a still-struggling James who, somehow, is pushing his feet into the ground and tipping the chair backward. It crashes over before Thomas can get to it, but a second later he tears the plastic bag open and James sucks in a deep breath that Tate doesn't see, but hears as he tears at the duct tape holding Kent's wrists to the arms of the chair, only it won't budge. He grabs his car key and pokes the tip into it and gets it going, freeing one side, then the other. He gets her on her back with her arms by her side. It's been years since he did any CPR training, and since then he has heard people advocate for using both chest compressions and mouth to mouth, as well as people advocating for chest compressions only.

He looks at Thomas as Thomas continues to pull the plastic bag from James's head. 'You know how to…?'

He doesn't even get to finish before Thomas is shaking his head.

'Here,' Tate says, and he reaches into his pocket for his phone and tosses it to him. 'Call for help.'

Thomas catches the phone. Tate tilts Kent's head back and breathes into her mouth.

Chapter One Hundred and Forty

Matthew Durry put up more of a struggle than Copy Joe thought he would have, having leaped up from his chair the moment Copy Joe got the bag secured around James's head. It meant Tate was able to make it up the stairs before Copy Joe could make sure Kent was dead, and right now all he can do is watch as Tate starts chest compressions on her. Which is a problem, because she's seen everything. He should have blindfolded her – only, he's not so sure it would have mattered. The look she gave him earlier when she woke up was one without surprise. Perhaps she saw something at his house, or maybe she just figured since she was abducted there, he was the one doing the abducting, which, when you think about it, makes perfect sense. And anyway, what was the point in blindfolding her when he was going to kill her anyway? And, if he's being honest with himself, didn't he enjoy the audience?

He did, and now that's a problem.

That is, of course, only if she wakes up.

Which means it's his job to make sure she doesn't.

He turns the cellphone off, then holds it up to his ear, and it's acting 101 when he says, 'Hello? Yes, yes, we need police and an ambulance ... Detective Kent has been hurt, I think she's dead. Detective Theodore Tate is working on her and ... well I don't know the exact address, but it's the apartment where Joe Middleton used to live. Martin Thomas. Yes, I can keep the line open.' Then he sits the phone on the dining table, then, to Tate, he says, 'They're sending people.'

Tate doesn't answer. His hands are clenched together as he maintains chest compressions on Kent. He's saying 'come on' over and over, as if his words will be the difference between her heading towards a bright light or running from it. When the movie gets made, he'll tell them he was the one who tried to save Kent, but for now he needs to stop Tate's efforts. He looks around the room. Tate's fate will need to be tied in with the rest of the scene. He just needs to figure out how.

Chapter One Hundred and Forty-One

James has no idea what's going on, or exactly who is here. The plastic bag has been removed, but whatever is over his eyes is still there. Somebody just made a phone call to the police saying Detective Kent was dead, which hurts, and that Mr Tate is here trying to help. How many others are here, and where is Hazel?

His chest is burning. His throat too. He hadn't even finished typing out a history for Angela Durry when his hands were duct-taped to the arms of the chair, then the bag put over his head. He thought he was going to die. His head still hurts from the blow it took from the floor when he tipped the chair back earlier, but actually, he was trying to stand. His hands aren't going anywhere, and, on his back with his feet in the air and with tape wrapped around his waist and the chair, he can't get any momentum to tip the chair onto its side. He's put on size and muscle over the last few weeks, but even if he'd put on twice as much he doesn't think it would be possible. However, being skinny does help, because he finds when he lifts his head he can at the same time bring his knees to his face. It's a strain, but he's able to work his knee at whatever is covering his eyes – he thinks duct tape, because as he hooks his knee into it and up, it pulls at his skin and his hair too. The man who ripped the plastic bag from his head must be too busy helping Tate to help James, or maybe he's pulling more plastic bags off faces.

The bottom edge of the tape shifts upward and light creeps in. The gap isn't large enough to see anything clearly, not at first, but he keeps working at it, and soon the gap is bigger, giving him a view of a ceiling with cobwebs growing across the lightbulbs. He can see Mr Tate to his left, hunched over Detective Kent, working to save her. To his right he can see a dead man on the floor with a knife sticking out of his chest at a perfect right angle, his lifeless face turned toward James. He must be the man who kidnapped him. James quickly looks away. He can't see the other man who's here, which means he's probably directly ahead, where James's own legs and the bottom of the chair are blocking the view. He pulls at the tape around his wrists but can't budge it.

He looks left again as Mr Tate frantically works at Detective Kent. He wishes he could help somehow. He looks back to the man who kidnapped him, and who...

Why is the knife no longer in his chest?

He has seen enough horror movies to know it takes more than a knife to keep a psychopath down, and this guy has ripped it out of his own chest and ... and what? The guy isn't getting up. He isn't doing anything. So where's the knife? He looks left at Tate. He looks straight ahead where the other man is in his blind spot. Could he have it? Yes, he does, because a moment later he comes into view and raises it.

Chapter One Hundred and Forty-two

'Come on, come on, come on.'

Tate keeps up the chest compressions, then checks for a pulse – nothing. He breathes into Kent's mouth – two long breaths – before clenching his hands together and going back to her chest. Her body moves as he pushes at her, her chin dipping up and down as if agreeing with his technique, but if she were, why isn't it working? That's one of many questions among others: will her ribs break? How long was she down before he showed up? How long for the others to arrive? Wilson was already on the way, will he have arranged an ambulance, or did that not happen until—

'LOOK OUT!'

He hasn't heard James talk before, but immediately knows it's him, knows what he's saying, knows what he's hearing in his voice isn't just a warning but fear too. He hunkers lower and twists to the side, knowing whatever last ditch Matthew Durry is making can't be a great one since the guy seemed all but dead, but even so...

It's not Matthew Durry, but Martin Thomas.

What the hell?

Thomas has the knife raised, blood rolling off the sharp edge and dripping onto the floor. There's no time to reach the gun in his pocket as Thomas brings the blade down hard and fast, so Tate does the opposite, and it's not a great option but it's the best one he has – he reaches up toward the knife but without an angle to block it. He pays for it too, the knife hits him in the forearm and even though it feels like nothing more than a pin prick, he knows the damage will be far greater. The knife carries on, but with the direction changed it harmlessly slices through the air, Thomas coming close to stabbing himself in the leg. As Thomas gets his balance to swing again, Tate, on his knees, reaches for his gun, gets his hand onto it ... only to find he can't tell if his hand is on it or not. He has no feeling in his arm, the pin prick now feels like an amputation, and sure looks that way by the amount of blood soaking into his jacket. He reaches across his body with his good hand, but it's awkward and he can't get his fingers into the pocket before Thomas is coming back at him. The tyre iron is too far away to be of any use, so he goes for the chair that Kent was tied into, barely getting it up in time to block the knife as it comes toward him, the blade sticking into seat. When he tries to stand to push Thomas back, he finds there is no strength in his legs. Thomas yanks the knife free and steps back as if to reassess his next best angle as Tate shakes his head, trying to get the world to snap back into focus. How much blood is he going to lose, and how much is enough to have him keel over and be an easy victim? He tries to get to his feet again, and again fails. He stares at Thomas. How many times have they met during re-enactments? More than a few, and Kent was so close with her theory – Thomas ticks all the boxes but one: he's not a cop, but he had access to plenty of them as he was taken though crime scene after crime scene.

'Why are you doing this?' Tate asks, but it's a stupid question because he knows why. He's doing it for the fame. It's why there's a plastic bag torn around his neck and duct tape hanging from his wrists. He's going to paint himself as the kidnapped victim who became the hero, and at the rate Tate is losing blood, the hero is exactly what Thomas will get to be – only one who wasn't able to save anybody else.

Thomas must think it's a stupid question too, because he doesn't respond.

'The police are on their way,' Tate says, trying – and failing – to stand once again. His arm, burning a moment ago, is now numb. He casts a glance to Thomas's left where James is staring wide-eyed at them both, only he's no longer on his back, instead he's twisted in the chair so his legs are pointing out to the side. James nods towards his feet, and Tate knows what he's saying. 'I know you didn't call them,' he adds, 'but I did, before coming in here.'

Thomas switches the knife into his other hand, and comes at him again. Tate is ready, and he lifts the chair and puts the last of his strength into standing, and he gets there too, and when the knife hits the chair again he drives forward with all his might, Thomas taking one step back, then another, and then he's tripping over James's legs.

Tate drops the chair and twists his jacket around his body so he can reach into the pocket with his good hand. Despite there being blood on the gun, he gets a good grip and points it at Thomas.

'Don't,' he says, as Thomas starts to get back to his feet. Christ he feels woozy. Kent still needs help and the world is swaying and he's used up the last of his strength. He takes a step to the side to keep his balance in check. He doesn't have long before passing out. Seconds, maybe. Blood is pouring out of his arm.

Help is coming, but it won't be here in time.

All Thomas has to do is wait for him to pass out, then he can stage the scene to look how he wants.

He can only see one option.

Chapter One Hundred and Forty-Three

James jumps when Mr Tate pulls the trigger, his ears immediately ringing loudly as he watches the bad man stagger back, his hands clutching at his stomach as he goes back down. Mr Tate goes down too, hitting the floor hard. Blood keeps flowing out of his arm. The bad man is slumped against the wall, his feet out in front of him. The knife has fallen out of his hand and is on the floor. He's looking around, but other than that he's not moving. Mr Tate drags himself to the knife, picks it up, then drags himself to James.

He slices through the duct tape holding James's right hand down. 'You need to help Rebecca.'

'Wha bout you?'

'Rebecca,' Mr Tate says, then he slumps against the floor.

James picks up the knife and slices through the rest of the tape. He can't walk, but he can crawl, even if it is badly, and he does that now, making his way quickly over to Detective Kent. He can remember every bit of the compulsory first-aid course they did in school. He checks for a pulse, doesn't find one, and goes about doing chest compressions. He is a minute into it when he hears people on the stairs. He yells out, and a moment later the room is flooding with police officers who don't seem to know what to do first. Four people are down, ranging from dead, to almost dead to very much alive. Two officers take over from him, and a third helps him away from the body and gets him up in a chair. Another works on Tate, checks for a pulse, and confirms he's still breathing. Another officer is talking quickly into a radio saying to send the paramedics in, who must have been just outside the door because seconds later they show up. He watches as they fight to keep Kent alive, while an officer uses a torniquet to staunch the blood flowing out of Mr Tate's arm. There's a cut that looks like it goes all the way to the bone, and James almost passes out when he sees it. More paramedics show up, two of them work on the bad man, but either there's little they can do, or they don't want to, because they quickly give up. The other man who was already dead by the time James managed to get the duct tape off his eyes is looked at, but just as quickly the paramedics make the call there's nothing that can be done for him either.

An officer comes to the realisation none of this is anything James should be watching, and he and another officer help him into the hall. There's nowhere to sit, and they end up resting him on the stairs. Then they hang around, unsure about what to do next as more people come and go. He recognises the detective from the other night – Eric Wilson – even though they never spoke. Wilson nods at him then disappears into the apartment. He keeps thinking the more time that passes, the worse it's going to be for Mr Tate and Detective Kent. He should have done more, and feels sick that he didn't, and feels even sicker that he can't figure out what he could have done differently. He couldn't help his parents, and just as equally he couldn't help Mr Tate or Detective Kent. If he could walk, he'd get as far away from here as he could. Best he can do is go to the warehouse. He closes his eyes and opens the warehouse door, but before he can go in, somebody is shaking his shoulder. He opens his eyes to see a paramedic crouching next to him.

'He's insisting on having a word with you before he goes,' the paramedic says.

James turns to see Mr Tate is in a gurney, being carried out of the apartment by two paramedics. The paramedic steps aside so the others can pause next to him. Tate reaches out with his good arm and grabs James's shoulder.

'You did good,' Tate says, his hand falling away from James's shoulder and swinging loosely a moment later. He looks like he's about to pass out.

'Whil 'Ective Kent be okay?' James asks, because one of the things they told him when he learned First Aid back in school is the longer you go without oxygen, the harder it is to come back … and if you do, you might not be coming back all the way.

'She's survived worse,' Tate says, and James doesn't like how that sounds.

'We have to go,' the paramedic says.

'A moment longer,' Tate says, and he reaches up, tries to grab James's shoulder again, but misses. 'I'll check on woo soom,' he says, and then his eyes close and he's gone.

James watches the paramedics carry Tate down the stairs, the staircase getting narrow when Hazel shows up at the bend. She steps aside so they can pass, and moments later Hazel is sitting on the step next to him. She wraps her arms around him and tells him everything is going to be okay, and it might be, but perhaps not for everybody. Either way, there's still one more thing he needs to do.

Epilogue

James walks the warehouse, his fingers running over the tops of the cabinets. In the two days since Martin Thomas was killed, he's spent a lot of time in here, going through memory after memory, saying goodbye to his parents. Of course he's been in the news a lot too – not just because of the interview the other night, or because of Nathaniel Perry, but because of the interest from the publishing world in his story. Doctor Wolfgang had been right in thinking people would be fascinated, but after what happened with Copy Joe, that interest has only compounded. An hour ago Doctor Wolfgang rang with news that there is a bidding war for the book, and that the latest offer has taken it over the one-million-dollar mark. James doesn't know if a million dollars is a lot of money like it used to be, but it sure is life-changing. It would mean more interviews. It would mean more people wanting his help.

He also had the news that Detective Kent was still in intensive care, but stable, making James hope that if she's creating a coma world of her own, it's better than the world she's absent from.

Last night he went to the hospital to see Mr Tate. He was okay, having already undergone three surgeries on his arm, and with more to go, but he was going to make a full recovery. He told James about Matthew Durry, and Durry's theory about pain tourists. It was something James was getting used to moving forward, that people see him as an adult when really he isn't, so they say things in front of him they wouldn't say in front of an eleven-year-old. Or maybe everything he has gone through has earned him that. After all, he saw one man with a knife sticking out of his chest, and he saw Mr Tate shoot another, and how many people have tried to kill him over the last week? These are things that tend to make you grow up faster. Tate explained how pain tourists were folks who were attracted to the pain and misery of others. It made

James worry that this would be his future, that people would bring their pain and misery to him, and would ask him to translate the fates of those lost into happy memories that were never real. Last week he thought that was okay, but last week was last week.

The warehouse ... he thought this building could be used to help people, but the price is too much. There will be others who will be willing to hurt him, or worse, hurt those around him. There will never be an end to it.

A million dollars on the table.

A million reasons that he needs to escape that future.

He opens the drawers and pulls out files at random and starts dumping them into the metal skip where all the old drywall and beams of wood were being tossed. One by one he removes the memories until the metal skip is full of them. He doesn't open any of folders. Doesn't read any of the past. The final drawer is the one he had to open with the axe, the one from the night he was shot. He removes the files and carries them into the new part of the warehouse where walls still haven't been painted and electrical cable hangs from the ceiling. He reaches up and pulls at the cable, running a length of it down to the ground. He flicks a red against a black, arcing them and creating a spark. It takes a few attempts before he can get the pages of the folder to catch, but he gets there. He picks it up and watches it burn, then tosses it into the metal skip along with all the others. It doesn't take long for the flames to reach the nearby walls, and from there the roof, and by the time the entire warehouse is ablaze, he's standing in the doorway watching.

He's no longer going to live in the past.

The door locks behind him when he leaves, not that it matters, because it will all be ash in a few moments anyway. He hugs Hazel in the lounge of their old house, which will soon be on the market.

'Is it all done?' Hazel asks.

'It's done.'